THE EXILED EARTHBORN

THE EXILED EARTHBORN

THE EARTHBORN TRILOGY BOOK 2

PAUL TASSI

TALOS

Talos Press

Talos books may be purchased in bulk at special discounts for sales promotion, corporate gifts, fund-raising, or educational purposes. Special editions can also be created to specifications. For details, contact the Special Sales Department, Skyhorse Publishing, 307 West 36th Street, 11th Floor, New York, NY 10018 or info@skyhorsepublishing.com.

Talos® and Talos Press® are registered trademarks of Skyhorse Publishing, Inc.®, a Delaware corporation.

Visit our website at www.talospress.com.

10 9 8 7 6 5 4 3 2 1

Library of Congress Cataloging-in-Publication Data

Tassi, Paul.

The exiled earthborn / Paul Tassi.

pages ; cm. — (The earthborn trilogy ; book 2)

Summary: "Lucas and Asha's continued survival hinges on gaining new allies they never could have imagined."—Provided by publisher.

ISBN 978-1-940456-38-6 (softcover) — ISBN 978-1-940456-47-8 (ebook)

1. Imaginary wars and battles—Fiction. 2. Extraterrestrial beings—Fiction. 3. Space warfare—Fiction. I. Title.

PS3620.A86E95 2015

813'.6—dc23

2015023690

Cover design by Paul Tassi, Victoria Maderna, and Fredrico Piatti

Printed in the United States of America

1

The war wasn't over. Not yet.

Lucas was shaking. He couldn't help himself. He'd faced battle after battle over the past few years, but never anything like this. Nothing could prepare him for the scene that lay before him.

How many did they say were out there? One million? Two? But the floating lenses around him were broadcasting to a hundred billion more.

He sat on a massive stage at the end of a long promenade. They told him they used to coronate kings there in the old days—back when monarchy was still an accepted form of rule. A few dozen massive statues of ancient warriors standing as tall as the giant trees in between them extended several miles out ahead of him. In the distance were the shining, colossal buildings that made up the heart of the sprawling city Elyria, the largest on the planet by far. It was balmy and felt like June in Portland. Before the world had ended, of course. They said it was always like this there, one of the many reasons it was chosen as the planet's capital. White clouds floated far overhead, but the sun shone brightly, nearly twice as large as its counterpart on Earth. But fortunately it was only half as hot. It was afternoon, but the crescents of two moons could still be seen in the sky. The other three had long since disappeared from view.

Lucas looked down to the ground, where archaic cobblestone had been meticulously restored and assembled for this very occasion. His black shoes had no laces; his dark pants and high-collared coat had no buttons. He scratched the back of his neck, which still annoyed him hours after a haircut. His close-cropped buzz had grown out, and a team of stylists had spent an eternity making sure every sandy brown hair was perfectly in place. And that was after spending half a day in wardrobe to assemble the outfit that would introduce him to the world.

Next to him was Asha, who had spent twice as long with her groomers, though she didn't need it. Her dark hair was done up in a series of elaborate braids that weaved in and out of each other like dueling serpents. Dark brown-and-gold makeup made her green eyes shine more brightly than ever. It was the most striking Lucas had ever seen her look, though that wasn't saying much, considering she had been covered in blood and grime a good deal of the time he'd known her. She wore an all-white ensemble, a counter to his dark suit. Her dress was wrapped around her like a fabric puzzle, and it was hard to comprehend how it was sewn. Noticing his leg was bouncing up and down rapidly, she put her hand on his knee to steady him. He caught her eye and she smiled.

Behind them stood Alpha, getting uneasy looks from the press in the first few rows, and assuredly billions of others around the planet. He had refused any attempt at custom-knit clothes; such coverings were deemed silly in Xalan culture, outside of battle armor. And letting him wear *that* would send the wrong message. Rather, the stylists had to be content with polishing up his natural gray plating as best they could before he had shooed them away with an annoyed growl.

To Lucas's right was Admiral Tannon Vale, the steely eyed soldier who had first picked them up when they entered the system. He'd since sprouted a light silver beard, and his chest was decorated with a pair of new accolades he'd won since they first met. A dozen more chairs around them were filled with military and political dignitaries. Lucas had heard many had been vying for a seat on the stage for months, promising all manner of payment and favors in order to be front and center at the most significant world event of their lifetimes.

High Chancellor Talis Vale, ruler of the entire planet of Sora, sat next to her younger brother. She rose as her undersecretary finished her introduction to the masses. Her blue eyes twinkled as she passed Lucas, and she briefly touched his and Asha's shoulders on her way to the lectern. She wore a flowing pale emerald dress that fluttered in the wind behind her as she reached the center of the stage. A hush fell over the crowd like a wave, and even those miles away became deathly silent, watching their leader begin to speak on hovering monitors.

"Greetings, people of Sora," she began. "Today marks a turning point not only in the Great War, but in our entire civilization's history. Today we learn we are not alone in this fight, or in this universe. Today you will witness the beginning of a new era."

Six months. That's how long it had been since the fateful battle aboard the Ark. Well, six Soran months, each of which were twenty days that were thirty-seven hours long.

Despite the initial findings of Tannon Vale's science team, it took an exceptionally long time for the travelers' impossible story to be fully believed. A dead planet, an extinct race, and a trillion-mile journey were too farfetched to be possible, no matter what the preliminary data said. The running theory became that they were some sort of Xalan science project—a covert-ops experiment attempting to replicate the creatures' original ancestors, the Sorans. Lucas, Asha, and Noah were each kept in isolation for months as endless tests were run on their biology. They extracted spinal fluid, brain cells, muscle tissue, and all manner of other bits and pieces meant to prove their claims. It was fortunately a painless process, but Lucas feared for the state of his companions while he was allowed no information or contact with them for what seemed like an eternity.

They were questioned about Earth, and Lucas was forced to paint as clear a picture as he could of the world and its entire history from memory alone. His vivid description of the Xalan invasion matched their own wartime history, and only when the genetic tests had been verified twenty times over did they start to truly believe him. Alpha provided them with exact coordinates of Earth's location, and they were able to catch their own glimpse of Lucas's former world through their observation equipment, albeit a place more brown and gray than it appeared in records. They lacked the ability to travel there, as the only two white null cores on the planet up to the task were firmly entrenched in two still-dangerous Xalan ships, but it was enough for them to loosen their grip and allow Lucas to see his companions during the third month of captivity.

The first of his old crew members he saw was Alpha, who had been stripped of his mechanical hand but was allowed to keep his translator collar for questioning. He greeted Lucas heartily and began attempting to recount the past three months at such a rapid speed Lucas couldn't keep up.

Next came Asha, who embraced Lucas fiercely when she saw him. Familiar feelings flooded back into him. She revealed nearly identical treatment at the hands of the Sorans, which had been firm and exhausting, but not abusive. But it was immediately apparent she was not pregnant, as she had been the last time he'd seen her. Before Lucas could open his mouth to ask, a new door opened.

Noah had been assigned a team of caretakers during his stay at the secret facility. Lucas was stunned to watch him led in by the hand by a nurse. The now much taller child toddled over to him and wrapped his tiny arms around his knee, his face beaming with a broad smile. At over a year old now, he'd taken his first steps in captivity without them.

The team led them to another secure area in the underground facility. When the sliding doors opened and he saw what was there, his heart soared in his chest. Asha saw the joy and relief on his face and smiled. Suspended in a tank in front of them was a small child. Well, the shape of a child. It was a fetus, three months old, connected to tubes and wires as it floated, suspended in the fluid. It was his child. Their child.

Natural childbirth had been outlawed for the last few hundred years on Sora. Fertilized eggs were extracted from the mother shortly after conception, and the children were birthed in units like the one that stood before them. Mortality rates of both mothers and infants became almost nonexistent. In the tanks, the children were laced with genes that would prevent all manner of future diseases and disabilities. Tears welled in Lucas's eyes as he stood in front of the tiny shape; they spilled over onto his cheeks when Asha told him it was a boy.

There was a sect that still didn't trust the three of them, and everyone was having a hard time believing Alpha was the first Xalan to truly turn traitor in centuries. But the waves and waves of scientific and tactical knowledge he bestowed upon the Sorans began to increase their goodwill toward him. He detailed the process of how the long-range white null cores were made, and though it would take at least a decade to properly synthesize the necessary element, the science team set to work under his instruction almost immediately to get the process started. The revelation that Xalans had conquered worlds like Earth and were using them for resources filled in many gaps in the military's knowledge. It had long been a mystery how they had sustained the war for millennia with such a resource-poor planet as Xala.

At long last, the Sorans realized they couldn't argue with the science anymore. The subtly different DNA, the vision of Earth, the tomes and tomes of knowledge about the colony planets and

Xala itself. Either it was the most elaborate, intelligent infiltration plan in Xalan history, a race of vicious creatures known for their brute force approach to warfare, or these strange visitors were telling the truth. Their cells became more comfortable, their meals more edible (it was miraculous to have solid food again, even if Lucas recognized nothing on his plate), and a dangerous decision was made. They would get their wish. They would meet Talis Vale.

She'd been observing them for months behind inches-thick indestructible glass, but she finally commanded her worried security team to let her see the travelers. Without restraints. Without guards. It was an insane idea to everyone but her, but Talis explained it was the only true test that would ease everyone's fears once and for all.

Lucas, Asha, and Alpha finally left their underground bunker and were taken to the palace itself in floating vehicles with completely blacked-out windows, though once inside they were made to wear blinding goggles anyway.

The light finally found them again in an exceptionally ornate room full of odd-looking furniture and walls adorned with paintings depicting epic battle scenes. Most looked ancient, with the Soran warriors clutching swords and spears. Eventually the artwork evolved into more modern warfare. The centerpiece of the room was a massive three-dimensional hologram with a label that read "The Battle of Gorgath." In it, Xalans and Sorans battled to the death by the thousand. Lucas couldn't comprehend how much time had gone into making something with such detail. Peering closer, he could see individual expressions of rage and horror on the Soran faces.

Talis Vale entered the room silently, and when they realized she'd arrived the three of them jerked their attention from the paintings toward her. The High Chancellor wore a simple blue dress, her silver hair done up into a pair of vertically aligned buns on the top of her head. She was clearly older than in the images they'd seen of her, but her skin was smooth and only a few creases lined her face. The room was free of guards of any sort, and they walked around completely unbound. This was the test. If they truly were assassins, this was their chance to kill the most powerful person on the planet with ease. It showed Talis had faith in them and in their story.

Obviously, there was no bloodshed as the group had no such murderous intentions toward a woman they'd traveled halfway across the galaxy to find. They chatted about Earth before the war, raising Noah on a spaceship, and other pleasant things. After a while, when Talis was satisfied she wasn't going to be killed by the outworlders who sat in front of her, she shared her true purpose with them.

"Your story is incredible, and the proof to support it is overwhelming. Your actions today have shown you are no threat to me or my people. I ask you, will you become our allies in this fight against Xala?"

Lucas leaned forward on the plush couch where he sat.

"Of course. But our people are gone. There's only us left."

Talis smiled.

"Yes, but you survived. I've fought with my advisors for many weeks about this, but I want you revealed to the world. I want billions to know that Sorans, humans are spread across the galaxy and have suffered at the hands of the Xalans as much as we have."

"More so," Asha said curtly. Talis continued.

"You are quite simply the greatest discovery in our world's history. We've been looking for life in the galaxy for countless generations, but finally, you came to us. And you *are* us. It's incredible, don't you agree?"

"I remember when my people first learned the truth of the web of Soran worlds," Alpha said, his collar communicator projecting his metallic voice. "It was impossible, extraordinary."

"I'll leave it to the scientists to fully understand how this came to be. But in the meantime, we have a more pressing problem.

Despite what this room may suggest, we do not relish war, and we have been fighting the Xalans for too long in this struggle that seems as if it will never end. Between the inspiration you will give our entire planet and the scientific knowledge we can gain from you, Alpha, this conflict may at last find a conclusion."

"But in what fashion?" Alpha asked. "You cannot reach the colony planets for years. Even if you could, you would find yourselves outmatched."

Talis shook her head.

"No, force alone has not worked for thousands of years, and it is not the ultimate answer we seek. The most important piece of information you've provided us with is that the Xalans have no knowledge of their true origins, and the people have forgotten we are their creators."

"We have not forgotten. We have been lied to," Alpha said. Talis nodded in assent.

"A monstrous lie to be sure. If what you say is true about instability in the planetary colonies, we can expose the truth your father discovered and your people will be free to overthrow their savage leadership. I imagine such a revelation would lead to this course of action, would it not?"

"It is possible," Alpha said. "But the Council has kept the secret for an eternity and silenced all those who would share it. What hope do we have of achieving a different result?"

Talis leaned over the table in front of them and popped a round blue piece of fruit into her mouth.

"That is a conversation for another day. But for now, I need to know you are with me. Are you ready to tell a hundred billion Sorans your story?"

Lucas snapped back into focus on the stage. Talis had been extolling their bravery and valor for a few minutes now, and the crowd was still silent after the thunderous news that aliens not only existed but looked exactly like them. Behind them, a giant bowl sat embedded in the ground, and out of it sprang two enormous holographic portraits of Lucas and Asha, floating for all the world to see.

Talis was wrapping up now. The main focus was always supposed to be on them, and Lucas jumped when he heard his name and saw her sweep her arm toward him and Asha, welcoming them to come forward.

"I give you the Earthborn, Lucas and Asha!"

He rose from his chair, as did Asha. She grasped his hand tightly and he could feel it was as clammy as his own. It appeared the dauntless warrior did fear some things after all.

This was as good a reception as they could have possibly received; Alpha had been right on all counts when it came to gauging the Sorans' reaction to their arrival. With the initial distrust and suspicion past, they were being welcomed as heroes. Practically gods.

Lucas's legs stopped quivering long enough for him to make it to the podium hand in hand with Asha. There was nothing resembling a microphone, but camera-bots swirled around, sending out every possible angle of the pair of them to all corners of the world. Behind them, the giant hologram had shifted to a mammoth globe of a blue-and-green Earth that rose fifty feet high in the air.

Lucas cleared his throat.

"Hello," he said to the masses, then froze as he realized he'd said the word in English. After all his lessons onboard the Ark and further training by Soran language instructors for this day, he stumbled out of the gate. Asha stepped in and saved him.

"Greetings," she said in perfect Soran, then turned back to Lucas with a sly smile.

"I am Lucas, and this is Asha," he said in the proper tongue. "And we come from a planet called Earth."

He could see the eyes of those in the front rows, wide with amazement. A few had even fallen to their knees—whether in reverence or terror, he couldn't be sure.

"Like you, we were stunned to learn that we had brothers and sisters across the stars. It is unfortunate our two civilizations could not have met during a time of peace, but because of the Xalans, our planet is now mere memory. All that's left are records and stories, which you will be hearing for days, months, and years to come."

All the information compiled on Earth from both their own testimony and Alpha's records was to be released on what the Sorans simply called the "Stream." It was a constant feed of information, communication, and entertainment that seemed like all Earth's media sources rolled into one. After the speech, the archive would go live and every Soran would be able to learn everything there was to tell about the lost planet of Earth.

"We learned we were one of many worlds full of humans"—*Oops*—"Sorans," he corrected, "that have been sacrificed to the Xalan war machine. These other planets were ravaged as Earth was, but we were the only world who could fight back."

The hologram behind them now displayed the various battle scenes of raids on foreign Soran worlds that Alpha had shown them aboard the Ark. The civilizations ranged in age from mere cavemen to the sorts of Industrial Revolution–era cities that once populated Earth. But none of them had the capacity to fend off the invaders the way Earth did. Its technology had been just advanced enough to ensure the mutual destruction of both itself and its attempted conquerors. There were gasps from the crowd as they watched the devastation unfold, and a few people actually screamed. The scene switched to a battle on Earth where a Xalan mothership was torn apart by a nuke dropped directly on top of it.

"We fought them off, but our planet was poisoned, dying. We soon learned of the far-off world known as 'Sora,' full of beings like us, and knew it was our only salvation."

Lucas turned to Asha, her hair blowing faintly in the warm breeze. She nodded and took over the speech as they'd agreed earlier.

"We escaped our planet on the last working spacecraft with the aid of a friend—an exiled Xalan named Alpha," she said.

The holograph changed to a view of Alpha sitting behind them, a stoic expression on his face. Countless pairs of eyes widened in front of them.

"We learned that not all Xalans are bloodthirsty; there are many who want peace. Because of his refusal to carry out the savage commands of his superiors, Alpha was branded a traitor and personally hunted by High Commander Kurotos across the galaxy."

Kurotos was the name Sorans had for Omicron, and he was a formidable figure in their history, infamous for his brutality across centuries of galactic combat.

"The Shadow killed his family on Xala for treason, a clan of scientists, and wanted to reclaim his considerable mind for the war effort. Alpha refused, and we aided him. After pursuing us all the way from Earth, Commander Kurotos boarded our ship as we reached Soran space. It was the last mistake he ever made."

The holograph showed autopsy footage of the blue-eyed, black-skinned Xalan lying dead in a Soran holding area. The crowd was too stunned by everything being said to even cheer. The silence of a million people in front of them was unsettling.

"We were welcomed warmly by your leaders, and a decision was made to tell the public our story. We want you to know that you are not alone in this fight. This war is about more than just the fate of your world, as the Xalans put every system, and every populated planet, known and unknown, at risk."

There was much they weren't allowed to say in the speech. They couldn't mention they captured Omicron's ship, which was now buried a few miles underground in a covert laboratory. They were advised to not mention the government's initial skepticism of their claims, or the fact that the Xalans were fighting a war based on false pretenses that had been uncovered by Alpha's father. Specific details of the final years of Earth were deemed too gruesome to share, and they were not to mention the eleven other humans Alpha had collected before meeting them that remained in brain-dead stasis after being extracted from the Ark. Such things were not "need to know" for the public, and revealing as much as they had already would be enough for the world to process. Lucas couldn't imagine if two Sorans had shown up on Earth and delivered a similar message on the steps of the White House.

"We have arrived safely now, but we did not come alone. We brought with us the last son of Earth, Noah . . ."

The hologram showed a beaming Noah playing with his beloved holoball. He tottered around the room onscreen ungracefully. His blond locks had grown longer and wavy.

". . . and soon, we will welcome our first son of Sora."

The image changed to the tank where the now six-month-old child grew. Lucas saw more than a few smiles on the faces closest to him. He began to speak again in place of Asha.

"We thank you for welcoming us into your world. As safe as we are here, and as hard as our journey has been, we will not be content to rest while the Xalan menace remains. As such, Asha and I will be enlisting in the Soran Defense Initiative, where we hope to contribute to the final resolution of this war. With one of the top Xalan minds now on our side, and your unwavering support, we will end this conflict forever. Thank you for accepting us into your home."

There was silence as Lucas and Asha stood uncomfortably at the podium. In front of them, humming generators provided nearly invisible forcefields that would screen them from the mob should things turn ugly. Lucas scanned the faces in front of them, searching for an answer as to what was about to happen.

Someone yelled. Then another, and another. Like a wave, people began to raise their right fists into the air, cheering as they did so. It was a sign of respect in Soran culture, and soon there were more than a million arms raised in front of them as the roar of the crowd became deafening. Lucas beamed as Asha bit her lip and gave a reluctant but dazzling smile.

Had they found a new home? In that moment, it certainly felt like it.

2

The speech earned Lucas many warm smiles and congratulations from the sorts of nobles and officers who had been peering at him from behind mirrored glass for the past six months. The Stream showed scenes of jubilation in many of the major cities across the planet, though there were already a few claiming the entire event was pure wartime propaganda. A political group called the Fourth Order said the newcomers were not from any such foreign planet but were just genetically altered Soran constructs meant to drum up support for the war. Further still, there were those who deemed the revelation a Xalan conspiracy led by the double agent Alpha, with genetic abominations Lucas and Asha set to usher in the end of Sora as they brought the government down from the inside. The team escorting Lucas tried to usher him away from the screens when such accusations cropped up.

But Lucas was still riding high on the thunderous cheers of millions of Sorans and nothing would derail his mood. He and Asha were separated and taken to yet another series of groomers who would prepare them for their next big event: the Earth Gala.

It was a gathering that had been announced weeks earlier, but the focus had been kept a secret. The now-revealed objective was that the party would personally introduce them to Sora's elite, from captains of industry to powerful politicians and military figures. Talis assured them they would be thoroughly annoyed by most of the people they met, but she'd never hear the end of it if they were kept secluded from her allies around the world after the news had been made public. Dignitaries had planned for the event for weeks, despite its secrecy, and had flown in from not only all over Sora but also from a few of the colonies planted on sparsely populated nearby worlds within the system.

The stylists mercifully left Lucas's hair the way it was, but they put him in a new suit that was a style meant for ultra-formal occasions such as this. It was similar to his old one, dark and high collared, but there were inlaid patterns of cobalt-colored fabric, supposed indicators of a high-class garment.

"You should be honored," a stylist said. She was an older woman with her hair done up like a tornado and colored varying shades of red. "This was hand sewn specifically for you by Jolo Houzan himself. His designs run upwards of a hundred thousand marks, even when they're not custom made."

Lucas knew neither who Jolo Houzan was nor if a hundred thousand marks was a large amount. He simply smiled and nodded and wondered how many marks were being invested into Asha's appearance next door.

After being kept in seclusion for so long, it was strange for Lucas to find himself being treated like a king over the course of the day. As he was being fitted, an attractive young girl with short auburn hair and sea green eyes came to take his pre-party food order. Sorans usually ate five meals a day. The only thing he knew how to describe was a slab of orange-ish meat he had been fed earlier; the rest of the holographic menu floating in front of him made no sense at all. Learning the language did not mean he knew much of anything about the specifics of life on Sora. But he did know that orange meat was delicious, which was proven true yet again when it arrived in front of him a short time later, hand-delivered with a lingering smile from the girl. "Seared Charo," the dish was called. He wondered what the animal it came from might look like. Though humans looked identical to Sorans, their wildlife was drastically different.

At last the flurry of servants and stylists left him, and he was able to sit in peace and enjoy the last bites of his meal. He stared into the mirror in front of him, barely recognizing the man looking back. He'd come a long way from the gaunt survivalist who had roamed around a desolate Earth, or the blood-spattered soldier who had killed too many aliens and humans to count in the past year alone. Before him was a regal-looking fellow with windswept hair, piercing gray eyes, and a healthy glow. And in a hundred-thousand-mark suit to boot. But he knew once he made good on his promise to join the Defense Initiative, this man would disappear.

It took weeks to convince Talis to let them enlist in the military. Finally she was swayed by her brother, Tannon, to let them sign on and become a public face for the war. The bravery of these newcomers, to have gone through so much and still be willing to fight, would inspire all of Sora, he said. And, judging by the public's reaction so far, he was right.

Lucas and Asha had discussed the matter between them. They decided they wouldn't be able to live with themselves if they let the war rage around them and did nothing. The creatures had taken away everything they loved, their entire world, and who was to say they wouldn't find another planet full of innocents and do the same to them? Even if they couldn't win the war outright, the Earthborn had to do their part to help. "Earthborn" was an identifier that had stuck, and as Lucas could see from the Stream on the opposite wall, the term was being used in headlines across the globe.

He glanced out the window that made up the wall to his left and watched the large sun dip down behind the reflective buildings of Elyria a few miles away. He was on one of the highest floors of the Grand Palace, and peering down he could barely make out the gardens below. Extending in front of him was the promenade where he'd addressed the world, and the giant stone guardians stood on each side, silently watching over the path to the glittering city.

The sky turned orange, then red, then a dusky purple as the sun finally disappeared completely. Above where it fell hung three round moons of differing sizes. Two more surely lurked behind him somewhere. Stars began to show through the darkness, despite the city lights below them. Sora's solar system was far closer to the center of the galaxy than Earth, and the Milky Way was at least three times brighter as the string of lights danced diagonally across the blackness. They called it the "Shining River" here, which seemed like a more appropriate nickname. Lucas realized that his sun was out there somewhere, a dead Earth orbiting it, filled with the ruins of his old civilization.

The door slid open behind him and there was a knock on the metallic frame. Lucas spun around in his chair and saw Asha standing before him.

The sight of her sent chills tumbling down his spine. She was now clad in a long cherry-red dress made out of a shimmering material that seemed to scatter the light around it. It was tied up around her shoulders, with makeup and a necklace of enormous jewels covering up the battle scars across her collarbone. As she strode toward him, a slit revealed her leg up to her thigh, and her neckline was equally daring. Her hair was down now and flowed over her shoulders in waves. Her lips parted into a smile when their eyes met. This was a far softer creature than the one he'd been traveling with for the last year.

"I've barely even recognized you today," she said, eyeing his new wardrobe.

"I know the feeling."

It was a relaxing to speak in English after being forced to converse in nonstop Soran for most of the past few months. He was even starting to think in the foreign language.

"They're nicer than my stylists back home, but I'm not so sure about their taste." She looked down at her dress and let the material slide through her fingers like water. Lucas forgot that Asha once lived in relative luxury herself as an actress, but it likely hadn't compared to this.

"You look . . ." Lucas started, at a loss for words, either English or Soran, to describe her radiance.

"That bad, huh?"

"No . . . I . . ."

There was no adjective. She fingered one of the large sparkling gems on her necklace.

"They told me that this belonged to some ancient queen. That no one's worn it in thousands of years."

"Are those diamonds?" Lucas asked.

"If they are, they're the biggest I've ever seen. Wars would have been fought over a treasure like this back on Earth."

"That's quite a gesture then. All I got was this designer suit from Jolo something."

"Well, you look good. And I don't think diamonds would help that outfit at all," she said with a smirk as she got up and walked toward the window.

"Quite a view," he said, rising from his chair to stand next to her. He watched her eyes dart from moon to moon. "It's a shame we're the only ones who get to see it."

"Yeah," Asha said. "But we're the ones who earned it."

"Still," he said, "I wouldn't say we're exactly the most noble representatives of Earth. If they all knew the things we'd done to be here . . ."

"Most of them would have done the same if they were in our shoes, and those that hadn't would be dead." She turned to him. "Why, who would you have picked to represent the human race?"

Perhaps she hadn't become gentler after all. Lucas leaned against the window.

"Someone more impressive than me."

"You were great today. Haven't you seen the Stream?" She motioned toward the holographic feed on the opposite wall.

Lucas laughed.

"Yeah, people think we're liars or spies."

"Not most of them."

She walked over to the screen and began sifting through the navigation system until she found the story she was looking for. Reading Soran had become as second nature as speaking it over the past six months, and the geometric symbols easily rearranged themselves into words in his mind. Asha pointed to the screen, which showed a crying baby accompanying the text.

"49,054 children born today were named Lucas. 18,324 were named Noah."

He smiled.

"What about Asha?"

". . . 85,941."

"Guess you're a crowd favorite."

"Well, I am the only Earth girl that made it here."

Lucas examined the story. "Hah, even Alpha got 3,200 little Sorans named after him."

"I'm sure he'll be thrilled."

There was another knock at the open doorway. It was an old man, at least by Earth standards. On Sora, he had to be around 150 or 160. Unnaturally extended life was commonplace on the planet, particularly among the affluent. He wore purple robes that hid his hands and feet completely. His white hair was cropped close to his head, and he was clean shaven. As he smiled, his blue eyes crinkled with a thousand lines.

"Pardon my interruption, but the event is about to begin," he said in a gravelly voice. "High Chancellor Vale has requested your presence in the Throne Room."

"The Throne Room?" Lucas asked. "She has a throne?"

"The room is a holdover from when the palace housed the royal family. But these walls have not seen a king in them for close to five thousand years now."

"So the High Chancellor is elected?" inquired Asha.

"Yes, and five years past, Madam Chancellor commanded 83 percent of the vote to secure her next term."

"Doesn't sound like much of a contest," she said.

"The Vales are a highly respected family on Sora. Her father, High Chancellor Varrus, was one of the most influential leaders in our planet's history."

"And what happened to him?" Asha asked.

An indicator light flashed on a piece of his robe, which was apparently laced with circuitry.

"I'm sorry, but we really must be going. I will be happy to elaborate on these matters at another time. I have been assigned as your personal ward during your time at the palace."

"Our personal ward? What's your name?" Lucas asked as he and Asha walked out the door.

"Apologies, my name is Malorious Auran. I've been Keeper of the Grand Palace for many, many years now. I've served both Vales and thirteen High Chancellors before them."

"I suppose you're the one to talk to about anything then. We're still learning our history here," Lucas said. "I'm Lucas, and this is Asha."

"I'm well aware," the old man said with a smile, shuffling ahead of them in long purple robes. "As of today, I have a newborn great-grandchild named Lucas."

Asha elbowed Lucas as she walked behind him. He grinned.

Lucas had only seen a few areas of the gigantic palace so far, but the Throne Room was by far the most impressive enclosed space he'd ever been in, on this world or his own. It was a mix of ancient art, advanced technology, and otherworldly architecture. Great stone columns held up a ceiling that was swirling with a floating replica of the entire galaxy, which spanned the length of the room. The walls were lined with a mixture of large oil paintings that were assuredly thousands of years old and holographic art pieces that were painstakingly detailed and popped out of their frames. A few even appeared to be moving.

Lush green plants sprouted out of the stone floor around the edges of the room, and Lucas wondered if they were always there or if they had been transplanted for this occasion only. In the center of it all was an enormous cornucopia of unfamiliar food that guests were sampling as they milled around it. Hoisted on a large spit was the skinless form of some great animal Lucas didn't recognize. It was hard to tell if it was feline, canine, bovine, or something else entirely. A neat row of glowing blue flames underneath kept the beast warm.

On the ground, guests chatted with one another. Many of the men had donned a look close to Lucas's own relatively subdued suit while others wore stranger ensembles. As they stepped out into the open, one attendee looked at them, then another, and within seconds the entire room had gone silent. Every eye turned in their direction, and they glanced at each other uncomfortably.

Mercifully, Talis Vale quickly walked over to them, downing the last of her drink and handing it off to a servant as she approached. She touched her hands to their arms while the old man who had escorted them shuffled off into the background after a short bow. Talis turned to address the crowd.

"Our guests of honor have arrived at last," she said, as everyone had now fallen silent. "And don't they look lovely? May I present Lucas and Asha, the Earthborn!"

There was a rousing cheer from the crowd. Lucas thought there were probably about three hundred guests in all. It was a far cry from the millions he had spoken in front of earlier, but this was an equally intense prospect, as everyone was transfixed by the pair of them. Talis kept her hands on their backs as they walked down the stairs onto the main floor. Lucas noticed an enormous old marble throne to his left.

"Don't worry," Talis said. "Everyone here has been instructed to mind their own business and not swarm all over the two of you the entire night, as much as they may want to."

A new voice came from behind them.

"And if they do bother you, let me know and I'll boot their asses out of here."

It was Tannon Vale, dressed in his military finest. He'd forgone his medals for a single pin that was a symbol Lucas didn't know. There wasn't a fleck of dust on his entire slate-gray uniform. He did, however, have an energy pistol on his hip. Lucas looked around and realized that at each pillar stood an armed guard clutching a large rifle.

"So you're running security?" Lucas asked.

"I run security for this whole damn planet, why should this party be any different?" he replied with a snort.

"How many death threats have we gotten so far?" Asha asked.

"About six hundred an hour," he replied. "But only 3 percent of those are from anyone who's actually dangerous."

"Tannon!" Talis exclaimed. "You're scaring our guests."

"They've seen worse, I can assure you. And besides, no one is within five miles of the palace who hasn't been put through ten levels of security, which includes all your little fancy friends here." He motioned to the crowd. Lucas still wasn't sure exactly how far a Soran mile was yet.

Talis turned to them with a reassuring smile.

"I promise you are perfectly safe here." She dimmed a bit. "Though I cannot say the same when you run off to join Tannon's army."

"It's your army, I just run it," the admiral replied. Suddenly his eyes widened.

"Oh, that reminds me." He turned and shouted toward a conclave of guests behind them, "Maston, get over here."

A tall, broad-shouldered man broke from the group and strode toward them. He too was in military dress fatigues, though his uniform was dark blue instead of gray and had a full array of commendations across the chest. Black curls of hair spilled down his forehead, and he had a pronounced dimpled chin like a cartoon villain. His brown eyes were deep and dark, and immediately worked their way up and down Asha. Annoyed, she cocked her eyebrow at him. He turned away from her with a smile.

"Yes, Admiral. How can I be of service?"

"You're first in line to meet the aliens. Lucas and Asha, this is Mars Maston, former Commander of the Fifth Fleet and current First Watchman of the Guardians. He's helping out with security tonight."

Lucas noticed a thin line that ran down the right side of his neck, parallel with his collar. A scar? It was the only visible imperfection on what was otherwise a flawless visage.

"It is an honor," Maston said, bowing deeply.

"Mars like the planet?" Lucas asked.

"Which planet is that?" he said, righting himself.

"Oh right, errr, it's one of ours." Lucas felt foolish.

"Well, I'd love to visit it someday," Maston said with a smile. "It's amazing," he continued, turning to Asha.

"What is?" she asked, eyebrow still arched.

"That the first contact we make with another species, they give us an ambassador that outshines our entire race with her beauty."

Asha rolled her eyes.

"I didn't need to fly a trillion miles across the galaxy to be hit on by soldiers. I had plenty of that at home."

"Don't mind him," Talis said helpfully. "He's been a charmer since he could walk. Trust me, I used to babysit him."

Maston looked a bit sheepish and veered the conversation elsewhere.

"I was impressed to learn that you two are enlisting in the SDI. That's quite a high calling after just finishing a war of your own."

"The highest calling," Tannon said. "And it's the real reason you have the honor of being at this gala, incidentally."

Maston looked confused.

"I don't understand."

"The Earthborn will be joining your Guardians."

A look of fury swept over Maston's face for a brief moment, but it was quickly wiped away and he forced a smile.

"But Admiral," he said, his voice dropping an octave, "the Guardians are the most elite unit in the entire Initiative. They're bred from *birth* for the squadron. It's not even possible to enlist."

"It is now."

"But sir, there's no way their skills will match that of the existing team. The Guardians have the finest genetic material on the planet. My best soldiers cost billions of marks to assemble."

The charm was gone, and his voice was now distinctly hollow and cold.

"They also have a bad reputation after your last few missions went . . . awry," Tannon said. "You need some good press, and these two joining up will turn them into heroes again in an instant."

"They are heroes, sir."

"Not recently."

Lucas felt the need to interject, though this was the first he was hearing about the Guardians or his imminent deployment to them.

"We've been fighting for years now, and outlived everyone on our planet. We took out an entire Xalan space station, and killed a Shadow general on his own ship."

Maston looked upward in a way that was dangerously close to an eye roll as he let out a sigh. Lucas wanted to hit him.

"Yes, yes, I've read the Stream."

"Then you should know we're ready for anything you can throw at us," Asha said menacingly.

"I very much doubt that."

"You have your orders, Commander. They'll report to you in a week," Tannon said forcefully.

"Yes, sir," Maston replied without breaking eye contact with Lucas.

Apparently Sorans didn't salute, or Maston was just overcome with anger as he turned and marched off into the crowd without glancing at either of them again.

"Oh, Mars," Talis said wistfully. "He's a royal pain sometimes, but underneath he's a fine soldier, and a fine man. And he's been through so much . . ."

"If he gives you any trouble, I can have him deployed to Thylium," said Tannon. They both gave him blank stares.

"The ice moon," he clarified.

Tannon glanced over his shoulder to where a large mustachioed man gave him a friendly wave from the other side of the massive banquet table. He returned it with a slight nod.

"Ah, damn it," he said, turning back to the group. "That's Madric Stoller, and he's about to talk my ear off for twenty minutes. Can you give me some backup?" he asked, turning to Asha. The man was indeed already starting to make his way around the table.

"What's in it for me?" Asha asked dryly.

"He's the second-richest man on the planet. Probably a good friend to make."

"He also ran against me last term for high chancellor," Talis added.

Asha shrugged.

"Interesting enough, I suppose." She turned to Lucas. "You going to be alright by yourself?"

Before Lucas could speak, Talis chimed in. "I will see to it he's well cared for."

That was good enough for Asha and she turned to leave, her iridescent dress swirling. They met Stoller as he approached, and his face lit up with delight as he was introduced to Asha.

"Come on," Talis said to him. "It's your turn to meet the masses too."

The next few hours were a blur. Lucas was paraded around to an endless array of dignitaries, nobles, provincial leaders, and planetary celebrities. Their names and faces all blended together after a while, and Lucas amused himself by trying to sample every piece of food on the central table at least once. A thought occurred to him as he was eating a pile of cubed red meat on a crystal plate while speaking to the Vice Emissary of Something-or-Other.

"Where's Alpha?" he asked Talis, who seemed glad to be talking about something other than the food shortage of the man's province.

"He was invited to the gala, of course, but he refused the offer. It's hard to blame him, as I can't guarantee many of these folks wouldn't be cowering in fear if he were here. Only a handful of people in this room have even *seen* a Xalan in person. He's down with the Shadow's ship, working with our scientists."

Lucas figured that's probably exactly where he wanted to be, but it would have been nice to have another friend around. Asha was currently surrounded by a throng of admirers hanging on her every word. Her hand gestures implied she was regaling them with tales of one of their past battles.

"If you'll excuse me," Lucas said to Talis and the emissary, "I think I'm going to get some air."

"Of course, my dear," Talis said, and the man next to her nodded. "Come find me later."

Lucas made his way through the crowd with all eyes on him. He figured that everyone he passed was probably dying to meet him, but knew they would be excommunicated by Talis if they bothered him without his permission. It was quite kind of her to make that rule.

He walked through a pair of armed guards standing stiffly at two pillars near the edge of the room. An open doorway led out onto a small balcony. The noise grew quieter as he stepped out of the grand hall. The brilliant display of stars was there once more, and he could see two smaller moons embedded in the sky, one full, one just a sliver. He supposed he was on the other side of the palace now, as the three he'd seen before were out of sight.

In the distance, tall spires of buildings glowed, lit up by pocket-sized null cores far smaller than the one that had powered their ship from Earth to Sora. Lucas wondered when or if he would visit the city of Elyria itself. Or anywhere else for that matter. The palace was gorgeous, but there was a whole new planet out there to see. He shipped off for military training in a week, and who knew what part of the world that would be in? Probably nowhere nearly as beautiful as this. Perhaps enlisting so quickly had been a rash decision, but it had seemed like the right thing to do at the time. But if he died fighting this war, he would get to see only a fraction of this wondrous place he had come so far to find. It was no wonder Alpha had called it a "crown jewel" that the Xalans sought as a prize at the end of the war.

Suddenly, a voice spoke behind him.

"Quite a view, isn't it?"

Lucas turned. A young woman in a sapphire-colored dress walked slowly toward him. Her blond hair was done up in a series of twisting strands that must have taken hours to arrange. Her neck and wrists glittered with the starlight reflecting off precious stones. As she drew closer, the moonlight illuminated her face. Her eyes sparkled at a distance, and it became immediately clear she was awe-inspiringly beautiful, with each facial feature perfectly measured and placed. And judging by the silhouette of her dress, she had a figure to match.

She stood next to Lucas without looking at him and put her hands on the stone banister in front of her, gazing out at the horizon. The guards hadn't stopped her from approaching him, which meant she had to be someone of high importance, even in a room full of the most powerful people on the planet. Lucas had forgotten she'd asked a question. She asked another.

"Did you have any cities like Elyria on Earth?" she asked. Her voice had a melodic quality to it that instantly made Lucas forget all about the stress of the party inside. He found his tongue.

"None like this. We had a few great cities. New York, Paris, Dubai, but none could match this."

She nodded.

"Yes, from what I understand your world was quite a bit younger than ours. But you do seem . . . civilized."

"Well, uh, thanks."

"You're welcome," she said with an earnest smile.

She was still staring off into the distance, and had yet to make eye contact with Lucas. She put her elbow on the banister and rested her chin on her hand. Lucas was trying to guess her age. Twenty-five in Earth years maybe? But it was always hard to tell on Sora, with so many procedures to make anyone look young through genetic reconstruction or therapy.

"Who are you?" he asked.

She finally turned to face him. A nearby lantern revealed her eyes, which were a shocking spectrum with flecks of blue, green, brown, and gold, all surrounded by a dark violet ring. Lucas had never seen anything like it before. Her irises were more captivating than the entire galaxy of stars behind them.

"I'm Corinthia, but most around here call me Cora. That'll happen when everyone's known you since birth."

"Since birth?" Lucas asked.

"Well, if you can call it that. My parents spent trillions on the genetics, and I don't even want to know where I was put together. A Vale has to be perfect, of course.

"I hear you have one of your own on the way as well. I suppose congratulations are in order. The First Son of Sora and all that. I'm sure they'll give him the best genes on the market. And probably some off market as well. Just avoid eyes like these," she said, motioning to her own. "Even at a hundred million apiece, the coloring isn't worth the light sensitivity."

"You're a Vale," Lucas said at last.

"Yes, yes, I know, the pains of being the High Chancellor's daughter. I must sound like a proper brat," she said, rolling her eyes.

Talis's daughter. He could see the resemblance now, vaguely.

"Not at all," Lucas said politely, determined to pretend he knew who she was all along.

"I do actual work around here, despite what they may say about me. I'm actually Chief Military Liaison for the Chancellor's office as of last year, so we'll be seeing quite a lot of each other. I hear you ship out with the Guardians in a week."

"So I'm told."

"Why would you enlist in the Initiative?" she asked. "You just got here after fighting a war, and now you want to jump into another one?"

"Well," Lucas said, "I do have a planet to avenge."

"And one to save as well," she added, her tone shifting from playful to serious. "Sora will be overrun in my lifetime if we do not find a way to end this war soon. Defenses are breaking down across the rim systems every day. They could be here within a decade. And truth be told, we don't have the strength to hold them off again."

She tucked a loose strand of hair back into a braid and continued. "I'm tired of war. We all are. Soran history is full of them. We've fought over land, money, race, religion. We had to fight our own creations, the machines, and now we're doing it all over again with the Xalans. We'll never learn."

"Earth wasn't so different," Lucas said. "Rarely a century went by without millions dying in conflict. It's human nature, I suppose."

"Ah yes," she said. "That's what you call yourselves, isn't it, 'humans.'"

"It's going to be hard to break that habit."

She fell silent for a minute and took a sip from the glass in her hand.

"Just promise me something, will you? Finish this."

Lucas raised his eyebrows.

"Your drink?" he said, nodding toward the blue vial she held.

"The war."

"That's a tall order."

"I know what they're planning, revealing the truth to the Xalans. It can work."

She really was well-informed.

"Convince the Xalans we can live in peace. Expose their leaders for the liars and murderers they are. Winning their minds is achievable. Wiping them out entirely is not."

A few trillion marks in genetic material had obviously made the woman in front of him poised, intelligent, and disarmingly beautiful. As she drifted slightly closer to him, Lucas realized it could be a potentially dangerous combination.

A shiver ran through her and she took a few steps back.

"It's a bit chilly out here. I'm going to return to the party, as much as it may pain me. I can't remember the last time this many windbags were in one room."

"Alright," Lucas said, chuckling. There was a raucous chorus of laughter from inside. "I'm going to wait a minute longer."

She backed away from him and spoke as she headed toward the entrance back into the gala.

"It was a pleasure, Earthborn. I'm glad you found us."

And then she was consumed in a ball of flame.

3

Lucas's back arched as the fiery blast that shot out from the balcony entryway flung him against the stone banister. He hit the ground conscious but disoriented, with pain surging through his body. A dull tone sounded in his ears while his eyes could only see enormous red spots.

He fumbled around on the ground, crawling forward, feeling bits of stone and glass under his feet, trying to understand what had just taken place. An explosion. A bomb. An attack. Immediately, his mind raced to Asha. He tried to stand, but the attempt resulted in an instant collapse to the ground. As his vision slowly came back into focus, he saw a pair of glassy, prismatic eyes staring back at him. Corinthia Vale lay on her side, her cheek and neck blackened, her tattered dress aflame. Her gaze was fixed and unmoving.

Lucas dragged himself over to her on his elbows and placed a trembling pair of fingers on her neck, confirming what he already knew. She was gone. Looking past her, the Throne Room was a hellish furnace of smoke and flame, and Lucas could hear screams coming from within. How had this happened? His mind swam as he tried once more to get to his feet, this time with greater success. He rose unsteadily, bracing himself against the railing. Corinthia lay still in front of him.

The ground shook as an armored figure landed on the balcony next to him, cracking the tiled floor. Jets protruding out of its back flickered with blue light, then went out completely. It turned to Lucas and revealed an assault weapon in its clutches and a face hidden by a helmet. The figure was a tower of black armor streaked with four blood-red lines intersecting across its breastplate. It was taller than Lucas, but too short to be Xalan. It raised the rifle and Lucas instinctively reached for a gun he did not have.

The figure's head jerked right and blood sprayed out of the side of the shattered helmet. The suit of armor dropped to the ground as if the body inside had evaporated entirely. A man strode through the flames from inside the main room. It was Mars Maston, uniform scorched and ears bleeding, clutching a long silver energy pistol. He met Lucas's eyes briefly, but his attention was soon caught by the body below him. He immediately dropped to his knees.

"Cora!" he yelled. "Cora!" He attempted to find a heartbeat as Lucas had and discovered the same sickening truth. He smashed his hand against the stone and turned a fierce gaze toward Lucas.

"Come, now!" he shouted as he rose to his feet, lifting the still smoldering Corinthia. He put her over his shoulder and clutched his pistol with his free hand. Lucas stumbled over to the dead invader and picked up his weapon, which strangely resembled a shortened version of the Xalan rifles he'd become intimately familiar with.

The scene inside was chaotic. The entire room was on fire and bodies littered the ground, including two armed guards on either side of Lucas as they entered. There were audible screams, but through the smoke it was impossible to tell where they were coming from. Lucas stumbled over a body. His ears still rang and smoke filled his lungs.

Ahead, two more armored figures streaked with red marched through the carnage, firing at those stirring on the ground or attempting to flee. They saw Maston and Lucas too late and were each met with a round to the skull. Lucas's instinctive shot from the energy rifle vaporized his target's head entirely, much to Lucas's surprise.

"Asha!" Lucas called out, but heard only unidentified shrieks in reply. "Asha!"

"This way!" Maston shouted as he pulled him in the direction of the large throne, Corinthia's body dangling down his back. The central serving table was in splinters and a circular blast pattern on the floor seemed to indicate it was the origin point of the explosion. In the distant smoke, more armored figures lumbered about. Lucas fired indiscriminately at them, but couldn't tell if he was landing any shots. How had they gotten past Tannon's security? Another one entered from the balcony they'd come from. It was clear this was an aerial assault. The newly arrived intruder took a pair of rounds from Maston and went down. Lucas saw palace guards enter from a passageway on the other end of the room and engage the armored troops as surviving civilians scrambled for safety behind them.

They approached the throne and Maston waved his hand, which drew out a holographic interface from the ancient, and now blackened, marble. He moved various virtual pieces around, and with a groan, the massive seat slid forward on the ground. At the base was square hole with a metal ladder.

"Inside!" Maston yelled.

"No!" Lucas replied as loudly as he could muster, ash burning his lungs. He turned back to the fiery room.

"Asha!" he yelled hoarsely as he walked toward the inferno. Maston tried to reach for him, but with Corinthia on his back and a weapon in his hand, he couldn't stop him.

And then, there she was.

Lucas saw two armored men dragging a woman with curled black hair over her face, clad in an unmistakable red dress and a jeweled necklace reflecting the flames around it. They went around the corner and out the balcony entryway on the other side of the room.

Lucas tried to sprint, but almost fell. He braced himself against the wall and continued forward as fast as he could manage. It was hard to even understand what hurt in his body anymore. A flood of adrenaline had shoved the pain away for later.

Stepping over another dead guard, he reached the opening. Rounding the corner with his rifle barrel, his sudden and unexpected appearance caught a man standing there by complete surprise. At close range, Lucas blew a hole clean through his armored torso and blasted off a piece of the stone railing behind them. As the man sank to the ground, Lucas saw what was ahead of him. His heart stopped.

The figure was clutching Asha with one arm while holding a snub pistol to her skull with the other. Lucas froze. The man gestured with the gun in silence. Slowly, Lucas let his rifle barrel drift toward the ground as the man's pistol retrained itself on Asha. She wasn't moving, and her skin and dress were a mess of black burns. But Lucas saw her chest rise and fall under the man's metal arm.

Lucas had dropped his gun far enough for the invader, and in a single moment he activated the blue jets on his back and fired the pistol. Lucas instinctively raised his rifle, which deflected the initial shot while the next two whizzed by his head and into the ground as the man soared into the sky at an incredible speed. Dropping the now superheated gun, Lucas ran to the railing. The blue lights of the jets were still visible as the pair of them kept rising into the cloudless night. Lucas looked down at the dead man, but his jet mechanism had been mangled by Lucas's shot, and Lucas quickly deduced that he couldn't somehow appropriate it to give chase. When he turned back to the sky, the lights were gone.

She was gone.

Lucas's forgotten pain returned all at once, and he collapsed to the ground, unconscious.

His vision was blurry when he woke. He could see lights and shapes, but couldn't make out what they formed. Lucas's head rolled from side to side and the shapes changed, but became no clearer. He was lying down, he thought, and tried to raise his arms but found it like trying to push through tar. A fuzzy blotch that must have been his hand waved in front of him.

"He's awake," a voice said.

Had he been captured too?

"Dial it back a bit then."

Pain. He winced and his muscles tightened.

"Not that much."

Relief, and his vision began to return. A man and a woman were standing over him clad in long silver coats. It was the woman who spoke.

"His injuries aren't severe. The vertebrae will heal. The burns are minor."

"Special case though," the man said.

"I know."

As his vision continued to return, Lucas saw the woman had short brown hair, dark green eyes, and severe cheekbones. The man was out of his field of vision now.

"Get him up, they want to talk to him. Keep him at 20 percent though."

Lucas felt pain return to his spine, but his mind became less cloudy. The woman unhooked several wires from his torso. He managed to sit up, though his back was angry with him for it.

"Over there," she said. "They're waiting."

Lucas looked over and saw that the room they were in was dark except for a brightly lit holotable in the middle. Figures were huddled around it and sifting through various displays that flew up from the surface.

Lucas stood up from the stretcher, which was immediately wheeled away into the darkness by the pair of attendants, a bevy of mobile machines along with it.

Walking was rough for the first few steps, but became easier as he found his footing through numb legs. He drew closer to the table and understood where he was. And where he was not.

He hadn't been captured like Asha; the appearance of Tannon, Maston, and Alpha confirmed that. The other men and women around the table he didn't recognize, but some were in military fatigues while others wore the suits of public officials.

Another attendant in a silver coat was applying something to Tannon's back. His uniform was scorched and his chin was dripping blood onto the shimmering surface of the table, but he appeared to be without mortal injuries. Maston looked similarly ragged. His once prim and proper appearance was transformed into a torn-up mess of ash and blood.

Across the table, Alpha was the first to spot him.

"Lucas," he said as the blue hologram on his translator collar flickered.

"Glad you could join us," Tannon said as he waved the silvercoat away from his back.

"Where are we?" Lucas asked, his voice sounding strange in his own head.

"A bunker under the palace. One of many. It doubles as a wartime fortress."

"How did I get here?"

"You have Maston to thank for that," Tannon said, gesturing toward the man across from him.

"I couldn't let two Earthborn leave us," he said in a tone that annoyed Lucas. But the man had just saved his life twice. As he moved into the light, Lucas could see a look of barely bridled anguish on his face.

"Asha, where is she?" His mind snapped back to the most pressing issue.

"That's what we're trying to figure out. We're attempting to make sense of this whole damn catastrophe. Get him up to speed."

A shorter man to Tannon's right spoke with a shaky voice. Lucas couldn't place his type of uniform.

"At 28:05, a device was detonated in the Throne Room from a concealed location inside the serving table. Its exceptionally small size and unique material composition allowed it to pass undetected through every layer of security."

The man waved and a three-dimensional vision of what looked like a microchip hovered above them.

"The thing was smaller than a fingernail," Tannon said. "Any bigger and it would have blown the whole floor to dust."

The short man continued.

"After the initial explosion, an assault team was dispatched from a ship of unknown origin. Casualties were high, but all members of the invading force have been killed or have fled."

"Who were they?" Lucas asked.

"Fourth Order," answered Maston through gritted teeth. "Their armor was unmistakable. But those weapons . . ."

"Fourth Order? Aren't they a political party?" Lucas asked, remembering the name from the Stream earlier.

Tannon scoffed. "A political party? They're rebels. A resistance group led by that fool Hex Tulwar. They've lashed out before, but I never thought they were capable of something like this. It doesn't make any damn sense."

"What do you mean?"

Another military official spoke. His unscathed uniform indicated he hadn't been in attendance at the party.

"The assault team simply appeared, and then disappeared. We don't know how they breached security."

An ash-covered woman spoke as she pulled up a readout on the table. She had to cough a few times before she spoke.

"Scans came back. No detection on motion, thermal, infrared. And nothing on video. They just . . . vanished."

A feed showed an attacker with a blue jetpack ascending into the sky. He slowed, then, in a split second, disappeared from view altogether in the cloudless black night.

Lucas had seen something like this only once before.

"Alpha, that's not . . ." Lucas said.

"It must be," Alpha said, his claws extended outward on the table. "The Sorans do not have the capacity for this technology yet. They cannot."

"What are you talking about?" Maston asked.

"They piloted a short-range cloaked Xalan ship. Study of their weapons and the explosive device will likely yield elements of Xalan technology as well."

"Impossible," Tannon said. "You're the first Xalan to even speak to us in three hundred years. What would they be doing working with the Fourth Order?"

Alpha looked nonplussed.

"Would you instead believe your underfunded resistance group managed to develop technology centuries ahead of your own by themselves overnight? It seems clear the two parties have conspired in an assassination attempt."

"Who was their target?" Lucas asked. "Asha? Is that why they took her?"

"You think you're that damn special, Earthborn?" Maston said, boiling with rage. "The most powerful people on this planet were at that party, and a good quarter of them are now dead! They wouldn't organize this just to snatch up a single useless Earth girl!"

That made Lucas push past two men and get right in Maston's face before a few nearby officers could separate them. Lucas backed down and his head throbbed from the surge of anger and whatever medication he was likely on. An obvious thought occurred to him.

"Where's Talis? I mean the High Chancellor?"

"She's safe," said Tannon quickly. "But mourning the loss of her daughter."

Corinthia. An image flashed in Lucas's mind of her being consumed in flame.

"Who was talking to *you* last I saw," Maston said venomously.

"She wouldn't . . . I was . . . There was no time," Lucas stammered. "She had walked inside when the blast hit. When I reached her . . . she was gone."

"There's nothing he could have done, Maston. Calm down," Tannon said.

"This whole damned party was for them! If they hadn't shown up in the first place—"

"I had no idea this would happen!" Lucas spat back. "Maybe if your security had been better, you'd have stopped this and she'd still be alive!"

Mars Maston lost what was left of his composure. He swung at Lucas's jaw and connected, his target too groggy to dodge the blow. Lucas hit the floor and Maston leapt on top of him. The officials around them scrambled to pull them off of each other as Tannon circled around the table, shouting at the pair of them.

The holotable lit up and the image that was displayed made everyone freeze at once. The top of the frame read "incoming transmission." Underneath it was Asha, battered, burned, and bloody. She was seated, her hands behind her back and her black hair hanging wet around her face. Her green eyes shone brightly through the feed and Lucas saw a familiar look of burning anger in them. Her mouth was covered by some sort of metal device that looked more involved than a simple gag. From the way her muscles were tensing, it looked as if she couldn't move an inch, and the mechanism was inducing a sort of paralysis. Lucas let Maston's collar slip from his hand, and the pair of them slowly got to their feet. The camera panned back and two armored men walked into frame, each with weapons drawn and pointed at Asha. Lucas's heart was thundering in his ears.

A new figure entered, one with no helmet or mask to hide his face. He was tan, with long brown hair and dark features. He wore a black uniform that was unbuttoned to his chest and had the sleeves rolled up.

"That bastard . . ." Tannon spoke slowly. Lucas looked at him. "That's Hex Tulwar," he clarified.

"Sir, this isn't just for us. It's taken over every layer of the Stream," the short man next to him said.

"What? How is that possible?"

"It seems your resistance is doing many impossible things today," Alpha said.

The man began to speak as he drew closer to the camera, which panned away from Asha. The background was dark and unidentifiable.

"Greetings, my Soran brethren," he said. His voice had an accent unlike any Lucas had heard on the planet so far.

"By now you've received word of the judgment that has rained down from the heavens on Elyria. The apostates of the High Chancellor have been made to pay for their misdeeds, and their facade has come crumbling down."

Lucas looked over at Maston, who was now seething at the monitor, not at him.

"We did not know what we would find when we infiltrated the gala of the vain and powerful this evening. After weeks of preparation, only this morning did we learn it was to celebrate the appearance of the two false idols known as the *Earthborn*."

He said it with the same sort of sneer Maston had.

"I hope that you are not foolish enough to believe these two are truly long lost relatives of Sora from some distant land. They are merely tools, pieces of propaganda created to further fan the fires of war."

The Fourth Order's statement decrying the Earthborn's validity on the Stream earlier that day was worded nearly identically to what Tulwar was saying now.

"This war has gone on for too long, and we want no more of it. For every ship that's vaporized, a hundred thousand Sorans could have eaten for a year. The cost of an antimatter missile could filter a million gallons of toxic water. And they have the nerve to celebrate this new chapter of conflict with a lavish party where the elite oppressors stuff their faces with fine food and drink as they worship these new idols."

The camera panned back to Asha who was still frozen motionless in her restraints.

"Now we put their lie to the test. If this Earthborn is as special as they claim, the last of her kind, they will pay to see her safely returned. It will be a ransom used not to kill, but to heal. The Fourth Order demands a payment of fifty trillion marks by tomorrow's moonrise, or we open up the idol and see if she looks like us on the *inside* as well."

One of the two guards brandished a long curved knife that flittered dangerously close to Asha's throat. Lucas's fists were clenched so tightly he'd lost feeling in them.

"We demand the funds used for war be returned to the people of Sora for peace. If they refuse to pay, and she dies, you'll know that your government has lied to you and the Earthborn are no more from another world than you or I. Surely the greatest discovery in Soran history is worth a few marks, no?"

The camera cut away from Asha and fixated solely on Hex Tulwar once more.

"Think, my children. Vales, I await your reply."

The feed cut to black and only a short string of symbols remained.

The room was silent.

"Trace?" Tannon said, but the woman next to him was already shaking her head.

"What the hell do we do now?" a rather frightened-looking military commander said from across the table.

"We leave her," Mars Maston said coldly.

"What?" Lucas exclaimed. "You have to be kidding. Just give them the marks!"

"Fifty trillion marks could finance our entire next campaign," Maston said, too close to Lucas's face once more. "Your . . . counterpart isn't worth a fraction of that."

Lucas clenched his teeth, but avoided lunging at the man again. He tried reason.

"If you don't pay, and they kill her, your citizens will think that we're just inventions of your government to drum up support for the war."

"You mean you're not?" Maston said mockingly.

Tannon slammed his fist down on the holotable, causing all the images on it to fizzle.

"You boys are forgetting a third option. We kick down their door, save the girl, and bring Tulwar to justice."

Maston had a confused look as he turned to him.

"They came here in an invisible ship, you can't trace the location of the transmission, and they've already carved out her tracking chip. How exactly are we supposed to find them?"

Tracking chip? Lucas quickly looked over his own body. They'd implanted him with something? And it had been cut out of Asha? Both thoughts were highly disconcerting.

"I've been chatting with our new friend here, and he has a way we can find her. Tell 'em," Tannon said, motioning to Alpha.

"Back on Earth," Alpha said, looking at Lucas, "I planted a chemical tracking element on you and Asha."

"What? Why?" Lucas asked. *Him too?*

"I required knowledge of your whereabouts in the early phase of our partnership, as I did not know if you were to be trusted. Later, it served to locate you as we journeyed to dangerous areas and were separated."

"Alright . . ." Lucas said hesitantly.

"The trace is still on you now. And Asha as well. It will be undetectable by this Fourth Order even if they were able to locate the more obvious Soran device. So long as they do not take her out of the system, the agent will still be traceable. I would, however, require a few hours to rebuild the device needed to detect the trace; it was destroyed in our last conflict aboard the Ark."

"We'd never reach her," Maston interrupted. "They'd detect us miles out and slit her throat before we could storm the place."

"He's got a point," Tannon said gruffly. "If there's one thing the Fourth Order is, it's jumpy. They've got more aircraft detection in Rhylos than ever after our last string of operations there."

"You are forgetting another gift you have been given," Alpha replied. "There is a ship in a bay a mile underneath us that would allow immediate and undetected access to anywhere on your planet."

Omicron's flagship stealth cruiser. Lucas had forgotten. It had the same cloaking abilities as the vessel the Fourth Order had used. But it was presumably much bigger, and much faster.

"Absolutely," Lucas said, energized by Alpha's plan. "Keep your money, let's just kill them all."

Maston was silent. He stared into the light of the holotable. Finally he spoke.

"For Corinthia," he said solemnly. "Put me on this infernal ship and Tulwar will be dead by dawn."

Tannon pushed back from the table.

"I'll talk to the High Chancellor. You," he said, pointing at Alpha, "start building that tracking device."

"At once," Alpha said. "But I need to be aboard my ship."

"And I need access to a few things as well," Lucas said.

Soon they were deeper inside the palace, down many levels past the dimly lit war room. Mars Maston had gone to assemble his

Guardian squadron, which had been assigned to the mission at hand, and the group had dwindled to only Lucas, Alpha, and the admiral.

When the doors opened, Lucas saw a sight he hadn't witnessed since back on Earth: the exterior of their savior ship, the Ark. The transport looked worse for wear after their frenzied firefight with Commander Omicron's troops, and much of the internal tech had been ripped out when the ship depressurized in the battle's final moments.

The entrance ramp descended and Alpha walked into the light, promising that there was enough material onboard to craft the tracking device he needed. Tannon then led Lucas to an offshoot room. Two Soran symbols were imprinted above the opaque door. Earth Archive.

Inside, Lucas was told he'd find what he was looking for. As he entered, he had the distinct impression he was inside the most significant museum on Sora, though one not open to the public.

Everything they'd taken from Earth and kept aboard the Ark was on display here. There was Lucas's desk, looted from the Scandinavian mansion. Asha's worn black tank top hung stretched out behind thick glass, a few dozen other pieces of clothing next to it, including his own. In another row lay books in secure containers on top of pillars rising from the floor. Approaching one, Lucas saw it was *The Picture of Dorian Gray*, every single one of its pages translated into Soran in a holographic screen below it.

Lucas turned a corner and entered a new section, one more relevant to his needs. A large display spanned the entire length of the wall, and this time the transparent energy field securing it promised to liquefy anyone who attempted to cross it. Mounted every few feet was a new gun labeled Earth Weapon along with a string of identifying numbers. There was his old boot pistol, shining more brightly than it ever had when he'd used it.

A cannibal's assault rifle, wiped free of blood and dirt. Standing vertically was an RPG that never ended up being fired in combat. As he reached the end, past two dozen weapons, he found what he was looking for.

"Open it," he said coolly.

A small man in a blue lab coat glanced nervously at Tannon, but the admiral nodded his approval. The energy field dispersed, and Lucas took his old friend into his hands. Natalie had been polished to an almost mirror shine, though the letters etched into its stock still remained. As Lucas turned it on, he could see that Alpha's technological hybrid appeared to be as fully operational as the day it was confiscated from him. The scientist next to him looked terrified as Lucas cycled through the modes from full-auto, to shotgun, to sniper, and back again. It had saved him many times over the years, and now it would help him save someone else.

But it wouldn't do it alone. Lucas slung Natalie over his shoulder and stooped down to pull out another pair of weapons, a long-barreled Magnum and a black-bladed sword only a few molecules thick. He clipped the revolver to his belt and mounted the sword so it crossed Natalie on his back. They were Asha's weapons, and when he found her, she'd need them to exact vengeance on those who had taken her from him. He turned toward Tannon and nodded and the two marched out of the room, leaving the skittish lab attendant to reinstate the force field over the armory. As they left, Lucas saw one last door they hadn't gone through. One simply labeled with the Soran symbol for "11."

Lucas was led into another large hangar area, though one far larger than the space that housed the Ark. It took him a minute to recognize the sleek ship before him, as he'd never seen Omicron's vessel in full light before. Previously, it had been in the blackness of space, reflecting starlight, or hidden from view altogether with the same advanced cloaking system that had been employed to attack the Grand Palace.

On the ground in front of the ship stood a formation of burly soldiers, each clad in gray fatigues and holding an energy rifle across their chest. Their eyes stared straight ahead, not daring to deviate from their path as their leader strode among them. Maston had assembled his Guardians.

It became obvious that Maston wasn't exaggerating when he said they were the finest genetic specimens on the planet, crafted using god-knows-what procedures for billions of the local currency. Every soldier here, male and female, was taller than Lucas, with many towering above him. They looked like a legion of comic-book superheroes, with bulging muscles and stone-cut jaws. Many looked more beast than man. Lucas caught the eye of a towering giant to his right when the soldier broke off his fixed gaze to eye the strange newcomer. If this was Earth, Lucas would have guessed he was Polynesian, but he still didn't understand the racial groups here.

Maston immediately strode up to Tannon, ignoring Lucas's presence entirely.

"You let him arm himself from the archive?"

"Would you prefer he take on the Fourth Order with a right hook instead?" Tannon replied.

"We could have issued him a rifle, that . . . thing he's using hasn't been fully tested yet. It could be dangerous."

"That's kind of the point," Lucas said.

"Dangerous to *us*," Maston clarified. "I've seen the preliminaries. If you overload the core in that weapon it would blow an entire ship sky high."

That much was true. Alpha had told him Natalie's power source could in fact detonate if it became unstable enough. All the more reason to take good care of his longtime friend.

"I've seen a feed of him using that loadout to kill a ship full of Xalan Paragons and their commanding Shadow. If we had the time, I'd have the mad scientist make one for every soldier in your unit," Tannon said.

Flustered, Maston walked back toward his troops.

"There's more than one way to kill a Shadow," he said, scratching at the scar on his neck.

4

Once Alpha's tracker had been built, the flight was going to take a mere forty-one minutes, despite the distance to Rhylos being equivalent to orbiting Earth about three and a half times. Omicron's ship was fast in the atmosphere as well as out of it. The newly appointed Guardian crew had taken to calling it the "Spear," likely due to its flat, elongated shape and razor-sharp nose.

Lucas was relegated to crew quarters and found himself sitting across from a familiar looking brown-skinned giant, the one who had been eyeing him earlier. His black hair was shaved into a wide mohawk that ran all the way down to his neck, and he had a bandage wrapped around his enormous left bicep, which was laced with a series of angular tattoos that resembled circuitry. Next to him was a pale, lean woman whose dark red hair had been roughly chopped short around her ears. Her blue-green eyes pierced Lucas with a glare that made him uncomfortable, but he was too preoccupied to be intimidated; Asha consumed his every thought.

They'd heard nothing from Hex Tulwar or the Fourth Order since the initial video message other than a brief transmission with instructions for delivery of a ransom payment that would never come. Rather, Alpha had used the chemical trace on Asha to reveal she was being held in a fortress buried deep inside the cliffs of Rhylos, a dusty continent tens of thousands of miles removed from the lush greenery of Elyria. Tannon had told him the nation had been in open rebellion for years, but civilian deaths as a result of SDI retaliation strikes had only strengthened the revolutionaries' cause, and nearby regions had begun to rally to Tulwar and his Order.

The only thing they knew for sure about this hidden installation was that Asha was still alive inside of it, and that was all that mattered. Lucas's thoughts were interrupted by a gruff voice in front of him. The man's.

"Did you truly kill Commander Kurotos on this ship, Earthborn?"

Kurotos. It took Lucas a second. Omicron.

"Yes, on the bridge."

"How," the man pressed. It wasn't really a question, only a statement of disbelief. A silver plate on his shirt read "Silo."

"I had help," Lucas said. "My . . . friends. We all nearly died trying, but his arrogance allowed us the upper hand."

"Impossible," the woman said, finally speaking. Her tag read "Kiati." Lucas didn't know if these were first or last names, or merely coded identifiers. The fatigues he had received and changed into were unlabeled. Presumably everybody already knew who he was. Kiati continued.

"You may be from this planet, Earth, but the stories they're telling about you? No one could survive that. Especially a fight with a Shadow."

"Maston did," Silo said, but Kiati shot him an angry glance and he said no more.

"He fought a Shadow?" Lucas asked, incredulous.

"He killed a Shadow. But it is not our place to reveal details of the Commander's history. Ask him yourself," Kiati said, still glaring at Silo.

Lucas leaned back against the wall.

"We're not exactly on the best terms," he said, rubbing his bruised jaw where Maston had struck him earlier.

"I heard he saved your life at the palace," Silo said, scratching at his bandage.

"That may be true."

"And that Corinthia Vale died in front of you."

Lucas sighed. Even if it was unwarranted, guilt did plague him. The blast was something unknowable, but the party in his honor? It was the perfect target for an attack with so many important guests in attendance there.

"She was gone when I reached her, there was nothing to be done."

He paused to form a question of his own he'd been meaning to get answered.

"Were she and Maston . . . involved? He seems pretty distraught over her death."

"We all mourn the loss of the High Chancellor's daughter," Kiati said with a stern face, but Silo had locked eyes with him and was silently nodding.

It was true then. He felt a touch more sympathy for Maston, and recognized his own fury would reach similar levels if it had been Asha murdered instead.

There was a ping from his chest, and he tapped his badge, where a holographic indicator tumbled out in front of him. The message that hung there told him to report to the communications center.

"Either of you know where comms is?" he asked hopefully as he rose from his seat.

Kiati simply stared at him, while Silo jerked his head to the right.

"Thanks."

Lucas was immediately lost after going down the first hallway. He'd only been on the ship once, and that was during a heated battle on the bridge that left him half dead. But as he continued, passing troops pointed the way to his destination. Some were already suiting up. It appeared that the Guardians had been training on this ship for some time, at least to the point where they knew their way around. They only needed someone to turn it on and fly it, a role Alpha now filled.

Comms was a large area buzzing with officers and flooded with an array of monitors everywhere he turned. As soon as he was spotted, a man ushered him to the rear of the room. A small screen floated up to his face, then tripled in size. Two familiar figures appeared. It was Talis Vale, and she was holding Noah in her lap.

"Madam Chancellor!" Lucas said, unable to hide his surprise. She was in a new ensemble from the gown she'd worn earlier, but bruising on her neck and face indicated she hadn't escaped the assault entirely unscathed. Dried tears were etched on her cheeks in two columns, but when she saw Lucas, she grinned. As did Noah, and the boy reached for the screen, trying to touch him.

"I've told you a dozen times to call me Talis, Lucas," she said with a weak smile. "It is good to see you well. I was thrilled to learn of your survival."

"I'm glad to see you're safe too, Talis. But I have to say I'm sorry for the loss of your daughter."

Her smiled faded.

"Thank you. I hope you don't mind that I've appropriated your child to help me through this difficult time. He's a constant source of joy, even in this darkness."

She bounced Noah on her knee and he giggled.

"Of course. I can imagine no greater protector for him."

Talis gazed off out of frame, her tone softer when she spoke again.

"I never thought I'd lose her. My sons, my husband, my father. Those deaths I knew in my heart would come someday as they fought impossible enemies millions of miles away. But Cora? She was supposed to be safe here. I cannot believe it."

Lucas didn't know what to say.

"I'm sorry."

But that didn't feel like anything close to enough.

She turned to face Lucas once more.

"The reason I called you here isn't to pine for the lost. I'm issuing you an order I hope you'll follow, even if you're a citizen of a planet other than this one."

"Anything."

"If you find Hex Tulwar in this mess after saving your companion, ensure he is captured alive."

Lucas was taken aback.

"Alive? After all that he's done? Conspiring with the Xalans? Killing your . . . killing so many?"

She shook her head.

"If you come home with his head, this will look like a covert assassination rather than a rescue mission. Even if his death is warranted, it will set the entire region on fire and we'll have two full-scale wars on our hands instead of one."

Her right hand was trembling as the other held on to Noah.

"As much as I want vengeance for my daughter, I won't put more lives at risk for my own vendetta. But I cannot say the same for Mars."

Lucas nodded.

"I've heard he and Corinthia were . . . close."

"That was kept secret by them, but it ended some time ago for reasons my daughter didn't care to divulge. But he never stopped caring for Cora, and I'm worried he'll tear Tulwar limb from limb if no one stops him."

Lucas rested his arms on the console in front of him.

"Why aren't you issuing this order to him? Or Admiral Vale?"

"I have, but if Tannon isn't on the ground, you can be certain none of the Guardians will intervene to stop Mars. He'd defy a direct order to avenge Cora even if it meant possibly spending the rest of his life in a cell."

"I'm not going to lie, I'd love to see this bastard dead as well, even if I just learned his name a few hours ago. He took Asha, killed innocents . . ."

Talis nodded.

"I understand, but he must face justice for his crimes in a civilized manner. If we execute him on the spot like barbarians, we're no better than the Order itself in the eyes of the world."

Lucas sighed.

"I'll do what I can, but Tulwar's death may be inevitable. Things are likely to get heated during the raid."

"All I'm asking is that you try, Lucas. It would be the best way you could honor my daughter. Hopefully Mars will understand that as well. Cora wanted peace above all else. Peace with Rhylos, peace with Xala. She would not want to be 'avenged' in such a fashion."

Noah squirmed in her arms.

"I know what you've done to get here. You've told us astonishing, harrowing tales of your will to survive. But you don't have to be that man anymore. You're a father now, whether you call yourself that or not. Be a man your children can admire, not fear."

That hit Lucas like a shot through the chest. He thought of his lost son, Nathan, on Earth, one he rarely saw even before the war, as he shirked his parental duties as often as he could. It was getting harder to picture his face.

"Take care of him for me," he said, motioning to Noah. Talis nodded with a strained smile and the feed went black.

Despite being told to remain in crew quarters for the duration of the flight, Lucas had little desire to return and play twenty questions with Kiati and Silo at his assigned station. Instead, he made his way to the bridge and, after a fairly long trek, the large central doors opened and he saw before him the place where his journey almost came to an end six months past.

The CIC had mostly been repaired, but a few of the consoles that Omicron had ripped out of the floor hadn't yet been replaced. Angular craters pocked the ground where they once stood. Lucas saw Maston and the admiral drawing up battle plans on the large central holotable. The last time he'd seen it activated was when Alpha's deceased father delivered his fateful message to them.

Maston saw him immediately and predictably began to protest.

"What's he doing here?" he said to no one in particular. "I thought I told you to remain in quarters."

"And I don't take orders from you," Lucas said coldly. "I'm not a Guardian."

"You wouldn't have even lived through training," Maston spat back at him.

Yet again, they were in each other's faces with someone about to be hit. Tannon walked up to them coolly, putting a hand on each of their shoulders.

"We're eight minutes from arrival, we don't have time for this shit," he said in an exasperated tone. "Lucas, on the ground you will obey Commander Maston for your own safety and the safety of the other Guardians. We don't do lone guns here. And you," he said, turning to Maston. "The man lived through his local apocalypse and killed a Shadow right where you're standing. Give him the benefit of the doubt."

Maston simply turned away and went back to the holotable. Lucas had no desire to provoke him further by relaying Talis's message, so he walked toward the figure sitting in the pilot's chair.

"Alpha."

The gray creature turned to him, cables connected to his temples. He nodded.

"Lucas."

The view out of the newly replaced central screen showed the curved edge of the blue planet rotating rather quickly ahead of them. They were in the outer atmosphere, the fastest way to get to their destination without being detected. They were cloaked, but flying too low at too-high speeds could damage any structures or aircraft nearby and give them away. The ship wasn't meant to run errands from one end of a planet to the other. Its usual destinations were trillions of miles away.

"How does this thing fly?" he asked.

"It is . . . pleasurable. The difference between this ship's capacity and the Ark's is like that between a [garbled] and a [garbled]."

Alpha's translator broke up when it couldn't find the necessary words to substitute into the analogy.

"I'll take your word for it," Lucas said.

"Perhaps when Asha has been safely returned, you can pilot the craft. You were quite skilled in combat with the Ark, and that was merely a transport vessel. This is a far more refined weapon."

"You should know, you built it."

"It was largely a creation of my father, though I did some work on the engine systems when I was younger. This ship brought Commander Omicron many victories, though often his enemies did not even realize it was present."

Lucas walked up to the viewscreen. The vista before him of the planet's curved surface was astonishing. He wished Asha were there to see it.

"What do you make of the cloaked ship the Fourth Order used?" he asked.

"It is hard to say," Alpha replied. "But I imagine it is a much, much smaller craft, and developed by someone with an intimate knowledge of the science."

Alpha became quiet for a moment.

"I would like to apologize in advance."

Lucas broke his gaze out the window and turned to him.

"For what?"

"For not being able to accompany you on this mission on the ground. I must remain here, as I am the only one trained to fly this craft."

"Of course, I never expected you would be coming. Why would you apologize for that?"

Alpha sighed.

"Asha is my . . . friend," he said, as if the word was foreign to him. "We have fought many battles together, the three of us, and I would not see her lost after the journey we undertook to get here."

"Neither would I," Lucas said firmly. "We'll get her back. Have you seen these guys?" he said, motioning to the hulking troops around him. "We have an army of monsters behind us now."

"But who is behind those we seek?" Alpha pondered.

"I guess we'll find out."

The blue edge of the planet turned red as land appeared over the horizon. Reading off Alpha's monitor, Lucas saw the famed cliffs of Rhylos were below.

"Suit up," Tannon called from behind him.

5

It was nearly dawn when they set out from the Spear. All five moons were still visible in the night sky while the sun lurked under the horizon.

The cliffs of Rhylos were indeed impressive to behold. A thousand feet of sheer red stone wound away from them for as far as Lucas could see. They'd landed on the muddy beach, where murky streams of brown water, spawned by a few trickling waterfalls on the sides of the cliffs, fed into each other. Clearly, a great body of water had flowed through here once, but not for ages, and the area was now desolate.

Advance recon had found multiple entrances to the underground base where Asha was being held inside the cliff. They made their way to the one at ground level. The darkness helped hide them from view on the ground, but it wouldn't for much longer, and they'd be much more visible climbing up the face of the massive cliff come daylight.

Lucas followed a long line of Guardians sprinting toward the rock wall. Rather than heavy battle plating, each wore a light mesh suit made of tough fibers that promised to stop a shot or two, but no more than that. It made their approach quiet and undetectable, as the stealth suits masked their biological heat signatures and heartbeats from any sensing equipment nearby.

It was impossible to see Maston, who was leading the charge a few dozen soldiers ahead of Lucas. There had been no time to train him in the formations and tactics of the unit, so Lucas was simply told to "stay in back," much to his dismay. And with Alpha at the ship's controls and Tannon running point on the bridge, he had no allies out here. He did, however, recognize a bandaged arm and a few tufts of red hair a couple yards ahead of him.

Lucas heard a few dull, concussive thuds up ahead he couldn't place.

"Three down," came Maston's voice over the comm. Gunshots. *So that's what silenced energy blasts sound like.* Lucas switched on Natalie's silencer as well, a firing mode he'd never had occasion to use in their past frenetic firefights. Their previous fights hadn't required the element of surprise the way this operation did. Lucas was convinced he'd suffered a bit of hearing loss from all the gunfire he'd endured over the past few years, much of it at close range.

The tail of the group caught up with the head, where Guardians were being ushered inside the ground entrance quickly by Maston while he radioed something back to Tannon. As Lucas and two more soldiers behind him made it through the entryway, Maston followed them and the large metal door snapped shut behind him. Inside, the three dead Fourth Order sentries were being stripped of their black armor, and a trio of Guardians were preparing to don the gear to replace them at their posts. One of them was already speaking into the radio collar of a dead guard in a language Lucas didn't recognize.

Maston was busy looking at a three-dimensional map of the complex. It was a maze of winding tunnels with no discernible pattern to it. Occasionally, a vast pocket was carved out, indicating an open space. Asha's tracking signal appeared as a faint dot on the far end of the labyrinth in one of the open outcroppings.

"She's there?" Lucas asked, sticking his finger into the holographic map, much the annoyance of Maston.

"It would appear so," he said coldly. "Unfortunately there appears to be no direct route to get there. These are ancient Lochni tunnels. We'll have to split up or we risk the entire unit being trapped or killed in these narrow corridors."

Lucas didn't want to know what a Lochni was if it was large enough to make a nest out of a thousand-foot cliff face.

The Guardians checked their gear in the dimly lit corridor around them. It was dawning on Lucas for the first time that these men and women were in fact risking their lives to help save Asha, as was the man he intensely disliked standing in front of him. But as Maston continued, his own primary objective became clear.

"Hex Tulwar will likely be in close proximity to the Earthborn. Her containment area appears to be the largest chamber in the facility, which is giving off the highest energy readings."

One female and two male Guardians had now fully donned the black armor, and Lucas saw the familiar four blood-red lines splashed across their breastplates. They looked similar to the invading force at the palace, but with no propulsion mechanisms on their backs. The large metal door opened and they sauntered out into the canyon, one continuing to chatter on the radio in the strange tongue. Lucas felt a hand jerk his shoulder plate.

"You," Maston said as he turned to him. "You're coming with me and Splinter Four. I wouldn't jeopardize another unit by forcing you on them."

Lucas scowled, but followed. There was no reason to continue sparring with Maston when Asha's life was at stake.

Splinter Four turned out to be one of eight units of six soldiers each that were being sent down the various spindly passageways of the cliffside stronghold. In addition to Maston, Lucas found himself marching alongside Kiati and Silo once more. Kiati didn't acknowledge his presence, but Silo gave him a curt nod. The other two soldiers were a massive, bearded blond man who reminded Lucas of a certain old acquaintance on Earth, and the other was a dark-skinned woman with a shaved head who was a good five inches taller than he was and built like an Olympic athlete.

The tunnel had a metal floor, but the walls were smooth stone. Sporadic lighting was implanted in the ceiling every few hundred feet, but it was still rather dark. Lucas checked his own micro version of the tunnel map on his wrist and found they were approaching an open area up ahead. He was in the rear and kept swinging Natalie around, peering through her infrared scope to ensure they weren't being followed.

Suddenly, Maston threw his arm up. The six of them split in half and pinned themselves to each wall. They stood perfectly still with their rifles fixed straight ahead. Lucas followed their lead and remained as motionless as he could.

Maston held up two fingers, his index and middle, and motioned downward. He then switched to his ring and pinky, and pointed those two up. Lucas was unsure of what exactly he was signaling, but no one wanted to break radio silence to tell him. Four enemies ahead?

Before he could speculate further, Maston clenched his fist and the other four Guardians sprinted around the corner with him. Lucas pushed off the wall and took off after them. He rounded the tunnel bend just in time to see the Guardians in front open fire. On the ground, he saw two guards being riddled with silenced plasma bursts. Above, Kiati and Silo had fired at two points Lucas couldn't identify, but debris rained down from the ceiling and he had a guess at what had just been destroyed. *Cameras.*

He didn't even get to fire a shot; the Guardian unit took out all their targets in seconds with extreme efficiency. Silo motioned for him to take one of the dead guard's arms, and they quickly moved him to the side of the tunnel, out of the light above them. A massive door stood before them, and Maston was checking readouts on his wrist.

"What is it?" Kiati asked him, breaking her usual stoic silence.

"I'm not sure," Maston answered honestly. "It would appear to be a hangar, though I'm not detecting any life inside."

"Sir," the dark-skinned woman said, sifting through a display on a small tablet. "I'm getting some bizarre energy signatures from in there."

Maston looked at a trio of squiggly lines in the palm of her hand. He shook his head.

"This doesn't make sense. Are you sure that's right?"

The woman nodded.

Silo held up a small chipcard he'd looted from the dead guard they'd just finished dragging.

"We going in?" he asked as he handed the card to Maston.

"It's the only way through, and we'll lose too much time if we backtrack. Just stay sharp."

Maston walked over to the side of the entrance and inserted the chip into a blinking console. The great metal door let out a groan that echoed throughout the hallway and slowly parted in the middle. Maston led the Guardians in, two at a time, and Lucas walked into the chamber next to Silo, whose eyes and gun darted to every moan and creak coming from within.

The room they found before them was circular and surprisingly vacant. There were mounds of scrap metal in small piles around the cavernous area, but otherwise it was completely barren. Looking up, Lucas saw the walls of the cylinder curve upward until they reached a massive, round skylight that was easily thirty feet in diameter and filled the room with an almost pleasant coat of moonlight. The six of them fanned out and began to explore the bowl, which appeared deserted. *Then why was it being guarded?*

Lucas was drawn to a particularly large mound of debris and walked toward it with Natalie raised. He heard electrical whirring, and as he circled around it, he found himself staring at a collection of consoles laced with holographic controls resting under a cascade of monitors. A workstation of sorts? As he approached, he recognized symbols that littered the screens. Xalan symbols.

"Guys," he whispered into the comm. "I think I've got something here."

Maston and the other five began to walk over to his position, but suddenly they all put fingers to their ears. The noise in Lucas's head was a cacophony at first, but soon dissipated into more recognizable sounds: yelling and gunfire.

"All units, this is Splinter Seven," came the frantic voice on the other end. "We're blown. I don't know how, but we were spotted. They've engaged us in the northeast tunnel. Gattio and Horva are down, I've been hit. Expect resistance wherever you are momentarily. Mission is now sparked."

"Shit!" Maston cried and flipped channels on his receiver. He patched himself into the enemy feed, which was broadcast out into the room. There was yelling in broken Soran.

"They're in tunnels two, five, nine, ten, and fifteen. Wait, six as well."

"How did they find the facility? How did we not we see them approach?" another voice asked. Lucas recognized it. *Tulwar.*

"We still don't know. I'll check—"

Tulwar cut him off.

"No matter. There will be time to dwell on your failures later. I must leave immediately. Kill the girl. They will earn no prize by coming here.

"Tell the Xalan to meet me at the craft. And you've encrypted our communications?"

"Um, of course," said the other voice nervously. There were a few tones of virtual keys being tapped, and the comm squealed before going completely silent.

Maston yelled into his chestplate.

"Are you getting this admiral? Mission's shattered, Tulwar's making a run for it."

"We'll head him off," came Tannon's voice through the speaker. "Pull everyone out."

No, they can't. Asha.

Lucas raced over to the cluster of monitors and whirled through the Xalan menus. It had been a while since he'd needed to read the language, but he could navigate the system well enough. He found the symbol for "holding," and the view that awaited him sent ice through his veins. It was Asha, hunched over in a cell with a lightscreen guarding the entrance. The barrier flickered, then disappeared. Four armored men strode in and formed a semicircle around her as she sat with her head between her knees, blood already caked on the floor around her. One brandished a long curved knife that Lucas recognized from the ransom video.

The feeds bathed Lucas's face in white light as they were all wiped completely. He frantically ran his fingers through the controls, but all were locked. The station had been shut down, and he no longer had eyes on Asha. He had to reach her. He ran out into the middle of the room toward the door on the opposite end.

As he found himself underneath the enormous light, the ground began to shake and he was thrown off balance.

"Readings spiking," yelled the woman to his right. Everyone clutched their rifles and spun in a circle as they searched for the source of the disturbance.

It surfaced next to Lucas. A twenty-foot-tall colossus of metal with a blank spherical face and bladed arms. Heavy golden plating coated its chest and shoulders and its legs were mammoth canisters that looked like they could crush a car. By the time Lucas raised Natalie, he was flying across the room from a thunderous iron kick that sent him crashing into a pile of debris.

"*Killbot*!" Maston yelled, and Splinter Four opened fire. The metal behemoth was peppered with plasma rounds as Lucas extracted himself from the scrap around him. There was no official diagnosis, but he'd broken ribs before, and the old, familiar surge of pain came roaring back to his insides. His suit released a stream of painkillers into his system and his vision blurred like he'd just taken his fifteenth shot of the night at the bar.

Mercifully, the effect was temporary. As he wiped his eyes he found the machine was gone. The rest of the team was searching for it, but it had presumably found a pile of metal to hide behind, or another floor panel to take cover inside. The thing could move fast. Lucas wondered if it was autonomous or if someone was directly pulling the strings inside. Hadn't advanced machines been banished for ages now after the last war? Whatever the case, this one was clearly predatory.

Lucas ignored the remaining pain radiating from his abdomen and flipped Natalie's scope to thermal. The thing had to be emitting heat, right? He swept across the room, finding only the yellow-red shapes of his teammates against the cold blue, when suddenly the thing found them instead.

The blond Guardian couldn't even formulate a scream as a razor-sharp blade plunged through the mesh armor on his back and out his chest. The killbot, as Maston had called it, materialized from behind a pile of metal it had blended into perfectly. It whipped its dripping spiked arm to the right, and the body of the soldier flew off of it toward the wall, a stream of blood following close behind it. The resulting sound when it struck the stone was something that would be hard to forget.

There was no time to linger on the loss of life, however, as the machine raised its bladed arm to reveal something Lucas hadn't noticed before. A barrel.

The concussive blast reverberated around the bowl like a bomb, and a crater appeared in the wall where Kiati had been standing moments before. Lucas thought her annihilated on the spot until he saw a flash of red hair dashing behind another scrap heap.

Lucas took the opportunity to finally aim down Natalie's sights. Throwing silenced mode to the wind, he let loose a spray of superheated plasma at the machine's torso. When that failed to produce more than few black scorch marks, he switched tactics. The barrel extended and he lined up a shot at what he presumed was the machine's head. The blank sphere was expressionless and mute as it recoiled from the singular blast that would normally decapitate targets with ease, but it was quickly apparent that no actual damage had been done. Another shot toward Lucas's position forced him to flee rather than continue to fire. The subsequent explosion nearly defeated him, and his ears rang painfully as he scrambled for cover.

Maston and Silo rained fire down on the machine, but despite its size it was surprisingly nimble and danced around most of the rounds almost gracefully. What shots did find their mark were clearly not getting past its heavy plating. The robot reminded Lucas of Alpha's mech used in their final stand against Omicron, but this was far more maneuverable than the bulky exo-suit ever was. It almost moved like a Shadow, the way Omicron had as he decimated the three of them on the bridge of his ship.

"Rana, spark it!" Maston yelled as he signaled to the dark-skinned female Guardian taking cover in the console cluster where Lucas had been. She nodded and threw out a blue orb from her belt that bounced as if it were made of rubber. Once it was within a few feet of the machine, it detonated and a visible pulse surged in a thirty-foot sphere around it. The machine shuddered for a second as electrical bolts rippled through its armor, but whatever the effect, it wasn't enough. It raised its bladed barrel arm and Rana couldn't move fast enough. The console enclave exploded, her along with it. Even fifty feet away, Lucas was spattered with blood droplets.

Gazing around the room, Lucas saw nothing but stone walls and closed doors. They were likely locked, and attempting to run and open one was asking to be annihilated by the metal behemoth. Lucas ducked as another blast rocketed over his head.

Maston, meanwhile, was formulating a plan. His energy rifle had been completely depleted, and now he was letting loose with his long silver pistol. But not in a frenzied manner; he was aiming at something. As the machine danced around, shots were being leveled at its backward-bending knee joints, and Lucas realized Maston was trying to land a shot in between the cracks of the armor plating. It was an almost impossible target, considering how fast the thing was whirring around the room, but a sudden shower of sparks indicated he'd found his mark.

The shot had hit some sort of mechanism, causing the machine to botch the landing of its latest jump and come crashing down to its knees. Its left leg shaking, it stood up, but remained motionless long enough for Maston to land another round inside its other joint, and it bent awkwardly back on its legs. Silo and Kiati were firing short bursts at its torso, also aiming for gaps in the armor. Another flash of sparks and the robot could no longer lift its right arm.

Lucas circled around behind the machine as it fired a series of bursts with its remaining good cannon. Despite its injuries, it was still attempting to get to its feet. As Lucas drew closer, it became apparent that something was . . . crawling on the machine. Smaller robots were pouring out of its joints, attempting to repair the damaged limbs. And it was working. The other arm swung upward, fully functional once more, and nearly took Silo's head off with a booming shot. Its legs sputtered as the microbots set to work on them next.

"It's auto-repairing!" Maston shouted as he attempted to pick off the tiny machines with his pistol, but for every one he blasted, two took its place.

Lucas shouldered Natalie and reached for the black-bladed sword on his back. In the next few seconds, he'd either be in pieces or one step closer to Asha. As the machine fired at the other

Guardians, Lucas sprinted up behind it as fast as the nanoenhancers in his suit would let him. He launched himself off a discarded cannon mount and landed on the killbot's wide shoulder blades. Inches away from the spherical head, Lucas could now see what he had been shooting at earlier. The entire ball was a cluster of tiny lenses, focusing and refocusing under a protective coating; a thousand eyes that could see everything at once. But they hadn't seen him, at least not quickly enough. A moment later, the robot was blind, its all-seeing eye rolling around on the floor after one quick swipe from the razor edge of the sword.

Unfortunately, its body didn't crumble with a mere piece missing. Without targeting, the arms waved wildly around, blasting enormous holes in every section of the room and blowing a pair of metal doors wide open across from them. Lucas bucked as the torso surged beneath him, but he was able to plunge the blade into a slit in the golden armor. A flick of his thumb on the sword's handle and electricity cooked the circuitry below to a crisp and smoke poured out of every crack of the machine. His suit insulated him from the surging energy. The killbot shuddered one last time before it froze completely, and the room was silent.

Lucas jumped down from the mammoth metal shoulders and immediately collapsed as the pain in his ribs returned. A hand waited outstretched in front of him. Silo's.

"You're the real deal then." Again, a statement, not a question. Lucas took his hand and lurched himself onto his feet. He spoke through shortened breaths.

"What was that thing?"

Maston walked over to the kneeling metal monster and picked up a smoking microbot from the floor. The spider-like machine was about the size of his palm, and burnt a crispy black.

"Something that isn't supposed to exist anymore," he said, casting a wary eye toward the mangled metal monster. He tossed the smaller bot to the floor. "In the Machine War, they just called them killbots. They were as deadly a fighting unit as the AI could produce, but this one is more advanced than any I've ever heard of. Morenthic plating, dark matter cannons, microbot repair. And it definitely never moved like that. State-of-the-art tech on a ten-thousand-year-old machine."

"I think the Xalans built it for them," Lucas said, motioning to the now smoldering station behind him. He saw a dark-skinned arm on the ground next to it. "That cluster was coded entirely in Xalan symbols."

"Fantastic," Maston muttered as he ran his hand through his sweat-soaked hair. "Alright, we're pulling out."

"What?" Lucas exclaimed, his focus jerked back to the mission at hand. "We have to find Asha."

"You heard Tulwar. She's dead. We need to regroup at the Spear and try to intercept him."

She wasn't dead, she couldn't be. Not like this. Lucas pressed him.

"And where do you think he's heading? There's only one chamber big enough to house a ship in here."

Maston mulled that over.

"Alright," he said. "You two take Rana and Chiron's Finals and help out Splinter Three in the adjacent tunnel. Once they're secure, get to the Spear."

Kiati and Silo nodded and spread out to attempt to salvage something from the bodies of the two fallen soldiers. Lucas and Maston began to run toward the now blasted-open doors across from them.

"What's a Final?" Lucas asked as he threaded the sword onto his back once more.

"A chip containing the last thoughts of a soldier for their family and loved ones," Maston said as he reloaded his gun while running. "We all record them in the likely event of our demise."

"And who should I give yours to if you die in the next few minutes here?" Lucas asked.

"None of your damn business," replied Maston curtly.

The pain in Lucas's sides peaked and another stream of liquid healing was released into his bloodstream. But it was thoughts of Asha, not painkillers, that propelled him forward.

Time blurred and the tunnels began to all feel the same as Lucas followed the tiny point of light on his wrist map. They encountered only minimal resistance in their trek to the central chamber, a few scrambling soldiers attempting to secure a location they would now never reach with smoldering holes in their heads. The comm chatter indicated that most of the Fourth Order troops had converged on tunnel six, where five Splinter groups attempted to hold them off as they retreated toward the Spear.

The main room they sought was up ahead. As they approached, the passageway was eerily silent, and he and Maston simply ran up to the large doors, as there wasn't a guard in sight. Presumably they'd all fled to the surface or were reinforcing the other tunnels under siege. Maston immediately started sifting through the controls.

"It's on lockdown. I knew this was a waste of time."

Lucas was frantic.

"We can get through. Another chip?" he asked hopefully.

Maston stepped back with his arms out.

"Do you see any guards around here?"

In frustration, Lucas raised Natalie and fired a round directly into the door console. The echo bounced around the curved walls. Maston glared at him.

"Is that how you open secure doors on Earth?"

But suddenly, the circular locking mechanism midway up the door began to turn. It was opening.

"You did not do that, trust me," Maston said. "Be ready."

The door's lock unspooled itself and the two panels slowly slid open. Maston and Lucas pointed their guns at the figure who stood there. It was a woman, whose dress was now a much darker shade of red. She held a curved blade in one hand, and her other was leveling an energy pistol at Maston's head.

"Asha!" Lucas cried, and she snapped out of her daze and recognized him.

He dropped his barrel and embraced her. She was slippery with blood. Lucas quickly pulled back.

"Are you hurt?" he said, checking her for injuries.

She shook her head.

"Not recently," she said hoarsely. "But I can't say the same for anyone in there."

In the room behind her was a trail of bodies. Some were armored, others wore plain black uniforms. None of them stirred. He should have known she wouldn't need saving.

"As delightful as it is that you're alive, we have more pressing concerns. Was Tulwar here? Where did he go?" Maston asked.

"Is that his name?" Asha said.

"We need to get you out of here," Lucas said.

"Well, quickest way out would be up there." She pointed behind her to a circular bay door on the ceiling. "Your friend got in a ship before I could get a shot off and flew out."

Maston didn't need to hear any more and was marching off in the direction of the exit port. Asha turned to follow him.

"Wait," Lucas called. "You'll want these."

He handed Asha her Magnum, then presented her the black-bladed sword.

"Such a romantic," she said as she grabbed him by the collar of his armor and kissed him deeply. Lucas didn't even care whose blood he was tasting.

Maston had located the controls, and the three of them stood on a platform that had once housed the ship. A few buttons later, the ground beneath them was rising and the bay doors opened up above. As they rose, Lucas could see Asha's handiwork from on high. The blood and bodies were strewn around the metal floor like some sort of nightmarish oil painting.

Daylight found them as they reached the surface, and what they saw in front of them brought a sick smile to Maston's face. Tulwar's Xalan ship, or what was left of it, was half sunk in the earth. Pieces of it were strewn all over the ground and smoke poured from the wreckage. A group of Guardians had laid waste to a number of Fourth Order soldiers and were now circled around two kneeling figures: Hex Tulwar, battered and bloody, and a skinny gray Xalan with green rings in his black eyes.

Above them hovered the Spear, its shimmer giving away its position from this distance even though it was cloaked. Alpha spoke in his ear.

"It was a simple shot."

Lucas grinned.

"I bet. I've got Asha."

"I can see that is the case; this is wonderful news. I will look forward to greeting her onboard."

As Maston stormed toward Tulwar, Lucas was jolted back into the moment. This was going to be ugly.

Before Lucas could get anywhere near Tulwar, Maston struck him with a hard right cross. And another. And another. The man was already injured from the crash, and his uniform was split open to reveal four dark scars slashing diagonally across his chest, the same pattern that adorned the armor of his troops. The Guardians looked on approvingly as Maston pounded on Tulwar. Strangely enough, in the midst of the beating, the man was . . . smiling. The Xalan next to him cringed with each fresh strike.

Lucas ran over and pulled Maston's elbow, delaying the next blow. Maston bolted up with wild eyes, his face spattered in Tulwar's blood.

"You better turn around and leave, right now, unless you want this to happen to you too."

"I can't do that," Lucas said. "I made a promise to Talis. He has to come back alive."

Maston growled.

"I heard her orders," he said, then paused as he considered something. "But there was nothing we could have done. Tulwar was killed in the crash as he tried to escape."

He turned to the Guardians that circled them.

"Wasn't he?" he yelled, and they all nodded silently in return.

Tulwar had gotten back to his knees.

"I died many years before today, Commander," he said as blood spilled out of mouth. "You should know that better than anyone."

Maston turned and hit him again.

"If you do this," Lucas said sternly, "you'll start a war with the entire region. You'll lose any intel he could give you."

Maston was breathing heavily, winded from his strikes. He rubbed his shredded knuckles.

"It's not what Cora would have wanted," Lucas said in a quieter voice that only Maston could hear.

Pacing back and forth, Maston flexed his fingers back into fists.

"Well, it's too bad she's not here to stop me."

Maston drew his pistol and pointed it at Tulwar, who was still smiling.

"My loves await me! My arrival will be celebrated by Kyneth and Zurana themselves!"

He raised his arms and eyes toward the heavens. The pistol started to shake in Maston's hand.

"Not yet," he said coldly.

He fired a single blast from his pistol. Tulwar's right arm detached at the elbow and he collapsed to the ground crying out in pain.

Maston bumped past Lucas on the way toward the Spear, shouting an order to his troops.

"Get him inside and stable. And secure that thing so it doesn't try to slit its own throat before we make it talk," he said, motioning to the Xalan.

"What the hell was that about?" Asha asked as Lucas turned toward her. Behind them, Guardians were swarming over the Xalan and Tulwar, who was still screaming in agony.

"A personal favor to Talis. Believe me, I wish he'd taken the headshot too."

"I wish *I* had," she said. "But I suppose Talis has her reasons."

The Spear landed on the cliff and troops began to file inside it. The sun had breached the horizon and surely the rest of Rhylos would soon be alerted to their presence if they didn't depart. Lucas took Asha's hand and the pair walked toward the ship.

"Who's Cora?" Asha asked.

When Lucas escorted Asha through crew quarters to medical, the Spear was already back over the vast western ocean. Though she'd avoided major injuries during her capture and escape, she was far from the picture of health. She wiped away the blood from her face and body as they walked, and Lucas could see burns sustained from the initial blast and bruises she'd acquired in captivity.

Rows and rows of Guardians eyed the pair of them curiously as they passed. Silo and Kiati were whispering to soldiers on either side of them, motioning to Lucas. Silo made a slashing motion with his arm, and it appeared he was recounting their encounter with the killbot.

Lucas passed a large, dark man with tears in his eyes. He held in the palm of his hand a floating hologram of a woman Lucas recognized. Rana, the specialist from his splinter team who had been slaughtered by the killbot. It was her Final. Her image was projected from the chip they'd procured from what remained of her body. She spoke softly, and Lucas couldn't make out what she was saying over the din of the room, but the Guardian who held her was visibly upset. A friend? A husband? But as Lucas passed he could see the resemblance. A brother. The man didn't look up as they walked by.

Further ahead, a group was crowded around a large floating monitor. It showed the same angle of security footage that Lucas had located through the Xalan station. Only this time it wasn't cutting out.

Four armed men approached a motionless Asha cowering on the floor of her cell. As one of them bent down toward her, she suddenly sprang to life and the Guardians watching jerked their heads back in surprise. In the footage, Asha grabbed the curved knife and slit two of the guards' throats before they even knew what was happening. She leveled another guard with a high kick and grabbed his sidearm as he staggered back against the wall. The knife was planted into his skull at the same moment an energy round was blasted into the face of the remaining guard. After a moment's hesitation, she pulled the knife out and ran to the main room. The camera shifted perspective to a wider angle in the central chamber and a blurry Asha was now tearing through dark figures, many of whom seemed to be scrambling to get away from her. Behind her, a ship rose into the port in the ceiling.

The Guardians all turned from the monitor to look at her as she passed. They nodded toward her, and she returned their sign of respect with a wink.

6

Despite Asha's insistence that she was perfectly fine after being forcibly kidnapped and tortured over the course of the past day, she was taken to the palace medical bay once they returned to Elyria. Anyone else who had undergone such an ordeal would likely have been scarred for life, but she'd already endured far worse on Earth and seemed eager to shrug off the whole incident. The men hadn't attempted to rape her in captivity, reportedly out of religious reasons. But their faith said little about abduction, abuse, and execution, it seemed.

After seeing she was taken care of, Lucas accompanied Maston down two hundred levels to the deepest, darkest corner of the Grand Palace dungeon where Tulwar was to be held until trial. The green-eyed Xalan had been taken to an adjacent holding room, and Lucas found Alpha peering through the one-way glass at him. It was hard to read Xalan facial expressions, but Lucas thought he saw one he could place: recognition.

"Do you know him?"

Alpha was snapped out of his gaze, surprised to find Lucas beside him.

"I do. He was a roboticist-turned-genetic engineer back on Xala. He worked with my father and me for many years before he was recruited for a project that caused them to cease speaking."

"The Shadows," Lucas said, an involuntary shiver working its way through him.

"Correct. He has since become a leading figure in the Genetic Science Enclave. How he came to be here, I do not know."

The Xalan was restrained in front of a metal table where his claws were bolted into the surface. Lucas had heard that when captured, Xalans would often kill themselves in order to avoid questioning, and they certainly weren't taking any chances with this one.

"Why is he here? Why is he working with the Fourth Order?"

Alpha shook his head.

"Conspiring with the Sorans for any reason was long thought of as blasphemy, but obviously it is a new tactic to attempt to destabilize the planet."

Lucas's ears were still ringing from the raid. He wondered if they'd ever stop this time.

"We fought a machine down there, something incredibly deadly, splicing ancient Soran tech with new weaponry and systems. It moved almost like a Shadow."

Alpha nodded.

"That is almost certainly his doing, as is the recent micro-explosive used in the attack and the cloaked transport vessel. He worked on the stealth drive with my father, and has apparently been able to replicate it on a smaller scale."

A freckle-faced young officer approached the pair of them.

"We're ready for you, uh, sir," he said, gazing up at the eight-foot-tall creature in front of him.

"You're going to talk to him?" Lucas asked, surprised.

"I will attempt to do so. He will die before he speaks to the Sorans, but he was a mentor to me in my youth, many years past."

He held up another translator collar like the one he wore.

"So you may all listen."

A crowd was gathering, and Lucas saw Tannon approach.

"Let him in," he said, nodding to the guard.

The door slid open and Alpha strode inside, ducking under the frame. The grizzled, angry look of the green-eyed Xalan immediately shifted into one of obvious shock. Alpha strode over to the table where he was restrained, clipped the translator collar around his neck, then circled around in front of him.

"I did not believe it when I heard," the prisoner said, his voice higher pitched than Alpha's. "The brightest hope for Xalan science in a millennium turned traitor. Slaughtering his own kind, cavorting with Sorans, and now making toys for them."

He jerked his head, apparently referring to his translator collar.

"You have no place to say such things, [garbled]."

Whatever the creature's name was, Alpha's translator couldn't pronounce it, which always seemed to be the case with Xalans.

"Undetectable explosives, stealth transports, energy weapons, combat machines. All crafted for your supposed enemy," said Alpha as he sat down across from him.

The green-eyed Xalan made a curt guttural sound.

"The Council made a ruling a few years ago when this project was devised. The enemy of our enemy is an ally. This planet now lies in chaos because of my work here. I accomplished what a thousand battleships could not. I struck at the very *heart* of this civilization," he said forcefully.

Alpha waved a claw dismissively.

"You struck, but missed. The High Chancellor lives. Your Soran puppet is captured. You will never see sunlight again, and they will torture you for years for intelligence."

"I shall give them nothing," he said. "And I am sure you have already willingly given them information no true Xalan would ever speak of, even under threat of pain and death. Such a thing is unheard of. You may in fact be the greatest coward in the history of our species."

"And what of you?" Alpha said, annoyed. "You speak freely now, though you must know there are Soran ears listening."

"I planned to say nothing, but your presence here . . . unnerves me. It is revolting to see one so promising lose his way."

The prisoner sneered at Alpha as he lowered his voice.

"Do you have any idea who they are sending after you now? After you killed the High Commander? The Council is furious."

"It matters not."

"You may not feel that way when the Desecrator darkens your door."

That made Alpha freeze.

"You threaten me a with a children's tale?" he asked.

"I do not, but you will learn that soon enough. He will teach you what sort of punishment a Xalan should endure when he turns his back on his own kind."

Alpha was angry now, and slammed his claw on the table.

"You accuse me of betraying my people? I received my father's message. I know what you and the Council have been keeping from us, all of us, for thousands of years. This lie has fueled our civilization to the brink of ruin!"

The green-eyed Xalan nodded.

"So it is true, you do know. It was a mystery why Commander [garbled] was pursuing you personally, but now it is clear. I pleaded with them to spare you. I told them I could bring you back and you could work under my tutelage as in the old days. But now I see how far gone you truly are. They were right; you should be dead like the rest of your clan."

Alpha was fuming at the restrained creature before him. The prisoner's green eyes glinted as he pressed on, his lips curled over his stained teeth in what looked almost like a wretched smile.

"Did Commander [garbled] tell you *how* your father died?"

Lucas looked nervously at Tannon, who was staring straight ahead, watching the conversation unfold, as were a dozen high-ranking officials around him. The creature continued.

"I know they told the public it was a targeted Soran airstrike, but that was a merciful excuse to hide his treachery."

Alpha's claws rattled on the table as he tapped them furiously. Lucas was growing increasingly uneasy.

"They restrained him in the Council chambers, and brought in your brothers, one at a time."

"Tannon," Lucas finally said. "Get him out of there."

The prisoner continued.

"After each charge was read, one of them was beheaded in front of him as he cried out."

"Tannon!" Lucas shouted, and a dozen heads turned to look at him, except those of the two creatures in the soundproof room. Alpha seethed and Lucas could see his muscles tensing. Alpha touched something on his metal hand and a mechanism somewhere in the room clicked. Tannon nodded to the guard who tried to open the door.

"Sir, it's locked. He's done something to it."

"Undo it, damnit!" Tannon roared.

"By the time they brought your sister in, he was weeping. It was pathetic. I could not believe this was the brilliant mind I once revered."

A sister? Alpha had never mentioned her in all their time together. Lucas banged his hands on the window to no avail. *Don't, Alpha. He's baiting you.*

"For the final, most poisonous charge of high treason, they cut her up piece by piece as she was still alive and screaming. It was the last thing he saw before he—"

Alpha leapt across the table and plunged his claws into the creature's throat. Soldiers yelled and fired at the seals of the door in an attempt to open it.

Black blood gushed out onto the table as the two locked eyes. The translator was still projecting the dying creature's thoughts.

"We could have . . . won this war . . . you and I."

"I will win it," Alpha said coldly, his teeth bared. "I will purge our people of monsters like you."

He ripped the creature's esophagus open and the captive Xalan collapsed on the table. Alpha was visibly shaking as he rested his bloody claws on the metal surface.

The door finally opened and soldiers stormed in with assault rifles pointed at him. Tannon marched in and Lucas quickly followed. Blood pooled around the creature's head and was dripping quietly onto the floor.

"Unauthorized execution of a restrained prisoner?" Tannon said. "I should have you share his fate right here, right now."

"I was . . . I did not . . ." Alpha stammered to find the words. Lucas had seen him fight when necessary, but this was a level of brutality he never expected from his friend.

Alpha looked up at Lucas with pain in his eyes.

"I was unaware of the specifics of my clan's death. I believed my sister would have at least been spared. She . . . was so young. She had nothing to do with any of it."

"I'm sorry, Alpha," Lucas said.

"And I am too," Tannon said. "But what about the intel we just lost? All you got him to say was what we already know."

Alpha shook off his shock momentarily.

"I extracted a large amount of encrypted data from his workstation in the Rhylos base. He would not have said anything further to me or you, but I may be able to glean useful information from what we recovered during the raid. I will set to work decoding it immediately . . . assuming I am not about to be executed or imprisoned."

Tannon sighed and rubbed his eyes with his hands.

"Get out of here and cleaned up. The rest of you, incinerate this piece of shit and make sure Maston doesn't do this to Tulwar next door."

Alpha walked to the door as soldiers parted in front of him. Lucas followed him toward the lift and could see he was still shaking.

"This war," he said with a wavering voice, "it has changed me, deeply."

"Not many of us still recognize ourselves," Lucas said. "I certainly don't."

"I must . . . I must decode his data. I am sorry you had to witness that."

He stepped into the lift with four armed guards accompanying him. Apparently Tannon wasn't letting him stroll around unmonitored after that incident.

"I would have done the same," Lucas said. The look in Alpha's eyes was one of haunting sorrow.

"Alpha, what is the Desecrator?"

Alpha glanced up at him.

"A story. Nothing more."

But there was no mistaking the expression of fear he wore as the doors closed.

Lucas returned to the holding block and found Mars Maston slouched against the wall opposite another pane of one-way glass. Inside was Hex Tulwar, his remaining arm restrained while his stump was wrapped in a bloody pressurized bandage hooked up to a nearby machine. He legs were firmly planted to the floor inside unmoving metal cuffs, and his shirt remained torn open to show his scars. His face was battered from the crash and Maston's subsequent assault. No one was questioning him, and he barely looked conscious. Lucas figured he must be on a steady flow of painkillers for the recent loss of his limb.

Maston was disheveled with his uniform unbuttoned and curled black hair covering his eyes. He rubbed his raw knuckles, which were split open from their recent contact with Tulwar's face. He spoke without looking at Lucas.

"If you're here to stop me from finishing the job, don't worry, everyone on this level has strict orders not to let me in there."

He turned to him.

"Though I hear no one made any such restrictions on your friend down the hall. I didn't think he had it in him."

Lucas stared through the glass at Tulwar, whose head was bobbing slightly.

"He was provoked."

Maston let out a short laugh. Lucas thought he smelled the all-too-familiar scent of alcohol, or whatever its equivalent was here.

"Provoked? You're going to tell me about being provoked when you stopped me from killing the man who murdered Cora in cold blood?"

Lucas sighed.

"No one cares about another dead Xalan. But they'll care about him."

He nodded toward Tulwar.

"Not for long," Maston said darkly. "We're already releasing evidence onto the Stream about his conspiracy with the Xalans. We got plenty from the raid, and even his allies will find it indefensible. The wildfire of the Fourth Order is about to be extinguished. And when it's his turn to be put down for good, I'll be the one to do it."

Lucas turned to Maston.

"When he was on his knees back there, he said something about being greeted by Kyneth and Zurana. Who are they?"

Maston scoffed.

"Pagan nonsense, though a belief half the planet used to share back in ancient times."

He scratched his head and continued staring straight ahead.

"Kyneth and Zurana were the first two Sorans. They arose out of the Blessed Forest a few million years ago and gave birth to our entire race. They eventually became worshipped as gods, and their followers believe they sit on the oak thrones, judging the dead who enter the afterlife."

"And you're not a believer, I take it?"

Maston shook his head.

"Almost no one is anymore. Well, no one but these fanatics who have twisted it into their own self-serving dogma." He motioned to Tulwar. "When we grew into this age of science, it seemed impossible for anyone to truly believe these superstitious folktales. And yet, some still persist. Religion was actually made illegal on Sora a few eras ago, but that was a disaster. After the Sacred Wars, we let people think what they wanted."

"The Blessed Forest, huh? We had a story like that back on Earth, but it was a garden, and there was a talking snake and some really bad fruit involved. A lot of people believed that one too."

"Legends are more interesting than facts, I suppose."

Maston was starting to slur noticeably now. He paused for a moment and stared past Lucas.

"Cora believed," he said quietly. "Not in all the bullshit in the Tomes of the Forest. But she believed in a greater power, that someone was looking out for her, for us. I mocked her for it, but some days I wish I had her faith. It made her so . . . peaceful. Even the deaths of her father and brothers she handled with more grace than should be possible. I never understood that kind of power. I probably never will."

He looked directly at Lucas.

"I-I don't have the ability *not* to kill Tulwar for this. What you said stopped me for a moment, but I'll never forgive him. Not like she would. I can't. And he'll never forgive me."

"Forgive *you*? For what?"

Maston waved him off. He reached into his coat and pulled out a small vial of brown liquid. He threw his head back and inhaled the entire thing. A few more clinked inside his coat.

"Why the hell am I talking to you anyway? I've had too many of these. Just leave me alone."

Lucas shook his head and turned to leave. If he kept that pace, Maston's vials would render him unconscious soon enough. But who could blame him? It had been a hell of a day. A hell of a year, for that matter.

Lucas left Maston to wallow, locked ten feet away from a man he desperately wanted dead. It was a tragic scene Lucas was finding hard to shake, and it had been a glimpse inside Maston's head that went beyond the pompous asshole from the party or the vengeful soldier he'd seen since then. Cora's death had hit him hard, and after learning something of their history, it was difficult not to feel for him. Lucas wondered if he would have been better off letting Maston beat Tulwar into oblivion back on Rhylos. What did Lucas care about the politics of this strange planet anyway?

But he owed Talis. She had faith in him when a dozen military officials were likely calling for his execution back when he was locked up, and had treated him with nothing but kindness ever since. If she wanted the murderer of her daughter to face justice alive, then so be it.

The lift doors opened and Lucas found himself on a level of the palace he'd never been to before. He double checked the virtual map on his wrist and found he was indeed in the right location, thankfully no longer deep under the planet's surface. There were people bustling around everywhere, and Lucas was relieved to spot a familiar face. *What was his name again?*

"Keeper Auran!" he called, motioning to the old man. The man smiled, adding a host of new wrinkles to his complexion, and he sauntered over to Lucas. His long robes were a rich green today with gold cords weaving in and out of the fabric.

"It is good to see you well," he said warmly. "After I left the Throne Room I feared the worst when I heard the explosion."

"Glad to see you weren't around either," Lucas said.

"Indeed. I've heard the lady is recovering from her recent brush with the Fourth Order?"

"She is," Lucas said as the pair of them walked down the hall.

"I must apologize on behalf of my planet that you would receive such a welcome after making the perilous journey you have."

Lucas waved him off.

"Trust me, if you came to Earth you would have seen wars and depravity a lot worse than your rebellion."

Auran sighed.

"We've had plenty of conflicts worse than this most recent flare-up. It seems there is no escaping them for Sorans, here or elsewhere."

"Can I ask you something?" Lucas said as he caught two older women staring at him as he passed. He could hear them whisper between themselves once his back was to them.

"Certainly," Auran said, his gait slow and methodical.

"Why does the Fourth Order hate the Vales so much? Or is it the government in general?"

"Ah," Auran said, nodding. "Someone needs to sit you down and give you a Soran history lesson someday."

"Haven't had much time for that yet," Lucas said.

"I suppose that would be true; you've been too busy making it."

"Making what?"

"History, of course."

Lucas chuckled. He sometimes forgot the weight of his appearance on Sora. Why people were staring at him left and right as he walked down the hall. His face was plastered across the Stream in every home. The stranger. The alien. The Earthborn.

"As for your question, it warrants an answer, but it's not one I can provide you with here."

Lucas was confused.

"What? Why not?"

"Though Talis Vale is a more friendly Chancellor than we've had in decades, she does have her sticking points. Speaking about that day within the palace is strictly forbidden."

"What day?"

"I cannot speak further, lest my voiceprint be tagged and transmitted to security. Even as Keeper of the Palace, I would be subject to punishment."

This seemed much too draconian for the Talis Vale Lucas knew.

"Alright, sorry, I wouldn't want to get you in trouble."

Auran shook his head.

"It is of no consequence. I can hardly blame her. It is, after all, the day she lost her father."

Lucas walked on in silence as he thought that through. If her father was High Chancellor before her, this unspoken day must have been when she assumed power. But how did that relate to the fury of the Fourth Order?

"In any event, we have reached your destination, Lucas."

Lucas liked that Auran referred to him by name; he was growing tired of being called "Earthborn" all the time. The pair of them stopped near a large opaque door.

"How did you know where I was going?"

Auran smiled.

"Why else would you be on this floor?"

The doors opened and they were greeted by chaos. Children ran everywhere, being chased by teenaged Sorans trying to corral them. The room was full of toys, both holographic and physical, and the walls were painted brightly with landscapes of blue mountains and red trees. Auran entered with him and he had to avoid tripping over a stuffed animal, species unknown. Looking around the room, Lucas found what he was searching for.

"Hah!" Auran exclaimed. "I see your son has already met my granddaughter. Hello, Kyra and Noah!"

At the sound of his name, Noah turned his head. He was kneeling on the ground next to a young girl, and was dressed in a light blue one-piece covered with seven-pointed stars. When he saw

Lucas, he shoved himself to his feet and ran over to give his leg a bearhug.

"Oo-cas!" he squealed.

"Hey, little man," Lucas said, hoisting him up into his arms. "Having fun?"

Noah nodded vigorously.

The little girl he was playing with had wispy blond hair, sparkling blue eyes, and a pair of deep dimples. Auran reached for her hand as she toddled toward them.

"This is my granddaughter, Kyra," he said.

"Hello," Lucas said and smiled at her. She grinned mischievously, but quickly hid behind Auran's robes.

"Her mother works in the consular office a few floors up."

The palace nursery was for the children of those serving in the Vale administration and working in the building on a daily basis. Lucas had been told Noah was brought here in order to socialize him with other children. At over a year old, he hadn't had any contact with anyone close to his age in months, and when he had, it was in a cannibal orphanage in god knows what conditions. From the looks of things now, however, he seemed to be adjusting just fine. Lucas eyed the burns creeping down past the sleeves of his tiny outfit. The kid sure was resilient.

"How old is she?" Lucas asked.

"About little Noah's age here, though I'm sorry I can't recall the proper Earth year translation. Arithmetic was never my strong suit."

Noah waved to be set down and he ran toward the little girl. He took her by the sleeve and the two of them wobbled off toward a brightly lit console projecting animated versions of nearby planets. Noah was a little too eager to get there and fell flat onto his butt, which made Kyra giggle.

"Born a trillion miles apart and already getting along famously," Auran said with a wink.

"I'm glad he's found a friend," Lucas said as he watched the two babble at each other. "Lord knows he could use one."

A few hours later, Lucas had seen Noah off to bed in a lavish nursery room near the top of the palace. The child had every toy and comfort in the world up there, but he still fell asleep each night clutching the holoball Alpha had made him aboard the Ark.

Now, Lucas sat in the darkened hospital wing, a few feet from Asha's bed where she lay sleeping. She'd had several microsurgeries throughout the course of the day, repairing torn muscles and hairline fractures, and now had been out for a few hours.

Lucas could not sleep.

His dreams had been strange lately, unsettling. Drifting off would likely yield some terrifying new vision, and so he staved off exhaustion for as long as he could. He found himself looking through a scroll, a small, thin, metal cylinder that projected a virtual piece of paper from its side. You could write and read on it, but its primary purpose was viewing the Stream. He sifted through the various news stories of the day, the majority of which were about him, Asha, Alpha, and Tulwar's attack on the palace. Lucas had the volume tuned into a frequency set that only he could hear it, so as not to disturb Asha. A newswoman dressed in what looked like a shirt made out of silver scales was showing footage from the early morning raid. Lucas saw the familiar sight of Tulwar side by side with his Xalan scientist after their capture. The video feed cut off before Maston showed up and started beating him into the dust.

Lucas flipped around some more until he discovered the search function. It was for the Palace Archives, a place Auran had told him might have the answers he sought about the Fourth Order and the Vales.

He was met with nothing. No results other than a simple page detailing the various atrocities committed by the Order over the years. And there were many. It seemed the palace assault wasn't their first bombing, and they'd targeted dozens of other government buildings on a variety of continents. Mysteriously absent, however, was any explanation of how the Order came into existence, or even what their stated goals were. The Soran term for "anarchists" came up frequently.

Lucas had another idea. He looked up when Talis Vale came into power. Records showed that it was on the eighth of Torsis in 24,440 CT. He didn't know what "CT" meant as a year indicator, but he knew Torsis was one of Sora's fifteen months. He entered the date into the search modifier. A singular result sprang up in front of him.

"The Fall of Vitalla."

He tried to enter the information page, but was met with a flashing red error message across the scroll.

Restricted Access: Violation Logged

Violation? It was true then, Talis didn't want anyone speaking about what happened that day, or apparently even reading about it. He wondered if someone was about to come arrest him, but a few minutes passed and the ward was silent. His scroll had returned to normal.

He tried to press his luck, attempting to enter a variety of links to "related stories" about Vitalla. He earned a new violation each time when he was met with the same foreboding message.

Midway through the list of terms, he came across one called "Send-off." He pressed it absentmindedly, assuming he'd get another violation, but was surprised when a video actually started playing. He was further stunned when he saw who was speaking in it.

It was Corinthia Vale, as gorgeous as when he'd seen her at the party, if not more so. She was standing on a stage that almost looked like it was made out of crystal. A line of dignitaries stood behind her including Talis, Tannon, and . . . Hex Tulwar? It couldn't be.

But behind them all was a familiar sight; the sheer red cliffs of Rhylos were unmistakable. A fleet of seemingly enormous ships hung in the sky behind them. Lucas's face was illuminated by the warm glow of the scroll as she began to speak.

"Greetings citizens of Rhylos, and the billions of Sorans watching on this momentous day."

The strong winds did their best to tear her blond hair from their braids, but they remained in place while the ends of her long dress danced about.

"I have been privileged and honored to have worked on the Vitalla project for the past decade, an idea sparked many years before I was even born. It represents the single greatest advancement in our history, and one that can help benefit the least fortunate among us."

She spoke articulately and with obvious confidence. A born leader. Or, from the way she had described herself, a bred leader.

"Rhylos has been ravaged by disasters both natural and unnatural throughout history. Many here live in poverty, struggling with the challenges of day-to-day survival, things most of us take for granted. We knew when the Vitalla project was created that it should benefit those who need it the most. It has been an enlightening experience working with Grand Cleric Tulwar, a man who wants nothing more than to see his homeland rise again."

Tulwar smiled. He clasped his hands together and made a small bow in her direction. His hair was shorter, his face absent of insanity.

"The land may be beyond saving, but the people are not. Vitalla will be their salvation, and the Rhylosi will earn a reward they've long deserved."

She motioned behind her. Lucas could see an enormous metal structure sitting on the cliff behind them.

"In a few hours, the largest convoy fleet ever launched from our world will make its way to Vitalla, a world outside our solar system we've spent the better part of a hundred years terraforming. One hidden from the Xalans and now filled with every resource and comfort a Soran could want. Cities stand erected, waiting to be filled. Millions of homes have been manufactured and will offer the people of Rhylos a long-awaited respite from their troubles on Sora. There will be plenty of opportunities available for all. Some may attend schools and be taught by some of the greatest minds our world has to offer. Others will find plentiful work farming and mining."

The live audience cheered, and Corinthia couldn't contain a dazzling smile.

"As this is the largest colony we've ever constructed, and the first outside our own solar system, there will of course be challenges. The journey to Vitalla, which begins today, will take just over a year. A hundred million citizens of Rhylos will load into thousands of our largest ships, which will take them there. The convoy will be personally escorted by my grandfather, High Chancellor Vale, and he will bring the might of the Soran military to ensure the path is safe, and the destination secure."

A gruff-looking man behind her gave a curt nod. He was Talis's father, the original High Chancellor Vale. Varrus, was it? He looked like an older model of Tannon and wore a perfectly pressed suit adorned with an incredible number of distinctions. Both Tannon and Talis eyed the taller man reverently, and the crowd cheered at the mention of his name.

"My mother will be acting Chancellor while my grandfather is away. Our homeworld is more secure than it's ever been. With Xala defeated soundly at the Battle of Golgath, they have been forced to retreat and regroup, and we have little to fear from them for some time. The Soran Defense Initiative remains in place guarding our borders while at the same time deploying troops to safeguard the passage to Vitalla."

The winds were picking up now, and Corinthia had to shield her face from stinging sand.

"I now invite Grand Cleric Tulwar to say a few words on the behalf of his people."

Another short bow from Tulwar and he strode up to the podium where he greeted Corinthia with a friendly embrace. He looked like no religious figure Lucas had ever seen, dressed in a short red coat with knee high boots and golden chestplate.

"Zurana bless us!" he said as he reached the podium, his voice booming around the canyon.

"Kyneth save us!" came the monolithic reply from the audience.

Lucas was jolted out of the scroll by an alarm sounding in the hall. He frantically looked to Asha, who hadn't stirred, and then watched as a number of silvercoats sprinted past their door and bustled into the next room. The alarm was silenced and Asha's head rolled to her left. Lucas bent across her bed and threaded her hair from her face back over her ear. When he turned back to his scroll to continue playing the video, he was met with a familiar message:

Restricted Access: Violation Logged

Repeated tries only yielded the same result, and finally his scroll shut down completely and refused to turn back on. Perhaps he'd violated one protocol too many. He tossed the device to the foot of Asha's bed and rubbed his eyes as he leaned back in his chair.

What had happened at Vitalla? The feed he'd just watched showed the Vales and Tulwar as allies, even friends. What sort of betrayal would spark an entire resistance movement pushing the planet to the brink of civil war? And how was Maston mixed up in all this? The thoughts plagued him as he eventually drifted off to sleep in the darkness of the medical wing.

7

Lucas awoke from a booted kick. He jumped and saw Asha standing over him, dressed in a fresh set of tight-fitting Soran clothes made out of an unidentifiable green-and-black material.

"Up and at 'em, soldier."

Lucas looked around groggily. She had a white bandage around her tan forearm and was favoring her right leg.

"They're letting you out?"

"I'm letting myself out. I didn't even need to be in here in the first place."

Lucas rolled his eyes.

"You were caught in an explosion, kidnapped, and tortured, all within the last day."

Asha scoffed as she began rifling through her pack.

"And I hear you fought off a robot the size of a semi-truck, and I didn't see anyone forcing you in here."

Lucas rubbed his sides, which still ached.

"You know, few cracked ribs, the usual."

"Whatever, I'm getting out of here." She kept digging through her pack. Her burns and bruises did look noticeably better. "Where the hell is my Magnum? And my sword?"

"Natalie's watching over them in the armory, don't worry."

She shook her head.

"You and that gun, I swear. It's like your daughter."

"Says the girl frantically trying to find her own weapons. Though I suppose that revolver is a priceless artifact here."

Asha stopped cold, a look of horror creeping across her face.

"Oh shit."

"What?"

"Speaking of priceless artifacts, I'm pretty sure I lost that ancient necklace full of fist-size diamonds I was wearing the other night."

Lucas laughed.

"Hah, maybe the Fourth Order will have their ransom after all."

"Not likely," said a voice from the doorway. It was Talis Vale, clad in a long purple gown that flowed over her feet. "It was a fake."

Asha didn't miss a beat with the sudden appearance of the High Chancellor. Box-shaped palace guards loomed behind her.

"What, you didn't trust me with the real one?" Asha asked.

Talis walked into the room while the guards stayed behind.

"No, no, that isn't it, my dear. The original was stolen from the palace vault a century ago, but we don't like to tell people that," she said with a wry smile.

The guards were eyeing Lucas, and he wondered if those were just the usual stares he got as the Earthborn, or if they were about to take him into custody for his apparently illegal inquiries into Vitalla last night. They made no moves toward him.

"I'm glad to see you up and about, Asha," Talis continued. "I wanted to personally come and apologize for your treatment at the hands of my . . . countrymen."

Asha waved her off.

"I was just telling him, it was nothing."

"If that was nothing, I can't imagine what your Earth must have been like."

"Well, the last few years certainly weren't great, as you've heard."

Asha paused, and her tone shifted into something more subdued.

"I was sorry to hear about your daughter."

Talis nodded.

"Thank you, though I suppose if anyone can share my pain, it's the pair of you. We three seem to have lost everyone over the past few years. It's a lonely place to be, but you should be thankful you have each other to help you through."

Lucas and Asha glanced at one other. If someone had told Lucas years ago that he'd fall for the woman who shot him and left him for dead in hundred-degree heat, he'd have laughed in their face. What a strange journey it had been.

"Also," Talis continued, "I have a humble request of the pair of you."

Talis's last request almost got him killed when he tried to stop Maston from executing Hex Tulwar. What would it be this time?

"If both of you are feeling well enough after your most recent ordeal, I'd like for you to discover a more pleasant side of Sora. One that doesn't involve imprisonment, war, or bloodshed of any kind. I want you to experience the best of our world, not just the worst."

They were both taken aback.

"Uh, what did you have in mind?" Lucas asked.

A few hours later they were speeding through the air in a luxury hovercraft far larger than others Lucas could see. It was the size of a small room and had a full array of drinks and beverages on a central table surrounded by plush seating that wrapped its way around the cabin. The windows were only tinted from the outside this time, and they had an amazing view of the surrounding countryside, which showcased vibrant forests of twisted trees and crisp blue mountains that surrounded the glimmering cityscape of Elyria. A constant feed of the Stream was plastered against the far wall of the vehicle, and it was tuned to a local sporting event instead of the news broadcasts that were usually focused on the war or, more recently, the two of them.

Lucas didn't understand the rules of the game onscreen. Two teams were flying through the air in colorful armored jet suits, clutching electric melee stun weapons, which they frequently used to incapacitate each other. There was a glowing, floating ball they batted around between them, and the object of the game appeared to be to get it into one of four light spheres hovering around the arena.

"Hey Silo, what's this called again?" Lucas called up to the front.

"Sakala," the large man replied from the driver's seat. "I played it in prime school before the SDI. We won the provincial championship three years in a row."

Silo had volunteered to head up Lucas and Asha's security detail on the trip into Elyria that Talis had arranged. Flying adjacent to all four corners of their craft were smaller armored vessels full of non-Guardian, palace-issue bodyguards meant to ensure their safe passage to and from the metropolis up ahead. The menacing gun barrels poking out from all angles of their crafts ensured there was no competing traffic within a few hundred yards of them.

"Try these," Asha said, tossing Lucas a bundle of orange fruit. They were attached to a central stem like grapes. They were completely round and almost translucent. Lucas popped one in his mouth.

"Not bad. It's like, mango . . . cherry?"

"I haven't tasted one thing here I can actually place," Asha said, tearing off a piece of oval-shaped bread and dipping it into a bowl of blue syrup. "But it's all fantastic."

Perhaps they were just used to eating cockroaches and dead Xalans for too many years, but the spread before them was undeniably spectacular.

"Don't eat too much," Silo said from the front. "You've got dinner reservations at the Golden Leaf later."

"Any good?" Lucas asked, his mouth full of orange pulp.

"The waiting list is several years long and a meal there costs more than I make in month, so yeah, it's good."

Silo had been somewhat friendly to him previously but was much more jovial off-mission. Another armored man sat up in the cockpit with him. His shoulder armor had a palace security emblem stamped on it. He never turned around or spoke.

"Well, maybe you can take Kiati there some time," Lucas said. Silo erupted with laughter.

"That'll be the day. Against regulation."

"Officially?" Lucas said with a raised eyebrow.

"Officially," Silo said with a broad smile and a quick wink.

Asha looked up from her syrup-soaked bread.

"Who's Kiati?" she asked.

"You missed a lot while you were busy being kidnapped," Lucas taunted. She ignored him and sipped a goblet of sparkling water she scooped off the table. Lucas did the same and found it wasn't water after all. He forced himself to set it down and gazed out into the magnificent metropolis that surrounded them.

Elyria was even more remarkable up close than it was from afar. The hovercraft drifted lazily in and out of buildings that shot up thousands of feet in the air from the floor of the city. Each was probably twice as tall and wide as even Earth's largest structures. Silo, doubling as their tour guide in addition to running security, pointed out which were residential, commercial, or owned by the government. Other hovercraft darted by them, most without anyone at the wheel. Pre-programmed routes through the sky took the citizens of the city to and from their various destinations, though after the Machine War, they were told, that was about as advanced as AI-controlled tech was allowed to be.

"Check this out."

Lucas motioned for Asha to come to his window and pointed toward a particularly busy corridor that seemed to be clogged in an aerial traffic jam. Her eyes scanned the vista until she saw what he was referring to. It was hard to miss.

To their left was a thirty-story-high digital billboard that showed a picture of Asha in the woven white dress she'd worn to the announcement ceremony days ago. Next to her was Lucas in his dark, high-collared suit. The photo appeared to have been taken as they made their way to the podium on the promenade's stage. The glyphic Soran symbols spelled out a tagline:

Earthborn—by Jolo Houzan. Worth a trip across the galaxy.

Asha sighed.

"Back to modeling again," she said, exasperated.

Lucas called up to Silo.

"Shouldn't we be getting some royalties for that?"

Silo glanced at the billboard.

"Not my department," he said, digging around in his suit. "But that reminds me. Courtesy of the High Chancellor."

He tossed a pair of chips toward them, which Lucas caught in his lap.

"Spending marks."

Lucas tapped the chip and a tiny indicator was projected from it.

AVAILABLE BALANCE—50,000M.

Asha found hers read the same.

"Is this a lot?" she asked.

"How much are on them?" Silo replied.

"Fifty thousand each."

Silo let out a low whistle.

"Damn, I wish I was an alien."

Too often in recent years, Lucas's most vibrant memories had been forged out of horrific events back on Earth or in space. Too many still haunted him daily, from the Xalan invasion, to the American wastelands, to the horrors of Kvaløya, to Omicron's onslaught. Today, however, was a unique experience. It was a time he would never forget, for all the right reasons.

Lunch was a served in an eatery nestled inside a massive aquarium. The menu consisted of the fish that swam all around them, each completely unique from any they'd seen on Earth. All of them wore holographic tags that, when pointed to, would produce information about the species along with preparation options. Lucas took the chef's recommendation of "seared Rostin," which was a shark-like behemoth with eight fins and four rows of teeth. After the meal arrived, Asha kept stealing bites from his plate when he wasn't looking. Apparently her "grilled Vorkal" didn't suit her quite as much.

They were then whisked away to a private show of the town's hottest stage performance, *Sora D'lorata Mus'tovi,* which loosely translated to "The Lost Lovers of Sora." The stage was a circular ring of ornate wood and metal that wrapped around the audience, and holographic backgrounds made it almost seem like they were living out a three-dimensional film. The story followed a soldier sent off to war who left his young love behind. When he returned, she had been forced to marry a cruel provincial tyrant who framed the soldier for murder after he attempted to win her back. The costumes indicated it was from a time period that pre-dated space travel, and Lucas could have sworn he saw a glimmer of a tear in the forever stoic Asha's eye as the soldier lay dying in his lover's arms in the production's final moments. Afterward, despite the show being performed by reportedly the most popular actors on the continent, it was the cast who wanted their pictures taken with the famed Earthborn, rather than the other way around.

Dinner at the Golden Leaf was a breathtaking event, mainly because the restaurant was on top of the tallest superscraper in the city, Stoller Tower. They could see for hundreds of miles in every direction, and a brilliant span of stars greeted them overhead while an invisible energy field kept the winds at bay. A staff of dozens waited on them hand and foot, and Lucas lost track of how many courses populated their meal as surrounding patrons looked over at them in wonder and envy. Lucas insisted that the ever-present palace security staff be given a meal as well, and though they refused initially, by the end of the night they were wolfing down thousand-mark plates of rare meat at an adjoining table. Silo couldn't stop grinning from ear to ear after he finished his enormous rack of Yutta ribs. Marveling at their size, Lucas wondered what sort of creature they were once attached to.

The final destination of the exhausting, enjoyable day was a return to the Grand Palace itself. Silo informed them that the mammoth structure had been destroyed and rebuilt a half dozen times over the lifespan of civilized Sora. Now, it stood as an amalgam of ancient architecture and state-of-the-art defensive tech. The tower was an impregnable fortress, daring anyone to try and knock it down again. Well, nearly impregnable, it seemed, given recent events.

As twilight descended, Silo left them at the hovercraft hangar, bidding them a good evening, not noticing the mark chip Lucas slipped into one of the pockets that hung off his armor as they departed. Despite the extravagance of the locales they had visited, everyone they encountered bent over backward to offer them everything on the house. With barely a mark spent, Lucas thought Silo could make better use of the funds.

Malorious Auran greeted them as they entered and escorted them to the highest levels of the palace. He explained this had been where they were meant to reside before the "unfortunate business with the Order," as he put it.

When the lift opened, a pair of enormous frosted glass doors stood before them. As they approached, elaborate carvings began to reveal themselves in the material. Lined faces of men wearing crowns, women with long flowing hair and sly smiles. Portraits of empires, risen and fallen long ago. Auran confirmed what the door suggested.

"The Eternity Room has been occupied by some of the most distinguished figures in Soran history when they came to visit the royal families or, more recently, the High Chancellors. Lords, kings, emperors, generals, heroes, and sometimes villains have all rested in comfort here, or in one of its many iterations throughout the ages."

He struggled with the heavy doors, and with an assist from Lucas, flung them open.

"And though you surely deserve a place among such legends, I beseech you not to break anything," he said with pleading eyes.

The room before them was more astonishing than anything they'd witnessed in Elyria. The ceilings were easily three stories high and completely covered in an elaborate mural. Figures that could have been kings or gods were locked in an epic struggle with celestial armies at their command, soaring through swirls of painted stars and planets.

On the ground, the floor was covered with a shimmering stone that almost looked wet, but was completely dry to the touch. Furniture was carved out of assuredly antique wood and inlaid with precious metals and fabrics. A kitchen area presented yet another cornucopia of food, though Lucas was far too stuffed to even think about sampling from it. Every few feet a new painting hung on the wall. None of them were the modern holographic art Lucas had seen around the palace. He ran his hand over a jewel-encrusted longsword that sat on a nearby table. An identifier said the weapon was nearly forty thousand years old, but the blade shone as if it had been crafted yesterday. Everything in the room was simultaneously old and brand new, artifacts somehow preserved precisely in their original state through science he couldn't fathom. As they drifted inside, enraptured by their surroundings, Auran stayed at the entrance.

"I won't bore you with further history," he said. "Though I could compose a novel about nearly every object in this room. I wish you two a good night, and do not hesitate to call if you need anything."

He tapped the communicator badge attached to his robes, and gracefully backed out of the room, closing the towering doors as he went.

Alone in silence, despite all the invaluable treasures that adorned the room, Lucas was only looking at one thing.

Her.

Asha stood facing him, wearing a bronze one-shouldered dress one of her many stylists had deemed appropriate for their night on the town. The lights had dimmed since Auran's departure, sensing it was far past the usual bedtime hour, and the room was soaked in moonlight from the wall of windows across from them. Asha was radiant. Ethereal.

The silence spoke more than words could. After six months of imprisonment and being torn apart, it was the first time they were truly alone and unencumbered since those sleepless nights aboard the Ark.

His buttonless jacket was flung across a twenty-sixth-century armchair, with his shirt not far behind. Her unclasped dress dropped to the floor and pooled out around her like water. As she kissed him, an old vein of passion ran through him with such ferocity it stole the breath from his lungs. She ran her hands across his chest, tracing the long, curved scar that ran all the way down to his hip. Her own skin was a familiar map of old battle wounds, long healed, one he'd memorized by touch. But here, now, it was like he was rediscovering her all over again, the way he had that first unreal night in the water chamber. It had been so long.

An hour passed before they even bothered finding the bed, tucked into another ornately decorated section of the suite. It was another two before sleep found them, and afterward they lay intertwined in the liquid sheets, the last king and queen of a dead planet.

Despite complete and utter exhaustion from the events of the day, and the activities of the night, Lucas awoke when a draft shook him. He felt around the bed and, as his eyes adjusted, saw an all-too-familiar sight. Asha was gone, still not comfortable enough to share a full night's sleep. With all she'd been through, it was hard to blame her, but still, it disappointed Lucas the way it always had on the Ark.

Here however, her disappearance was a bit more worrisome. The Ark was a shoebox compared to the palace, and a search of the entire room revealed she hadn't relocated to another section. Lucas felt panic rising in his chest and considered contacting palace security.

Stopping to collect himself, he decided against such a reaction. She hadn't been taken again. Not here, not in silence. He had an idea of where she might be.

The elevator ride was a long one, going from one of the highest floors of the palace to one of the lowest, several thousand feet underground. When he reached his desired level, the attendant stationed there recognized him immediately and waved him through. When Lucas asked if he'd seen a half-dressed Earth-girl come by, he replied with a sheepish smile and a nod toward the direction of the floating text over the adjacent entryway:

Earth Archive

The doors parted and Lucas found himself once more among the rows of glass cases full of his old possessions from the Ark. Hearing footsteps on the other side of the room, he moved toward the section where he knew he'd find her.

But she wasn't there. The armory rows sat empty, displaying all their appropriated guns along with their current loadouts. Natalie sat mounted next to Asha's Magnum and sword. She hadn't come for them after all. *What's she doing here?*

The room was so deathly silent he could actually hear her breathing the next row over. When he turned the corner and saw her, he understood.

It was the book section, filled with collected Earth tomes from Milton to Rowling. But she wasn't reading. Rather, the enclosure she was looking into held only two pieces of paper. Photos.

The first was charred around the edges, but clearly displayed its subjects. In it, Asha smiled peacefully with a glittering ring on her finger, wrapped in the arms of a handsome young man with blue eyes. Below that was another picture, one far more mangled. Only faint traces of a woman and her child could be seen. Lucas's wife. His son.

Upon seeing the photo, one he had thought lost a long while ago, the same feelings stirred in him that were surely storming inside her. Pain, sorrow, love, things buried away for years now. It was a life lived so long ago, it felt like fiction most days. But not now, not in a moment when he could look into their eyes again.

"I don't know if it will ever stop," she said solemnly, not looking at him as he stood next to her.

"It won't," Lucas said as he brushed his fingers against the glass separating him from his family.

"It's not just Christian, it's all of them. Everyone I lost. Out there, you couldn't think about it. Each day was all about your next drink, your next meal, your next near-death experience. There was no room for them in your head. But here?"

"It's quieter," Lucas finished her thought. "You can hear them all the time."

She finally looked at him, an old fury burning in her eyes, rekindled once more by the image before her. But the wrath was mixed with sorrow, brought on by a loss she could likely never truly recover from.

"The anger is always there. Just under the surface. Like it's going to burn me alive if it doesn't have a place to vent," she said, and he could almost feel the heat radiating off her.

"I know," said Lucas, recalling the constant rage that propelled him through the past few years. Rage that still simmered within him at all hours of the day. But like her, grief was carved deep into his heart. A permanent mark that would forever stain his soul.

"This life, it's not for me," she continued. "I'm no princess. I don't need to be rescued. I don't need to be spoiled. I don't want to be some political pawn or celebrity idol here. I want to actually matter."

"You matter," Lucas said, swallowing his own emotions.

"I don't, not yet. I've done nothing here but get myself captured by some separatist idiot. What makes you think we can do anything to help end a ten-thousand-year-old war?"

Lucas paused as he considered the question and shoved remaining thoughts of his family into the prison of memory where they usually resided.

"Alpha."

"What, the message? You honestly think that will work?" she said with crossed arms and obvious skepticism.

"'The supreme art of war is to subdue the enemy without fighting.'"

"Okay, Confucius."

"Sun Tzu, actually. I think they've got his book over there." Lucas motioned toward a pillar a few yards away.

"No amount of firepower will win this war for good the way things are going," he continued. "Only when the people lose faith in their leaders will Xala be weak enough for us to strike a blow that actually cuts to their heart."

"Since when are you a military strategist?" Asha asked.

Lucas shrugged. "I like history. No reason to repeat Earth's mistakes here."

"Still, it can all seem pointless sometimes."

Asha leaned against the glass and played absentmindedly with the ends of her short, sheer nightdress.

"I want to show you something," Lucas said. "Come with me."

They were still underground, but only twenty or so levels beneath the surface. This time they were met by a pair of smiling female silvercoats who led them into a room secured by a twenty-inch-thick metal door. The attendants returned to the other room as they walked toward what lay in the middle.

"You matter," Lucas said. "You matter to him."

Their unborn son was decidedly human shaped at six months, though would likely still fit in the palm of either of their hands. Asha stroked the glass of the tank when she reached it. The child was suspended in a viscous, aqua-colored liquid. Tiny tubes threaded out of him, including a synthetic umbilical cord attached to whirring machines next to the enclosure.

"You matter to me," Lucas said as he came up behind her and rested his hand on the back of her neck.

"I'd be lost here without you. So would Noah. So would he," he said, motioning to the fragile child before them.

She remained silent for a while.

"God dammit," she said. "You're good. Playing the unborn kid card. You son of a bitch."

She grinned, but the smile gradually faded.

"You know, it's strange. Even being so far removed from the child, from this 'pregnancy,' I can still feel him some days. I swear yesterday I felt him kick . . ."

Her voice trailed off, but soon she returned to the point Lucas had been attempting to make.

"Yes, of course I'll stick around to complete this weird family unit. Someone has to make sure these kids end up normal."

Lucas laughed.

"One pulled from the wreckage of a smoldering cannibal village, the other bred in a tank who will never step foot on his home planet? I think we've got our work cut out for us."

She nodded.

"I guess it has to be more than just revenge, then. We have to fight to make sure they can grow up in peace," she said, looking at the tiny creature inside the tank. "They should never have to live through the kinds of things we have."

"They won't," Lucas said firmly, even if he wasn't entirely convinced of the statement himself.

As they made their way out of the incubation room, Lucas noticed a familiar-looking door. It was the same symbol that hung over a room near the Earth Archive, and he'd seen it again just a few minutes ago when they'd been down there. *Can't hurt just to take a peek.* He pulled Asha toward it, and she looked up at the Soran glyph floating above the entryway.

"Eleven?" she asked, translating the symbol. "What's in there?"

"I think I know," Lucas said, but was surprised when he was greeted by a rather rude "Not Authorized" message that flashed at him from the control cluster when he attempted to open the door. Asha figured it out.

"You think it's our old crew?" she said, referring to the eleven brain-dead humans Alpha had collected from all over the globe before he met them. They were meant to be "scientific specimens" to take back and study on his home planet. Lucas instinctively scratched his largest scar. There were a dozen originally, but after sustaining horrific injury at the wrong end of a plasma rifle, one had donated half its collection of internal organs so that Lucas might live.

"I do," Lucas said. "But I don't know why they'd lock us out of here." The controls were still unresponsive, and after a third attempt to navigate them, the cluster shut down altogether.

"They let us wander around the armory freely, but not in here to see our old friends? What are they up to?" Lucas tapped the steel as he studied the elaborate locking mechanisms woven throughout.

"I don't know; the last time we opened a lock like that, it turned out I'd been sleeping next to a nuke. Some stones are better left unturned," Asha said as she moved toward the exit. Lucas furrowed his brow and gave the door one last pound before turning to follow her.

8

For the week that followed they lived cozily in the lap of luxury, each day another Talis-orchestrated sightseeing trip to the finest parts of the capital and continent meant to wash away the stresses of the Fourth Order assault. Each night was a circus of pleasure that far outclassed the evenings spent on the floor of the water chamber aboard the Ark. Some days felt like a lucid dream, while others were interrupted by nightmares that haunted Lucas with reminders of what he'd done to get there.

Reality came knocking when Lucas woke the morning before Guardian training was supposed to commence. He found himself staring at a feed of the Stream on the opposite wall through bleary eyes. As the room came into focus, he saw that Asha was sitting on the edge of the bed, already dressed and put together.

"Get up," she said when she saw he was awake. "There's about to be some serious shit going down around here."

The Stream was in total disarray as live newscasts and recorded video footage were spliced together, while text stories fluttered around the borders, each with different reports on what was happening. After a few minutes of processing the calamitous coverage, Lucas could make out the main details of what had occurred.

A planet called Kollux was, or at least had been, a major Soran military installation. Four hours ago, the small planet was besieged by an overwhelming Xalan force that had all but wiped out every major facility on the rocky surface. Three hundred thousand soldiers were annihilated almost instantly, caught unaware by a fleet that was supposed to still be wounded from the failed Earth campaign. They'd besieged the planet's bases from the air, and then dropped ground forces for face-to-face clean-up. It reminded Lucas of the war his own planet had recently endured. An orange-haired woman with obviously frayed nerves, who was reporting the story on one of the larger Stream feeds, assured viewers that Soran forces were already on the way to assist the remaining troops (provided there were remaining troops) and ensure the Xalan fleet didn't advance further. Kollux was in a star system light-years away, but according to the Stream, this was the furthest Xala had pushed since the homeworld strikes of the previous millennium.

The various screens floating around the horizontal video band showed footage of furious firefights on land, in the air, and in orbit around the planet. Several of them cut to black after particularly raucous explosions, and in all of them, it was clear who was winning. It wasn't the Sorans.

Lucas put on a shirt and pair of pants extracted from an oversized wardrobe stocked with a myriad of outfits meant to fit him and Asha.

"Have you heard from anyone?" he asked her. She sat on the bed, still glued to the projected newsfeed.

"I got pinged to expect orders shortly," she replied.

"Does that mean we're going?"

"I hope so," she said through gritted teeth as she watched all-too-familiar scenes of devastation play out on the feed in front of her.

A mix of fear and excitement rose up inside Lucas. As appealing as the past week of lavish comfort had been, he found he had an itch for vengeance that seemed like it would never leave him. They'd both made a promise to the Guardians, either to join them or at the very least help them if Maston was too stubborn to officially bring them onboard. They'd proven themselves in their dealings with the Fourth Order and earned the respect of at least some of the soldiers, though likely not Maston himself. The war was moving too fast for training.

On one of the screens, a screaming Soran soldier was being torn apart by two armored Xalans with gigantic bladed weapons. The camera, likely attached to the helmet of an adjacent soldier, soon flew into the air after the Xalans turned toward it, and then rolled across the ground a few feet away.

"Jesus," Lucas said. "They show this to the public?"

"Best way to drum up support for the war effort, I suppose," Asha replied. "How could you not be calling for the complete destruction of Xala after watching this?" It was true, Lucas could feel the anger rising inside him as the images onscreen too closely mirrored the war on his home planet they'd barely survived.

The screen flickered for a moment, then was consumed by a shot of a singular man, Tannon Vale. Asha stood up from the bed and Lucas joined her. He looked exhausted and disheveled. When he spoke, it was directly to them. This was not a widely projected address to the nation.

"Good morning, Earthborn, if you can call it that."

"What can we do?" Lucas said hurriedly.

"This event is an extreme cause for concern, if you haven't figured that out," Tannon said plainly. "It means the war is closer than it's been in centuries, and I'm afraid we might not survive another push like the one twelve hundred years ago. Their technology has evolved too rapidly, and we've been too caught up in our own civil strife."

His voice dropped.

"They could take Sora," he said quietly. "They could finally do it. We've never seen them this strong, even with their supposed losses on Earth."

Asha repeated Lucas's earlier sentiment.

"How can we help? Are we shipping out to Kollux?"

Tannon shook his head.

"Kollux is gone, despite what the news reports are saying. Wiped out completely. The Xalan fleet is already three systems away, their mission accomplished. It was a surgical strike on a forward base they know will take us decades to rebuild. But they won't wait for that. They're going to keep coming hard and fast after this. We need a distraction."

"What kind of distraction?" Lucas asked.

"I've been talking to your scientist. He's pulled something off the salvaged data core of that Fourth Order Xalan at long last. Something we can use."

"What is it?" asked Asha.

"I'll let him explain. He's down below waiting for you. I'm en route to Kollux to see if there's anything to recover from this godforsaken mess. I've instructed Maston and the Guardians to escort you to where you're going.

"Keep me posted on your mission progress. I'll be back on Sora before you get there."

"Tannon," Lucas interrupted, ignoring seniority and title. "Where the hell are we going?"

Tannon eyed something offscreen for brief moment before turning back to the lens.

"Somewhere you can make waves."

Despite the fact that Soran scientists all over the continent were bending over backwards to offer to help Alpha with his research, he had made the unusual request of being allowed to work in his old laboratory aboard the Ark. He'd been working on the white null core synthesis process initially, but had recently been consumed decrypting the data looted from the Fourth Order raid.

Lucas and Asha arrived at the hangar level and made their way into their old vessel, beaten and battered as it ever was. It was almost eerie to tread through the same corridors they'd spent so much time in. Glancing into the battle-ravaged CIC, memories of the heated firefight that took place there flooded Lucas's mind. The viewscreen remained shattered; a jagged hole was the only remnant of the central holotable. Storage crates once used as cover were peppered with burn marks and holes.

As they navigated toward the lab, the dead had long been cleared away, but black blood still stained the walls and floors. A thick layer of dust blanketed everywhere they walked, and three-pronged footprints had been tracked all throughout the corridors. The ship was dead. Why was Alpha still holed up in here?

When they finally did reach their destination, they saw that despite Alpha's refusal of Soran labor, he had accepted their technology to aid his endeavors. The room across from the lab, which had once held the stasis-bound humans, was now full of equipment running independent processes while he worked in the adjacent area. His lab had been completely stripped and refurbished with shiny new pieces of machinery that whirred and hummed and made the entire room feel alive. In the middle of all of it sat Alpha, sifting through data on a virtual screen raised out of his desk.

"There's no place like home, eh?" Lucas said. Alpha twitched, startled at hearing his voice. Apparently he hadn't registered they had entered the room. His work did tend to absorb him completely.

"'Home' is a term that no longer has particular relevance to me," Alpha said. "Did Admiral Vale send you down here?"

"Yeah, he did," Asha said, poking at a nearby device hanging from the ceiling. "What exactly is going on? What do you have to do with Kollux?"

"Nothing," Alpha replied. "Our mission is a great distance away from that location."

"And what is our mission? Tannon said you'd pulled something from the core of, uh, I never did catch his name . . ." Lucas said uncomfortably.

"I would not acknowledge his memory by speaking it," Alpha spat out through his translator, his face full of the same contempt Lucas had seen in the interrogation room.

"But his work has proved useful. Most of it was being eaten away by a corruption algorithm by the time I reached it, but there were pieces that are quite valuable. One in particular."

There was now a tangible excitement exuding from him, an energy Lucas had never seen him wear before. He motioned for them to come around to his side of the desk. He flung his claws outward and the screen he was working on expanded. In front of them were portraits of a dozen Xalans, each colored a variable shade of gray. Lucas could translate at least one word in the header: DANGEROUS. Alpha elaborated.

"These are the leaders of the Xalan resistance, the sect that wishes the eternal Soran war to end and the Council to be overthrown and replaced with proper leaders who truly have the well-being of Xala at heart. Should we be able to reach any of these figures, they would be of invaluable help in spreading the message of my father to our people."

Lucas was scanning the text under the pictures for words he could decipher. He saw terms like BOMBING, ASSAULT, REBELLION, and TREASON repeated frequently. Alpha motioned to one of the portraits and it grew to consume the entire screen. It was a Xalan who was almost pure white. It had larger eyes than Alpha's with rings of sky blue. Not the ice cold glare of the Shadows, but a softer gaze.

"This is [garbled]," Alpha said, his translator again refusing to convert Xalan names to anything understandable.

"Ah," he said as he stopped himself. "Refer to her as . . . Zeta, I suppose."

Another Greek letter. If they ever met more than twenty-four Xalans, Alpha was going to be out of luck fashioning identifiers for them.

"She is an old friend, and one I must admit I was shocked, and thrilled, to find on this list. We studied together a century ago at the Institute of [garbled] and both came from science-minded families, a common ground over which we formed a bond. We became . . . close."

His eyes trailed off to some faraway place for a moment before snapping back toward them.

"When I became drafted into my father's work fashioning weapons systems, she was tasked with designing interplanetary communication relays that could transmit orders instantaneously from Xala to the colonies, or vice-versa."

He scanned through a number of data entries below her picture. "Though stationed trillions of miles apart, we kept in contact for years, until one day, she disappeared. I feared her dead, and had no reason to believe otherwise. During any leave I had from research, I scoured the colonies and Xala for her to no avail. She was gone, and no one could tell me what had happened to her. Until I discovered this."

He pointed toward the screen.

"This decrypted file says that she was arrested twenty-three years ago for setting up backchannels for the resistance to communicate across planets, precisely when she vanished. She was sentenced for extermination, but escaped custody in transit and piloted her prison ship to [garbled]. To a nearby colony planet. She has not been heard from since, but the resistance communication network remains online. The coding of the backchannels is sufficiently complex that the Council believes she must still be running it remotely, and so her name remains on this list."

Lucas studied the text. He could make out phrases that Alpha was glossing over in her file. "Resisted High-Level Interrogation" was one of them. Meanwhile, Asha was already thinking ahead.

"This sounds great, but how exactly do we find your girlfriend if she hasn't been seen in two decades on this planet?"

Alpha was taken aback.

"Girl . . . friend? That Earth term has no bearing here. If you are implying we were . . . We were simply interested in the same—" he stammered.

"Alpha!" Lucas course corrected. "How do we find her?"

He nodded and went back on point.

"Long ago, we spoke in secret of the resistance and possible ways to aid them. Minds like ours see no purpose in war, and the desire for change was a seed planted in us during our youth as we witnessed the atrocities of the conflict and the effect it had on our people. She grew up to deliver on her promise, whereas I did not."

His eyes were downcast.

"You are now," Lucas said. "That's what matters."

Alpha ignored him and continued.

"We developed a communication system lest one of us be captured. It was a deeply encoded frequency only the pair of us would have access to."

He paused, and let out a sigh.

"Every day after she disappeared, I monitored the frequency to no avail. Either it had been discovered or disabled, or wherever she was being held was blocking the signal. I checked the frequency when I came to Earth. I checked the frequency when I met you. I checked the frequency until the day my signal reader was destroyed when we fought Omicron."

"You never mentioned this before," Lucas said.

"It was of no importance to you; why would I?" Alpha said, but Lucas remembered seeing him on the Ark's security monitor working late in has lab some nights, staring hard at a screen with a resigned look on his face.

"When I saw her name on this list, the first thing I did was to rebuild the device needed to locate the signal."

He threw up a garble of lines onto the screen that were pulsing with repeating frequency.

"I checked it, and it had been reactivated."

Lucas's eyes widened in surprise.

"You talked to her, after all this time?"

Alpha shook his head.

"Though the signal is active, it is too scrambled for anything resembling auditory or visual communication."

"Then how does that help us?" Asha said, immune to what had been a rather touching story, Lucas thought.

"Though we could not speak, I traced the signal back to its origin point. I found her."

He cycled through the controls in front of him and brought up a planet streaked with green and brown with only faint hints of blue, identified by indecipherable Xalan symbols. A dot of light was pulsing in one of the greener areas.

"This is the colony planet [garbled]. I leave it to you to invent a Soran or English name for it. Less than half the size of your Earth, it once was mostly covered in a lush jungle, but after being harvested for its water, 92.4 percent of the forests have died out. Only a few still remain, and Zeta is in one of them."

The blinking light seemed to indicate where exactly they'd find her. Lucas supposed a jungle was an easier place to hide than a desert.

"[Garbled] was the last planet discovered and pillaged before Earth. Its Soran, or *human* population, if you still prefer the term, was quite primitive, and has since been purged out of existence. The Xalan colony there is the least populous of all our off-world homes, but more arrive every day as refugees from the ever inhospitable Xala. The resistance is rumored to have a strong presence on the surface, though I do not know the full extent of the operation."

"Fantastic," said Asha with now genuine enthusiasm. "So we go there, find your girl, give her your father's message, and spread it to the resistance to mobilize the population?"

"She is not my . . ." started a flustered Alpha. "But yes, that is something resembling the plan I have devised. If we can incite open revolt on [garbled], something the message could achieve, it would buy Sora time as the Council is forced to deal with an uprising. With any luck, the message would spread across all the colonies shortly after. Mass rebellion across the entire population may itself be enough to end the war once and for all, though I fear swift and bloody retribution from the Council."

"In any case," Lucas said, "this sounds like our best option. Our only option, really."

"Indeed it is, as direct military strikes against Xalan forces will only result in further stagnation and depletion of resources, something both sides should have learned by now."

"Then what are we waiting for?" Asha said. "Let's get on the Spear and head out there."

Alpha fell silent, and the hovering screen went blank.

"As elated as I am to find [garbled], to find Zeta alive, it is not all good news I have discovered inside this core."

"What do you mean?" Lucas asked cautiously.

Alpha flung up another document. Lucas quickly translated the title. ORDER FOR EXTERMINATION. As he kept reading, a knot began to tie in his stomach.

"Alpha, what is this?" he asked breathlessly.

"It appears the threats of my old mentor were not unfounded. The Council has indeed sent a new party to bring me to justice for my purported crimes. The Desecrator."

There was an image accompanying the text, but it was blurred beyond recognition, like someone had tried to snap a shot of a car speeding by at a hundred miles an hour.

"The Desecrator?" Asha asked skeptically. "Who, or what, the hell is that?"

"I only know the stories I was told as a child. The Desecrator was a monster of alleged Soran origin. With the help of their ancient, wrathful gods, they created a being to terrorize the population of Xala without quarter, without mercy. To desecrate our homeworld to its very core. If your allegiance to Xala was anything but steadfast, he would prey on your weakness and consume your soul. The Sorans bred him to look like us, but he wielded unholy powers that could tear apart any foe."

"That sounds familiar," Lucas said.

"Indeed it does. Though the legend predates the psionic mutation of the Chosen Shadows. It may be the case that the Desecrator is something else entirely, something new. Or rather, something old."

"Stronger than Omicron?" Lucas said, almost in a whisper.

"Unknown," Alpha said. "There is no further information about the Desecrator here. His existence is apparently such a guarded secret even those assigned to handle him may not know the full extent of his origin or abilities."

"What does this mean for the mission?" Asha asked, undeterred by the new threat.

"Whatever he is, even the Desecrator could likely not reach us on Sora. But offworld? If the Council catches wind of our plan, they will likely dispatch him along with any additional troops needed to secure us. The order you see before you is unmistakably specific in its instructions. I am not only marked for death, but the pair of you are as well."

An unwanted chill shook Lucas as he stared at the blurred image of the Desecrator. The Council must have acquired full knowledge of their role in the murder of Omicron, and wanted blood in return. And now they were sending . . . what exactly for them? Lucas was sure he didn't want to find out.

"How do we know this all isn't a trap?" Asha asked.

"We do not," Alpha said. "But if there is a chance Zeta is alive, I must go. And if there is a chance she could help us, we all must go."

After a painful goodbye from an inconsolable Noah and another visit to the incubation chamber, Lucas and Asha descended back underneath the surface. Down in the hangar, the Spear was being hastily outfitted for another round of travel, and the small Guardian squad that had led the raid to recover Asha and capture Tulwar had doubled in size for the scope of the mission at hand. The existence of the Xalan sub-colonies was a revelation only a few months old, and due to the Spear's exceptionally advanced white null core, this was the furthest any Soran would travel out into the galaxy. A historic occasion. Still, there were ripples of discontent through the troops.

"What's up with them?" Lucas asked Silo when he found him next to Kiati as usual. Both were unarmored, yet still towered over him. She spoke before he could.

"Many Guardians are upset we are being drawn away from helping our brethren on Kollux in pursuit of some scrap of information pulled off a traitor's data core," she said, her voice dripping with contempt.

"It's a scrap of information that could end up turning the entire tide of the war," Lucas said, annoyed. He no longer had tolerance for Kiati's attitude. She was beginning to sound like Maston. *And speak of the devil.*

Maston strode toward them in full uniform. His appearance was meticulous, a far cry from the broken-down man Lucas had encountered outside the interrogation room.

"Get onboard," he said to all four of them. "We don't have the time to debate these orders. They are simply that: orders."

Lucas was surprised he wasn't raising hell like Kiati. She and Silo nodded and turned to walk onto the entry ramp with dozens of other Guardians.

Asha began to speak, but Maston cut her off.

"Your personal weapons are already in the armory. Get into your fatigues on that ship in the next two minutes or I swear to Kyneth I'll leave you here, Vale orders aside."

He did an about-face and left them standing looking at each other before either could even respond. Maston wasn't messing around today. Lucas wondered how many of the lost on Kollux he had known.

Lucas and Asha stood in the first row of over a hundred Guardians who had assembled in the still-under-repair CIC of the Spear. Maston stood at the foot of the holotable and was issuing instructions for the voyage ahead.

"By now you've all read the brief and know where we're going. They're calling it 'Makari,' which, for the non-Ba'siri speakers, means 'turning point' in the old tongue. I don't know if this place will be the salvation our newly appointed heroes claim," he said, casting a hard glare toward the pair of them. "But it is our job to find out, and honor the memories of the fallen of Kollux as we do so. Is that clear?"

"Yes, Watchman!" came the cry all around them, one that used Maston's official title as leader of the Guardians.

"Using this new Xalan hypercore, the trip is a mere sixty-eight days. The majority of you will be in cryo for that time, and will wake up refreshed and ready to serve. If you have been designated otherwise, report to me after this briefing."

Lucas was not surprised to see that his set of orders had deemed him one of the chosen meant to speak to Maston. Asha had the same notation on her own display.

Sixty-eight days? That meant by the time they returned, if they returned, their child would be ready to be "born"—if the word was still appropriate—even with the additional time in the birthing tank normal on Sora that extended past a human's nine-month pregnancy. And Noah would grow ever older, another stretch of time away from his surrogate family, with only Malorious Auran to take care of him. It was another reason to ensure that their mission was a success.

Lucas blocked out Maston's last few points, one of which brought a rousing cheer from the soldiers around him. Upon hearing "dismissed," he and Asha remained where they were. Most of the soldiers filtered out to the cryo area. The Xalan pods had been stripped out and replaced with ones suited for Soran biology, which didn't have the unfortunate side-effect of unleashing scarring flashbacks or outright madness.

A few Guardians were filtering toward the front, however, including Kiati and Silo. Lucas counted twenty in total. When they were all assembled, Maston launched into a new set of directives.

"Congratulations. You lucky few have been chosen to stay out of cryosleep in order to help our newest recruits not kill themselves or us once we reach Makari."

Lucas couldn't contain a look of surprise as all twenty hulking soldiers turned to glower at the pair of them. Asha interrupted Maston.

"Really, we're fine," she said. "Wasn't the Fourth Order raid proof enough we know what we're doing?"

"How can something so lovely be so dense?" Maston wondered aloud to the snickering Guardians. Flames flashed in Asha's eyes, but Lucas put his hand on her arm to prevent her from tearing his head off.

"This isn't just about you and your inexplicable ability to stay alive. The Guardians are a single unit, and only as strong as their weakest. Despite the admittedly adequate combat skill the two of you possess, you know nothing of the tactics, techniques, or training of the Guardians."

Asha was still fuming from the insult and had likely not heard a word he'd just said.

"Every man and woman here was bred to be a warrior before they were even born. They have strength and intelligence natural biology like yours cannot possibly compete with. You are inferior."

That did it. Asha lunged at Maston, but he deftly moved to the side, caught her with a haymaker blow, and slammed her down on the holotable. Lucas sprang to her aid but was leveled by a high kick from Maston that landed just under his jaw. He released Asha, shoving her toward Lucas who was struggling back to his feet.

"You know nothing, Earthborn," he said smugly, his demeanor closer to the time they'd first met. He'd clearly locked Corinthia away in some dark corner of his mind now.

"But we will do you the honor of teaching you as much as you are able to learn."

Adrenaline was flowing through Lucas like lava, but he restrained himself from further assault, as did Asha, surprisingly. A single trickle of blood streamed from her cut lip. Lucas could now shift one of his molars with his tongue. Maston continued talking as if nothing had just happened.

"You twenty have been chosen as the best possible instructors for these new *recruits,*" he said the word contemptuously, "and will spend the duration of the trip molding them into something resembling half an actual Guardian."

More stifled laughter.

"Space and equipment is limited aboard this craft, but most exercises will require only your body, and your mind," he said, turning back to them.

"Dismissed."

Asha stormed out of the CIC without a word, and most of the other Guardians followed her. Maston stayed at the holotable and started sifting through data on Makari, ignoring Lucas.

"I don't understand you, Maston," Lucas said to him. He didn't look up.

"That's probably for the best."

"All we want to do is help."

"All I want to do is get this over with," he replied, scrolling through three-dimensional terrain maps. "Tulwar's trial starts the week we get back."

"You realize this mission could change the entire course of the war?" Lucas said emphatically.

Maston turned to glare at him.

"What do you know of our war? What you've read in scrolls? What you've seen on the Stream? Have you smelled the air after Golgoth? Have you walked through the ruins of Bedlam? Have you heard the screams at Vitalla? You're a tourist at best, a dangerous distraction at worst."

"Isn't it enough that I watched my entire planet burn, along with everyone I loved?" Lucas growled.

"Not everyone," Maston said.

Lucas realized the conversation had become a recursive loop and began to walk away. A thought stopped him.

"What happened at Vitalla?"

Maston flashed him another look of anger, but as he turned back to the screen before him, Lucas was surprised to see his expression shift into something resembling anguish, if only for a brief moment. The silence said Lucas should press no further, and he was tired of dealing with the man anyway. Lucas rubbed his bruised jaw and winced.

He approached Alpha in the central command chair. Alpha was running through a pre-flight checklist of sorts, and green indicators seemed to say the Spear was ready for another galactic journey.

"They do not trust me," Alpha said with a twinge of sadness as Lucas came to stand beside him.

"They're here, aren't they? That's enough."

"I cannot understand how they fail to realize the importance of this mission. They think I have set them on, what is the phrase? A 'fool's errand.'"

Lucas shook his head.

"It's not that. They lost a lot of friends today and wish they could be helping. Exploring a planet light-years in the other direction is a hard sell. They probably think we should be attacking this colony, not infiltrating it."

Alpha revved the engines and the entire ship rumbled.

"That would be an unwise tactical decision."

"Well, the Vales have faith in you, or else they wouldn't have greenlit this. And you know Asha and I always have your back."

"That is appreciated," Alpha said. His six-fingered mechanical hand was speeding through a control cluster. The viewscreen before them opened to reveal the hangar doors.

"Besides, you'll get to see Zeta again."

Alpha's face brightened instinctively.

"I hope that is indeed the case."

"Tell me," Lucas said wryly. "When you said you became . . . close with her. Were you—"

Alpha sighed.

"You and your kind's notions of romance. Such things do not exist in Xalan culture. Most pairings are arranged from birth. Zeta was promised to an army commander for the duration of the time I knew her."

"And who were you promised to, before all this?" Lucas asked.

"Someone I would not deem a suitable match. Being sent to the Earth campaign allowed me to temporarily escape my obligations. My treason freed me from them entirely. I am sure my promised partner was elated."

"But Zeta?" Lucas asked. "She would have been a 'suitable match'?"

"We shared many common interests and goals, yes. Physically, we would have made a better pairing, as well, than our assigned matches. Light coloring is a good indicator of fertility and quality genetics in females. And I have never seen anyone with a coat as pure as hers."

"So you thought she was cute."

"You have a way of simplifying things to the point of annoyance."

The hangar doors were starting to open.

"Well, you know," Lucas said. "Her treason has probably freed her from her obligations as well."

The thought struck Alpha like a silent thunderbolt, but after pausing briefly, he resumed his duties at the controls.

"Just something to think about on the way," Lucas said with a masked smile.

"You may want to find a seat," Alpha said, motioning toward one of the two smaller chairs that were on either side of him. Lucas saw that Maston had occupied one already. It was comically oversized for his frame, meant for an eight-foot-tall Xalan. Lucas walked toward the rightmost chair.

"He's not authorized to—" Maston began. Alpha held up his metal claw to silence him.

"I require his presence on deck. Secure your restraints and cease verbal communication."

Alpha answered to no one here. It was his ship, whether Maston liked it not. Realizing that reality, he did as instructed with a scowl.

Vibrations.

Tunnel.

Daylight.

Elyria.

Blue sky.

Black sky.

Stars.

Planets.

System's edge.

The blue-green haze of a space-time wormhole.

No matter how many times Lucas made this kind of journey, it would never fail to take his breath away.

9

Lucas stared down at the pile of vomit he'd just created on the floor of the poorly lit storage room. He heaved again, but found himself choking and coughing this time instead of evacuating.

Maston wasn't joking when he said the Guardians were perfect physical specimens, and trying to live up to their level of strength and vitality seemed like it might kill Lucas before they even reached their destination. The ten pounds he'd gained sampling all of Sora's finest delicacies before shipping out certainly hadn't helped matters, but in the past few weeks he'd lost all that and then some.

His body had endured hunger, thirst, exhaustion, and pain out in the wilds of a ruined Earth, but what they were putting him through almost made him miss the wastelands.

"Again," said the instructor in front of him, a dark, towering man roughly the size of a Volvo. Today was Fight Day. It was exactly what it sounded like.

"Just give me a—"

His plea was interrupted by a seismic slam to the face that propelled him back against the wall of the fiber cage.

It was like this every Fight Day. Lucas was thrust into a makeshift pen and got his ass kicked by Guardian after Guardian. He'd fought Axon, the man in front of him, a few times now, and it had always gone something like this.

Another lightning jab, this one to his twice-broken ribs. Pain at this point was becoming as commonplace as breathing, which was one of the purposes of the exercise, he was told. They'd patch him up with tech that allowed him to heal at ten times the rate of any medical supplies on Earth, but all it would do would be to get him healthy enough to be destroyed again.

Though his trainers consisted of both male and female Guardians, he was kept separated from Asha for practically all hours of the day. The reason given was that they couldn't become reliant on each other; they first had to draw only on themselves in order to learn to become a solid member of an ironclad team like the Guardians.

"Get your goddamn guard back up!" Axon bellowed at him.

Lucas raised his forearms just in time to deflect a tree-sized arm flung toward him, but couldn't react in time to catch the surprise follow-up knee to his kidney.

There were also Survival Days, something Lucas thought he should excel at due to his past few years on Earth. But they were more daunting than he anticipated. During one he was forced to tread water in an unfiltered tank for hours until he lost consciousness. After he did so, he found a Guardian dragging him out of the drink and expelling the water from his system with a hearty slap on the chest. They'd test his mind by locking him in a storage crate for what felt like eons, alone with only his thoughts and without the ability to move, see, or hear.

Lucas's favorite were Marksman Days, as they were the only ones without physical abuse. Well, that wasn't strictly true. Using a variety of energy weapons, including Natalie, which he had been approved to equip, he shot at jury-rigged moving targets in the galley for hours. Each miss was noted and various punishments would be added on to Fight or Survival Days. Another few hours in the box. Another opponent in the ring.

Today there was only Axon, but that was enough. He might as well have been two people.

Lucas sidestepped an uppercut that would have likely taken his head off. He countered with a high spin-kick that caught Axon on the cheek. When that didn't faze him, he looped around and tried for another strike at the back of his right knee. This time, Axon caught his leg and jabbed his elbow into Lucas's thigh. He was far too hoarse to cry out, but below the impact point, he could no longer feel a thing as his overloaded nerves simply shut down.

There was almost never a time of the day where Lucas wasn't in agony. The line between training and torture was a fine one, but Lucas was determined not to show weakness by complaining to Maston. He would survive. He would become one of the monsters if it killed him.

And it might.

Axon raised both his fists clasped in an axe handle and attempted to smash Lucas's head down through his neck. He rolled out of the way and hit Axon with a hard cross that actually made him stagger. Using the rarely seen opening, Lucas lunged off his good leg and flung him toward the cage's cables. Axon staggered backward for a moment, but suddenly planted his foot firmly in the ground. He stopped moving, Lucas didn't. He flew up and over the man's shoulders and came crashing down on the outside of the ring. He landed with a crack on the metal floor. He resisted the urge to puke again.

"Enough for today," Axon said. "Get him wrapped up."

A familiar tuft of red hair bobbed its way around the side of the cage. A familiar frown followed it. Kiati was assigned to keeping Lucas alive through this, and he'd discovered she was actually a practicing silvercoat in addition to her regular duties of death and destruction. Silo had been assigned to Asha's training squad, as Maston had deemed him too "friendly" with Lucas based on their past interactions. Kiati had no such conflict of interest.

"Hold still," she said as she jerked his arm toward her. She sealed a gash with a hot liquid that solidified within seconds. Hiking up his shirt without permission, she sprayed him with a stinging mist that would reduce his abdominal bruising significantly by the time he hit cryo that night. Sleep. It was the only thought driving him most days. He got twelve hours in his frosty cryochamber each night, with the twenty-five that followed spent almost entirely in hellish training.

More liquid was poured over his tattered knuckles, which had gotten the worst of their limited interaction with Axon's face. Kiati shone a piercing blue light into his eyes that somehow alleviated the nearly constant headaches he suffered on account of repeated blows to his skull. The feeling was starting to flood back into his dead leg now, but it felt like a thousand fire ants were attempting to burrow their way into his bone marrow.

Kiati always went through these motions as quickly as she was able, and she hadn't warmed to him any in the past few weeks. During their little recovery sessions like these, he'd been able to extract exactly three pieces of information from her: her birthplace (Gahren, off the Shining Coast), her length of service (twelve years so far), and the cost of her "kit," i.e., the pool of custom-tailored genes used to create nearly all Guardians. She rang in at a cool 42.8 billion marks, as the intelligence required for master medical training cost extra. All of that was spent on utility, with little going to inconsequential things like cosmetic appearance. Her severe features and pale skin reminded Lucas of the intimidating statues that stood guarding the Grand Palace promenade back home. She wasn't unattractive, but was certainly no Asha or Corinthia Vale. If she could ever hear these sorts of thoughts, she would likely beat him so badly even she wouldn't be able to put him back together again.

"Done," she said flatly as she finished wrapping a numbing bandage around his forearm.

"Hey," Lucas said as she turned to leave, curious to get at least one more piece of information out of her, "how long have you known Silo?"

She stopped and considered whether to answer or keep walking. She usually chose the latter whenever he asked her anything.

"We were in the same graduating class at the academy. We ran the Cell together."

The Cell was the place where Guardians were normally trained on an off-world moon, and pieces of the program had been replicated on the Spear, which was what Lucas was currently enduring.

"Was it this bad? Honestly?"

She scoffed.

"Worse. Gravity is 1.1 there. Imagine doing everything you've done here with twenty pounds of allium attached to each of your limbs."

Lucas wasn't sure what allium was, but he got the point. Just when he thought Kiati was being unusually chatty, she was already walking out of the room.

He struggled to bring himself to his feet. The treatments wouldn't really start to subdue his pain for another hour or two.

With all the battles he'd won over the past few months and years, it had been easy to feel almost invincible. Like there wasn't anything he couldn't beat with enough firepower, luck, or skill.

He didn't feel that way anymore. Despite being treated like a god on Sora, he had now been thoroughly reminded of how mortal he truly was.

After comparing bruises and war stories of the day with Asha over dinner, which consisted of an amorphous, protein-rich goo said to help muscle regeneration, Lucas searched the ship for a quiet place to do his homework in the precious two hours he had before cryosleep. The after-hours work assigned to him was mostly technical, like how to hack a virtual lock or understand the various readouts on his power armor.

He'd been exploring the ship a lot recently, and was interested to see which sections had been stripped and retrofitted for Sorans and which had been left in their original Xalan state. The craft was far larger than the Ark. That ship, though a trusty steed, had been a junk heap of a transport, while this was one of the finest weapons in the Xalan arsenal. The difference in quality from materials to design was very noticeable, and when he could, he talked to Alpha, who loved to explain all the detail that had been packed into the ship at the hands of his father. Lucas didn't understand half of it most times, but it was clear he was residing in the pinnacle of Xalan ingenuity. It was shockingly advanced for a race barely ten thousand years old.

The room Lucas stood in front of today was on the highest level of the ship, and the holocontrols informed him that it was restricted. Every inch of the ship had been searched by the Sorans, so the lock was crafted by them, rather than being of Xalan origin. Lucas got an early start on his homework by cracking it in a matter of minutes using a circuit overload technique and soon found the metal barricade sliding open in front of him.

Like many of the areas of the ship, the room was all but empty. Everything from foreign technology to harmless decoration had been stripped away and was likely currently housed in either a museum or a laboratory, much like what had happened with their own ship after they arrived. The only objects that remained here were a large metal desk fused to the ground and an attached chair, a wall-mounted Xalan sleeping pod, and a mural that could not be removed, as it was carved into the surface of the far wall.

Lucas knew where he was.

The figure depicted in the image was unmistakable. It was Commander Omicron, clad in his slim armor, one arm raised to the heavens, the other clutching what appeared to be a dead Soran. Beams of light, or some other energy, were being emitted from his triumphant form, and Lucas could translate the inscription above it.

HONOR. COURAGE. POWER.

Quite the egoist, Lucas thought to himself as he ran his fingers over the grooves of the mural, which he could now feel was carved an inch deep into the surrounding metal. He supposed Omicron wanted a permanent mark on his flagship, and what better place to put it than in his private quarters?

Lucas kept tracing the curves when he felt one of the standalone pieces near Omicron's kneecap click. It was a subtle, momentary feeling, but pressing his face to the wall, he could see that the piece was just slightly more indented into the surface now. He tried to push it in further and pull it back out to no avail. But it had moved, he was sure of it.

He started scanning the mural for more individual pieces that might also move. There were a large number, as the picture was an exceptionally detailed carving. Some were a few inches thick, others merely millimeters.

It took him a half hour to find the next one, buried in a cluster near the dead Soran's shoulder. Twenty minutes after that, he found another in the gravel beneath Omicron's feet, and again, a familiar click could be felt. Eventually, he had to grab a nearby storage cube to stand on to reach the top of the mural. There was one in a particle of an energy ray, another nestled in the creature's breastplate. Lucas found a final switch in the seemingly obvious location of Omicron's eye. He pressed it, and heard five other simultaneous clicks. Looking around, he could see that every switch had reset.

Shit.

Every piece he'd found had popped back out, and he'd almost lost track of where one or two had been. He stopped to think.

There must be an order to them.

Six switches. Six ways he could press all of them. He brought up his wrist readout and quickly calculated that there were hundreds of possible combinations. It was strange to see a manual lock in a world where almost everything was secured electronically, but he supposed in many ways this was far more secure. And what the hell was it guarding? Surely the sweeper team had missed this when they stripped the ship. Lucas ignored the pain of the day's training wracking his body and set to work.

Gravel. Knee. Breastplate. Eye. Particle. Shoulder.

Click click.

Gravel. Knee. Breastplate. Eye. Shoulder. Particle.

Click click.

Gravel. Knee. Breastplate. Shoulder. Eye. Particle.

Click click.

Each time Lucas recorded the sequence on a scroll so he wouldn't repeat it. What was apparent was that this was going to take a very long time.

Lucas eventually stopped looking at his wrist; he didn't even want to know what time it was anymore. He was dreading dealing with a Survival Day on nonexistent sleep, but he'd become obsessed with the puzzle before him.

Particle. Eye. Knee. Gravel. Shoulder. Breastplate.

Click click.

Particle. Eye. Knee. Gravel. Breastplate. Shoulder.

Click click.

According the scroll, this was attempt number 435. He had gotten the movement down to a science over the past few hours, hopping up and down the storage crate to monkey around to the various areas on the massive mural. It had become both a mental and physical workout, and the constant pumping of his heart was expelling blood from a few of his wounds from earlier in the day.

And then—

Particle. Knee. Breastplate. Shoulder. Gravel. Eye.

Click. KA-CHUNG.

Lucas almost fell backward off the crate as the entire wall sank backward a solid few inches. Every piece he'd pressed remained fixed in place. This was it.

He stepped down and put his fingers in the grooves of Omicron's leg armor. He pulled hard to the left and the metal plating groaned as it slowly shifted sideways.

Before him was a series of glass cubes that protruded from a metal wall a foot or two behind where the mural had been. It wasn't a vault, but appeared to be a display case of sorts. Each glass box had an object floating inside it and a Xalan number above it. Underneath "1" was an ornately painted gold-and-black musket pistol unlike any Lucas had seen in Earth's history books. "2" was a sharpened stone axe held together by fine leather strips with long red feathers dangling off the grip. "3" was a curved hand scythe with what appeared to be a solid diamond blade, while "4" was the broken head of a ridged bronze spear. "5" was an obsidian ceremonial knife with a human skull as the pommel. "6" sat vacant. Lucas tapped on the boxes, but if there was a way to open them, he couldn't see it. The weapons looked permanently encased inside.

After a minute of delirium due to a lack of sleep despite utter exhaustion, he suddenly understood what was before him.

Trophies.

The five items had to be from the colony worlds Xala had conquered and occupied over the years. Judging by the fine design of each piece, a great warrior had likely wielded each of them at one point, defending their planet from the Xalan horde. Either Omicron had taken these personally, or he'd collected them. Surely he wasn't old enough to have traveled to each planet himself.

Earth's "6" box sat empty, but Lucas had a feeling that, had the fight aboard this ship gone differently, it would have been Natalie encased in the clear material before him. Three more numbered boxes sat underneath the first six. *Never hurts to plan for the future, I guess.*

Below them all, near his waist, was one more fixture on the wall. It was a single small pane of transparent glass propped up on a pair of small hooks. Lucas took the object into his hands and turned it over. It was completely blank and somehow felt smoother than glass. Soft, almost, yet simultaneously solid. After sliding his fingers across it with no response, Lucas attempted to put it into his pocket. The lack of sleep was now affecting him deeply in the ghostly hours of the night, and it slipped across his pants and clattered to the floor. After a second of his stomach being flipped upside down, it was apparent that the object hadn't cracked or even suffered a scratch, despite being exceptionally thin. Lucas breathed a sigh of relief. He turned to the display case and pulled the metal mural over it, leaving the trophies to sit idly in the darkness, trillions of miles away from their vanquished owners.

After cramming in a precious few hours of cryo, Lucas had to wait until dinner the next day to find Alpha. Still drenched after a marathon session in the water tank, he made liquid footprints as he trudged to the CIC on legs that would barely support him. Alpha sat flipping through star maps and signal patterns in the central chair. His eyes widened when Lucas showed him the glass square.

"You got this from a covert compartment in Omicron's quarters?" he repeated, still skeptical of Lucas's detective abilities.

"Yes," Lucas said, suddenly chilled from being damp. "The only other things in there were trophies from the colonies. Preserved period weapons the Soran civilizations wiped out there."

Alpha nodded.

"Depending on their age and who owned them, they are likely invaluable artifacts. It is no wonder he kept them secure."

"But what is this?" Lucas said as he jabbed his finger into the glass square. It left no fingerprint.

"A [garbled]. Again, I am not sure of the translation. A personal . . . log, perhaps?"

"A journal?" Lucas said helpfully.

"That may be an apt description. Though the [garbled] is no simple scroll or book."

"What do you mean?"

"It only responds to the biological signature of the person who ordered its creation, without exception. There is no amount of hacking or decrypting I could possibly do to activate it. And any trace amounts of Omicron's DNA would not be sufficient either. A substantive sample is required."

"That means . . ." Lucas said warily.

"We would have to wait until we return to Sora to extract Omicron's body out of storage. I would likely have to reanimate some of his cells to get the [garbled] to recognize his presence."

"Well shit," Lucas said, disappointed that his treasure hunt had yielded a dead end. But at least Alpha seemed to think it was possible to unlock at some point, provided they survived the trip.

On the way back to the makeshift mess hall, Lucas saw a battered Asha talking to Maston in the hallway. Lucas shoved the glass square into his pocket so Maston wouldn't ask about it. He'd decided it would be best to keep its existence secret from the Sorans, should they confiscate it before he got a chance to see what was on it. Asha smiled painfully as he approached, her chin bruised. Maston wore a familiar scowl.

"How's Alpha?" she asked, seeing where he'd just come from.

"Fine," Lucas nodded. Her face looked how his felt, and it was clear they weren't going any easier on her. "Calibrations. The usual."

"The bond you have with that creature is . . . disturbing," Maston said piously.

"*That creature,* as you call him, has advanced your tactical military knowledge of Xala more than anyone in your history," Lucas countered. "What are you doing here anyway?"

"Maston is heading up my training squad now," Asha replied.

"That's Watchman Maston to you," he corrected.

Asha rolled her eyes.

Maston was training Asha now?

"Why?" Lucas blurted out.

Maston considered the question.

"Your . . . companion shows promise," he said. "I cannot say the same for you."

Mind games. It was almost too obvious. Was Maston really going to try to pit them against each other like this? Lucas had to repress laughter.

"Yeah, I bet she does. She's killed more Xalans than you, I reckon."

Maston looked amused.

"I very much doubt that."

Lucas pressed.

"You're training her now, huh? Did you do that?" he motioned toward her purple bruises.

"She failed to correctly block a number of my strikes."

"Or maybe you just like beating on women?"

Maston turned red and stepped toward Lucas who met his gaze and didn't back away.

"Training is over for the day, boys. At ease," Asha said, parting the two of them. Maston turned and stormed off without a word. Lucas couldn't stand this new version of Maston, which was, in effect, the old version of Maston. He'd completely shut down the side of him mourning for Corinthia. At least publicly.

As he rounded the hallway corner, Lucas turned to Asha.

"Seriously?"

Asha rested her head against the wall.

"Yeah, yeah. Well, it wasn't my call. And besides, he may be a dick, but he knows his shit, that's for sure. After seeing him fight, I'm glad he's on our side."

"I'm not so sure he is," Lucas said. "I don't trust him."

Asha cocked her head.

"Because he'll try to kill me, or try to sleep with me?"

Lucas was surprised to hear her correctly vocalize his thoughts.

"Either. Both. Who knows with him? He's got a past so dark it's illegal to even talk about it."

Lucas relayed what he knew about Vitalla to her, and she listened intently.

"Interesting," she said. "I'll see what I can dig out of him when he's not yelling at his henchmen to beat the shit out of me. Or doing it himself."

"Say the word and I'll knock that smug smile off of him."

Asha looked at him sternly.

"I can handle myself, thank you very much. And I'd be careful with how many of his buttons you press. Earthborn or not, I can see him trying to take your head off someday soon."

"He can try."

Lucas couldn't focus his vision as he drifted in and out of consciousness. He was being carried somewhere, and he could hear voices around him.

"What the hell, Wrev? You weren't supposed to kill him."

"He told us to go as hard as we could."

"Which would *obviously kill him!*"

Lucas felt liquid dripping down from his ear. He couldn't move.

"Those *were* the orders," came another voice. Axon.

"You do realize he's not tank-grown like us, right? There's no way he could keep up with one of us going full tilt, much less two."

Lucas was trying to remember what had just happened. His memory was jumping around like a skipping record.

"He's tougher than he looks," came the first voice.

"I don't care. It's my job to ensure he's alive and that's pretty damn hard to do when I have to deal with bullshit like this. And you can tell the Watchman I said that!"

It was Kiati, her shrill voice raised in a yell Lucas had never heard before. Images began to swirl in his head. The ring. Two opponents coming at him with furious, terrifying intensity. They were out for blood, and lots of it.

Lucas tried to speak, but could barely move his lips.

"Shut up," Kiati said sharply, recognizing the gesture. "It's too dangerous for you to even be awake right now." She turned a dial and Lucas blacked out entirely.

A dream found him. A familiar scene buried in his mind. Everything was hazy with the colors distorted and constantly shifting. This was no pod vision, but a memory nonetheless.

He was lying on a tile floor, clad only in a towel, several inches shorter and a few dozen pounds lighter. His head was throbbing. When he sat up, he felt the blood drain quickly downward, threatening unconsciousness. Looking around he saw lockers, showers, and her. He blinked.

"Wh-what just happened?"

The girl before him was slowly coming into focus. She had wavy blond hair with bright blue eyes. Her lips parted to reveal an ivory smile.

"You *are* alive. That's good. The nurse should be coming down soon."

Lucas rubbed his forehead with a skinny arm. He realized that he was naked under the towel draped over him and quickly wrapped the end of it around his backside.

"The nurse? What happened?" he said, disoriented.

The girl laughed.

"Yeah, that *would* be a moment to forget, I'd say." She swept a dangling strand of hair over her ear as she knelt next to him. She wore a crimson-and-white Salem Sun Devils cheerleading uniform and had similarly colored ribbons in her hair.

"What are you doing in our locker room?" he asked, looking around.

"Nope," she said, slowly moving her head from side to side.

Lucas saw a curious absence of urinals and began to scramble to his feet.

"Oh shit."

"Whoa there," she said, holding her hands out as she rose with him. "I don't think you should be walking yet. That was quite a hit."

Lucas felt the lump on his head. The girl realized he needed a full explanation.

"The football guys ran in here and tossed you on the ground," she recounted. "You tried to sprint out of here, but you slipped on the wet floor and rammed your head into that locker."

She pointed to one nearby with a large dent in it.

"The other girls all ran out of here screaming, but I figured someone should make sure you weren't dead."

"Uh, thanks," Lucas said, uncontrollably red from embarrassment. As soon as she said it, it all came flooding back to him. The yelling, the struggling, and him being thrown naked into a room full of cheerleaders who were about to head out for practice. This was literally his worst nightmare.

He looked around for any additional clothes he could throw on to cover his bony frame, but there weren't any. This wasn't his locker room after all.

"Why'd they do that anyway?" she asked. "Aren't you *on* the team?"

"Yeah," Lucas said, shifting uncomfortably. "But I'm a freshman, so . . . you know."

"On varsity?" she said, taken aback. "*Puh*, you'd think you'd be their hero. None of their sorry asses ever made varsity their first year, I'll tell you that. They're just jealous."

"I doubt that," Lucas said. He could hear water dripping in the shower stalls behind her. She put her finger to her lip, considering something.

"If you want, I can get my brother to kick their asses for you."

"Your brother?" Lucas asked.

"Captain of the hockey team, could bench press any one of them."

Lucas smiled sheepishly.

"Nah, that's okay. I can fight my own battles."

The girl put her foot on a nearby bench and retied one of her shoes.

"Then you should. They won't stop. Not unless you stand up to them."

Lucas scoffed, but found he was surprisingly at ease talking to this girl, despite the present circumstances.

"They're all twice my size, what am I supposed to do?"

"Hit the biggest one as hard as you can. That should be enough."

Lucas smiled and looked down at the pattern of the tile.

"Alright, but if I die, I'm blaming you."

She looked over at him.

"You know, you better go get suited up or you're going to be late," she said.

"Oh right," Lucas said, forgetting he still had a full day of practice with those miserable assholes ahead of him. He turned to leave, then stopped himself.

"Thanks, uh, for staying," he said.

"No problem. What's your name, anyway?"

"Lucas."

"Sonya."

When he opened the door, it wasn't the hallway of Salem High. It was a vacant abyss that forcefully pulled him from the entryway like he was being sucked into a black hole. He was flung out into the darkness, which brightened until it was a blinding white.

10

He shuddered as he woke. Though he was no longer sleeping in the Xalan pods, they seemed to have altered his unconscious state long after the fact. He'd had a few dreams like that one recently, memories real yet unreal, but almost verbatim how they'd happened in his own life, no matter how many years it had been. That was the first time he ever met Sonya, and he found tears in his eyes when he blinked. It was strange to see her so young again, the girl he fell in love with who years later would be his wife. Who years after that would be dust in a crater in Portland. He shivered again.

Lucas could hear yelling, though it felt like his ears were stuffed with cotton. As the room came into focus, it was Asha screaming at Kiati, who in turn was screaming at the sorry-looking pair of Wrev and Axon, still coated in much of his blood. Lucas saw a three-clawed hand pass over his face and, mustering all his strength to turn his head, found Alpha working on his wounds, beads of sweat dripping down his tough gray skin.

Maston. Maston had done this. To teach him a lesson, to send a message, or some combination of the two. It was Lucas's last thought as he drifted back into blackness. He would pay.

He would pay.

The next day, Lucas waved away the narcotic medication that was keeping him in a constant haze. He was tired of a fogged head and wanted to embrace the pain that plagued him. He never wanted to forget how this moment felt, as he lay in complete and utter agony. Every muscle and bone screamed from underneath his skin. Through careful breathing and almost zen-like focus, Lucas pushed away his body's cries. Asha, Alpha, and even Kiati pleaded with him to accept more painkillers, but he refused. He could feel the scratches of the microscopic nanobots sewing his bones back together and mending torn tissue. His blood ran rich with healing compounds that would bring him back from the brink. In tune with every fiber of his body, through the constant pain, he felt himself healing, hour by hour, day by day.

After hearing the laundry list of his injuries read out by Alpha with scientific precision, Lucas was sure if this were back on Earth, he would have never made it back to his former state. But here? There seemed to be no such thing as an irreversible injury. Silo showed up to visit one day and talked him through the time he'd had his arm blown off by a proto-nade. There was a thin line running down his shoulder where they grafted on a new one, grown from his own cells in a matter of weeks. By comparison, Lucas's healing process looked downright simple.

Six days. That's all it took for Lucas to pluck the wires from his body, stand up in the med bay, and demand to start training again. Maston hadn't come at all the past week to witness his handiwork, and Lucas was determined not to let him win. Accompanied by his training contingent, the eleven of them marched with Lucas to the CIC where Maston stood gazing out the viewscreen. He turned with that same sickly smile he always wore when attempting to make Lucas's life hell.

"Let me guess," he said. "After your recent . . . training accident, you wish to be put in cryosleep for the remainder of the journey?"

Lucas had to suppress a burst of rage when he'd heard the words "training accident," but managed to speak calmly.

"Actually," he said, keeping a civil tone that mirrored Maston's, "I look forward to completing the program."

It very obviously caught Maston off guard.

"There is no way you would be physically able to continue after your ordeal."

Alpha spoke from a few feet away near the commander's chair.

"You underestimate both the healing regimen I prescribed, and the tenacity of the individual in question."

Matson pretended not to hear him.

"In your absence, your companion has made great strides in her training. You are behind."

"I'll catch up," Lucas said, his blood starting to boil.

"You can't," Maston sneered. "Axon, prove my point."

"Excuse me, Watchman?" Axon said confused.

"Show the Earthborn that he is not ready for Phase Two."

"But sir, he just got out of the med bay minutes ago."

"And he and his . . . *doctor*," he jerked his head toward Alpha, "claim he's all put back together again. Now *show me* or I'll put you out an airlock for insubordination."

Axon looked uneasily at Lucas as the rest of the group spread out around them. His eyes apologized in advance, but Lucas didn't care. His blood had dropped in temperature about forty degrees. He flexed his hands and clenched them into fists. Tiny wounds where tubing had entered his veins were still red between his tendons. He'd been fighting Axon long enough to know what his opening would be. A calamitous swing from the right followed by sharp uppercut with his left. Lucas had been floored by either blow many times. But not today.

"Hit the biggest one as hard as you can."

The behemoth lunged at him with the familiar combo. Lucas ducked under the haymaker and immediately shifted right to avoid the incoming uppercut. He then dodged three lightning quick jabs that pummeled the empty spaces over each of his shoulders and avoided the heel kick at the tail end of the pattern. As Axon wound up for another punch, Lucas shifted to his back foot. The swing missed his nose by a quarter inch and was so forceful that Axon stumbled two steps forward in its wake. That was all Lucas needed.

Lucas pushed off his legs and drove a straight right directly into Axon's jaw. His eyes were vacant before his feet left the ground and he crashed to the deck with a thud, all three hundred-plus pounds of him almost leaving a crater. Every pair of eyes around them widened, including Maston's. Axon didn't stir. Lucas's hand was on fire, and he was fairly certain he'd rebroken a pair of fingers. He walked to stand over Axon who was now blinking his eyes, unsure of what had just happened. Extending his left hand downward, Lucas helped pull him back to his feet.

Maston's voice wasn't so gleefully malevolent now.

"Report to the training chamber tomorrow," he said coldly. "Perhaps you'll be of some use to this unit yet."

Lucas turned and walked out of the CIC, leaving the other Guardians to marvel at his handiwork. A small smile crept across his lips.

Phase Two was far more instructive than destructive. With his body now forged into metal on the backs of countless Fight and Survival Days, it was time to learn what exactly to do with it. Fight Days were no longer mindless assaults. He ran through a variety of actual tactics from modern and ancient Soran fighting styles. Kal M'so. Jartanne. Baali-stanno. Words Lucas didn't know, but each came with a set of deadly techniques that would allow him to dominate his opponent, no matter their size. In his training, Lucas heard the story of Sha'len, the Baali monk who defended his mining vessel from a Xalan raiding party using only his bare hands. He would later rise to become a field general in the SDI. There was a power in these schools of martial arts that would take a lifetime to truly unlock, but even the highlights were shaping Lucas into a deadly weapon.

Standard tools of warfare weren't to be forgotten either. Lucas began running through practice assault formations with all members of his training squad in full combat gear. He learned how to clear corners, breach doorways, engage enemies behind cover, and a host of other tactics that made him part of a singular unit with the rest of the squad. Though they still towered over him, no one dared think of him as a weak link any more.

What little he saw of Asha before, he saw even less of her now. Phase Two training left almost zero free time, and even meals were inhaled on the fly. He'd occasionally pass by her training chamber, watching her practice the same techniques he was learning with her own squad. He silently cheered when she landed a cross kick on Maston during a training bout, but his stomach clenched when he took her by the leg on her next try and slammed her down to the ground like a paper doll.

Lucas had gleaned select pieces of information in passing from his squad as he trained. It was revealed that for all his physical prowess, Maston was not tank-bred. He may have had good genes, coming from a long line of military nobility, but no one spent billions to purposefully craft him the way the other Guardians had been assembled. His skill and power was earned, much in the same way Lucas was trying to earn his own now. Still, it didn't make Lucas hate him any less.

Graduation day was fast approaching, but Lucas was kept in the dark about what his final test would be. He'd passed all his Phase Two training exercises with flying colors since his stint in the med bay, and he'd grown stronger and tougher than he'd ever been on Earth or aboard the Ark. He felt like he was ready for anything as he was called to assemble in the large water chamber on the fifth-level deck. The room was cavernous and tanks three stories high glowed blue with liquid fuel for the Spear. In addition to the twenty training Guardians, Maston, and Asha, Alpha was present as well, looking around nervously as he didn't want anything in the room to sustain damage during whatever was about to happen.

The chamber was dark, with only the ambience of the tanks shedding light on the group. Maston spoke in a solemn tone once they were all in place.

"High marks in training exercises are one thing, but to be a Guardian there has to be more to you than what can be read off a scroll. You've proven you deserve to be in this chamber, but that's all you've proven. Today we will see how deep your commitment to our continent and our planet runs. Needless to say, because of your . . . place of origin, you have more to prove than any Guardian who has come before you."

Lucas wasn't sure where this was going, but it sounded sufficiently ominous. It was freezing in the vast room, and the air smelled like burnt metal.

"The female is first," he said, as if he were talking about zoo animals. "Secure him below." He motioned toward Lucas. Wrev and Axon gestured for Lucas to exit the room. He wouldn't get to see her trial? He supposed it was in order to not give him an advantage by knowing what to expect. He locked eyes with Asha one last time before the metal doors shut behind him. She smiled, but Lucas caught a glimpse of panic in her face.

A full deck below in a small storage space, Lucas was left alone. He hadn't even bothered asking either of the guards who waited outside the door what was happening, as they were obviously sworn to silence. Lucas couldn't hear a sound from upstairs and tortured himself envisioning every sort of scenario he could be facing. It would have been annoying if Maston had pitted him and Asha against each other, something he had half expected, but that clearly wasn't the case. Lucas was secretly hoping he'd have to face Maston himself in some sort of duel, but there was nothing to indicate that was what lay before him. His knee was bobbing up and down uncontrollably like it had the first day on the promenade in front of millions of Sorans, but Asha was not there to steady it.

Lost in his own head, Lucas was unsure how much time had gone by in the cramped storage room before Axon and Wrev reentered and summoned him to return to the water chamber. As the doors opened, the Guardians all stood before them, but Asha was nowhere to be found. The metal floor beneath his boots was wet and seemed like it had been cleaned mere moments ago.

"Where is she?" Lucas demanded of Maston who stood in the middle of the group with his arms crossed.

"Is she hurt?"

Silence.

"Did she pass the test?"

Silence.

"Answer me, damn it!"

"She is alive," Maston said coolly. "But one more word and you will fail automatically."

Lucas held his tongue, forced to be content with his answer. Though "alive" could have any number of different caveats attached to it. Lucas eyed the wet floor worriedly.

"Your final trial begins now. A single opponent. Defeat him, and you will be welcomed into our ranks. Fail, and we will tolerate you on this mission, but you will never be Guardian."

Lucas cared less about being a Guardian and more about proving to Maston that he would not be beaten. He would win.

"Step forward," said Maston to no one directly. But the recipient of his command obeyed nonetheless.

Silo.

Lucas knew the game here. Maston had picked a Guardian that was a friend of his. Surely under threat of excommunication, Silo would be forced to go full-steam at Lucas, but it could have been worse. Lucas had already knocked Axon out cold, a man even bigger than the enormous Silo, and he'd also faced two opponents in the ring at times. Silo would certainly be a challenge, but he felt confident. Lucas nodded at him, but Silo surprisingly refused to acknowledge him. He was taking his newfound role of challenger seriously. But his face told a different story. He looked . . . angry.

As amiable as the two had been, Lucas had never seen Silo fight for more than a minute or two at a time when he'd glanced into one of Asha's training sessions. Presumably she had been assigned to fight someone from Lucas's squad. He looked around the room and saw that Kiati was missing as well. Were they in the med bay? It had likely been a brutal brawl, knowing the two of them.

Lucas was snapped out of his thoughts by Maston's voice.

"Begin."

Silo charged at him with the force of a ten-ton elephant and a roar to match. Lucas barely reacted in time to roll over the top of him and avoid the human battering ram, a move he'd picked up in training a week earlier. He was light on his feet and dodged swing after swing from Silo, landing a few of his own inside the man's ribs. Unfortunately for Lucas, it felt like he was pummeling metal.

Silo fought like a man possessed, and it was clear his rage was somehow authentic. A thrust punch straight out of a Jartanne scroll caught Lucas in the solar plexus and rocketed him a few feet backward while he tried to keep himself from tumbling to the floor. Another few swings connected shortly after and Lucas found his head spinning as he desperately avoided seeking comfort on the ground. He caught Silo's neck with a well-executed high kick and jammed an elbow into his eye on his next spin. Lucas was a fan of Baali-stanno ever since he'd heard the story of Sha'len, the Xalan-slaying monk. As Silo was practically as tall as a Xalan, it seemed like the appropriate technique.

Every expression in the room was unchanged as the two traded blows in the dim light. Even Alpha was stone-faced, and for once not constantly checking a readout or data nodule on his wrist display.

Lucas was cut and blood spilled into his eye, which he was forced to rub away with grimy hands. Silo too was bleeding, and red gushed from his mouth and dripped onto the floor below, mixing with the water that had recently cleaned it. Lucas imagined Asha's bout had yielded similar results.

But it was far from over. Silo charged in with another flurry of strikes, which were lightning quick for a man of his size. Lucas blocked what he could, but found aching ribs and growing nausea in his gut after the assault was over. He bought some time by hacking away at Silo's knees with a series of low kicks, another Baali-stanno tactic, and temporarily paralyzed one of Silo's legs with a punch to his quadriceps in a specifically targeted nerve cluster. Silo had to limp back and shake the rust out of his dead leg, his eyes still burning with anger. Fighting this intensely made sense from a following-orders perspective, but why the unbridled fury?

There was little time to consider as a quick roll and a lunging grab from Silo had Lucas in an unfortunate headlock. He hammered away at Silo's midsection with his free hand, and only when he slammed his skull into his chin was he able to shake himself free. Two quick blows to the ear made Silo back off once more.

Exhaustion was setting in now as Lucas's hands and feet felt like they were dipped in lead. For each new barrage of strikes, his knuckles became even more mangled, and it was no longer fair to assume the blood on each combatant was their own.

Lucas caught a boot to the chest that reminded him of a certain kick from a towering metal robot just a few weeks earlier. Silo had a power behind his strikes that was physically impossible for Lucas to match. Writhing on the ground, he barely rolled away in time as Silo came crashing down onto the metal grating with a knee meant to cave his head in.

Speed was the only option. Lucas flipped up to his feet and caught Silo in the chest and face with three quick kicks in succession. Avoiding another straight kick, he punched Silo in his extended kneecap, causing him to land painfully in the wake of the kick. Another two blows and the leg was even more useless than it was before. It only took one more low sweep to get him to the ground.

He tried to rise, but Lucas planted a boot on his shoulder and shoved him down. He tried again, but Lucas floored him again with a straight punch that shattered the bridge of his nose, causing blood to spray everywhere. One last time, the bloodied man tried to get up and Lucas brought down both his fists in an axe handle that knocked him out completely.

He had won.

Hadn't he?

Lucas looked around the room. There were no cheers, there was no celebration. Even Alpha looked grim. The mood was tense, but Lucas's heart rose as the room's doors opened and Asha limped inside. She was very obviously hurt, but alive as Maston had promised. She'd missed the fight, but would be there to see him pass the test. But she too wore a stoic expression like all the rest.

Maston eyed Asha as she entered, then slowly walked toward Lucas.

"He's out. I beat him," Lucas said with his arms extended. "Is that it? Do I pass? Or do you want a piece of me too now, Watchman?" Lucas's mind was hoping that was the case, but there was no way his body could handle it.

As he approached, Maston took out his silver energy pistol. Lucas tensed instinctively, but the gun remained at Maston's side until he reached Lucas. When it was lifted, the handle was presented first, the barrel pointed at Maston himself.

"You've won," he said coldly. "Now end the fight with honor."

Maston pressed the gun sideways into Lucas's chest and released it, forcing him to catch it on instinct.

"What?" Lucas said in disbelief. He couldn't mean—

"Kill him."

Lucas looked down at Silo who was slowly coming around.

"You're insane," Lucas said. "You'd have me kill one of your best men, for what?"

"For his failure," Maston said, now walking backward away from him. "Any Guardian who would fall in this arena to someone with inferior genetics and limited training does not deserve to wear the uniform. He has outlived his usefulness. The combatants agreed to this stipulation after they were chosen."

Lucas looked down at the gun, then over at Asha. There were tears in her eyes, and Lucas realized something. She'd come back, but where was Kiati? She hadn't . . . This was a joke, right? A setup. But things started to add up in his mind. The clean floor, the rage in Silo's eyes. What had he just witnessed before Lucas came in? What would make him fight so viciously? Asha stared into his eyes and mouthed two words.

"Do it."

Lucas's head was spinning. He was in cryo, right? In a pod maybe? This was just a nightmare. She couldn't have . . . But Lucas thought back to the woman who had left him for dead on Earth, the one who had tricked and murdered her way through the desolate landscape, surviving at the expense of others. He thought that person was gone, but maybe he was wrong. Maybe deep down she'd never changed.

"Do it," she whispered again, this time more fiercely.

Lucas looked down at Silo who was now blinking at him through bruised, bloody lids. Lucas raised the pistol with a shaking hand. Silo nodded weakly toward him, finally returning Lucas's sign of respect from the start of the fight. The rage in his eyes had subsided.

Lucas's finger twitched, coming within a millimeter of the trigger. Every muscle in his body was contorted into knots. He was nauseous, dizzy, and in anguish, though not from the fight he'd just endured. This was asking something impossible.

It was impossible.

"No," he said forcefully as he threw the gun down on the floor. It clattered toward Maston, who looked up with that same hateful smile.

"Congratulations," he said. "You've failed."

"I don't care," Lucas said angrily. "I'm not a barbarian. I don't need this." He turned, but stopped as Maston called again.

"You really should see this," he said. "Don't you want to witness your companion's triumph?"

Lucas turned back and saw a holoscreen being projected into the middle of the room. It was so large, the three-dimensional figures in it were actually life size, and rested on the ground where Asha and Kiati's fight had taken place. Asha watched the reenaction of her own bout intently, nervously glancing up at Lucas periodically.

After going blow for blow, each side battered and bloody, Asha finally landed a knockout kick under Kiati's jaw that sent her sprawling. Again, Maston approached her with the gun and uttered similar words to her as he had to him.

Lucas didn't want to see this, but he was rooted, unable to tear himself away. For what seemed like a year, she leveled the gun at Kiati's head, shaking as he had. Then, without warning, it fired. The recorded echo boomed throughout the chamber as it assuredly had when it was live. Asha staggered backward, dropping the gun. But then Lucas saw something that almost knocked him over.

Kiati slowly rose up from the ground, unharmed by a blast that didn't actually fire a thing at her. The image disappeared and Maston walked into the center of the chamber.

"Rewired test fire mode," he said, pointing to an indicator on his gun. "Says it's live, but no energy output."

Lucas felt even more sick.

"Of course I wouldn't sacrifice a single Guardian to either of you, are you mad?"

He was almost laughing now.

"But it proves you lack the will to make the hard choices. Out there, mercy will get you killed. Will get all of us killed, or worse. And that is why you will *never* be one of us."

"Do it," she'd said. She tried to tell him it was all a ruse, but he didn't understand. But how had *she* done it, believing it would kill the woman in front of her? It was hard to believe. And it was ugly. Very ugly.

In the med bay a short while later, Alpha was treating Lucas's wounds, which were numerous, though he wasn't on the brink of death like a few weeks ago. Three beds down was Kiati, sleeping off her injuries sustained during her encounter with Asha, but still very much alive.

"These Sorans," Alpha said as he shot cauterizing gel into a cut on Lucas's chest, "their cruelty almost rivals that of the Xalans. Though in Paragon training, death would not have been a mere illusion."

"I'm done with them," Lucas said. "All of them."

"All of them?" came a voice in the doorway.

It was Asha. She wore fresh fatigues with a winged Guardian emblem stamped on the sleeve. An emblem both their uniforms had long been missing.

"I shall leave you two to discuss present circumstances," said Alpha as he shuffled past her and out of the room.

"I told you to do it," she said. "I wasn't supposed to come back, but I had to try and let you know."

"And who told *you* to do it?" Lucas asked, his question laced with anger. "You had every reason to believe you'd kill her," he said, motioning to the unconscious Kiati nearby.

"And how many times did you pull the trigger in that situation back on Earth?" she shot back.

"I didn't with you."

"Only because Alpha stopped you. I saw the look in your eyes. You would have left me in that crater with a hole in my head without a second thought."

Lucas wasn't sure he could deny that, given the situation at the time, but he pressed on undeterred.

"This was different. This wasn't about survival. This was about joining their little murderous club."

"Are we honestly going to lecture each other about murder here?" she said, annoyed.

"Kiati and Silo are not cannibals or separatists trying to kill us."

"You think they're our friends?" she was shouting now. "You think they would have hesitated to snap our necks if Maston ordered them to?"

"Yeah," Lucas said, "I've seen what Maston's orders can do."

"He was teaching you," Asha said. "You were stronger than you ever were after that ordeal."

"Now you're defending Mars Maston?" Lucas said in disbelief. "A man who ordered me to be beaten half to death and did god knows what on Vitalla?"

"Vitalla wasn't his fault!" Asha blurted out, almost immediately realizing her mistake.

The resulting pause was an eternity.

"He told you about Vitalla?" Lucas asked slowly. "And you didn't tell me? What's he done to you?"

Asha remained silent.

"After this, I'm going straight into cryo for the last week of the trip," he said. "I'll see you on Makari. Have fun with your new squad."

By the time he finished, she was already storming out the door.

The anger didn't leave Lucas as he fled the med bay and rushed upstairs to the vast cryo room that housed the sleeping pods for the entire crew. Most were already full. The Guardians who slept there had been on ice for months, the rest were vacant, meant for him, Asha, and their training squad. They slept there each night, but not under "deep ice" as the Sorans called it, which was for prolonged unconsciousness lasting weeks, months, or even years. But that's the sort of asylum he was seeking now.

Alone in the room, it felt like a cemetery. The only light came from the closed pods where other Guardians rested. He didn't care to say goodbye to Asha, to Silo, to any of them. He'd had it with this whole damnable ship and crew and wanted nothing more than to shut the entire events of the day out of his mind in deep sleep until they finally reached this wretched planet. He figured he would have probably been better off just spending the whole trip in cryo like so many of the others onboard.

He stripped down to nothing but a pressurized mesh bodysuit, the standard outfit for deep ice as the system needed direct access to all the vital organs to keep everything running smoothly in hibernation. In his "personal effects" compartment he crammed Omicron's glass device, the only thing of value he had with him. Additionally, he'd quickly swung by the armory to grab his most trusted ally on the ship, Natalie. It was against regulation, but he pulled her into the pod anyway. There was no telling who might attempt to steal or dismantle her while he slept. He didn't trust anyone here anymore. Rage was perhaps tipping him into paranoia, but he didn't care. Lying down inside the chamber, he tapped the control sequence on the interior wall that would automatically wake him when they arrived. Natalie lay upright near his feet (deactivated of course), taking up precious space in the cramped area.

The machine started to spool up and a series of restraints threaded themselves across him, securing him in place. The device doubled as an emergency lifepod should the moment call for it. Next, cables snaked out of the walls, and Lucas winced when they dug into his skin at various points all over his body. None of this was necessary as a precursor to nightly sleep, but it was mandated for long-term rest. If it weren't for the madness-inducing nightmares, he much preferred the comfortable setup of the Xalan pods with their gel backing and simple halo. This seemed downright medieval in comparison.

The last stage of the process was the lid, which slowly lowered down with a creak. The rest of the chamber became obscured behind the frosted glass.

Lucas felt liquid relaxation flood into his veins. His anger was washed away in minutes, and he watched a blue substance work its way into his arms and legs. Soon after, the liquid switched to green, and his head started to grow fuzzy. He embraced the darkness in which he'd rest for the next ten days until they landed. At last he'd have some peace.

Mercifully, the dream that followed was far more placid than the ones he usually endured.

He sat on a platform, a broken-off piece of pavement floating in space all by itself. Sparkling stars surrounded him, but the vision ahead was an even lovelier sight.

It was Earth. Old Earth. Facing forward, the planet took up almost his entire field of vision and was a spectacular painting of blue, green, and white, the colors it had once been known for. North America was in front of him, and he could see its southern counterpart curving under the globe down by his feet. The entire planet turned ever so slowly in front of him.

After what seemed like an eternity of staring at the sphere, the platform suddenly buckled and sent him tumbling toward the Earth. He'd had this dream before, and he'd ended up in the Portland crater. He had no desire to return there, but as he sped through the atmosphere, found he was heading a little farther south. California.

Opening his eyes, Lucas found a different vision in front of him. Bacon sizzling in a pan he was holding. He blinked and looked around the room. The kitchen was large and full of dark-wooded cabinets with glass fronts and granite countertops. Bright morning light streamed in through the windows. It was a place he'd never been before.

A little boy wandered sleepily into the room from the hallway and took a seat at the table across from the counter.

"Daddy, is breakfast ready yet?"

Lucas stared at him. It was Noah, probably about three years old, but still very much recognizable with bright blue eyes and distinctive blond locks. His arm had no burns that Lucas could see.

"Daddy!"

"Um, uh, almost," Lucas stammered as he poked the bacon around. A stack of steaming pancakes sat on the counter a few feet away. Looking around, he could see that the house he was in was gorgeous, with lofted ceilings that gave way to skylights. Massive couches sprawled across the living room, gathered around a stone fireplace devoid of a fire.

Lucas saw the bacon starting to burn and quickly pried it off the pan and onto a nearby plate. He brought it and the pancakes over to the table where Noah eyed them hungrily.

"I swear you're going to make us all fat."

The voice was one he knew instinctively. He turned and saw Asha descending from a spiral staircase nearby. She wore a form-fitting navy dress and heels with an oversize necklace. She also had an enormous diamond ring on her finger. Lucas looked down at his own hand and saw that he too wore a band.

In Asha's arms was an even younger child, little more than an infant. One with wispy dark hair, her eyes, and his nose. Their other son, one not yet given a name. She set him down in a high chair across from Noah and then grabbed a couple nearby oranges from a bowl and started peeling. Lucas just stood at the table in shock.

"What are you staring at?" she said. "Start eating! I'm on set today after dropping these two off, and you've got that huge meeting in what, like an hour?" She looked at her watch.

"Uh, yeah, right," Lucas said, not sure what she was talking about. He looked down at his own outfit and saw he was wearing a slim gray suit with a sapphire tie. He slowly sat down and started eating breakfast. The pancakes tasted as good as they ever had when he used to make them years earlier. The baby in the high chair waved his arms around and babbled until Asha fed him a tiny piece of orange. He grinned happily.

Noah was drawing on a piece of paper with crayon in between bites of bacon.

"What are you working on there?" Lucas asked him.

Noah slid the paper over to him. On it was a simple drawing of a stick-figured family, their own, judging by the hair colors, and then a larger figure with slightly elongated arms and an oblong head.

"Who's this?"

Noah looked exasperated.

"Uncle Alpha!"

Lucas's eyebrows lifted in surprise, but he didn't miss a beat.

"Ah yes, of course. It's a really good picture of him. I must have had something in my eye. And what's this?" Lucas asked, pointing to a black scribble with neon blue circles on its right edge.

"His spaceship, it was *soooo* fun riding in it last week!"

Lucas played along.

"Yes, it was, wasn't it?"

Asha laughed.

"I'm surprised I even still have a job," she said. "Why would anyone want to watch movies anymore with them here?"

For the first time, Lucas looked out the window in the living room. When he saw what was there, panic surged through him. A mothership hung in the distance over downtown Los Angeles.

But then he kept looking. Walking down the street were two Xalans. Not dressed in power armor, but in their natural greys. As they passed, another walked by, this time talking with a woman walking her dog. *What the hell?*

Lucas slowly shifted his view to the fireplace. A photo sat framed with a plaque next to it. It was of him and Alpha shaking hands. The engraving read:

"This commendation recognizes the outstanding work you have done on behalf of the Interspecies Initiative after first contact. The citizens of two worlds thank you for your invaluable assistance."

"Everything okay?" called Asha from the table. The baby and Noah had turned to look at him as well.

"Yeah, fine," he said, noticing an ID badge on the counter with his picture on it. Underneath his name it had his title, "Director of Interplanetary Relations, North America." A US government seal followed.

"Alright, well, that's enough pancakes for you," Asha said.

"But I want another one!" Noah moaned.

"Nope, we're going to be late. A little help here?"

"Sure."

Lucas cleared the table and hoisted the baby out of his high chair. He passed him off to Asha, who scooped up a large purse and took Noah by her other hand. Lucas followed them out onto the driveway. After the boys were buckled into car seats in a silver SUV, Asha turned to Lucas and wrapped her arms around his neck. She kissed him, letting her lips linger far longer than any unhappy housewife would. He felt . . . passion.

"Alright, don't be too late tonight," she said as she released him. "And don't let that Ambassador Omicron boss you around; he's a prick."

"He is . . ." Lucas said, his head still swimming.

"Bye, I love you."

Lucas was stunned at his own words, ones that had never actually left his lips when speaking to Asha.

"I love you too."

And ones that had never left hers either.

The car pulled away and Lucas was left in his driveway. He stared up at the sky where Xalan ships zoomed overhead like lightning bugs.

Clouds started to form above him. They darkened, then reddened.

No, Lucas thought. *No, I want to stay.*

But it was too late. The ships were gone. The house was gone. He was standing in a new crater. He forced his true set of eyes to open.

His head swam, his vision was still black, but he knew he was awake. A bizarre dream, but a welcome one. He'd often wondered in quiet moments what life might have been like had he been able to start over with Asha on a reborn Earth. Perhaps the drug cocktail gave the user a pleasant insight into their deepest desires as a programmed side effect to make the cryosleep go more smoothly. The scenario presented of the Xalans coming in peace was the furthest thing from what had happened, but it was an intriguing alternate reality.

Now awake, Lucas wanted to go back to that world. To their children. To her. A peaceful, loving Asha that didn't seem to exist in the real world. Old pain resurfaced as he thought about her recent demonstration of mercilessness, and the fact that she seemed to be getting too close to Maston, in one way or another.

Lucas's vision was slowly coming back. The cables had retracted from his body, leaving dabs of healing gel in their wake, and the restraints slid off of him and back into the base of the unit. He was surprised to see Natalie up near his shoulders now, rather than at the south end of the pod. He blinked and saw something he didn't understand. The opaque glass had long cracks running through it from top to bottom, and light was flooding in.

Too much light.

Sunlight.

11

Lucas was having trouble moving inside the chamber. His arms and legs were stiff from lack of use, though muscle stimulants inside the unit were supposed to keep them refreshed while he slept. The wall controls were unresponsive when he waved his hand where a hologram should have appeared. Scouring the coffin-like environment around him, he searched for the manual release. When he found it, the lever was jammed and no amount of force seemed to budge it. The cracked lid shifted slightly, but some sort of mechanism was clearly broken within.

Panic was starting to set in now, both from claustrophobia and the clearly damaged nature of the pod. Why was it so light outside? The worst sorts of thoughts began to flood into Lucas's mind as he banged on the glass in a frenzy. The cracks didn't spread any further, and it was time for a last resort. He brought Natalie down from his shoulders and pointed the barrel at a twenty-degree angle toward the lid by his feet, which was as high as the gun could be raised before it met the glass. Switching to silenced mode so he wouldn't deafen himself within the chamber, he fired one, two, three, four shots. On the final one, the weakened glass shattered altogether.

Oh god.

He wasn't in the cryobay any more. He wasn't even on the ship. Lying on his back, his field of vision was a thick canopy of enormous, leafy green trees. Sunlight streamed through the treetops and made its way into his quickly shrinking pupils.

Am I still dreaming?

He climbed out of the unit and staggered to his feet, his muscles burning as they were put back to work. All around him the jungle called out, chirps and screeches from unseen creatures lurking nearby, or far away.

His bodysuit was torn in a few places, and he felt bruised patches of skin all over himself as he surveyed the forest. There was only one explanation for all of this, and he had to somehow prove it. Scanning his surroundings for the tallest climbable tree, he found one a few yards away from the downed cryo unit. Slinging Natalie onto his back, he ascended through the branches painfully as his body struggled to reactivate its core functions. Star-shaped leaves whipped against his face, and the bark felt sticky, which thankfully helped him keep his grip. The ground became more and more distant below him while the white sun got brighter.

Finally he burst through the forest canopy, nearing the top of the tree. He found a branch wide enough to sit on and, shielding his eyes with his hand, he looked out onto the horizon. It was true, then.

Plumes of smoke were rising from areas all over the vast jungle, with one enormous column coming from an area a long distance away. He didn't need to see the wreckage to understand what had happened. The Spear had been destroyed upon reaching Makari, and an unknown number of the crew with it. His heart raced and threatened to beat right out of his chest. It was getting harder to breathe.

Where were the others? Could they possibly be alive? He was. But he had the security of a cryopod. Who knew what state they were in when the ship broke apart. What the hell happened? Was there some mechanical error, or had they actually been shot down by the Xalans? The stealth drive was supposed to get them in and out of there safely. Lucas's head was dizzy trying to imagine what might have occurred, and what the fate of everyone onboard could have been. A hundred feet in the air was not an appropriate place to pass out, and Lucas quickly scrambled down the tree, taking note of which direction the largest stream of smoke was.

He collapsed on the ground when he reached the base of the tree. Sap trickled down into his hair and onto his shoulders as he attempted to mentally pull himself together. It was still hard to believe this was actually happening.

Controlling his breathing, he slowly brought himself back from the brink of hyperventilation. It was time to take stock of the situation. First, the cryochamber.

He crawled a few feet over to it and searched inside. Immediately disappointing was the discovery that the comm transponder within was as nonfunctional as the rest of the electronic features of the unit. He retrieved Omicron's glass square from the personal effects compartment and found a welcome bonus next to it. There was a panel labeled Emergency Kit he hadn't seen before, as it was practically behind his head. He wrestled it open and sifted through the contents of the pack.

Inside was a very small knife, but one that was exceptionally sharp. There were a few packs of powder labeled survival supplements and a rubberized canteen that would expand if filled with water. A few tiny vials of healing gel were there to seal wounds, and a small hollow metal circle produced a blue flame in the center when he rubbed his thumb around the outside. It wasn't much, but it was something. And of course he still had Natalie.

Another thought occurred to him as he slung the pouch over his shoulder. If the ship had either crashed or been shot down, the Xalans here would be out hunting for survivors. He'd seen how good they were at tracking living organisms through heat and heartbeat, and for all he knew they could be on top of him in the next few minutes. It was unclear how long he'd been unconscious after the cryochamber crash landed. Yes, this was a sparsely populated colony according to Alpha, but who knew how many troops were stationed nearby that could be sweeping the area? What was obvious was that he couldn't stay in his present location.

He did one last search of the unit and set off toward the largest column of smoke he'd seen, where he figured he'd find the bulk of the wreckage, and with it possible survivors. It was also likely he'd find Xalans there by the time he reached it, but it was a risk he had to take. Where else could he even go? He didn't have the coordinates of their contact Zeta's location. His only hope was to try to regroup with whoever was left before the Xalans reached them, or him. If he was alive, others had to be, right? He refused to let himself believe anything else, and he knew Asha and Alpha were alive. He felt it, as strange as it sounded, and it drove him forward with purpose.

The jungle was unforgiving. Even if most of the planet had been rendered desolate by the Xalans stripping it for resources, they'd crashed square in the middle of one of its last thriving rainforests. Thick vines and branches barred his way, and his bare feet were being shredded by the forest floor. The air was so humid it felt like he was wrapped in a thermal blanket, and he had to tear his bodysuit to his knees and elbows to avoid passing out.

So far, he'd only seen glimpses of the local wildlife. A millipede-type creature the size of his forearm slithered up a tree trunk. He swatted away clusters of what looked like tiny red mosquitoes that were equally as annoying—and presumably as disease-bearing—as their distant cousins on Earth.

His first truly bizarre encounter was with an animal that could only be described as the nightmarish union of an octopus and a snake. It was about ten feet over his head in the trees and, fully extended, probably as long as he was tall. It had two yellow eyes with black slits and four green, scaled tentacles that it was using to swing from tree to tree. As it passed over him, he could see a mouth on its underside full of razor-sharp teeth. Not knowing its intentions, his rifle remained pointed at it until it swung out of sight.

Along the way he collected water housed in nearby leaves, draining it into his canteen. Feeling weak, he inhaled one of his precious few "supplement" packs and found the chalky taste quite a bit more off-putting than the gaseous nutrients he'd had for months on the Ark. But it did spark some energy inside him, and he pressed onward, periodically scaling trees to ensure he wasn't going in circles. The smoke was still a long way off, though he was getting closer to one of the smaller plumes nearby.

Eventually, he saw what was burning through the trees ahead. He readied Natalie. It was hard to tell what piece of the ship he was looking at when he reached it. It was a fifty-foot swath of the hull rising out of the ground, with an unknown length of it buried beneath the dirt. Moving cautiously around the wreckage, the inside revealed a control cluster he recognized; it was part of the comm unit. He waved his hand across each darkened station he could reach, but no controls flickered to life. That would have been too much to hope for, he supposed. Detached from a central power source, it was all useless. Realizing there was nothing of value to be found, he hurried back into the jungle in case the smoke had attracted any unwanted parties.

It was about an hour later when he found the first body. The cryopod was completely smashed open when he came upon it, and a short distance away lay the mangled remains of the Guardian who had broken free from the enclosure. She lay crumpled against a tree trunk, the impact of which had likely killed her, judging by its splintered base and the awkward angle of her neck and other obviously broken limbs. He didn't recognize her. Through the blood that coated her face he could see tan skin and long dark-brown hair, the latter of which was unusual for a militaristic Guardian woman. She must have been one of those who stayed in cryo for the duration of the trip, as she wasn't a part of either his or Asha's training squads. He raided the emergency supplies from her pod and then, out of curiosity, opened the personal effects compartment. Inside was a tiny metal disk no bigger than a quarter. When he tapped it, a three-dimensional image shot out. A little boy with brown eyes and curly hair was sticking out his tongue in a universally recognized expression of goofiness. Lucas felt a twinge of a smile for a moment, followed by sadness as he glanced back toward the dead woman. He straightened out her body on the ground, gently placed the hovering image on her chest, and continued his trek into the increasingly dark jungle.

Lucas couldn't shake the feeling that something was following him. He'd felt it at the wrecked comm station, and it had stayed with him since. His eyes were constantly darting all around the murky jungle, but he couldn't see anything resembling a threat. If the Xalans were stalking him, why didn't they just attack? What were they waiting for?

The small white sun began to set overheard and, as it disappeared, a cover of dark clouds filled the sky. Minutes later, the clouds opened up and unleashed a downpour that drenched Lucas to his core. Soaking wet and covered in mud, he hoped it would make him harder to track, but he had to stop until the rain let up; it had become impossible to move forward through the torrential sheets of water.

He used his knife to collect some of the largest leaves from the surrounding plants, some of which were as big as his torso. Laying them across a pair of nearly parallel branches, he managed to erect a makeshift shelter that gave him some respite from the hammering rain. Though he'd been sweltering earlier, a deep chill now set into his bones, and the water was creeping dangerously near the top of the small boulder he'd taken refuge on. The surrounding area was starting to flood pretty heavily, and he watched an amphibian of some kind with webbed feet and two flat tails paddle by him through the water, unperturbed. Lucas gripped his arms and shivered on the rock. Even through the rain he still felt eyes upon him, somewhere in the dark jungle ahead.

After a few hours, the rain let up, and Lucas was able to heat himself up using the tiny flame from the survival kit and a series of muscle expansion techniques taught to him in Guardian training that kept his blood pumping. Night had officially descended, and Lucas thought it wise to scale another tree to figure out where he was now and how the landscape might change as he journeyed through the night. On the ground, he was surprised to see there were still streams of light piercing through the trees, presumably from a moon. When he reached the top, his jaw dropped at the sight.

There was a moon all right, but one no less than twenty times bigger than the ones around Sora or Earth. It shone brilliantly, reflecting the light of the dwarf star Makari orbited. The surface was littered with craters, the fine detail of which could be easily seen since it was so close to the planet. Lucas stared, transfixed, as it slowly rose from the horizon. Lost in its beauty, ten minutes went by before Lucas even averted his gaze.

And then, another couple of hours later as he marched through the forest, the moonlight was gone, the sun quickly rising again. Lucas had long grown accustomed to the thirty-seven-hour days of Sora, and of course the twenty-four-hour ones of Earth. But what had it been, ten hours to complete a full cycle here? He'd have to ask Alpha about it later.

Alpha. Surely he had the coordinates to find Zeta. Had he survived the crash, Lucas was sure he would have made his way to her and was probably already devising a plan to rescue the rest of them. That's the sort of thing he excelled at. Perhaps he was in the next clearing. Maybe the next one.

Maybe the next one.

But as he pressed onward, Lucas found no rescuers, nor pursuers. He did stumble upon a plasma cannon mount torn off the Spear and another dead Soran body, this one skewered in the branches about twenty feet in the air. After a short climb, he found it was another unrecognizable face. The corpse was a man this time, with a shaved head and long limbs. Lucas left him on his perch and turned to leave with no nearby cryochamber to salvage supplies from. A dark thought occurred to him. Could he possibly have been the only one who survived the crash?

Lucas stopped as he heard a distinct crack in the forest. Then another. And another.

He'd heard similar noises from the brush before, but this was different. These were footsteps. He scrambled up a tree across from where the dead man hung and hid behind the foliage. He minimized his breathing and lowered his heart rate as much as he was able, which was exceptionally difficult when he saw what was below him.

A squad of five Xalans moved through the jungle and into the small clearing where he'd just been standing. All wore light armor and held energy rifles, but one had a display hovering in front of him projected from his wrist. Lucas was too far away to read the symbols, but looking through Natalie's scope he saw something he recognized immediately. A heartbeat monitor, beating to the tune of his own pulse. He readied his rifle as the creatures began looking around the forest.

One raised his head and let out a loud roar. He pointed at the body in the tree, and the rest of his squad turned to look in the direction of his finger. The creature tapped the heartbeat display and then motioned up at the carcass.

They think he's still alive.

The squad found a way to quickly test their theory. Taking aim, they shot out the branches holding the man up with three quick bursts that caused a flutter of leathery winged creatures to fly up and out of the tree. The corpse cascaded awkwardly down the remaining branches and landed on the forest floor with a dull thud. The Xalans quickly ran up to it, guns at the ready, but the lead creature soon started shaking his head and growling as he stood over the obviously dead body. He pointed at the monitor, which was still pulsing with a live heartbeat.

So much for that.

The squad quickly realized the implication of the discovery, that another Soran lurked nearby, and started to fan out around the clearing. A few looked up and started to scour the trees, and fiddled with the scopes on their rifles.

Thermal.

Lucas couldn't remain hidden for more than another few seconds. He'd only have one shot at this.

The first creature didn't hear the piercing round that went directly through his skull, but the rest of his squad did. As they turned to look at their fallen comrade, Lucas was halfway to the ground. He used the creature twenty feet below to break his fall. They both hit the ground and became a tangled mess of limbs. Lucas ignored the sharp pain in his right leg and jabbed his survival knife into each of the creature's eyes. The blinded Xalan let out a painful howl as Lucas extracted himself from his lanky form. He got off a spray of rounds that tore into a third creature still reacting to the initial shot. Before his corpse even hit the ground, Lucas rolled away behind a nearby stump, which was fortunately about six feet in diameter and provided ample cover. Plasma rounds from the two intact creatures splintered the wood all around him and he stayed as low as he was able, sliding into the muck. He could still hear the cries of the injured Xalan, now forced into combat without eyes.

Lucas looked at the pooling water around the stump, which still hadn't receded from the downpour the night before. It gave him a reflected view that showed the two creatures were splitting up, working their way around each side of his barricade. They growled at each other in low tones, a contrast to the high-pitched squeals of their wounded counterpart.

Formulating a plan of attack in a split second like Guardian training had taught him, he whipped out to the left of the stump and cut the first creature in half with Natalie's area-of-effect "carnage" setting. The other Xalan opened fire and one of the shots tore across Lucas's arm, blackening his skin and making him cry out in agony. He unloaded another shotgun blast. At range, the particles spread out and merely peppered the creature. Still, it was enough to burn, and the creature flailed around with holes spattered across his chest armor and exposed arm and neck. Apparently it was too hot for a full bodysuit out in the jungle.

The creature staggered backward, still clutching his gun. Lucas flipped Natalie back into full-auto mode and marched forward, sending a spray of rounds his way that brought him first to his knees, then flat on his face. Smoke rose from the exit wounds as Lucas reached him.

Nearby, the blinded Xalan had finally located his gun. Lucas walked over to him and kicked the rifle out of his hand, and the creature let out a desperate cry. His wrist display still showed the heartbeat monitor, and the pulse was beating exceptionally fast now as Lucas was surging with adrenaline.

Blood streamed from the Xalan's eyes, one of which still had the knife stuck in it. He lashed out blindly with his long talons, catching Lucas by surprise. A claw grazed Lucas's cheek, but as he jumped back, further swings missed their mark by a few feet. Lucas briefly thought about attempting to question the snarling creature before him, but without Alpha's translating abilities, there was nothing useful he could get from him. Well, almost nothing.

After the final creature lay sprawled on the ground with a smoldering hole in his forehead, Lucas unclasped his wrist display.

After playing with the controls for a minute he finally found an option that read IGNORE CURRENT SIGNATURE. When pressed, the monitor went dead, no longer tracking his own heartbeat. He snapped it to his wrist, though it was meant to fit a far larger creature and took up most of his forearm. Quickly sifting through the rest of the bodies, he couldn't find much that would be of use to him. Their armor was too bulky to wear, their guns too heavy to carry. The holodisplay he currently wore would have to do. He had to move, as god only knew what sort of attention that firefight had drawn from other search parties nearby. And still, the feeling that he was being watched never left him, even with all the dead around him. He sprinted off into the forest, leaving their bodies to the jungle.

Lucas's singed arm and hurt leg were giving him trouble as he continued on, and it was another few hours before he even noticed the tiny piercing pain in his neck. He flinched when he went to scratch the area and his fingers brushed against a tiny sliver embedded in his skin. Stopping his trek, he carefully pulled it out with his thumb and forefinger. A red drop of blood was at the end of the centimeter-long protrusion. It was small and barbed and looked to be a little longer than a bee stinger, though that was exactly what it felt like. He'd waded through all manner of foreign insect swarms on his journey, but hadn't thought much of the various bites he received. Sure, they itched, but this was different. Looking in the reflection of his survival knife, the area around where the stinger had been was dark red, almost black. Lucas pressed on it gently, drawing out another few crimson drops. He searched within himself to try and see if he could find any adverse symptoms other than a small amount of discomfort. Yes, he was fatigued and dizzy, but anyone making their way through such a hostile jungle with barely any food or water would likely feel the same. He shoved it to the back of his mind. Just another ailment he'd need treated when he finally found Alpha. *If* he found Alpha; it was getting harder and harder to believe what he was telling himself in order to stay motivated.

The rain started again, and shortly after, night fell once more, the ten-hour cycle starting anew. After two torrential downpours it was getting harder to see any smoke from the wreckage rising from the jungle, but Lucas still trusted that his gut was taking him the right direction. Still, he was growing concerned that he had yet to find anyone else from the ship alive. Worry gave way to exhaustion as his internal clock was spinning, and he propped himself precariously on a branch about thirty feet off the ground. The feeling that something was watching him had now left him, and he felt fully alone in the noisy jungle as he unwillingly drifted off to sleep.

Lucas woke with the dwarf sun rising quickly, spreading light through the mist in the air and the droplets on the leaves all around him. If it wasn't for the looming specter of death that seemed to emanate from the forest, it might have actually been rather beautiful. The smoke from the wreckage was nonexistent now, but spherical Xalan probes strafed the skies, looking for survivors from on high. Whether they could detect him or not was anyone's guess, but Lucas had tuned the heartbeat monitor clamped to his forearm to track both Xalan and Soran signatures, though the display had been quiet since he'd starting using it. He hoped it was actually working.

As Lucas moved through the wet brush, a dry scratching began to claw at the back of his throat. He tried to quell it with a swig from his canteen, but it did little to abate the feeling. He cleared his throat and kept trudging forward. A pair of scaled tree octopi swung through the branches a few dozen feet above him. Loud bird calls screeched nearby, though the creatures themselves were hidden from view. At least he imagined they were birds.

Lucas scratched the bump on his neck. It had expanded and the discoloration was now seeping into his collarbone. This was no bee sting. He rubbed another dab of med gel on the wound, but so far the treatment had no effect. There seemed to be a constant dull hum in his ears in addition to his newfound throat issues. He needed to find some help, and quickly.

A few more steps later faint pulses displayed on his heartbeat sensor, but he couldn't tell if they were Soran or Xalan. He took a step forward and they disappeared. He took a step left and they were still gone. Only when he shifted right a solid three paces did the jagged lines return to the screen projected in front of him. Lucas clutched Natalie tightly and upgraded his brisk walk to a light jog in that direction, as much as it pained him. He wiped sweat from his brow as he kept glancing from the jungle ahead to the monitor. Five distinct lines had now appeared. One Soran heartbeat and four Xalans, still a good distance away. He drew upon all his remaining strength to start sprinting.

Gunshots. Lots of them. Lucas brought his pace down to a crawl. The sounds seemed to be incredibly close. He crept through the vines and ferns and tried to make out if there was anything up ahead. He couldn't just run in there blindly, lest he catch a plasma round to the face before he even got a shot off, but it tortured him knowing a Guardian was out there fighting for their life the way he had earlier. It could be Asha for all he knew. He had to help.

But soon it became clear the person might not need his assistance after all. A Xalan heartbeat flatlined on the display while the others were racing a mile a minute. Lucas heard a few more gunshots and then another pulse went silent. He resumed running, determined to come to the aid of whoever this was, should they need it. He almost tripped over the first Xalan body, draped over a log with a long wooden spear sticking out of its neck. A few feet further and another Xalan soldier lay with a series of smoking holes across its body.

Lucas bounded over a collapsed rock formation, scattering a bunch of tiny lizards living within. His heart monitor showed another flatline, along with the Soran's heartbeat that was slowing down. Way down. Lucas burst into the clearing.

A few feet in front of him was another dead Xalan, this one without a head entirely. But the more pressing concern was a tall Xalan trooper standing with his back to Lucas, aiming his rifle at a figure whose bloodied, bare feet were visible between the creature's legs.

Lucas didn't even slow down as he sprayed a burst of plasma into the Xalan's back. The creature spun around in agony, just in time to take one last shot to the head. He crumpled in a heap, and the air was sucked out of Lucas's lungs when he saw what was lying on the ground.

It was Silo, bathed in black and red blood, propped up against a small boulder with a Xalan energy rifle a few feet out of his reach. His injuries were severe; a series of black plasma scorches peppered his thighs and torso, and deep claw marks were engraved all over his body, with a particularly nasty pair running across his face. His pulse was barely registering on Lucas's monitor.

"Holy shit," Lucas exclaimed breathlessly. Silo's eyes lit up when he saw who was standing over him. Lucas quickly dropped to his knees and, with shaking hands, took out the med gel he'd collected from his pair of survival kits.

Silo made an attempt to laugh, causing blood to erupt from his mouth, which he spat out through choked breaths. He spoke, taking pauses as he attempted force out the words.

"It's not . . . going to do anything," he said weakly. "Save that for yourself, you'll . . . probably need it."

It was true. The small vials of gel were simply disappearing into the gaping holes all over his body. There wasn't enough to stitch one of the gashes up, much less all of them.

"It's fine . . . I . . . I just need to find someone, and they can come help," Lucas said frantically, his hands now slippery with blood.

Silo shook his head.

"There is no one. And if there was, they couldn't do anything for this."

It was clear Silo couldn't move his arms or legs, which were sprawled out uselessly around him. Lucas wasn't eager to see what his spine looked like if the rest of him was this mangled.

"They'll fix you. You people can fix anyone."

"There's no fixing dead," Silo said with a painful chuckle. "Even we . . . haven't figured that one out yet."

Lucas emptied another gel vial into a wound.

"Stop," Silo said calmly.

"*Stop*."

Lucas finally obeyed, and dropped a quartet of now-empty vials on the ground. His head was throbbing and he felt like he was on fire.

"You don't have much time, you've got . . . got to get out of here. They'll be coming."

It was Lucas's turn to shake his head.

"No, I'm not just going to leave you here." A thought occurred to him. "Do you know what happened to the ship? Was it shot down?"

Silo winced before speaking. The ground was drenched beneath him.

"Seems like it, though I can't say for sure. I was in cryo, woke up . . . out here. Been running around for a few days. Ran into these guys with only a makeshift pike, but I think I did . . . pretty well."

Silo attempted a smirk. The slashes across his face made Lucas cringe just looking at them.

"You know, I never got to thank you . . . for those credits," Silo said.

"What credits?" Lucas said, caught off guard by the shift in topic.

"That . . . 50,000 marks you threw me back in Elyria. Might have been pocket change for the Earthborn, but that's a lot . . . a lot where I'm from. Sent my little brother . . . to flight school."

"Oh," Lucas said, embarrassed. "It was nothing."

"Maybe, but that kid's going to be an ace pilot someday . . . thanks to you."

"It's more because of you, I'm sure," Lucas said.

Silo pressed on.

"And I'm sorry about the fight on the Spear. They . . . juiced me for that. Made me so mad it was like you'd just slept with my sister or something."

He paused, drawing a wheezing breath from punctured lungs, and continued.

"I would have killed you without thinking twice. Even without the drugs I'd have to do it . . . under orders. But you didn't."

Lucas put his hands on his knees.

"Where I'm from, you don't kill your friends. For any reason."

Silo laughed.

"Guess your lady . . . forgot that rule."

"She's forgotten a lot of things," Lucas said darkly. "But come on, we've got to get you out of here, let's go."

He bent down, slung Silo's arm over his shoulders, and attempted to lift all three hundred pounds of him. Lucas barely got six inches up before he collapsed to his knees under the mass of dead weight. Silo started coughing and wheezing, more blood pouring from his mouth.

"You still don't get it, huh? This is it. I can't even move, and you . . . you look about three steps away from the Oak Thrones yourself. Just take this, and get . . . out . . . of here."

Silo looked downward, and Lucas saw a chip hung on a cord around his neck.

"Your Final?" Lucas said as he snapped the cord and took the device into his hand. Silo nodded.

"Who do I give this to?" Lucas asked.

"You'll know."

Silo's circuitry tattoos on his arms and shoulders had been ravaged and his bodysuit was torn to the waist. Across his blood-soaked, muscled chest was a string of curved text. Through the gore Lucas could make out what it said.

"Forsaken are the strong who do not protect the weak."

Involuntary tears were welling in Lucas's eyes, and he felt like he was about to pass out. Lucas could hear new heartbeats from the device on his wrist.

"Go," Silo said, recognizing the danger.

Resisting every urge to stay and fight and die, Lucas finally turned to leave.

"Wait," Silo said, considering something. "One more thing . . . before you go."

Lucas looked at him and understood.

Don't ask me to.

"I . . . I'm going to need you to break your rule."

No.

"No warrior's death for me if they find me like this. I'd do it myself, but I can't."

Lucas stared at him. It was the same sight as on the Spear, the same broken friend with his life in his hands. But this time the stakes were different. This was mercy. Wasn't it? That's what he'd have to tell himself.

"Alright," Lucas said, his voice a whisper.

"Don't worry," Silo said with a weak smile. "The way things have been going for you, I'm sure I'll see you . . . soon enough."

"I don't doubt it," Lucas said, attempting to keep his composure. He thumbed around with Natalie's options, fingers trembling.

"You know," Silo said, looking out into the trees as Lucas circled around to stand behind him. "It's kind of nice here."

His voice was growing fainter, as was his heartbeat. The other pulses on the display were becoming more pronounced. Lucas couldn't risk him expiring naturally in time.

"It is." He raised Natalie, the rifle's mode switch set to Carnage. He didn't want to leave anything behind for the Xalans to experiment with.

"I'll see you around, Lucas," said Silo as he stared out into the clearing.

"Sure," Lucas said, his stomach one giant knot.

The echo of the blast would haunt Lucas for an eternity. The jungle roared in disapproval. He sprinted off into the darkness, his head pounding and vision bleary.

12

Lucas had killed many people over the years, but none had shattered him like what he'd just done. None had that much weight that would now be forever attached to his soul. He kept telling himself it was a kindness given the circumstances, but that didn't scrub the image from his mind.

He tore through the jungle like a madman until the heartbeats on his monitor finally faded. He'd lost them, for now. But when he stopped, it didn't register with his quickly deteriorating body. His thoughts were fractured, and he no longer had any idea which direction he was going after two days of careful navigation. His face was hot and flushed and the air smelled like putrid milk all around him. The right half of his torso itched furiously, and he started cutting away his bodysuit in a frenzy. On his chest a series of black-and-red tendrils crawled down under his skin from his neck wound. His vision was blurred; the jungle's hue shifted from green, to blue, to orange. And then he saw him.

A hallucination. A ghost. One and the same. Lucas stumbled toward him and his swollen tongue tried to form words. He only managed to get one out.

"Adam."

It was him, or at least a spectral vision of the man who'd been Sonya's sibling but whom Lucas had thought of as a brother; Lucas had always been the one he had to look out for.

"Hello, Lucas, it's been a while."

It certainly had. Lucas hadn't seen him since the wedding, and after that, Adam had shipped out on his next tour. His last tour.

Here he was, standing in the jungle exactly as Lucas remembered him. Bright eyes and dress blues. He was a fixed force in Lucas's vision as the rest of the jungle seemed to vibrate around him. Lucas's fingers were starting to go numb, and his rifle felt like it weighed a metric ton. He slung it over his back.

"Can you h-help me?" Lucas pleaded with the vision before him.

"Why do you need help?" Adam replied coolly.

Lucas flexed his fingers, but couldn't regain feeling.

"I'm a-alone out here."

"You've always been alone."

That feeling of being watched was back, more pressing than it had ever been. Lucas could feel the presence in the jungle around him somewhere.

"Who's out there?" he called.

"They can't hear you, Lucas," Adam said calmly.

"Yes they can. Where are you?" he shouted again, spinning around in a circle so violently he almost fell. A brightly colored flock of red birds flew across his vision, startling him. He couldn't tell what was real and what wasn't anymore.

"Is he really dead?" Lucas whispered, his brain burning inside his skull as his thoughts returned to Silo.

"Yes."

"Are you?"

Adam remained silent. Lucas knew the answer, even in his delirium.

"Why did you have to go back?" Lucas screamed at him. "The w-war was over!"

"Wars are never over, not really. Peace is a necessary illusion."

"Who are you?" Lucas yelled.

This wasn't Adam, the kindhearted Marine Lucas once knew. This was a demon, a twisted manifestation of Lucas's own subconscious tormenting him.

Adam merely smiled. The right half of his face became mangled. Slowly he shifted into the autopsy photo Lucas had seen after the IED tore through him.

"You know."

Adam decayed completely. Standing in his place was a creature like none Lucas had ever seen before. It was an enormous wolf-like animal covered in black scale plating separated by tufts of dark crimson fur. A serpent-like tail writhed at its other end. Its paws revealed curved talons six inches long and, when it snarled, rows upon rows of white teeth glinted, surrounding a forked tongue. Standing on all fours, it nearly met Lucas's gaze, and he couldn't look away from its piercing yellow eyes. He knew these were the eyes that had been burning into him throughout his trek around the jungle. They blazed through him now, staring straight into his soul. Was this death? Had it been stalking him all this time, waiting for its moment to strike?

Lucas couldn't even lift his arms to unsling Natalie from his back. His body wasn't letting him. He stood there frozen, the rest of the jungle spinning around him, lost in the creature's gaze.

"*Naali*," came a voice in the ether. "*Chit-ka'lik*."

The animal broke eye contact with Lucas and walked a few feet to the right. As Lucas turned his head to follow him, he felt a piercing pain in his neck. He grasped at it and pulled out a long needle coated in a viscous green gel. It fell from his fingers and he collapsed on the spot. The last thing he saw was the face of a child with dark skin and wild hair. White tattoos circled his features and his hazel eyes watched Lucas slip quickly into unconsciousness.

Fevered dreams in the darkness. Only voices. Too many voices. Too many from days long past.

Michigan.

"Sir, do you know why I pulled you over?"

"I may have been going a bit fast coming out of that turn."

"Sir, have you been drinking tonight?"

"No! Well, I had a couple a few hours ago, but that was—"

"Sir, I'm going to need you to step out of the car."

"But I have to get home, I'm—"

"Sir, step out of the car."

"Seriously, please just—"

"Sir."

Oregon.

"He was sitting there for *two hours*."

"I know I'm sorry I—"

"Two hours. He tried to walk home by himself. If Jean hadn't seen him—"

"I set a reminder in my phone, it just didn't—"

"You need a reminder to make sure your own son is safe after baseball practice? Where the hell are you anyway?"

"Work, it's just crazy here and I lost track of—"

"Is that a fact? Because when I called Mark he said you left three hours ago."

"I had to—"

"Wherever you are, just stay there. We deserve better than this."

"I know."

Florida.

"I'm sorry, but I need your car."

"What? Who the hell are you? Get away from me!"

"I really am sorry, but you need to get out, now. I have to get back to my family."

"Look I don't know what—"

"This things started shooting. It's a war out there. My family is on the other side of the country and every airport on Earth is shut down. I need your car."

"This is a $90,000 Range—"

"I'm sorry to have to do this."

Louisiana.

"What are you doing, Greg?"

"I'm done."

"Just take a step back. Let's talk."

"No more talking. No more walking. I'm done."

"We're almost to Texas."

"You don't know where we are."

"We're almost to Texas."

"I don't want to go to Texas. I don't want to go anywhere, anymore."

"Greg, take a step back. The whole group is watching."

"If they were smart, they'd be up here with me."

"Greg—"

Colorado.

"Any last words?"

"Eat shit."

"Okay then."

"The others will find you."

"They won't. And cannibals shake so much they can't even aim straight."

"We can, we're military."

"Who isn't these days? Why are you in my camp?

"I like that gun. And those canned peaches. Would've gone great with your liver."

"You're insane. You all are."

"We're survivors."

"You're not."

Lucas opened his eyes, but the darkness didn't leave him. He blinked, but there was nothing but a rich black void. He was lying flat and could barely move his arms and legs. Voices were whispering a ways away from him.

"Hello?" he called out to the void.

The whispering stopped.

"*Sinaa-sti vindala ki'lek,*" came a voice speaking an unfamiliar language from down by his feet. More whispering and the faint sound of hurried footsteps in the dirt.

"*Chun saunto,*" came another voice, this one much deeper.

Lucas still couldn't see. He felt sweat pouring down his face. He raised his right arm to his neck and touched a goopy paste that was spread there. The itching had ceased but his insides still felt like they were cooking.

"*Kala lo'tonti, Rokaan ma'l loro 'Soran.'*"

Now there was a word Lucas recognized.

Where was he? He felt around the surface he was lying on. It was a kind of mesh netting that appeared to be woven out of tiny branches. The sides were held up by solid wood logs. Lucas's lack of vision was starting to cause him to panic. Was he permanently blind? What had happened to him? The last thing he remembered was the wolf and the child. A child? It couldn't have been. Another hallucination.

"Lucas!" came a booming metal voice he would recognize anywhere. Every muscle in his body breathed a collective sigh of relief.

"Alpha," he said hoarsely.

"Indeed!"

The enthusiasm in his friend's voice was palpable, even if Lucas couldn't see it on his face.

"I was elated to hear the *Kal'din* had stabilized you after your *Moltok* sting. I have been informed that the toxin of that insect is among the most deadly in the forest. Thankfully, across generations the *Oni* have developed a treatment that reverses the effects."

Kal'din? Moltok? Oni? Lucas didn't understand any of these words. But first questions first.

"Why can't I see?" Lucas asked.

"It is a side effect of either the Moltok poison or subsequent cleansing treatment. I am assured it is temporary. In most cases."

Most cases? Alpha was reassuring as ever.

"What happened to the ship?"

Alpha fell silent before his tone turned dire.

"Upon entry into the atmosphere of Makari, we were shot down by a highly concentrated barrage of surface-to-air ordinance. The ship broke up and was scattered throughout the jungle."

Then it was true.

"How is that possible?" Lucas asked incredulously. "What about the stealth drive?"

He could hear Alpha moving around him.

"They must have improvised a way to detect the ship, knowing that we had appropriated the vessel. It was likely relayed by [garbled], by my mentor before his capture at the Fourth Order base. They may have predicted we would attempt to reach the colonies on a mission such as this for sabotage or other purposes."

Lucas felt the medicinal goop in between his fingers. There were coarse grains in it. His brain felt numb.

"Where's Asha? The rest of the crew?"

"Many Guardians died in the crash despite the safety systems onboard the Spear. Others landed in the jungle. Some are still there. We can track their vital statistics remotely from here and locate them, but retrieval has proved . . . difficult due to Xalan interference. They scour the landscape hunting down survivors."

Lucas was starting to get groggy. Someone was lathering more paste on his neck. The corpse-like odor burned his nostrils, but fogged his mind.

"Yeah . . . I know, I ran into a few of them. But Asha . . . Where . . ."

"She has been located and is presently en route with her Oni escort. Her vitals are stable."

He was floating up toward the blackness, trying to keep his thoughts straight.

"Where is . . . here? Where . . . are we?"

"That is something better explained with the benefit of sight."

Lucas hoped that was something that would find him again. He succumbed to the all-encompassing abyss.

When Lucas woke this time, the blackness had been replaced by a bleary light and amorphous shapes. With each blink, his vision became a little clearer, and finally he rubbed his eyes to the point where his surroundings were finally revealed.

He was in a stone chamber lit by open flames all around him. There was no one else in the room, but on the ground nearby lay a collection of various primitive-looking bowls and tools covered in the gray paste that was caked onto most of his right side. Reaching up to his neck wound, he found that the enormous lump had subsided under the solidified goo. His thoughts were no longer jumbled, his insides no longer burned. Feeling a tinge in his left shoulder, he looked down to see a small metal disc attached to his skin. He attempted to pry it off, but it was deeply embedded. Part of the healing process, perhaps.

Rising to his feet, he was unsteady, but able to walk. As he moved toward the thatched door, he found the walls were full of pictures carved into the stone. In one of the biggest murals, a large object loomed in the sky, and an army of stick-figured tribal warriors sat below it, heaving spears and arrows upward. The last stand of a doomed people, something he could empathize with.

Opening the door, it became immediately apparent that he'd spoken too soon. They weren't a dead race after all.

Before him was a village, bustling with activity, housed in its entirety inside the largest cave Lucas had ever seen. Bits of sunlight poured in from holes in the ceiling that appeared to be at least a thousand feet above them. Below, humans milled about between buildings made out of stone, wood, and the occasional sheet of metal. Astonishingly, they'd somehow survived the devastation of their people countless years ago.

Those closest to him stopped and eyed him as he passed. Everyone here had dark caramel skin with brown or black hair and a hunted look in their eyes. Most had white tattoos coating parts of their body, and the villagers wore a combination of animal furs interspersed with metal pieces that looked like they'd been torn from sets of Xalan power armor. Clusters of armed men talked to each other, eyeing Lucas suspiciously. They wielded spears, bows, axes, and knives, though a few were brandishing modified Xalan energy weapons.

Even underground, plant life still thrived. There was mossy grass under Lucas's feet and trees were rooted along the outside of the settlement, which looked to be a few dozen buildings housing several hundred of these tribal humans. Or Sorans, he supposed.

Lucas's blood froze when he saw a troupe of Xalans, clad in full power armor and clutching rifles, near one of the warrior groups, but they merely eyed him like the others. What the hell was going on here?

A wild-haired child ran past Lucas and into one of the huts nearby. A second later, Alpha emerged from the entryway with a white-skinned, blue-eyed Xalan in tow.

"Miraculous!" Alpha exclaimed in Soran. "I was told of the Kal'din's healing abilities, but I did not expect primitive medicine to achieve results this significant so quickly."

"You do not need to persist in referring to the Oni as 'primitive,'" said the creature behind him. "They are a race that has survived longer than many more advanced cultures."

The white Xalan spoke through a translator collar like Alpha's, surely one he'd given her, as the device was of his own invention. Her voice was tinged with metal as well, but somehow it had a softer quality than his.

"Apologies," Alpha said to her before turning back toward him. "Lucas, this is Zeta, the contact we came here to meet."

Lucas gave a slight nod, which she returned. You didn't really greet a Xalan with a handshake.

"Of course, I've heard a lot about you."

"And I, you," she said. "Though the tales I have heard over the past few days are almost impossible to believe."

"What is this place?"

Alpha glanced toward Zeta, who began to explain.

"Nearly a thousand years ago, the Xalans sacked Makari, as you call it, like they did your planet. The indigenous people here were the Oni. They were a young culture, and only as advanced as what you see around you. As such, they had no true means to fight back against the Gal'krai or 'sky demons' as they deemed their invaders. Their population of a mere hundred million was decimated by the superior force. Armies that had previously conquered entire continents fell in a matter of hours. Great cities were razed along with the vast forests in which they resided."

The Oni were starting to gather around them now, listening to Zeta who was also motioning with her hands as she spoke, communicating to them in a sort of sign language. A tall, lanky Oni warrior sidled up next to her. His dark green eyes scanned Lucas up and down. He was more heavily tattooed than the others around him, with black-and-white markings weaving in and out of each other all over his body. His hair was shaved into winding patterns on his head and he had a scar that crept up from his jaw and crossed his lip. He wore a chestplate of black metal, lifted from a "sky demon" corpse, no doubt, and had both a long, thin energy rifle and a dark, metal-tipped spear slung across his back. A string of marble-gray claws hung around his neck. Xalan claws. Zeta continued.

"The remaining Oni took shelter in the myriad cave systems scattered throughout Makari, where they have lived since the invasion. Many pockets of the surviving population have been hunted down over the years, but some persist. Some like the *Khas'to* tribe you see before you."

Upon hearing their tribe's name, the Oni around him gave a brisk shout.

"I discovered them after I crashed my appropriated prison ship here some years ago. I was severely injured, but they came to my aid and nursed me back to health when they easily could have executed me. I am told that my unique coloring indicates that I am not a sky demon like the others, but rather a *Holoi*, a "white spirit." An opposing force to the evil, meant to aid the Oni and see their people rise again. It is a title I have attempted to live up to these past years. I outfitted each Khas'to with a device to mask their biological signatures from detection, and they are able to live in relative peace here in *S'tasonti*. 'Sanctuary.' They no longer have to move around constantly to avoid detection."

She pointed to the shoulder of the man who stood next to her. There sat a metal disc like the one on Lucas's own arm. Looking around, he could see that every Oni here wore one.

"In return for my aid, I have been allowed to live here among them and assist the Xalan resistance movement on this planet and many others. The other Xalans you see here are my personal escort and are loyal to our cause."

The quartet of tough-looking Xalan soldiers continued to glare at Lucas.

"The man to my right is Toruk, chieftain of the Khas'to. He is overseeing the rescue of the surviving members of your squad. In fact, he was leading the group that brought you back."

Lucas's eyes widened as the giant scaly wolf he'd seen in the jungle wandered out from behind a hut. *So it wasn't a hallucination.* It ignored Lucas and plodded toward Toruk, who reached out to ruffle the patch of fur on the top of its head. His eyes never left Lucas. With his power armor and rifle, tribal tattoos and trophy necklace, he looked like some kind of strange pirate, lost in time.

"Come," Alpha said. "There is much to discuss."

Inside the largest hut in the village, Lucas was surprised to see a collection of machinery that rivaled the CIC of both Xalan ships he'd been in. The walls were lined with floating monitors and a central workstation was alive with light and sound. It was entirely out of place in their present surroundings, but Lucas figured it must be Zeta's base of operations.

"Alright," Lucas said. "I need some more answers. Where's Asha?"

Alpha projected a floating display from his mechanical hand. It was a topographical map of the local landscape, and there were a flurry of red, black, and green dots pulsing all over it.

"What am I looking at?" Lucas asked. Zeta was busying herself shifting through pieces of a video. The video that Alpha's father had made before his death.

"Each Guardian is implanted with a tracking chip so their location might be known in circumstances like these. It monitors their vital statistics along with other pertinent data relating to their biology."

Lucas squinted and could see tiny names next to the dots. Wrev. Danna. Kali. Corvin.

"Living Guardians are red, the deceased are black."

Lucas searched the litany of black spots until he saw the one he sought, Silo's. He had been secretly hoping that entire event was some sort of disease-induced dream, but no. He still had Silo's Final on him as well, he discovered.

"And the green clusters?" Lucas said pointing to the dots, which were grouped together.

"Those are rescued Guardians or Oni warriors. We have been sending them out in waves in order to retrieve the survivors. Their *vornaa* are expert trackers, though I have outfitted them with a copy of this readout as well."

"Vornaa?" Lucas said. "The wolf?"

Alpha nodded.

"It is a nearly extinct, carnivorous species, native to the area, that the Oni have domesticated over time. I am told it was not an easy feat."

Lucas spotted a cluster of green surrounding a red dot. Asha. They were moving toward the indicator of the village where there was another, larger grouping of green dots, his own included.

"So she's on her way back?"

"Indeed, Asha should be here in less than a day. Reports from the search team indicate she is without serious injury and in adequate health. More so than you were, to be sure."

Lucas looked over the entire map in front of him.

"What's the final count then? How many did we lose?"

Alpha checked a readout.

"Of the 106 crew members onboard the ship, forty-eight died on impact. Twenty-three more have perished in the jungle since the crash almost three days ago. Twenty-five have been found and brought back to the village."

"Where are they?" Lucas asked.

"Most are being treated by the Kal'din. He is the medical overseer of the community, trained by generations of his own people, and given further knowledge and tools by Zeta."

Zeta remained fixed on her monitor. It showed the segment of the video where the evolutionary pattern of the Xalans over generations could be seen.

"The healthiest Guardians have gone out with the Oni in search of other survivors."

"How many are still out there?"

"Ten. Three are on their way back. Four have rapidly deteriorating vital signs. The rest are stable. Teams are en route to almost all of them."

"We lost two-thirds of the entire crew. And the ship," Lucas repeated.

"That is correct."

Alpha looked dejected. He clearly blamed himself for the loss of life and the impending failure of the mission.

"How did *you* get here?" Lucas asked.

Alpha's eyes were downcast toward the map.

"I will admit some guilt pertaining to how easily I survived the encounter. The Spear had contingencies for the pilot when the destruction of the ship was imminent. As it broke apart after the unexpected assault, I was absorbed into a highly secure chamber that weathered the chaos with ease. Inside, I still had access to many of the ship's core functions. This tracking program, Zeta's signal. As quickly as I could, I made my way here and attempted to explain myself to the Oni. Had Zeta not appeared, I would have likely been skinned alive and had my teeth and claws removed one by one. It is a tribal custom for captured Gal'krai here."

Zeta strode over to the two of them. She was just a few inches shorter than Alpha. She too wore nothing, but other than her pale complexion and bright eyes, there was no visible difference in biology between the two of them. Lucas had yet to determine how Xalans reproduced, as it certainly wasn't obvious.

"Imagine my surprise when [garbled]. Excuse me, when *Alpha* arrived at my door after all these years. I had assumed he was dead along with the rest of his clan, though I activated our backchannel signal as soon as I was able in the hopes that he was not."

Alpha chimed in.

"I have spent the two days after my arrival attempting to explain our present circumstances to Zeta. Why we came. What we can hope to achieve. And of course, I shared my father's truth with her."

Zeta looked shaken. A freeze frame of Alpha's father's face hung on a monitor across the room.

"It was . . . difficult to process," she said quietly. "To think that our entire existence is built upon a lie? It is almost unfathomable. The scope of this deceit is truly astonishing, even for a ruling body as corrupt as ours. Hundreds of thousands of our own people must have been killed to prevent this secret from getting out. If the public knew our history, that we were created by the Sorans from their own DNA, the unrest would destabilize the Council."

"Then you think it will work," Lucas said.

Zeta nodded.

"I do," she replied. "But the challenge of disseminating the message throughout the colonies and Xala so that all may see it at once is great. And that is without considering the obvious fact that all of you are now stranded here without a ship. I am told you have two sons who need you back on Sora?"

"That's right," Lucas said, his thoughts turning to Noah. How lonely he must be without the pair of them, even if he was surrounded by palace staff. And their second child was scheduled to be "born" from the tank when, in a month? Two? He and Asha had to make it back to them.

"We have to find a way out of here."

"That will be an arduous process," Alpha said. "And there is much to plan in order to ensure the success of our mission."

"The success of our mission?" Lucas exclaimed. "Most of our crew is dead and our ship is in pieces. How exactly is our mission going to be a success?"

"We have reached Zeta, as intended. She is already working on a broadcast algorithm for our message of truth. For every ally we have lost, we've gained two in the form of the Oni."

"No offense," Lucas said, "but they don't look like the most well-equipped bunch compared to the Guardians, who would have been here in full armor with high-tech weaponry in tow."

"You should not underestimate the Oni," Zeta said. "They have survived here for thousands of years, and the jungle is littered with the carcasses of Xalans who have died at their hands. In fact, the local military base calls this [garbled]. 'The Black Forest.' Entire platoons have been swallowed up by the Oni as they have attempted to navigate the jungle. The more superstitious Xalans believe them to be ghosts of the old civilization, haunting them for their crimes against the planet's people."

"And what do the Oni believe about us arriving here?" Lucas asked.

"There used to be those on this planet that shared your skin tone, many, many generations ago. I have told them that you are *Rokaan.* Descendants of the once-great mountain tribes who have come to fight alongside them. They are wary of new faces, but can see you are obviously Oni as well, which builds a bridge of trust. Though to you they would be called Soran. Or human, as you said on Earth. All the words mean one and the same now. I will never understand your people's presence all throughout this galaxy. And now knowing that the Xalans are not a sovereign race, merely a Soran genetic experiment, it appears you are the only true species that populates the stars."

"And yet here we are," Lucas said, "practically extinct on a half dozen planets, save one."

"We will try to reverse that with our work here," Zeta said.

"So what's the plan now?" Lucas asked, turning to Alpha.

Alpha scratched an old scar on his chest.

"Zeta is working on her algorithm and I am attempting to formulate a path off this planet."

"And what can I do?" Lucas asked. He noticed that Natalie lay propped up against a console and immediately walked over and grabbed the rifle. Alpha had likely placed it there for safekeeping. It was one of his best creations, after all.

"There is one more matter we need you to attend to, if you feel able to take on the task," Alpha said.

"I've been in way worse shape than this," Lucas said. It was true, and his body had learned to live with minor discomforts like burns and fractures for years now. With the poison out of his system, he was refreshed.

"There is one last Guardian in need of rescue."

Lucas already knew what was coming next.

"First Watchman Mars Maston."

He'd seen his dot on the map a fair distance away from camp. The area he was in had been shaded red for some reason.

"Why hasn't a team been dispatched to him already?"

"One was," Zeta said, looking sorrowful. "But they were lost in *Ai Los'ri Vin-taasa.*"

"What is that?" Lucas asked.

"The Dead City."

Lucas's face remained blank. She elaborated.

"It is the two-thousand-year-old husk of an ancient Oni metropolis. It lies in ruins deep within the jungle, and it is most unfortunate your colleague landed there."

"Why?"

Alpha was growing nervous as Zeta spoke.

"Legend has it the Gal'krai, the Xalans, handed the city over to a powerful beast some time after they invaded, one they did not want living among them. It hunts in the jungle by day, sleeps somewhere within the walls by night. While the Oni have hunted Xalans in the Black Forest, the creature has been hunting them. They quickly learned that stepping foot in the city itself was certain death. None have survived to even report back what the beast looks like."

"Fantastic," Lucas said. "How is Maston even still alive, then?"

Alpha spoke now.

"Readings indicate that his cryochamber has not yet opened, and his tracking signal is coming from underground. Most likely, both the Xalans and the creature do not know he is there."

Maston was still asleep? That would be quite a wake-up call if they managed to reach him. Something occurred to Lucas.

"A beast they didn't want living among them . . . Alpha, that's not—"

"The Desecrator?" Alpha said. "For all our sakes, I hope not. That would be an exceptionally unfortunate stroke of luck if the abomination were being kept on Makari."

"The Desecrator?" Zeta said incredulously. "You believe the creature to be the subject of an old children's tale?"

"It is more than a story, it seems. I discovered actionable intelligence of the creature's existence, and the fact that it had been tasked with our extermination."

"Well, perhaps you will be fortunate and it is halfway to [garbled] by now looking for you, and will have to make a long return voyage."

"Perhaps," Alpha said, but did not sound confident.

13

Lucas stopped by a large hut that sat on the edge of a crystal-clear lake within the cave. It housed more than a dozen injured Guardians, some Lucas knew, others he didn't recognize. His old sparring partner Axon was unconscious and feverish, stricken by some sort of jungle ailment like Lucas had been. He was being treated by the Kal'din, a witch doctor of sorts, using a combination of herbal remedies and Xalan technology. He waved a metal stick with a blue light on the end of it over Axon's body like it was a magic wand. His face was hidden behind an elaborately carved mask, and he had two outstretched handprints tattooed on his bare chest. Lucas wanted to thank him for his role in his own recovery, but the language barrier prevented him from doing so. The Kal'din barely acknowledged his presence as he darted from patient to patient. Lucas could see a number of Oni warriors were lying on wooden mats as well, many nursing fresh wounds.

In the rear of the room lay a pile of Guardian armor and weapons that had been salvaged from the forest during the search for survivors. It wasn't much, but it was enough to be useful, and Lucas slipped into a stealth suit, as full-scale war plating was not ventilated or maneuverable enough for the murky jungle. In addition to Natalie, he took an energy pistol, a pair of pulse grenades, and a combat knife that could be lengthened into a machete if the situation called for it.

Soon he and his newfound party were marching through the dreaded jungle once more. Because of the forbidden place they were headed, this "Dead City," Zeta and the Oni had pulled out all the stops when assembling the team. Zeta had ordered her entire personal guard to accompany Lucas, and Toruk had volunteered to come as well, bringing three of his best warriors with him. Also in tow was Toruk's vornaa, which Lucas learned roughly translated to "bloodwolf." But mere minutes after they set out, it bounded into the jungle to scout ahead, as was apparently customary for a bloodwolf escort. It's why he'd felt hunted during much of his time in the forest.

Though the Xalans and Oni could communicate to each other with a series of gestures that Zeta had developed over the years, Lucas had no such way to converse within his own group. To rectify that, Zeta donated her translator collar to the leader of the squad, a tall Xalan corporal who had a pair of automatic plasma submachine guns strapped to his hips. It took him some time to get accustomed to it and they traveled mostly in silence for the first few hours. Lucas was the first to break it.

"How far to the city?"

"[garbled] is [garbled] away from our present location," the Corporal replied, immediately frustrated with his translator's inability to relay the Oni name of the city or a presumably Xalan unit of measurement.

"How many days?" Lucas tried.

"Two, if we keep this pace," said the Corporal, grateful for the rephrasing.

They were making fantastic time through the jungle, led by Toruk. There weren't exactly paths, but there were definitely moving through less dense brush, routes the Oni assuredly took when they went hunting for food, or for Xalan troops.

Lucas took a sip from his canteen. His leg felt noticeably better, and healing gel had almost regrown all the burnt-away skin on his arm. The dark stealth suit reflected the sunlight with its mirrored microfibers and kept him cool. All in all, it was a far more pleasant experience than his last time out there, half naked and half dead. The eight fearsome-looking warriors to his front and rear helped put his mind at ease, as did the bio-signature masking device implanted into his shoulder. He was now a hunter, not the hunted.

Surprisingly, the dark fell without rain, and the group made a small camp in a clearing they deemed safe enough to stop and rest in for a bit. The Corporal took a small bowl out of his pack and placed it on the ground. When activated, a white, barely visible flame shot out of it and heated up the surrounding area quite nicely without giving off too much light. As humid as it was in the day, it got rather frigid when the giant moon came out. Toruk was chewing on a piece of fruit he lifted from somewhere in the jungle, while his Oni brethren had taken to the trees to scout and slumber. The Xalans were seated on a downed log, each cleaning their guns, grunting to each other occasionally. Lucas attempted to chime in.

"So why did you join the resistance? You all look like you come from the military," he asked.

The Corporal turned to him.

"Indeed. Our team served on [garbled] for many years. I have killed more Sorans than I care to count."

The tone sounded more despondent than boastful.

"What made you switch sides?"

The Corporal grunted to the men around him, presumably translating. Turning back, it was a while before he spoke.

"Many of us grew up together in [garbled], a small village on the homeworld. We only were allowed to see our clans sparingly, often deployed on missions for months, even years."

The faces around him were solemn, as was his own.

"We were sent to the siege of [garbled], where we assaulted an extra-solar Soran base. It was a prolonged affair, and quite far from home. When the battle was over, we were exhausted and wanted nothing more than to see our clans again back on Xala."

He lay his rifle against the log. The enormous moon could now be seen through the trees up ahead.

"When we returned home, our hearts broke. Over the year, our village had been ruined by famine. The Council had issued a tax meant to pay for a new warship, at the expense of food and water for a string of local settlements along the [garbled] coast. Even our wages sent home to our clans were appropriated. They were left with nothing."

He stared straight ahead at the trampled leaves underneath his clawed feet.

"My mate, my six sons and four daughters were already in the ground when I arrived. The same was true for many of my men."

This was the sort of thing Alpha had told him was happening, but to hear a firsthand account of it was unsettling.

"When our leaders kill more of their own citizens than the Sorans, the time for intergalactic war is over. The time for civil war is at hand."

Lucas nodded.

"Can't fault you for that."

"And you?" the Corporal asked, his voice shaking off any hint of sorrow. "Is it true you and your mate are the last survivors of Earth campaign?"

"More or less," Lucas said. "We brought a child as well, and have another on the way."

His "mate." He wondered what Asha would think if she heard that. She'd likely be back at the Oni village in a few more hours. He was glad she was alive, but hurt feelings still lingered after what had taken place on the Spear.

"You must despise my people, for destroying your world."

Lucas chuckled, which caught the Corporal off guard.

"Yeah, most. But a few of you aren't so bad."

"The Oni have been hospitable, but to have true Soran allies is a welcome development for the movement. Your High Chancellor actually sanctioned this?"

"It was practically her idea," Lucas said, taking another swig of water. "Peace with Xala is good for everyone. Preferably peace by way of the death of your Council and all the corrupt who support them."

"Then we are in agreement," the Corporal said. Toruk turned his head in their direction as if he were about to speak, but went back to eating his meal, carving out the pit of his red fruit with a jagged knife.

As the night progressed, it was Lucas's turn to take watch up in a tall tree. He found a particularly wide branch that would suit his purposes. The giant moon was lofted in the sky again, though it was waning a bit now. The light it gave off masked most of the stars around it; only a few could be seen outside of its radiance. The forest was still and mostly quiet except for the occasional jarring screeches from some of the local wildlife. Their path had hooked around the base of a mountain. It was in the exact opposite direction Lucas had been traveling earlier. Far off in the distance, Lucas could see the lights of what looked like some sort of settlement. A Xalan city? It didn't appear to be very large, but it was hard to tell.

Lucas jumped when he saw a pair of eyes peering at him from an adjacent tree. It was Toruk, who had somehow managed to scale the massive trunk in complete silence. He was munching on something else this time, a piece of charred meat skewered on a sharpened branch. Where had he gotten that? Lucas was further surprised when Toruk spoke.

"I know you truth."

His Soran was heavily broken, but understandable.

"What?" Lucas said, incredulous. "You speak Soran?"

"Yes," Toruk said. "Small."

"How?"

Toruk took another bite of his meat.

"White Spirit Seat of Great Knowledge. Learn many thing."

Seat of great knowledge? It took Lucas a minute, but he thought back to how he'd learned Soran for the first time in, the programmable captain's chair aboard the Ark, which transmitted training through neural wiring. Zeta must have a similar model in the Khas'to settlement somewhere.

"Need learn new ally tongue."

The words were scattered, often pronounced wrong and lacking any semblance of grammar, but it wasn't bad for probably, what, a few hours in the chair at the most between rescue missions? Alpha must have programmed it for him on the fly. Toruk continued.

"I know you truth."

"My truth?" Lucas asked. "What truth?"

"White Spirit say you mountain people. You no mountain people. You *Mol'taavi* people."

No more wild sounds came from the forest; the night was completely still as the two of them spoke.

"Mol'taavi?" Lucas asked.

"Mol'taavi." Toruk said, pointing upward at the moon overheard. "Fall from sky. You brothers of Saato. Sisters of Valli."

"Saato? Valli? I'm sorry I don't understand."

"You forget. All forget. Mol'taavi home ancient Oni. Saato, Valli first man, woman. Rule over Great Jungle of Ak'tai. Cover all Mol'taavi. Jungle burn. Oni sent here."

Lucas was trying to make sense of all this.

"Sky demon turn Mol'taavi white ash. Now sky demon burn Makari jungle. Saato, Valli spirit send you. You help. You kill sky demon with White Spirit and Oni. Bring great magic. Great courage."

Another creation myth, it seemed. Toruk and the Oni apparently believed the giant moon, Mol'taavi, to be their original home where the first Oni, Saato and Valli, lived. After their forest was destroyed, they came here, to Makari. Was that right? And who were Lucas and the Guardians supposed to be? Some sort of resurrected spirits of the old homeworld? Falling from the sky probably had helped bolster that myth.

But what good was attempting to explain Earth and Sora now to this man? That the Xalans weren't demons, that their technology wasn't magic. Such concepts would be impossible for Toruk or his people to comprehend. Lucas now knew what it must have felt like for Alpha to try to explain to them how a water-powered null core opened a rift in space-time for intergalactic travel. So Lucas decided to go along.

"Yes, it's true. We are from Mol'taavi, but you can't tell anyone. Saato and Valli's spirits are not supposed to interfere with the Oni," he improvised.

Toruk smiled broadly, which was odd for a man as menacing looking as him strapped with ancient and modern armor and weapons and the claws of a dozen dead Xalans around his neck.

"I knew, I knew," he said, still smiling. Lucas had apparently made his day with his confirmation.

Lucas had a flashback to a conversation he'd had with a drunken Maston a few months back.

"Kyneth and Zurana were the first two Sorans. They arose out of the Blessed Forest a few million years ago and gave birth to our entire race."

Two original humans in a place of lush greenery. Taking into account Earth's own similar tale and now this new Oni story, this was starting to sound less and less like coincidence. There was a connecting thread here that was starting to gnaw at Lucas. Why there were planets of humans scattered across the galaxy had always been a mystifying thought. As they branched out to new worlds, it appeared there was an answer out there somewhere, but Lucas felt like he'd put together three pieces of a thousand-piece puzzle. Alpha would be better at analyzing this, were he not occupied with attempting to save civilization itself.

Toruk had his hand stretched out and Lucas realized he was offering him a piece of his cooked meat.

"Uh . . ." Lucas said as he eyed it.

"Even brother of Saato need food. Eat."

Lucas was rather famished and took it from his hand. It crunched when he bit into it, but the taste was pleasant, almost pork-like.

"Not bad," he said. "No good food on Mol'taavi these days."

Toruk tried not to fall out of the tree as he burst with laughter.

It wasn't until the next day, when they rounded the back side of the mountain, that Lucas caught his first glimpse of the Dead City. Dark stone towers could be seen rising from the jungle above the tips of the trees. Toruk's bloodwolf had returned to them a few hours ago and it was somehow communicated that Maston was indeed in the city, and there were no other enemies nearby. How the two managed to converse in that level of detail was a mystery, but one that would remain unsolved, because the bloodwolf bounded back into the jungle after receiving fresh orders from Toruk.

A few of the Oni started whispering to each other when they saw the pillars, and they clutched their weapons a little tighter. They'd progressed through the jungle without incident, invisible to Xalan forces, but that was no longer what they had to fear if the rumors were to be believed.

Eventually the trees started to thin out and glimpses of a wall could be seen up ahead. It was cracked and broken down. The rock it was made of was dark and smooth. Lucas presumed it was volcanic, but now was not the time to ask Toruk for a history lesson. As they moved inside the city, they began to get a scope of its size, something that couldn't be seen from the forest. Though many former buildings were no more than piles of decaying wood at this point, many were chiseled from the same black stone and stood resolute against the greenery that had engulfed them. They could see the wall curved around the city, and the towers they'd seen from the jungle were a few hundred feet high. There were six of them stretching back toward the eventual end of the city, which seemed to be quite far away. Only two were fully intact; the rest had been broken off at various points.

Though simple homes stood at the outskirts, the buildings became more ornate as they moved toward the center of the city. What black-stone buildings were not destroyed had glyphs and murals carved into them. The outer wall of what appeared to be some sort of temple had an interesting scene in the stone. A dozen Oni knelt before two figures, each with their right hands raised. Behind them was a large sphere. Mol'taavi.

There were no references on any of the murals to the Xalan invasion like there had been back in the Kha'sto cave village. Lucas assumed the city had been destroyed too fast for such stories to be told here.

Lucas's wrist map told him Maston was still about a mile away. This really had been a massive metropolis once, and Lucas couldn't even see the outer wall anymore through the maze of structures.

The jungle was silent here. Lucas had long grown used to the cries of various alien animals out in the forest, and the quiet was unsettling. When he rounded the next corner, stepping over a collapsed statue, he understood why no living things dared to tread here.

In front of them was an open stretch of town with a central stone sphere. All around it lay the bones of countless creatures, each in various stages of decay. Some of the bones had been swallowed into the ground by encroaching moss or vines, others lay atop the greenery.

There were few full skeletons to be found, so it was hard to tell what many of them were. Some of the bones were tiny, others enormous. Toruk picked up an odd-looking one and turned to Lucas.

"Vornaa," he said.

It didn't take long to find a human ribcage, then a skull, and another, and another. If this was the creature's feeding grounds, it appeared it had caught many Oni over the years. Lucas was surprised to find a few Xalan skulls amid the bone piles as well. Did this thing eat its own? Was it even Xalan at all? Lucas shivered involuntarily as he moved around the spherical statue and saw a huge skeleton, picked clean, with bones shining a brilliant white. The skull was larger than he was, and it had at least three rows of foot-long teeth. An obvious carnivore. It had long arms, legs, and a tail, but if Lucas didn't know any better he'd say the shape of the skull looked rather . . . prehistoric, to borrow from Earth's timeline. Lucas saw another similar creature in pieces a few dozen meters away, crumpled up against a collapsed pillar. What the hell was this thing to be able to take down rival predatory beasts this large?

Lucas kept his eyes fixed on his surroundings, as did the Corporal, Toruk, and their respective men. He glanced down at the map and saw Maston's signal was coming from just a little further ahead. They moved out of the graveyard clearing and into a section of destroyed buildings, which were tricky to navigate. Lucas hopped from stone to stone, the stability sensors in his suit steadying him. The Oni leapt with no such aid, but didn't seem to need it.

Finally, he stopped short when he found there was no place left to jump. Rather, a large hole stood in front of him, newly disturbed dirt around its edges, blackness obscuring the view of what lay inside. But according to Lucas's locator, he knew what he should find. Maston.

As he reached the lip, he opened his palm and shone a light from his mesh fiber glove into the opening. He could see the ground about a dozen feet down. Without hesitation, Lucas leapt down. His suit took all of the impact, and the other eight quickly followed him, eager to get out of the open where unknown dangers lurked.

But underneath the Dead City, things felt hardly less imposing. The crater had torn a new entrance to an underground catacomb system built by the original occupants of the city. It smelled of dry mold and everything was coated in a solid inch of dust. Stone tombs stood upright all around them, visages of those within them etched onto the lids. But there was only one coffin that interested Lucas, one made of metal and glowing blue a few feet ahead.

Lucas quickly scanned the cryochamber and the results matched what the indicator had told him. Despite being battered and cracked, the pod was still intact, and Maston was alive inside it. Lucas used his knife to pry open the stuck hatch.

Inside was Maston, far too peaceful-looking for the present circumstances. He had dried blood on his forehead and neck, some sort of injury sustained during the crash, but nothing too serious according to the sensors. Lucas fiddled with the controls, which were still functioning. It must have been why Maston was still under while Lucas had been forced awake. Swirling his hand around, Lucas undid Maston's restraints and an orangish liquid flooded through small tubes into his veins.

Lucas jumped when Maston's eyes sprang open, jolted awake by the chamber's wake-up cocktail. They immediately dilated from the sunlight shining down into the hole, though it became clear he couldn't actually see much of anything.

"Who's there?" he said hoarsely, and Lucas offered him his canteen.

"It's Lucas," he said.

Maston blinked rapidly, attempting to clear his eyes, and tried to sit up, pushing the water aside.

"Why are *you* waking me up? Have we landed yet?" he slurred.

After successfully sitting upright, his next move was to try to stand.

"Maybe you better stay seated."

Maston remained surprisingly calm as Lucas gave him the rundown of the events of the past few days. He didn't hyperventilate the way Lucas had when confronted with the enormity of the situation. Years of military training had forged his nerves for moments like this. Or he'd just experienced disaster too many times to be shaken by it now.

"And this place?" he said when Lucas reached the end of the tale. "What is it?"

He looked around the crypt and out the sunlit hole in the ceiling.

"They call it the Dead City. It was a metropolis before the Xalan invasion, a ruin after. But there's something that lives here now. Something very dangerous, and we need to get the hell out of here."

"What is it?" Maston asked, eyeing the Oni and the Xalans suspiciously. Both parties returned his glare. The Corporal nervously glanced at his wrist readout. There was the faint signal of a heartbeat.

"Something so deadly that two separate civilizations tell ghost stories about it," Lucas replied. "Can you walk?"

Maston brought himself to his feet and nodded.

"Bring anything for me?"

Lucas motioned to the Corporal who unslung a Soran energy rifle from his back and handed it to Maston. They hadn't hauled along any armor, so he'd have to make do with just his bodysuit and a spare pair of boots.

"Use it well, Soran," the Corporal said coldly. "I hope you prove to be worthy of this much risk."

"I am," Maston replied curtly.

"Must go," Toruk said impatiently. He was right, they'd already wasted too much time down there.

They hoisted each other out of the hole and back into the sunlight, which was already fading at the end of yet another exceptionally short day.

They were moving much faster now, keeping low and bounding from rock to rock quickly and quietly. Maston was keeping up, and seemed to have lost little of his strength in the chamber. The tall, dark obelisks cast long shadows over the remains of the city. They ran past the crumbling temple and returned to the boneyard clearing.

The dwarf sun was now directly above the central spherical statue that Lucas assumed was a representation of the moon Mol'taavi. But there was something else atop the stone, bathed in the white light. Something that moved ever so slightly.

"My prey comes to me. Strange."

The voice came from the Corporal's translator collar, much to everyone's surprise. It was intercepting and interpreting the brainwaves of whatever lay before them.

Lucas crept closer, Natalie trained on the top of the sphere. The figure shifted again.

"An alliance. Xalan and Soran. Perhaps a worthy challenge after all these years."

The creature's voice was low and gravelly, and though its speech patterns were strange, short, and halted, it boomed with a gravitas the Corporal's did not.

"We have no issue with you," Lucas called out without thinking. He was shocked the beast could speak. Judging by the bones around them, he was expecting something snarling and savage. This creature was neither. Not yet, at least.

"The voice," it said. "The face. It is you. One of the three."

Uh oh.

"Searched the stars for you. Yet here you are. The others not far behind assuredly."

It was him, then, the Desecrator. Alpha's worst fears realized. Lucas took a dangerous step forward and the sun dipped below the trees. He could now make out the figure before him.

The creature was indeed a Xalan, of sorts. He was perched on the stone orb like a coiled snake, ready to spring. Even at this range, his massive size was apparent. Rather than select patches of armor plating across his torso and shoulders, he appeared to have natural protection everywhere, even down his arms and legs and creeping onto the sides of his face. He wasn't wearing a shred of artificial armor, as he presumably had no need for it. There were no weapons in either of his hands or on his person, but his claws were jet black and a solid foot long on each of his three-pronged hands and feet, triple the size of a normal Xalan. A parted mouth revealed similarly enormous teeth. Most notable of all was his coloring, a shade of dark, hellish crimson Lucas had never seen on another Xalan before. His eyes were black with rings of fiery orange that flickered in the dying light. This was no Shadow. This was something . . . else.

"Red demon," Toruk muttered. "Old evil. Great power."

"What are we waiting for?" Maston growled at Lucas, his own rifle raised. "Shoot it."

"It can reason, it would be a waste not to try," Lucas whispered back to them fiercely.

The Corporal was having none of it and took over his collar with his own voice again.

"This is an abomination!" he roared. "Another of the Council's wretched creatures."

The voice switched back.

"Fool. I am a creation of gods."

"Of devils!" the Corporal shouted.

The creature leapt off the sphere and landed with a crunch on the carpet of bones. Standing up straight, Lucas's suspicions about his size were confirmed. The creature towered over them. While most Xalans were seven or eight feet tall, this one was easily twelve.

"I am the future," it purred. "I am what is to come."

"You are mad," said the Corporal, holding both of his guns outward. His hands were trembling slightly.

"I know you're an outcast," Lucas called out to him. "Your own people want nothing to do with you. You don't have to do their bidding."

The Desecrator turned toward Lucas.

"I serve no one!" he snarled. "But your actions demand vengeance."

He flexed his lengthy claws outward and a low guttural sound rose out of his throat.

"You killed him," he said. "Share his fate."

So much for reason.

The Desecrator bent down and his armored muscles bulged. Something long and almost transparent sprang out of his back.

Wings.

He shot up into the air just as Lucas regained enough composure to pull his trigger. The rest of the group followed suit, but the Desecrator wove around in the air, dodging every round with ease.

"What the hell is this thing?" Maston shouted as he unloaded a stream of plasma into the sky. The Desecrator's wings were almost insect-like. Far above them, they fluttered so fast they were a complete blur in the air. Suddenly they stopped vibrating, and he started to fall. More accurately, he started to dive.

"Concentrate fire!" Maston yelled, back in commander mode already. Everyone obeyed, but even in his breakneck descent, the Desecrator was able to duck and weave around the incoming fire. A few rounds did manage to strike him, but appeared to glance off his plating harmlessly. In an instant, it was too late to stop him.

He crashed into the middle of their line, slamming into the Corporal with such force Lucas could hear bones shatter, and bowling all of them over. As Lucas scrambled to his feet, he saw the Desecrator swing his right claw upward. With it came the Corporal's head, dripping blood onto the already red arm that held it.

One of the Oni warriors leapt bravely toward the Desecrator, swinging a large axe in a downward arc. It found enough of a gap in his armor to draw blood as it crunched into his collarbone, but the Desecrator quickly countered with a forceful kick. The three enormous claws buried themselves in the Oni's chest and gut. From the placement, it looked like they'd gone through both lungs and his stomach. Blood spurted out of his mouth and the Desecrator wrenched his foot to the ground, the man underneath it. More bones cracked and the Desecrator launched back up into the air on his wings as the rest of the group opened fire.

A low voice crackled in the collar wrapped around the newly headless body of the Corporal.

"Blasphemer."

A bloodied axe clattered to the ground from on high, having been dug out of his armor. The Desecrator looped around again and this time the dive was more of a line drive as he skimmed just a few feet above the ground. As two of the Xalans fired away, he caught one with his right claw and the creature spun around awkwardly, cascading into a nearby bone pile with a deep slash across his throat. The Desecrator landed next to him and ripped the energy rifle from his claws. Aiming quickly, he put down the second Xalan with a round to the skull. Maston tried to dive out of the way but caught a blast in the shoulder. From the ground he returned fire and grazed the creature's neck plating, causing him to leap backward behind one of the colossal skeletons for cover.

Lucas saw an opportunity and tossed a pulse grenade over the top of the skeleton. They hadn't managed to salvage any explosive grenades, but he'd learned the electric killing power of the pulse variants could wreak havoc on a nervous system. Lucas followed it up with a shotgun blast that tore an enormous hole in the skull.

It propelled the Desecrator backward just as the grenade exploded. A blue sphere of energy and light consumed the creature and made Lucas's skin prickle, even at a distance.

The Desecrator was disoriented and Toruk took advantage of the moment of weakness. He sprinted forward, leapt up and over the skull, and jammed his black-tipped metal spear into the Desecrator's chest. The rare metal cut through the armored plating and hit its intended target. The creature let out a roar that the collar couldn't translate, and he violently whipped his arm around, catching Toruk with a backhand that sent him flying all the way back to the central statue in the clearing. The effects of the pulse grenade were only temporary, it seemed, and the creature stretched out its wings and hovered a few feet above the ground. He dodged an attempted sniper shot from Lucas and ripped the spear out of his chest. Whirling around, he slung it at the final Xalan resistance fighter, who took it directly in the heart, the force of the throw pinning him to the ground.

Before Lucas could even blink, the Desecrator had flown over to the two other Oni warriors who had been firing their appropriated energy weapons, hitting mostly air for the duration of the fight. Lucas winced as he saw them dismembered almost instantly by the fearsome razor claws of the creature. Limbs and organs dropped unceremoniously to the ground. One man lay in pieces while the other was on his knees. The Desecrator hoisted him up, two claws hooked under his ribs, and as Lucas watched in horror, he sank his teeth into the man's face. Wrenching backwards, the Desecrator tore the man's head from his body before he let the skull and attached spinal column drop to the ground, joining the sea of bones at his feet.

A dazed Toruk had a fury in his eyes when he saw what the demon had done to his men. He turned to charge once more, but Lucas called out.

"We need to get out of here!"

It was the first time Lucas had felt the need to flee from a fight in a long while, but it was clear they were grossly outmatched by this monster. He turned to Maston who nodded in assent, clutching the black burn on his shoulder. He was a soldier smart enough to know when to retreat.

Lucas had to physically intercept Toruk as he raced toward the Desecrator and drag him toward the wall of the city. The creature stood over the butchered corpses of the two men and roared so loudly a plume of black birds shot out of the nearby trees. He sprang into the air, and his wings hummed as he raced toward them. It seemed that even if they wanted to escape now, they couldn't.

In desperation, Lucas flung the last pulse grenade toward the Desecrator as he sped toward them. He attempted to spin out of its radius, but when it erupted, the energy field consumed him once more. His flight pattern became erratic and shifted hard left. Maston turned and fired a trio of rounds that hit his right shoulder and threw him further off balance. He was unsteady, but still in pursuit.

The three of them raced through the destroyed houses toward the wall, but the jungle likely wouldn't save them; they were simply moving out of the creature's home and into its hunting grounds. Lucas heard another sound from up ahead. Snapping twigs and crunching leaves. Something else was coming.

A figure burst from the brush ahead of them. It was Toruk's giant bloodwolf, sprinting straight at them at an incredible speed. Lucas had to veer to the right to avoid colliding with it, and it shot past him without so much as a glance. Lucas turned to watch the wolf leap up onto the roof of a nearby house, then launch itself into the air. After a few seconds suspended in flight, it crashed into the Desecrator, latching its jaws around his throat, and the two of them tumbled to the earth with a thud out of sight.

"Naali!" Toruk cried as he stopped and turned around.

"No!" Maston shouted. "This is our shot, let's go!"

Lucas looked at the rage and sadness in Toruk's eyes, but nodded in agreement with Maston.

"We'll all die," he said solemnly.

Toruk turned back and sprinted toward the jungle. Lucas and Maston followed and a painful howl could be heard echoing out of the city behind them.

It was hard to tell when they stopped running. The sun had gone down and hours had passed before they finally ran out of adrenaline. Toruk had years of conditioning in the jungle, Lucas had his stealth suit to aid him in recovery, and Maston seemed to be driven forward only by pure force of will, despite his severe plasma burn. Lucas almost doubted whether he didn't have Guardian tank-bred genetics buried in him somewhere.

Eventually they came to a halt deep in the forest and Lucas almost collapsed when the fatigue caught up with him. They hadn't seen the Desecrator since the bloodwolf had intercepted him, but it was likely the creature, however brave, couldn't have slowed the monster down for long.

"Must stop," Toruk said, finally showing signs of being winded. "Make camp fast, go home. Hidden for now."

He tapped on the metal disc on his arm. Maston had been tossed one as they ran and he too was now undetectable by traditional Xalan biological tracking. Though Lucas wondered if the Desecrator had more primal means of finding his meals.

Soon they had a small white fire burning, and Toruk had killed and descaled a nearby tree octopus, which he called *lo-bai*, and was handing out samples to the pair of them. It tasted vaguely squid-like, but seared in the fire it wasn't half bad.

"What's your wolf's name?" Lucas asked. Toruk looked confused.

"Your vornaa?" Lucas clarified.

"Naali," he said, his brow furrowed. "Belong father. Wise vornaa. Old vornaa. Fierce vornaa."

"Fearless vornaa," Lucas said.

"Naali alive. Red demon no kill."

Lucas nodded silently, keeping to himself the fact that he very much doubted that statement.

"What a goddamn mess," Maston said, rubbing his head. "We should have known they'd figure out a way to detect their own damn ship. This mission was idiotic."

"We reached our objective, now we just need her to complete her end with the transmission and we can get the hell out of here," Lucas said, attempting to keep the faith the way Alpha had.

"Get out of here?" Maston said, eyebrows raised. "Our ship is in a million pieces, as is most of our crew. Sora literally does not have a vessel that can reach this place within several lifetimes. We're castaways in this hellhole."

"Saato aid brothers," Toruk said confidently.

"What the hell is he talking about?" Maston asked.

"It's a long story," Lucas said. "The Oni believe we come from their moon, Mol'taavi, to aid them in their fight."

He pointed upward to the huge shining orb above them. Maston just shook his head.

"I don't even want to know."

The fire flickered and Toruk was busy finishing off a lo-bai tentacle. A large welt had formed across his chest where the Desecrator had struck him. He threw some gristle into the fire and climbed up a nearby tree to keep watch.

"So who did we lose, specifically?" Maston asked, his voice growing quieter.

Lucas pulled up the terrain map on his wrist display. The forest was filled with only black dots now, and there was a larger green cluster in the village. He was elated to see Asha's name among them. He turned the readout toward Maston, who scanned through the names of the deceased.

"Jano, Yuttori, Moloy, Wrev, Tuya, Corvin," his voice trailed off as he read the names.

"Silo?" Maston said, spotting the dot.

Lucas nodded.

"Yeah, I was with him. I . . . did it, actually."

"You did what?"

Lucas sighed.

"When I reached him, the bastard had taken out a full Xalan recon squad with a wooden spear. But they messed him up bad. Paralyzed. I couldn't move him, couldn't let him be captured alive. I . . . I killed him."

Lucas fought back against the lump rising in his throat. He wanted to avoid giving Maston yet another reason to deem him weak.

Maston simply stared at the fire.

"You understand the lesson then. Why sometimes we must be willing to kill even those who . . . do not deserve the fate."

Lucas shook his head.

"It wasn't like on the ship."

"Perhaps not, but both triggers took strength to pull. At least you managed to get it right the second time."

"What do you know about that kind of sacrifice? I can't imagine there's a person alive you wouldn't kill in a second if you had to."

Maston's eyes flashed with anger.

"Why do you persist to presume to know me?" he spat back at Lucas. "You kill one friend and believe yourself worthy of pity? I have done things that do not just eat at my soul, but feel like they have erased it entirely."

"What have you done?" Lucas pressed.

"You want to know?" Maston snarled in the firelight. "You want to know what happened at Vitalla?"

Maston spoke. Lucas listened.

14

"Rhylos had it rough from the beginning. Fifty thousand years ago, before anyone invented so much as a light switch, they constantly found their land pillaged by their neighbors who were after its abundant resources. They were once a peaceful people, but were forged into warriors over time. Much of it was against their will, of course, their populace ravaged by conquering armies, but they grew stronger with each new generation.

"They held fast to their faith. They always maintained that Kyneth and Zurana had revealed the Tomes of the Forest directly to their ancestors. They believed the pair kept them safe from harm, but after enduring so much, it's hard to believe that idea persisted. Again they were razed during the Sacred Wars and had to build themselves up from nothing. They were largely spared during the machine uprising, but suffered huge losses in the next war when the first-gen Xalans took up arms. Years after that, they were hammered by the first of the homeworld strikes in the Great War. And, to top it all off, a massive earthquake shook the life out of them barely a century ago. Heartache was simply a way of life even as the rest of the world thrived around them.

"When we discovered Vitalla nearly a century ago, it was our first reason to celebrate in a long time while the Great War droned on. It was a planet far more hospitable to life than any we'd discovered to date. Sure, we'd built bases on moons and extra-solar planets, but they were always domed colonies surrounding by inhospitable landscapes. Vitalla was different.

"It wasn't filled with lush greenery, but it was rich with rare minerals and had enough surface water to sustain life. The weather was too severe to allow for anything larger than microbes to exist. But with some modifications, we believed we could artificially raise the temperature enough for a colony to thrive.

"Once we started talking about a settlement, a spark was ignited inside Corinthia. Her sole mission in life became to ensure the colony went to Rhylos. She'd been doing aid work on the continent practically her entire life, and she pleaded with her grandfather Varrus to allow the Rhylosi to be the ones transplanted there.

"It was a hard argument to dismiss. Rhylos was now little more than a wasteland, its people only surviving on the charity of other nations. They were a resource drain on the entire planet, and the idea was that on Vitalla they could be put to work farming and mining resources to be shipped back to Sora for the war effort. Hex Tulwar, then Grand Cleric of Rhylos, happily agreed to the bargain with Varrus, and Cora's idea, much to her delight, was approved. Though she was young, she threw herself into the project, spending almost every waking hour planning the details of the voyage and eventual colony.

"The discovery revealed further good news: Vitalla was in the opposite direction in the galaxy from Xala. It was unlikely they could even reach it. But regardless, the exact coordinates of the planet were trusted only to a select few. Even Cora and myself didn't know precisely where it was. In spite of all of this, a military escort would be required to ensure the millions reached the destination safely. The escort would be made up of a large portion of our forces, but at that point our homeworld defenses were strong enough to hold off a direct Xalan assault, at least temporarily. We'd spend a year going there and a year back, leaving behind what personnel we could spare to guard the colony.

"I'd just been promoted to Varrus Vale's right hand. He wanted to personally be a part of the mission, and said it would be 'unifying' for the planet to see him go and ensure the future prosperity of the least fortunate of our people. His advisers protested the decision, but he always was quite the stubborn old fool. We boarded his flagship, the SDI *Nova*, and began the journey alongside the largest migrant fleet ever assembled.

"Much can happen in a year, and much did. I'd grown up with Cora, as our families had been close for generations, though our interactions had usually been at a distance. I'd always viewed her as something of an entitled prat, and the rumors of her genetic price tag in the trillions certainly didn't help that perception. But to see her so passionately involved in the plight of Rhylos, and trying to ensure a future for its citizens, erased any previous notions I had of her. There was a great deal of good inside her. Far more than there was in me.

"For as long as I'd known her she'd been linked to the rich and handsome of Sora's elite. A baron here, a duke there, all arranged by her mother, all of which bored her to tears, she later told me. This trip was the most exciting thing her family had ever allowed her to do, and fortunately for me, there wasn't a duke or prince in sight.

"I don't know what Corinthia saw in me, but I didn't care. Every eye on a ship full of thousands was on her whenever she passed, and somehow, some way, she'd chosen me. I'd been with my fair share of Sora's most beautiful, but Cora was in a class all her own. At times she barely even seemed Soran, like some sort of celestial being that had graced us with her presence.

"We made plans, big plans. After Vitalla had been settled, we'd return to Sora and buy a home in Landrift Valley in the Sorvo Republic. She'd help another impoverished people, and I'd be with her whenever I wasn't out on assignment with the SDI. I imagined if it was anything close to what that year had been like, I could live the rest of my days as the most fortunate man alive.

"We finally reached Vitalla, in all its gray and brown glory. It wasn't much, but it was more than Rhylos had, and it could be fixed up into something that wasn't half bad at all. Advance construction crews had flown out years earlier to set up the framework for the colony. Cities were already built, waiting to be populated. Mining tunnels were dug and the equipment was all laid out to ensure the new Rhylosi economy could be up and running right away. The images we were sent from the advance team made it look like a rather fantastic place.

"I never got to see it. I was stuck a few thousand miles out in orbit aboard the *Nova* to keep an eye on things while Varrus took a shuttle down the surface. The christening ceremony was the whole reason he'd come, an attempt to look like some benevolent ruler by providing the poorest among us their very own planet. Cora wasn't with him; she stayed on the *Nova* with me. Despite all her work on the project, she wasn't there for the glory. She'd given the send-off address and was content to let Varrus have his moment, not to mention her mother absolutely forbade her from stepping foot on the rock. There was real work to be done after all, and she was busy mapping out the daunting process of getting the population settled in the colony over the next few weeks before we returned home.

"They waited until the moment they knew all of us would be watching. Right as Varrus finished his blustering speech, they emerged from the dark side of the moon. No one knew how they'd discovered the place or how they'd gotten there, but it didn't matter. The Xalans had found Vitalla.

"It was mass chaos. They split their forces in half, and cleaved us in two. They landed ground troops on the surface and flooded the now-inhabited cities with soldiers. The bulk of their fleet turned their attention to us, the military escort, in orbit. There were more missiles in the air than stars, and we lost a worrying percentage of our capital ships in the first few minutes. The *Nova* was wounded, but could fly. I tried to coordinate Varrus's orders shouted from the ground as best I could, but Xalan forces were quickly closing in on his position.

"Scrambling through the monitors of the battle, I saw we had been boarded. The enemy troops were already ravaging the lower decks, and we had to divert all attention from the war outside to our own more imminent threat.

"I hid Cora away in the floor paneling between decks and raced down to the armory, where the fighting was the fiercest. When I arrived, I found dozens of bodies, both Soran and Xalan, and the failing gravity drive of the ship was causing pools of blood to periodically rise into orbs all over the room. Each time the drive kicked back on, they'd drop to the floor and splatter. It was a scene that will never leave me.

"When the ship stabilized, I crept around a stack of bodies and saw the lone survivor of the conflict. Well, 'survivor' isn't the right word. He was tall with black skin and haunting eyes of ice. This was one of the mythic Shadows I'd always heard about. And I was now just another soldier who would never live to tell the tale.

"And yet, I did. I barely remember more than a few seconds of what happened next. The lights were flickering on and off, and as we fought we were repeatedly hoisted up into the air by the sputtering gravity drive. He wasn't one of the new-era psionics, but he was one tough son of a bitch. Fast. Strong. It was unreal. More than once I was saved by a power fluctuation or a random jolt from the drive that sent him flying off me. In the end, I'd been shot twice and gored more times than I could count. He somehow ended up with a knife in his skull. Later they'd tell me that 70 percent of my body was covered with scar tissue. I had to grow an entire new skin suit for transplant. I only saved one wound as a reminder, a slice on my neck that would have been the end of me if gravity had remained intact for another millisecond.

"A group of soldiers found me, and a team of medics patched me up as best they could before they hauled me back to command. If I was conscious, I was still in charge. We'd fought off the boarding party, but by the time I reached the bridge it was clear we had to retreat or else we'd lose the entire fleet. The intact half of our ships followed the *Nova* to safety the next planet over while the remaining Xalan ships locked themselves in a ring around Vitalla, with a hundred million Rhylosi and our High Chancellor in their clutches.

"It was an hour before the executions started, beamed to our ship through the very broadcasting equipment that was supposed to stream the christening. The soldiers who accompanied Varrus on the surface were forced to kneel on stage as, methodically, their heads were turned to ash by energy blasts. These were men I knew. Men I'd fought with. Most met their fate with stone jaws and steel hearts, but a few died screaming.

"I finally managed to get a wormhole comm line open to Talis, now acting chancellor with her father captured. She informed me that I was the highest-ranking officer still alive, and the remnants of the fleet were mine to command. As we talked through rescue strategies and escape plans, they were now killing civilians by the hundreds across the other cities of the colony. Soon it became thousands. Their goal was clear, even if they couldn't verbalize it.

"'Come save them,' they seemed to be taunting. 'Or watch them die in agony.'

"It was too much to bear. The Rhylosi died on our viewscreens burning, melting, or choking on gas. After another hour, they detonated the first city from orbit. A hundred thousand gone in an instant. Cora was sobbing, my men were screaming in my ears to attack; to save them.

"Talis saw it differently. Why would they taunt us like this if not to bait us into a trap? Who was to say that there wasn't another hidden fleet somewhere in the system, waiting to pounce as soon as we moved back into range?

"The risk was too great. If we lost what was left of the escort fleet in a misguided rescue attempt, it wouldn't just be disaster at Vitalla; it would take us years longer than it already would to rebuild the ships and retrain the men we'd lost. The Great War could slip from our grasp, and Xala might finally have the opening they needed to make a final push into Sora once and for all.

"As Talis told me this, we saw onscreen they had identified Hex Tulwar as a leader in the christening crowd. They dragged his family up on stage. A beautiful wife, two sons, three daughters, not one over ten. I'd never seen a man fight so hard for anything. He killed the two Xalans guarding him with his bare hands and raced toward his wife and children, but a Shadow commander tore his chest open before he could reach them. Just before he lost consciousness, he watched his family obliterated by a hail of plasma.

"Cora screamed and screamed, pleading with me to help. But I saw the truth in what Talis said. We could lose everything. I wanted to make sure this was what she was telling me to do.

"'What about your father?' I said to her. I heard her choke back tears. And after a long while she whispered, 'Sora will survive.'

"And so, on the orders of the acting High Chancellor, I told the escort fleet to leave. As our cores spooled up to make the leap out of the system, I could see the Xalans figure out what was happening. They dropped a cascade of antimatters across all the outskirt cities, killing millions in an instant. A last ditch effort to provoke us. But we continued our escape.

"Then they brought Varrus on stage. He stood defiant right until the moment his head came off. It was the last thing we saw before the cores activated. Vitalla had fallen. We survived."

Lucas stayed silent when Maston finished his story, awestruck by what he'd just heard. The night chirped away and Toruk was still above them in the trees somewhere. Maston spoke again.

"Cora couldn't even look at me after that. Even though her mother had given the order, it was me she had watched carry it out, and she'd hold me responsible in the years that followed. She wasn't hostile or cruel, but after what we had, her indifference to me was crushing. I became like a stranger, allowed only small waves and polite smiles when the situation called for them."

"What happened to Hex Tulwar?" Lucas asked.

"What *exactly* happened to him? I've no idea, but eventually he and a small band of Rhylosi escaped Vitalla and made it back to Sora in a half-destroyed transport. Knowing what I know now, that was probably when he made a deal with the Xalans for Talis's head. He blamed the Vales and me for the massacre of his people and family. It didn't take him long to whip up support for a revolution once he returned and explained how the fleet had abandoned them."

Maston threw a leaf into the fire and it vaporized.

"In the Tomes of the Forest, the First Order is to serve the gods. The Second is to revere the planet. The Third is to resist evil. The Fourth Order is to protect the weak. I forget the exact wording."

"Forsaken are the strong who do not protect the weak," Lucas interjected, remembering what had been tattooed on Silo's chest. His friend had been religious, though not a zealot it seemed. Maston nodded, ignoring why Lucas would know the phrase.

"Tulwar made sure the entire world knew how we'd broken the Fourth Order, and so his movement had a name."

"And you've been fighting them ever since," Lucas said, many things now coming together in his mind. "Was there ever a second Xalan fleet? Would you have been wiped out if you tried to save them?"

Maston stared into the flames.

"I ask myself that every single day. I imagine Talis Vale does as well."

"Why'd you tell Asha that story?" Lucas pressed.

"Your counterpart is a rare creature," he said. "She possesses many of the same qualities as Cora, incredible beauty paired with an unconquerable spirit. She is an echo of the woman I once called my own."

Lucas began to feel his blood simmer a bit, but Maston continued.

"Treasure her," he said sternly. "Know how fortunate you are to have someone so exceptional at your side."

Lucas relaxed. Maston wasn't competing for her, then, it seemed.

"You've proven yourself capable as well," he said. "You have a talent for both ending and saving lives. Not many would have braved that city and that creature to rescue someone they couldn't stand."

"Well, I'm hoping you can help get us out here," Lucas said.

Maston nodded.

"Perhaps I can."

Rising to his feet, he spoke to Lucas without looking at him.

"That is the last time you question what I know of sacrifice."

After Toruk came down from the trees, it was Lucas's turn to try to grab a little rest. But as he sat on a pair of branches staring at Mol'taavi, none found him. Maston's story was incredible, horrifying. Lucas had killed many bad people to stay alive, but few good ones. His own experience executing Silo had shaken him, so he could only imagine how Maston felt with the lives of untold millions latched around his neck for the rest of his life. And losing Corinthia the way he had. Perhaps the man had earned the right to be difficult and hostile, but at times he had seemed borderline psychotic. The man did have him beaten half to death onboard the Spear, after all. Another of his "lessons" perhaps, as Asha maintained? He did finally appear to be coming around to Lucas as an ally rather than an adversary. Lucas had risked much to save him, and perhaps staring into the burning eyes of the Desecrator had melted Maston's frozen soul just a bit. Too bad Silo wasn't here to see his commander finally come around and embrace the wretched Earthborn.

Silo. Lucas remembered something. He dug through the pack attached to his stealth suit and, moving aside Omicron's square, found what he was looking for. Silo's Final. Lucas placed the chip in the palm of his hand and tapped it. Immediately an interface popped up, a list of names. "Madi, Rula, Koto, Velia, Kiati."

Lucas tapped the first one. A three-dimensional image of Silo appeared before him from the chest up. His hair was longer, he looked at least a few years younger. Lucas wondered how often these were recorded or updated. As Silo spoke, Lucas felt his blood go cold.

"*Sa Madi*," he said, smiling widely. "I hoped you would never have to watch this, but in my line of work, it's bound to happen sooner or later."

Holographic Silo paused to take a breath.

"I'm sorry this had to happen the way it did with *Padi*, with *Brota*. I can't imagine how much your heart must ache now after all this. Just know that you'll see us again in the Forest one day."

Lucas paused the video. He hadn't spoken of it, but it seemed Silo was religious enough to believe he was headed to a better place. This Blessed Forest Maston had told him about. Lucas wondered if it was controversial for a Guardian to have a Fourth Order tattoo. Even if the sentiment was a good one, the group that had adopted the name was bloodthirsty, ruthless, and the most destructive force on Sora.

Lucas hovered over the pause button, but didn't resume playback. This was private. It seemed the video was for his *Madi*, mother, he assumed by the reference to "*Padi*" as well. Lucas looked down at the other names. Brothers? Sisters? Friends? He stopped at the one he recognized, Kiati. *Just a few seconds can't hurt.*

"Kiati," Silo began, "who knows if you'll outlive me, but I bet you will. You were always the smarter one with your fancy medical package and those record-setting cog scores."

Silo still smiled, but looked pained.

"I'll always remember that week of shore leave after Golgath. I don't care that you told me to forget it. One of these days you'll come around again, but if you're watching this, maybe it's too late for us. You were the best thing I found in this dark storm of war. I know you'll go on to do great things, and someday, I'll see you in the Forest. I'll save you a spot. I know you don't believe, but you'll see. You'll see."

Silo briefly looked off camera, then turned back.

"I hope you never see this. I hope we made it through."

That was enough for Lucas. He deactivated the chip and slid it back into his pouch. He pulled up his wrist display that showed a pulsing green dot labeled Kiati back at the underground village. She'd returned from a rescue mission of her own, saving one of the other stranded Guardians. Lucas was not looking forward to telling her how Silo died, nor giving her his Final. There had indeed been something between them once, long ago. The knot in Lucas's stomach that had formed when watching the video had not yet gone away. Silo was a good man. Lucas had seen too many of those die these past few years.

The remainder of their trek through the jungle was uneventful and they took no further breaks. Either the Desecrator had lost them, or simply stopped pursuit. Toruk frequently let out a low sharp whistle that blended in with the rest of the forest's noises, and Lucas thought he knew the purpose. He was trying to call his bloodwolf back to him, but there was no way the creature could have survived his attempt to stall the Desecrator. The bones they saw of much larger creatures the monster had killed were proof of that. Each time his whistle was met with silence, Toruk seemed to grow a little more despondent.

The entrance to the village was actually a narrow holographic stone in the earth that didn't warrant a second glance. The illusion was perfect. They passed through the image and down into the cave system unseen and, after a short trek, came to the underground lake and the settlement itself.

There was no parade to greet them, only a worried-looking crowd of Oni wondering why so few had returned. He watched Toruk regale his people with tales of his warriors' bravery as they faced down the terrible monster in the Dead City. Lucas had the unfortunate task of relaying to Zeta the news that her entire team had been killed in action.

"It cannot be," she exclaimed, her pale face growing whiter. "All of them?"

Lucas nodded.

"They were such fine soldiers! I have known Corporal [garbled] for nearly a century. The man has survived more battles than I can count."

Lucas glanced over at Alpha.

"He'd never fought anything like this before, I'll tell you that."

"You said it had *wings*?" Alpha asked, curious more about the discovery of the Desecrator than the death of those who fought him.

"Yeah," Lucas said. "A dozen feet tall, claws like scimitars, and it was red. Blood red. I've never seen anything like it."

"Nor have I," Alpha said. He looked worried.

"No psionic abilities, so far as I could tell," Lucas continued. "If it is a Shadow, I don't know what kind it is."

Alpha sifted through some data on a scroll.

"The Shadow transformation process is meant to spark premature evolution in our species. Perhaps through a different sort of experimentation, this Xalan went down a . . . different path. One I have certainly never seen replicated."

"Well, you can dissect it after we kill it," came a voice from behind them. Lucas knew who it belonged to from the first word. He turned around, already smiling.

Asha stood in the doorway of the hut clad in a torn stealth suit with her trademark sword crossing her back. Her hair was wild from the humidity and her skin had darkened in the sunlight to the point where she almost looked like a native. In her right hand she held a familiar object, the white null core they used to travel to distant star systems with relative ease. It was shaded, but still illuminated the room. She dropped it on the ground haphazardly, causing Alpha to cringe, but before he could chastise her, she was already across the room with her arms wrapped around Lucas.

She gripped him so tight he thought he'd rebroken a rib, but the happiness he felt seeing her alive outweighed it. All the anger he'd felt toward her on the Spear and afterward was erased in an instant. She was here. He hadn't lost her. Not yet. She pulled back and wore a wide, bright smile. One he hadn't seen in far too long.

Alpha said they needed to talk further later, but he allowed Lucas some reprieve to recover from his recent outing. He and Asha made their way to the edge of the lake and sat perched on a ledge about a dozen feet up from the crystal clear water. Colorful fish could be seen swimming in schools below, while light shone in from the openings in the roof of the cave. Toruk had told him upon their return that those gaps were also covered by holographic images meant to look, from the outside, like the forest floor. Though he had called them "fool shields," as it was the best term he could come up with.

Asha attempted to tame her hair as she told Lucas the story of her own awakening in the jungle. She pointed to a bandage around her arm and said that, while she hadn't run across any Xalan search parties, she was forced to battle a lizard-like creature the size of a pickup truck that wasn't terribly pleasant. Fortunately, like Lucas, she'd slept with her weapons inside her pod, which had greatly increased her chance of survival right off the bat.

The search team eventually found her, but she wasn't borderline psychotic the way Lucas had been after his Moltok sting, and she had remained conscious for the return trip. She peeled the bandage back to reveal a few swaths of skin missing in jagged patterns that were obviously bite marks. She'd wanted the bring the lizard's head back with her as a trophy, but it weighed far too much to be worth carting around in the heat.

On the way back to the village, her group of Guardians and Oni ran across a large chunk of the engine bay of the downed Spear. After clearing out a few enemy Xalan troops attempting to comb through the wreckage, she spotted the white null core, detached from its housing and barely visible in the mud. Understanding its usefulness, she brought it back with her, much to Alpha's delight. It wasn't as heavy as it looked, she said.

The two of them sat with their feet dangling off the edge of the precipice, watching the fish swirl below them.

"Well, this is a goddamn disaster," Asha said, echoing Maston's earlier sentiment. It was a relief to have a conversation in English again. "We lost most of our escort and our ship and the thing that's hunting us happens to live next door. Fantastic."

"It is less than ideal," Lucas said, staring out at the opposite wall of the enormous cave a few thousand yards away. "But at least we're still alive."

"Seems to be our curse," she said distantly.

"It won't last forever."

"What the hell motivated you to go back out for Maston? Especially after all that shit with Silo and your fever? If anyone deserved a break, it was you."

"You were right," Lucas said. "He's an asshole, but a useful one. If we're going to figure out a way out of here, a plan is better with him than without."

Asha turned to look at Lucas.

"About Vitalla . . ." she began. Lucas waved her off.

"He told me," he said. "All of it. And you think this is a disaster. I can only imagine what Sora was like when that happened. No wonder they were so happy to see us. Lord knows they could have used a bit of good news right about then."

Asha scoffed.

"Yeah, because we're being terribly useful so far. We got half their nobles blown up, I was kidnapped, and now we've stranded or killed most of their finest soldiers an impossible distance away from home."

"Well, we found Zeta," Lucas said.

"Ah yes, the great 'White Spirit,' huh? And what exactly is she doing that's so helpful? I don't hear Alpha Senior's message being broadcast around the galaxy yet."

Lucas shook his head.

"I don't know what the plan is anymore. Something must be wrong."

"That's the understatement of the year," Asha said.

There was a commotion from back at the village and Lucas stood up to look down at what was going on in the square. A large group was gathered, watching a bloodwolf limp its way into town. Its pace was a crawl, and it was dragging both of its hind legs. Lucas was too far away to get a proper view, but he could see enormous gashes on the creature even from this distance. Toruk burst forth from the crowd and wrapped his arms around the bloodwolf's neck, and other Oni rushed toward him with what looked to be medical supplies in hand. A few other smaller bloodwolves emerged from nearby huts and ran to greet their lost pack leader.

"Well, how about that," Lucas muttered to himself. "Tough old bastard."

That the animal survived its encounter with the Desecrator was a miracle, though to expect the wolf to have killed it was far too much to hope for. But still, it was a heartening sight. The brave beast taking on the supposed pinnacle of evolution, and surviving.

"What's that?" Asha asked, also rising.

"Hope," Lucas said.

15

Lucas rose the next morning after a mercifully dreamless sleep. He was in a hut close to the bank of the lake, and as he sat up he could hear the bustle of the village outside. Underneath him was a stretched skin coated in a striped fur, pulled from the local fauna, no doubt. Light crept in through narrow windows cut into the sticks that made up the forward wall of the enclosure.

He looked down at Asha, her bare skin still pressed against the fur. They'd stayed up half the night talking about what had happened back on the Spear. Silo, Kiati, Maston, all of it. Asha admitted Maston had a cruel streak, but Lucas had to admit in turn that he was an effective commander. Lucas had learned the hard lesson Maston was trying to teach when he found Silo wounded in the forest. Asha recognized that some part of her still felt trapped on Earth, where instinctive killing was second nature. It was why she was willing to execute Kiati when the moment called for it. They'd come so far, but still held on to pieces of their old selves, for better or worse. But they realized that, whatever their lingering issues, nothing had broken between them, they spent the other half of the evening not talking much at all. In the end, there wasn't much time for sleep.

Lucas noticed a pulsing light from the sleeve of his crumpled stealth suit. After crawling over to it, he realized Alpha was pinging him to go to Zeta's hut. Time to figure out just what the hell they were going to do now.

He sat down on the fur floor and tried to nudge Asha awake. On the third try, she rolled over and grinned sleepily at him.

She stretched her arms overhead and the morning light bathed her body in such a way Lucas forgot about how tired he was. Alpha could wait a few minutes longer.

They arrived at Zeta's a while later to an annoyed Alpha expressing confusion that he had requested their presence some time ago. Zeta quickly shushed him and attempted to veer him back to the task at hand. Lucas was puzzled to see that Alpha looked wet, his gray skin glistening. Also present in the room were Maston, who now wore a pressurized bandage over his shoulder, and Toruk, who was idly thumbing through his claw necklace.

"Now that we have all managed to respond to my summons," Alpha said as he cast an eye toward Lucas, "we need to discuss present circumstances."

Zeta spoke next out of another translator collar, though this one looked more hastily improvised then her first, now lost in the Dead City around the neck of the Corporal's headless corpse.

"I regret to inform you that the action you seek, to disseminate this message to all Xalan systems, is not possible from our present location."

"What? Why not?" Lucas asked.

"Since your arrival, a void veil has been dropped over this entire planet. No communications in or out. Or even between installations on the planet itself. Nothing is allowed other than the singular military channel, which still allows access to the troops directly. The general populace is simply in the dark. The Council knows what you are attempting to do and is taking drastic steps to ensure you cannot achieve your ends. I cannot even broadcast the message to this entire planet, much less all the colonies from here."

"A 'void veil'?" Asha said. "How the hell do we lift that? If they can just shield entire planets from communication, there's no way to even accomplish what we're trying to do with the message."

"You're going to love this," Maston said from behind her, his arms crossed.

Zeta continued.

"The only way to disrupt the veil is to trace it to its origin."

"Xala," Lucas said breathlessly.

"Correct. It is also the only location where I can ensure I am able to broadcast the message to every colony, every citizen at once. Otherwise, broadcasting to select groups would just make each a target as the Council seeks to contain the fallout."

"Contain with mass murder," Alpha muttered. Zeta nodded.

"In our present circumstances, there is simply no other method of mass delivery that would be viable other than broadcasting from the veil's point of origin itself, central command on the home planet."

"We have to go to Xala itself?" Asha asked, incredulous.

"Yes, but you also have to take *me* to Xala itself. Though I have been able to create the necessary broadcast algorithm, I am the only one with the knowledge to implement it into the Xalan galactic network."

"You can't do this?" Lucas said, turning to Alpha.

"I could attempt to do so," Alpha said, "though Zeta has a dramatically better chance of completing the objective, as she has had intensive experience with the system for decades. She actually built most of it. I am no match for her prowess in this area."

Lucas walked over to the metal desk in the center of the room and sat on the edge.

"We seem to be fast-forwarding here. How are we supposed to do any of this when we can't even get off this planet?"

"There is . . . something I must show you," said Alpha. Lucas glanced at Maston and he shrugged with his bandaged shoulder.

Alpha ushered them out of the room. Toruk crossed in front of Lucas and was muttering something to himself.

"What did you say?" Lucas asked.

"Broken chariot," replied the chief.

Lucas followed him out into the village square, and Toruk began speaking to the Oni nearby.

"*Holoi ba'to suuta. Ba'to suuta.*"

Some of the Oni whispered to each other while others raced to nearby huts to spread the message, whatever it was. Soon there was a large group following them. Even a few of the rescued Guardians were now with them, moving with the growing crowd down to the shore of the underground lake.

When they got there, Lucas looked around and saw that Alpha had disappeared entirely.

"Where the hell did he go?" he asked Asha. "What's going on?"

"I have no idea," she said, shaking her head. "But knowing him, I'm sure it's something insane."

The Oni were all staring at the vast lake in front of them. A hush fell over the crowd. Maston and the other Guardians were scratching their heads and looking around.

Zeta stepped forward to stand next to Lucas.

"I never thought this day would come."

"What day?" Lucas asked, but before she could answer, he felt the ground start to vibrate. Dark silt slid toward the water, and ripples scattered across the normally tranquil surface.

From under the water, a spectrum of white and blue orbs shone up from deep underneath the surface. The Oni let out a collective gasp, and Lucas took a step back in amazement.

The lights grew brighter and brighter until, finally, what they were attached to broke through the surface of the lake.

"What the . . ." Asha's voice trailed off.

It was a ship, assuredly of Xalan origin, but far older and boxier than the models Lucas had seen over the past few years. As it rose out of the water, seaweed hung off it like wet hair, and there were hundreds of barnacles attached to its hull on all sides. Lucas actually saw a large rainbow-scaled fish flopping around on top of one of the engine mounts before it managed to dive back into the water.

"Want to fill us in here?" Lucas asked Zeta as Maston and Asha drew closer.

"This is the ship in which I arrived," Zeta said as she observed the craft slowly rotating in the air. "It's a prison vessel used to shuttle high-risk inmates."

"How did you escape?" Asha asked.

"After my capture, during transport to sentencing, I overrode the security protocols and released those incarcerated within. We let loose the psychopaths, imprisoned for insanity and violent crimes, who killed the guards. Then my fellow resistance fighters and I killed the surviving criminals. Unfortunately, the plan went awry as the ship was damaged in the conflict. I ended up being the only one to survive the crash."

She motioned to the largest hole in the roof of the cave where the sunlight came in. It was hard to get a sense of scale, but it looked to be the same size as the ship before them. Lucas could see the sheen of the holographic imagery that shielded the opening from view up on the surface.

"I ended up in the bottom of the lake, and it was a full week before the Oni found me. You have heard the rest of that story already. After we made S'tasonti a permanent settlement, I made sure to keep the ship in working order as best I could, should I ever need it again. It is immune to rust and other maladies, even housed underwater, but it was a challenge to repair the damage from the hijacking and subsequent crash. However, even with everything repaired, its [garbled] core was depleted, and it could never leave the system again. At least not until now."

"The Spear core," Asha said slowly.

Zeta nodded.

"You are our unwitting savior, human. With the long-range [garbled] core you salvaged from your downed ship, we now have a chance of returning you to your home, and of continuing on to Xala for the final dispersion of the message."

The Oni were scrambling to move fishing boats so that Alpha could park the tail end of the large ship on the beach. It was bigger than the Ark, but smaller than the Spear. As it drew closer, it really did look ancient. Lucas's knees buckled as the metal monstrosity landed with a thud on the sand a short distance away, scattering the Oni.

"There is no way that thing is airworthy, much less spaceworthy," Maston said.

"For all our sakes, I hope you are incorrect," replied Zeta.

"And we're just going to fly this thing out of here, completely undetected by the entire planet that's hunting us? I'm guessing you don't have stealth drives in ships a thousand years old," Maston continued.

"Very astute, though the facilitation of our escape is a problem I was hoping that you could help us solve, commander."

Maston stayed barricaded in with Zeta, drawing up battle plans, while Lucas and Asha headed toward the Khal'din's medical hut, where they were to get loaded up and ready to ship out. They weren't clear on the specifics just yet, but they were told their escape attempt would take the combined might of the surviving Guardians and every Oni who could hold a weapon.

In the tent, the injured and whole mingled as everyone dug through the salvaged supplies to find a collection of armor and weapons that suited them. With adequate recovery time, nearly all the surviving Guardians were now standing, thanks to a combination of their resolute genetics and the healing techno-magic of their caretaker. A few however, were missing entire limbs, an ailment that would need to be remedied off-planet.

Even the Kal'din himself was strapping on a ragged suit of armor, and he wielded a metal and bone scythe taller than he was. He still never said a word nor took off his mask, but seemed ready for a fight as he did last minute touch-ups on the wounded.

Lucas milled through the crowd until he saw a familiar shock of red hair up ahead. Moving his way through Soran and Oni, he gave her shoulder plate a tap. He couldn't hide his surprise when she turned around.

Kiati wore a bandage wrapped around her head that covered her left eye. Jagged cuts poked out from underneath the bloodied fabric.

"Jesus Christ!" Lucas exclaimed in English, ignoring that she wouldn't recognize the expression. "What happened to you?"

"Got ambushed returning from hauling back Celton," she said, jerking her head toward a silver-haired male Guardian a few feet away who was missing most of the fingers on his left hand. "Lost the eye to proto-nade shrapnel. Xalan who threw it lost his head."

"Does it hurt?" Lucas asked.

"No, it feels like I dipped my face in a cool river," she snorted.

"I mean, should you be fighting?"

"They'll grow me another one back on Sora. But I'll have to fight to make it there first. All hands on deck here, as you may have noticed."

Lucas fingered the chip in his pocket.

"Look, the reason I wanted to find you was because of . . . Silo."

She nodded briskly.

"I already know. I saw the blacklist."

"Yeah, well, not sure if anyone told you, but I was with him when he died."

She raised her eyebrows. Well, her eyebrow.

"That so?"

Lucas pulled the Final out and held it in his outstretched hand. "I figured you could get this where it needs to go."

Kiati took the chip and tapped it. The list of names came up, including her own. Her eye widened, and she quickly shut the device off.

"Did you watch this?" she asked, her tone arctic.

"No," Lucas lied. She seemed to relax a bit. "But I know you were . . . friends. I'm sorry."

"Stupid bastard was always going to get himself killed one of these days. What'd he do? Eat a poison mushroom?"

"Killed four Xalans with a makeshift pike before they took him down," Lucas replied.

Kiati scoffed.

"Only four?"

Her face remained stern, but Lucas could see wetness creeping into her one visible eye. Tough talk wasn't enough to block the grief within. Lucas didn't feel the need to give Kiati the full rundown of his involvement in Silo's last moments, at least not right now.

"We should have gotten out after Golgath . . ." she muttered, mostly to herself.

"Golgath?" Lucas pried, recognizing the name Silo had mentioned during his message to her.

She looked up at him.

"Never mind," she said. Whatever had gone on between them, Lucas wouldn't hear her side of it here or now. He turned to leave.

"Thank you," she said after he'd gotten a few steps. Lucas turned back and nodded before continuing on. She tapped the chip and stared at her own name in the list.

16

Lucas tapped his foot nervously as he sat in one of the prison ship's turret chambers. Nearly a half day had passed before Maston and Zeta finally got their plan of action together, and Lucas could hardly believe it when they'd told him.

There were many obstacles standing in the way of leaving the planet alive, but the most immediate was a Xalan spaceport located near the coast a short distance away. Lucas had seen its lights from his earlier trek through the jungle, and it was reportedly quite a sprawling facility. If their escape in the prison ship sounded any alarms among the Xalans, that base would be the closest one launching ships to pursue them. Simply put, it needed to be wiped out completely in order for them to make it to the outer atmosphere safely. If they could do that, there was a fair chance they could reach the edge of the system and activate the null core to head home. After the spaceport was gone, the rest of the fleet in the area would be scrambling to figure out just what the hell happened, and they likely wouldn't notice a simple craft such as theirs passing through so many others like it. Prison ships were all over this planet, as resistance troops and Oni were constantly being rounded up and transported for questioning, sentencing, and execution. Zeta had one of her undercover Xalan resistance agents activate the prison ship using his biology so it wouldn't be flagged or tracked by her or Alpha's traitorous signatures. A lengthy hack had made the process permanent.

Maston and Zeta's plan had many moving pieces, all of which would have to align at the correct time in the correct order for them to succeed. First, Zeta, piloting the ship, would sweep across the air hangars that held the largest ships stationed at the spaceport. Lucas, Asha, and Alpha would be in three of the craft's six heavy gun turrets. The rest would be filled with a few Guardians who had lost legs and couldn't join their squadmates in open combat during phase two.

After the ships were crippled, they'd need to destroy the rest of the base to ensure they didn't call for help. Zeta asserted that she could block their communications temporarily, but the equipment and personnel needed to be decimated so reinforcements would be delayed after they left.

On the ground, Zeta's undercover agents inside would open the main gate, letting the Oni troops flood in from the jungle and seize the base with the help of Guardians dropped from the prison ship into the higher levels of the base. Hopefully all of this would be enough to overrun the spaceport completely, and with no ships to chase them and no one alive to call for help once they left, they could cause enough of a delay to get away cleanly.

As mad as it all sounded, it wasn't a hard sell to the Oni, who were eager to help their newfound warrior brethren by eliminating an installation that had plagued them with a constant supply of Xalans in the past. They'd never be able to take a base this fortified by themselves. Equally raring to go were the Guardians, who desperately wanted to leave Makari and return to Sora. The fact that the way to get there was to plow through a battalion of Xalans was a bonus, as there were many, many dead to avenge littered throughout the forest.

Lucas's seat rumbled as the prison ship's engines fired up. They slowly rose from the beach inside the cave, and Lucas could see the remnants of the Khas'to tribe assembled to see them off. Only the very old and very young remained. All other members of the village, men and women old enough to wield a spear, were already armed to the teeth and sprinting through the forest outside en route to the spaceport.

As they reached the ceiling of the enormous cavern, the figures below became mere insects. Lucas saw a flicker of light as they passed through the opening at the top of the cave, and then immediately the holographic barrier resealed itself, a perfect image of rocks and brush to hide the gap from above.

They struck a leisurely pace over the jungle toward the spaceport so as to not draw suspicion. Algae and barnacles had been scraped off the ship so it didn't look quite so decrepit, but most prison transports were pretty battered anyway. From his perch, Lucas could seen dozens of drones strafing the jungle, still hunting for them. For the moment, it looked as if none had noticed their emergence from the cave, a move that had been carefully timed by Zeta after analyzing their patrol patterns.

Down in the jungle below, Lucas saw a trail of green specks through his window display. It was the Oni, tagged and visible only to them so they could monitor their progress. They were nearly to the spaceport, having left quite some time ago so the assault could be properly coordinated. Toruk was communicating to them from the ground, and relayed that they'd already dismantled four Xalan patrols they'd come across, all quickly enough to ensure the troops didn't broadcast their position back to base.

Lucas brought up a series of three-dimensional displays that rotated in front of him. One was of a large Xalan capital ship, three of which were docked at the spaceport ahead. Alpha had highlighted the engine power nodes in red. If they were destroyed, it would disable the vessels. A few other images showed a couple of smaller single-pilot fighter and bomber variants. Some were housed in the ships themselves, others would be out in the open and needed to be eliminated. If not, even without white null cores, they could chase them into the outer reaches of the solar system, and the prison ship would likely not survive their pursuit.

Lucas's leg still hadn't stopped shaking. It didn't matter how many battles he'd lived through, fear wasn't something that could be erased when there was this much danger present. Days like these were why he still jumped at shadows each night. Not knowing whether he would survive the next day, the next hour, took a toll on his mind, which felt like it was fracturing a little more with each new upheaval. The luxurious comforts of Sora seemed so far away now. Earth was so distant it didn't even feel real anymore. He brought up a monitor and saw Asha staring at her own display.

"You alright?" he asked through a private channel. She looked at her monitor when she heard his voice.

"This is no Kvaløya," she said. It was true. They were assaulting a secure military installation, not some run-down Scandinavian fishing village. The only things working in their favor were Zeta's inside men and the element of surprise. Lucas flipped to another feed, where Maston was in a cell block going over assault tactics and blueprints of the compound with the remaining Guardians. There were so few of them now. They'd lost, what was it, 70 percent of the squadron between the crash and the jungle? And most of the rest were injured or ill. It was time to see what a few trillion in government-grown genetics actually bought.

The ship rounded the side of the mountain and the spaceport could be seen up ahead. It really was enormous, and Lucas nervously eyed defensive gun turrets pointing out from various corners of the outer wall. Zeta said her spies would be able to deactivate the automated defense systems of the facility, leaving them to deal with organics only, but that was a hard gamble, which made Lucas uneasy.

The dwarf sun was starting to set now, and the light refracted off the ocean behind it. This place did have a certain beauty to it at times, but while it was still populated by bloodthirsty Xalans, there was no chance to return it to its untainted former glory. They'd have to win the war and then some in order for Toruk to get his planet back.

The central comm channel started to light up with untranslated Xalan hailing requests as they approached the station. Though Lucas couldn't understand the growls, they were clearly inquiring as to why an unscheduled prison ship was arriving at their base. Zeta spoke back to them in Xalan, reciting her practiced story about capturing a troupe of Oni warriors, explaining all the Soran life signatures onboard. After much debate, Zeta convinced the operator to allow them entry to the hangar area to set down and discuss the miscommunication in person.

The ship slowly glided toward the hangar area where Lucas saw the large capital ships looming. On the deck below, there was a long line of fighters with Xalan pilots milling about. Lucas gripped his controls tightly and shifted in his heavy armor plating. No stealth suit this time; this was an all-out assault that would require his armor to catch a plasma round or two (or dozen) on his behalf. Natalie was hooked to his chair and his pistol and knife were strapped to his chest. He put on his helmet and a litany of display readouts sprung into his line of sight, attempting to work in synergy with those of the Xalan turret in front of him. The combination was a garbled mess, and he decided to remove his helmet for the time being to avoid confusion created by the pairing of two different technology systems. They hadn't had time to retrofit any of the Xalan readouts on the ship to Soran other than a few key words. FILTER switched in and out of thermal and infrared views. FOCUS cycled through potential targets on the viewscreen. FIRE was self-explanatory.

Alpha broke in on the central comm.

"This is it," he said solemnly. "Fire on my mark."

The prison ship was starting to dip low, though Lucas knew it would never touch the ground. In his viewscreen, the engine compartments of the capital ships in front of him were highlighted, and his fingers hovered over the turret's dual triggers.

They were only a few dozen feet from the surface now, and Lucas saw a Xalan pilot staring up at him from the ground. Was the glass opaque enough to obscure him from the outside? The Xalan tilted his head, then turned to shout something to the other pilots nearby who gathered around him and also looked up at his turret bay.

"Alpha . . ." Lucas said as commotion started breaking out on the ground below.

"Engage," came the mechanical reply.

Lucas swiveled the turret down toward the cluster of pilots that had assembled at the behest of their colleague. His first pair of shots liquefied most of the group, as armor-piercing artillery turned on organics was like emptying an Uzi into a box of crackers. He kept firing until nothing stirred in the smoking hole, and then pivoted upward to tear into the cockpit of the nearest fighter.

Behind the line of planes on the deck, the three docked capital ships were being lit up as the other five turrets focused their fire onto the highlighted compartments, which had been opened up for maintenance and were particularly vulnerable. Two ships had been crippled in the first few seconds with targeted strikes, and now the third was attempting to take off under fire. Lucas turned his turret toward it and let loose on the engines. The ship got about five hundred feet in the air before a huge explosion inside the hull shorted out the lights of the engines, and Lucas watched as the massive craft fell back to the hangar floor, almost in slow motion. When it hit the ground, it didn't stay there. The gigantic ship tore through the metal floor and sank deep into the highest levels of the base. With a painful groan, it pulled much of the hangar bay down with it, and the smaller ships parked on the deck began to slide down the newly sloped surface and into the jagged hole the ship had created. Pilots scrambled to stay on their feet, but many were leveled by their own ships and equipment and were swallowed into the pit. The two other capital ships that had initially been disabled tumbled off the edges of their platforms and landed with deafening crashes in the jungle below, shaking the entire facility. Nothing was going to be taking off from the hangar now, as that entire section of the base had ceased to exist.

Alarms sounded all over the spaceport. The prison ship rose up from the collapsing hangar and turned toward the center of the base, where troops were starting to scramble. They rained down fire on all the Xalans they could see, and Lucas breathed a sigh of relief when he saw that the defensive auto turrets remained still. Zeta's inside men had done their job. Well, one of their jobs at least.

The original plan had been to drop the Guardian squadron on the hangar, but the surface was too unstable with the area in ruins, and Zeta relayed over the central comm that she was looking for a new place to touch down safely.

The monitors showed Alpha and Asha firing at troops on the other side of the ship while Lucas did the same. The enemy soldiers were shredded by the artillery fire and the structures around them were reduced to rubble as explosive canister rounds the size of footballs ripped through them. But even after being caught off guard, the troops were starting to get in position to return fire on the ship, and there were simply too many to target. Where were the Oni?

Lucas flinched as plasma peppered the hull near his turret. He returned fire, but the ship veered so that he took a chunk out of the structure behind the Xalans instead. More and more of their shots were connecting; the prison ship was a rather large target lacking significant maneuverability. They were too far into the base to be able to evade properly, and suddenly a raucous explosion from somewhere underneath Lucas rocked the entire craft.

"Zeta, Alpha, talk to me!" Lucas yelled as the ship started lurching hard to the right.

Alpha broke in, but the comm was going fuzzy.

"[Static] stabilizer took a [static] hit."

Then Zeta:

"Have to [static] set down [static] repair."

"This is not the time to stop for a tune-up!" shouted Asha, her voice bursting through the static and gunfire. On her monitor, Lucas watched her take a shot and blow a pair of Xalans to pieces even as the ship was spinning.

"No [static] option," came Zeta, and the array of flashing warning lights and alarms all around the turret seemed to back up her statement. "Brace [static]."

There was only a split second between her warning and what happened next. The ship spun around and Lucas suddenly saw nothing but an enormous wall in his viewscreen, a wall that shattered like china as they plowed directly through it. Lucas was almost pitched off his seat, barely held in place by ill-fitting restraints meant for a much larger creature. His stomach dropped as the ship fell a few stories and hit the ground with a jarring thud that shook Lucas to his core and made his ears ring.

His controls were unresponsive, and only emergency lighting was flickering in the turret bay. Outside the viewscreen in front of him there was nothing but a mass of swirling smoke. Lucas unclipped his restraints and staggered to his feet. His helmet was nowhere to be seen, but Natalie had been flung into the glass in front of him. He scooped up the rifle and headed into the bowels of the ship. Comms were completely silent, though sporadic gunfire could still be heard outside. Lucas ran down the hall and saw an electronic panel in flames as thick smoke filled the corridor. Would the ship be able to get airborne again after this?

"Asha . . . Asha," he called in between coughs into his armor's communicator, but was met with silence. He stumbled around the dimly lit corridors of the ship, and had to bring up a display of the craft to understand just where the hell he was and where he was trying to go in the unfamiliar vessel.

Eventually he pried open a stuck set of doors and found himself staring at a large collection of Guardians, along with Asha and Alpha, all assembled in a large storage bay with a massive door at one end. He breathed a sigh of relief, but that sparked another fit of coughing as his lungs were still inundated with smoke.

"What's going on?" he managed to get out as all eyes turned to him.

Alpha was dressed in a full set of Xalan power armor, which made him look far more menacing than usual. He spoke first.

"A [garbled] strike hit the [garbled] and we now need a period of time to perform repairs."

The exact specifics escaped Lucas through the mistranslation, but he got the idea.

"Here? Now?"

Maston was uneasy.

"We have no time to debate this. Xalan forces are amassing outside as we speak."

"Defend the ship for as long as you are able," said Alpha. "I will stay back and assist with repairs, which can hopefully be made with haste."

"Where are the Oni?" Asha asked.

Alpha looked grave.

"We lost communication with them some time ago. We must assume they met with some form of resistance."

Gunfire was growing louder, and it could be heard striking the hull outside.

"We're moving out, now," Maston said emphatically.

"Agreed," Alpha said. "I will inform you of our progress once I can bring communication systems back online."

He exited through a door in the rear of the room, and all eyes turned to Maston.

"Form up!" he bellowed. "Position 202!"

The formations Lucas had learned on the Spear rushed back into his mind. Yes, he'd failed his final exam, but that didn't matter now. He took his place down on one knee in a line of Guardians with their weapons pointed toward the exit bay doors. A row stood behind them, their weapons facing forward as well. Asha was right next to Lucas, and Maston stood behind the pair of them. In the corner, the newly cycloptic Kiati ran her hand through a cluster of floating controls.

It seemed like an eternity as the bay door opened; the wall became a ramp that slowly descended from the ceiling on a path to make contact with the earth. As it did, the smoke cleared and they could see what lay before them outside.

They were on the ground level of the base, and there were dozens, hundreds of Xalan troops standing or crouching with energy weapons leveled at them. The remains of the spaceport were crumbling or blazing around them, ravaged by their airstrike. The two groups eyed each other, neither daring to fire first, but it was clear who had the upper hand. The Guardians were cornered and vastly outnumbered. *This is about to get ugly.*

A tall Xalan with slate-gray skin strode toward them. Lucas recognized that his armor had the Xalan symbol for "Commander" on the breast, embossed in gold. He pointed at them and began snarling unintelligibly. A call for surrender? Four other menacing Xalans strode to take places at his side, their armor's markings implying they were lieutenants of some sort. The hundreds that surrounded them started creeping slowly forward. Were they trying to capture them? Lucas could only imagine what horrors lay ahead if they were taken alive rather than slain here and now. But the Guardians would never let that happen. Neither would Asha. Neither would he.

Maston raised his hand, and when it dropped, all hell would be unleashed on the army in front of them. He held it aloft for five seconds, then ten, then—

Down the central road running through the base, they heard a loud groan at the opposite end of the spaceport. The colossal gate that stood there was slowly opening, and a dull roar could be heard from up ahead.

The Xalan troops started to look around nervously, not wanting to switch their focus away from the phalanx of Sorans in front of them. One of the lieutenants made the bold move of pivoting fully around to see what was going on, his back turning toward them. When he saw what approached, he let out a loud yell that caused nearly everyone to turn around, the commander included.

Two Xalans near the rear of the assembly took plasma rounds to the head and slumped over. One caught a spear through his heart while a half dozen more were pelted with arcing arrows. Through the legions of troops in front of him, Lucas could see what was plowing through them. In the distance, the dark skin and white tattoos of the Oni were unmistakable.

The Xalan commander turned back to the Guardians, stretched out his claw, and yelled something that assuredly meant "fire." But as he did so, the lieutenant who had been the first to turn around pulled out an energy pistol, leveled it at the commander's temple, and pulled the trigger. The creature's head exploded and the air became instantly misted with black blood. The other three lieutenants couldn't process what was happening, as one got a claw in the throat while the other two were dropped by another pair of headshots from the traitorous Xalan's pistol.

The Guardians watched in confusion, Maston's arm still raised, as the Xalan lieutenant pulled out a red piece of cloth and shoved it into his upper arm's plating. It was the sign of the resistance Zeta had told them to look out for. He was one of hers.

Maston's arm fell. The entire area roared to life as gunfire was traded between armies. The Xalans had their attention split between the rampaging Oni and the Guardians before them, and it largely negated their advantage of numbers. The undercover Xalan dove out of the crossfire and proceeded to dismantle two other soldiers hiding behind a downed piece of a nearby building before bounding out of sight.

Lucas had set Natalie to full-auto mode, and he sprayed a constant stream of plasma out into the smoke. He connected with a trio of Xalans perched on a nearby rooftop, and they dropped from it like dead birds after the rounds had pierced them.

"Forward!" came the order from Maston, and the group all stood up and marched out of the loading bay into the street ahead, continuing to fire without a second's rest. Out in the open, without adequate protection, their close proximity was making them easy targets, and a few Guardians took hits and went down. Lucas expected Maston's next order from their training exercises.

"Break!"

Their singular unit shattered into thirty-odd pieces, and the remaining Xalans lost their targets in the smoke and rubble. Guardians streamed into nearby buildings, and Lucas could hear the screams of the Xalans being butchered within. It was time to start cleaning house. No one could be left to relay the attack to other bases in the area or in orbit. The facility's communications were being jammed by Zeta presently, but that effect would dissipate once they left. *If* they left, rather, as looking behind them, their downed ship, buried in a collapsed building, didn't exactly look like it was going anywhere. But there were larger tasks at hand.

Lucas sprinted forward down the street, making sure to keep Asha in his view through the chaos. Natalie's barrel retracted, the gun shifting into close-range shotgun mode forever identified by the Xalan symbol for "carnage." And carnage was exactly what it created as it blew apart Xalan troops left and right on the road, shredding armor and flesh and bone alike.

Asha, meanwhile, had her own way of dealing with close-quarters combat. Her guns were holstered and she grasped her black-bladed sword tightly in her hands. Lucas could barely keep up as she sprinted down the street, leaping over craters formed by their own assault with the prison ship. She cleaved the legs of one soldier, then whipped the blade around to slice through the midsection of another. Dodging a blast leveled from a nearby rooftop, she flung her sword at the culprit. As it struck him in the chest, she drew her Magnum and put a pair of fission rounds into the face of the soldier in front of her. A slight flex of her wrist caused her sword to shoot out of the dead Xalan on the roof and race back into her hand as fast as the electromagnetism in her wristband could propel it. Once reunited, she used it to removed the head of a nearby trooper whose attention was directed toward Lucas.

Lucas watched the decapitated soldier sink down to the ground and blasted through a lanky Xalan ahead of him. His constant use of the carnage setting was causing Natalie to overheat, something he'd never actually encountered before with the revamped weapon, though he'd never been in a firefight this intense. He shouldered the rifle as steam poured out of its cracks and unholstered his sidearm and knife from his chestplate. As he did so, a round whizzed by his ear and, touching it, he found sticky red blood on his black-gloved fingers. Still running forward, they were approaching a cluster of Xalans who had their backs turned to them and were focused on the marauding Oni warriors ahead. Lucas popped off two shots from his energy pistol, dropping a pair of unaware soldiers, and he sank his knife into the spinal column of another who howled as he collapsed to the ground, paralyzed. Whipping the knife out, Lucas flicked it into its elongated machete form and swung it around where it buried itself in another Xalan's throat. The resulting spray drenched Lucas in black blood, though at that point his armor was already slick with it. The latest kill drew the attention of another cluster of a half dozen troops, two of which proceeded to eat a pair of plasma rounds while three more were carved up by Asha's blade from behind before they could fire a shot. The final soldier was dragged away with his head clamped in the jaws of a nearby bloodwolf.

Lucas spun around to shoot another Xalan, but as he turned, found he was half a second behind and there was a barrel already pointed at his unfortunately unarmored head. Lucas's stomach felt like he'd just fallen off a building, but the gun didn't fire. Rather, the Xalan gave him a curt nod, and Lucas saw the red cloth tied around his arm. Another insider. Perhaps the same one from earlier. It was hard to tell.

The creature flinched and cracked off a shot that nearly deafened Lucas, but he quickly saw a Xalan soldier writhing around behind him, having caught the round in the neck. Asha stuck her sword through his chest, causing him to go still, and looked up at the resistance fighter. But he was already gone, having disappeared into the smoke to continue the fight elsewhere.

The remaining Xalans were retreating now, but they were caught on one side by the Guardians and the other by the Oni. Lucas looked up and saw Axon on a rooftop, clutching an enormous spinning plasma cannon, raining down brimstone on the confused troops attempting to flee into the building beneath him. Through the haze on the road, Lucas saw Toruk burst forth in full war regalia, impaling a Xalan on his spear before riddling another two soldiers with plasma rounds from his rifle. Retracting the spear, he thrust the blunt end backward into another Xalan's midsection and then whipped around, the razor's edge opening the creature's throat from a solid eight feet away.

Lucas felt a jolt as someone grabbed his shoulder plate, but as he spun around with his machete, he saw it was Maston.

"You, you, and you," he said, motioning to Lucas, Asha, and Toruk. "Come with me."

Maston was flanked by a quartet of Guardians whose helmets were hiding their identities. All were covered in a thick coat of dust and blood.

"Where to?" Lucas shouted over the roar of the battle that surrounded them.

"Central comms hub. Insurance," Maston yelled back. He looked free from injury, but blood was seeping through the bandage on his shoulder where his armor had been torn away.

Something exploded a few dozen feet away and they were showered with bits of metal and stone that stung like wasps. It was enough to motivate them to head inside, and they followed Maston into a burning building that already had dead Xalans lining the corridor.

Maston kept checking his wrist readout, and the group wove up and down narrow halls and ascended oversized staircases to higher levels. Occasionally they passed a shattered window that showed the fighting raging outside.

From around the corner ahead came the dull thumps of plasma bursts, and as Lucas rounded it he saw the corpses of two unarmored Xalans freshly killed by Maston's Guardian escort. One stirred briefly and Asha barely glanced downward as she put a round in his skull while she stepped over him.

When they reached the top of yet another staircase, they came upon a vast room full of blinking consoles and loud alarms. Inside were a half dozen Xalans attempting to use the unresponsive equipment. They all turned to look at the group that had just entered the room. The terror on their faces was unmistakable, regardless of their species.

Only three had weapons anywhere near them, and Maston shot the first two before they could reach their rifles. The third went down to one of the other Guardians, and the other three attempted to flee toward the rear door. Lucas let off a pair of shots with the now cooled-down Natalie that connected with the lower back of the closest one. Asha hit another in the arm, knocking him off balance and sending him crashing into a nearby desk. But before either could take further action, Toruk was already hurdling a holotable in front of them. He landed on the back of the one Lucas had shot, driving his spear into his chest. He then leapt over a workstation and brought the spear around, which planted itself into the neck of the second Xalan clutching his wounded arm. Finally, just as the third fleeing creature reached the door, the spear shot into his back, pinning him to the metal after a powerful throw from Toruk a solid fifty feet away.

The rest of the room stood silent after the display of murderous athleticism. Toruk ignored their stares and set about pulling a claw from each of the three dead bodies, which he then threaded onto his necklace.

Maston was also walking around, but not to collect trophies. Rather, he was planting explosive satchel charges on the most important-looking pieces of equipment.

"So this is it?" Lucas asked.

Maston nodded as he set another charge, this one fixed to the base of the holotable. "The bulk of their long-range broadcasting equipment is in here. If we detonate it all, it shouldn't matter that our jamming signal fades after we leave."

Lucas jumped as one of the Guardians took a shot at a Xalan who had the misfortune of stumbling into the room. The creature promptly crumbled into a heap at the doorframe. The soldier holstered her pistol, removed her helmet, and ran her gloved hand through her wet red hair.

"How many of those are you planting?" Kiati asked, her one remaining eye glaring intently around the room.

"Eight should do it," Maston said as he finished activating the final device. The alarms kept blaring, and the entire room was a strobe of white and red lights. When Maston finished, he motioned toward the rear door and the group moved out as Toruk removed his spear from the entryway. Rather than go out the way they came, they kept moving up until they reached the light of the open air. They spilled out onto a roof and, following Maston's lead, sprinted across the surface until they were a solid thousand feet away from where they'd emerged. Across the chasm of the street below they saw where the prison ship lay buried in the side of a structure. A contingent of Oni had surrounded it and were fending off advances from Xalan troops. Lights were starting to flicker inside the craft.

Up ahead, a few levels down on another rooftop, Lucas could see Axon fighting with a pair of Xalans. He'd dropped his massive gun and was pummeling them with his bare fists. He cracked one across the jaw so hard they could see his gray teeth fly through the air, even at a distance. The second managed to dig his claws into a crack in Axon's armor, which caused him to roar with rage, and he slammed his hands down onto the creature's arm, snapping it cleanly and producing howl of agony. Axon finally reached for a pistol and shot the wailing Xalan in the leg, then, as it dropped down to eye level, in its forehead. For good measure he put a round into the unconscious Xalan already on the ground.

"Axon!" Maston called out to him. "Join up!"

Axon turned at the sound of his name and raised his hand toward them. He was perhaps two floors down from their position, but a distance that was easily climbed with the help of mechanized power armor.

Axon took one step forward and was instantly split in half.

A millisecond later the loud, piercing crack that accompanied the shot echoed all around the walled compound like a thunderclap.

Lucas froze, staring at the pieces of the man as blood was spattered in a huge arc around the point of impact. A hole had been torn through the roof just to the left of the body.

Maston was shouting something, but Lucas's ears were ringing and the words were indecipherable. Suddenly, the entire head and torso of the Guardian next to him erupted, and the blast sent all of them flying on the rooftop. Again, Lucas's ears could hear nothing but a high-pitched whine, and he looked at the mangled corpse a few feet away, which was now two legs, an arm, and nearly nothing else.

Lucas turned his head and began searching for the source of the slaughter as he scrambled to his feet. With Asha a step ahead of him, they ran for cover behind a large cooling tower. Another ear-splitting shot tore a mammoth hole in the roof next to them, and they were pitched off their feet again. Both landed behind the tower, neither having sustained injury, and Kiati, Toruk, and the other Guardian were already there. But when they turned around, Asha let out a gasp.

Maston lay near the latest smoking hole. His right leg had been blown off and was a dozen feet away from his body. He wasn't moving, and there was an exceptional amount of blood everywhere, both his and that of the Guardian who had already been turned into pulp a short distance away.

He can't be dead.

It was Kiati who spoke next.

"Cover fire!" she yelled, and Asha, Toruk, Lucas, and the remaining Guardian snapped out of their daze and started firing anywhere, everywhere they could toward every possible sniping vantage point they could see. It served as enough of a distraction for Kiati, who sprinted out to Maston and pulled his body back to the cooling tower. With his armor, he must have easily weighed three hundred pounds, but Kiati's own suit assisted her with the weight. Between adrenaline and the armor's enhancement, she could have pulled a car if she needed to. Lucas stopped firing long enough to peer through his scope, and he scanned the direction the noise of the shots had come from. In the distance, he located a figure perched on top of one of the wall's defunct auto-turrets all the way across the base from them, but before he could zoom in further, a shot rocked the top of the cooling tower and rained stone debris over all of them.

Kiati looked at Maston's leg, which was severed midway up his thigh. His pressurized undersuit had already grown over the stump, sealing it up with a combination of heat and med gel. Within seconds, blood had stopped leaking from the gaping wound.

Scanning him with her hand, Kiati checked her wrist display, which showed an image of his circulatory system.

"He's alive," she said. The heartbeat on her readout was painfully weak.

But Lucas wasn't looking at Maston; he was peering back through his scope, focusing on the point in the distance. He increased magnification to twentyfold and saw the figure clearly.

It was the Desecrator, standing atop the turret a solid two miles away, holding a rifle as tall as he was. A railgun of sorts, judging by its devastation. The creature was already lining up another shot.

Lucas shot first, his crosshairs aimed squarely at a point between the Desecrator's burning orange eyes. After he pulled the trigger, the resulting milliseconds seemed like hours.

But at that distance, Lucas had overestimated his marksmanship. The round actually struck the railgun itself rather than the creature holding it. The shot knocked the Desecrator off balance, though he immediately attempted to return fire. Through the scope, Lucas could see smoke erupt from the railgun's barrel, but no shot fired. Frustrated, the Desecrator threw the weapon down with a pantomimed roar, and managed to dodge Lucas's second shot by launching himself up into the air. Lucas lost track of him. He dialed back the magnification on his scope, but soon saw his wings buzzing as the creature burst through a column of smoke. He was coming.

"We need to move," Lucas said, turning back to the group huddled behind the tower.

"We have to get him back to the ship," Kiati said. Maston was still unconscious at her feet. The other Guardian had now removed his helmet to reveal a brown-skinned man with a shaved head, blue eyes, and blood streaming from his ears. Lucas was surprised to find his own were bleeding as well.

"What was that?" Asha asked.

"You're about to find out," Lucas said.

With the ability to fly at blinding speeds, the Desecrator had already reached the rooftop. He skidded to a halt on the surface, his claws tearing through the metal as he came to a stop. His wings fluttered, then retracted into his armored back.

"Holy shit," Asha exclaimed when she saw him.

The Desecrator let out an ear-splitting shriek. The creature scratched his neck and Lucas saw that there were a pair of scars on the armor plating there. Fang marks from Toruk's brave bloodwolf, he assumed. But there was something else on his neck. A collar with a little blue light on it.

"Useful device," came the deep-throated metallic voice projected out of it. "The races have not spoken in so many years."

"Yeah," Asha called out. "And what do you want to talk about?"

The creature looked surprised.

"It is you. The other. Something so small. So dangerous. Intriguing."

Natalie's barrel never left the creature's head, and Asha had her Magnum pointed in the same location. Kiati and the other Guardian circled around to the sides of them, their own weapons drawn. Maston's leg lay a few feet in front of them like a fallen tree branch.

"Your assault here was brave. Foolish," the creature rumbled.

"Foolish?" Lucas said. "We've won the battle. Look around you."

It was true. In the streets below, the last of the Xalans were being systematically butchered by the Oni and the remaining Guardians. Some of the troops were fleeing out of the central gate, chased by a pack of bloodwolves, but an Oni sniper who had climbed the wall was picking them off as they reached the entrance. When he turned in their direction, Lucas could see the warrior wore the familiar carved mask of the Kal'din.

The Desecrator snorted.

"So long as I live, no battle is won."

"Well then," Lucas said. "We'll have to see about that."

He reached down to his belt and pressed a button on the detonator clipped there. He'd pulled the device off Maston before he'd emerged from behind the tower.

The charges in the comms hub detonated, and the entire building buckled from the blast. The Desecrator was momentarily thrown off balance by a section of the structure caving in near his feet. The fireball dissipated just as it reached him, but by that time, a hail of plasma was already heading his way from the four of them. He caught a few rounds in his armor plating before launching back into the air. His hands went behind his back and returned clutching a pair of enormous pistols, which discharged rounds at them at a furious pace. They were forced to roll out of the stream of shots and return fire as he looped around in the air, flying high over the street.

The Desecrator was now drawing fire from not only them but the other troops below. He turned his weapons toward the ground and shredded a pair of Oni leveling shots at him with ancient-looking power weapons. Curving around, he took a shot in the arm that caused him to drop one of his two guns. But with the second pistol he lined up a shot and blew the head off a Guardian on a second-tier rooftop.

His flight path shifted and became a beeline straight toward their group. In an instant he was on them, and Asha rolled just under his hooked claws as he passed by. The brown-skinned Guardian next to her wasn't so lucky. The claw caught him in the shoulder and he was hoisted off his feet and into the air as the Desecrator arced upward. A few flashes of movement several hundred feet up in the air, and the Desecrator released the soldier. His body eventually landed on the roof, deeply cratering the metal. His head followed a second or two later, and cracked the way an egg might if tossed from a similar height. Lucas felt a surge of nausea.

Immediately the Desecrator was diving, and swooped down toward them once more. This time, Asha was ready with her sword. The creature saw the blade at the last second, and swerved right to avoid it. He crashed into Kiati, who was pitched backward and tumbled off the roof. As the Desecrator flew away from them, Lucas and Asha rushed to the edge, breathless for what they would find. The adjacent building Kiati had landed on was only a few stories down. She was stirring, her armor apparently absorbing most of the impact, and in flash there were Oni swarming around her, attempting to help her up. Asha turned to Lucas. The pair were now the only ones left on the roof.

The Desecrator had landed in front of the cooling tower and now stood between them and the downed Maston on the other side. Their backs were to the edge of the rooftop, and a short ledge was the only barrier between them and a fall far worse than the one Kiati had just endured.

In a flash, the creature drew his remaining pistol like an otherworldly gunslinger. Lucas and Asha both fired a shot, their weapons already raised. Her revolver round went straight through the barrel of his weapon, causing it to explode in his hand. Lucas's shotgun blast peppered his torso at range and propelled him backward into the crumbling tower. Smoke rose from the smoldering spheres across his body, and the explosion of the gun had taken one of his fingers off.

"Enough of these toys!" he roared through his collar and thrust his wings forward with an incredible amount of force. Before either of them could get off another shot, they were flung backward through the air from the resulting gust. Lucas threw his arm out to catch Asha, who went diving off the roof, in the process dropping his rifle, which bounced away from him. They locked hands and Asha crashed against the side of the building, hanging over the edge. Lucas swung her upward, and the collective strength of his suit and muscles propelled her back over the lip and onto the rooftop once more. Looking down, Lucas saw that their guns were a solid five feet away. The Desecrator was already airborne and hurtling toward them on furiously beating translucent wings.

But there was something else flying toward them. Toruk hung suspended in midair, having launched himself out of his hiding place inside the destroyed cooling tower. He'd disappeared when the railgun first opened fire, but Lucas hadn't noticed until this moment. And neither had the Desecrator. As the red demon lunged toward them, Toruk leapt onto its back, driving his black-bladed spear down all the way through the creature's chest. Blood sprayed out of the armor plating as the Desecrator let out a piercing howl. He crashed to the roof and, as he did so, flexed his wings, which launched Toruk forward. Lucas reached for him, but the warrior sailed over the edge and dipped down out of sight as he fell. A scream was caught in Lucas's throat.

Asha was already on her feet and sprinting toward the Desecrator, who was struggling to get to his feet. She lunged at him with her sword, and he rolled to avoid the swing. Standing upright, he pulled the spear all the way through his chest and then whipped it around so that Asha barely had time to deflect it with her blade. He thrust forward and she backflipped over it, cutting off the head of the weapon. The Desecrator now held a rather useless metal pole. Lucas was on his feet and rushed over to see where Toruk had fallen.

Toruk was there all right, standing on top of the hull of the now functional prison ship that had caught him. The craft was rising quickly, and as it shot over the edge of the rooftop, its shadow engulfed all of them. The Desecrator looked up in surprise.

The foremost turret of the ship fired a blast that hit the creature directly in the chest. The resulting impact launched him off the far side of the building and he tumbled into the gray smoke below in complete silence.

Asha was knocked backward by the explosion, but she quickly regained her footing and ran with Lucas to the other side. The structures below were ablaze, and they couldn't see anything through the smoke.

"Is he dead?" Asha yelled over the roar of the prison ship's engines.

"I don't know," Lucas shouted back. "But we don't have time to find out."

That displeased Asha, who continued to scour the area, but there wasn't a trace of the beast.

Alpha broke through on their armor comm.

"Has the issue been dealt with?" he asked, as though he were troubleshooting a tech support call.

"For now," Lucas said.

"Come," Alpha continued. "It is time."

Lucas and Asha left the edge of the roof and ran back toward Maston, still sprawled unconscious behind the cooling tower. Lucas hooked his armor onto his back and carried the man like a rucksack as they walked toward the ship, which was now slowly turning around and lowering its exit bay ramp. Inside were a dozen or so Guardians, including the banged-up Kiati. They were the few who had survived the assault.

As they made their way inside, the ramp was raised and they started to ascend. Lucas peered out the window and saw the spaceport in ruins below. The hangar was completely annihilated. The other structures within were almost entirely consumed in flame. The Oni swarmed the street like ants and would mop up any remaining troops before anyone discovered they'd taken the base, though the smoke would soon be spotted now.

Reinforcements hadn't come. They'd pulled it off. The loudest covert assault of all time.

The forest disappeared beneath them and the curved edge of Makari could soon be seen from the viewscreen as they continued to rise. Kiati was tending to Maston, and Asha had passed out sitting against the bay doors. Lucas felt like he was about to collapse as well.

In the rear of room, he saw Alpha playing with some controls with Toruk next to him, having slipped inside the ship after he landed on it.

"What are you doing?" Lucas asked.

"Sending our friend home," Alpha replied, typing coordinates into the display in front of him.

"You don't want to come back with us?" Lucas asked, turning to Toruk. "To Mol'taavi? You could help us."

Toruk shook his head.

"Khas'to need Toruk. Oni need Toruk. Must protect. Must protect until big Mol'taavi army come. Kill all sky demon."

Someone had filled him in on their plan. Lucas was worried the Oni would think they were abandoning them by leaving.

"We will come back, Toruk. Thank you for giving us your White Spirit. She will be the one to help us end this. She will give you your planet back."

Lucas didn't have the heart to tell him it would be a full decade before anything resembling an army could even reach Makari because of the time it took to synthesize new white null cores. He wondered if he'd ever see the man again.

"You not fail. I know you secret," he said as the door slid up in front of him and he ducked into a cramped-looking cockpit.

"Another secret?" Lucas asked with an eyebrow raised. "What have you figured out this time?"

Toruk smiled.

"Goodbye Saato. Valli keep you strong," and he nodded toward the sleeping Asha across the bay.

They weren't emissaries of the gods. They were the gods?

Lucas turned back to say something, but the door had already slid shut. Toruk was gone.

Alpha tapped a few more virtual keys, and with a muted whooshing sound, the escape pod was jettisoned from the ship. Its engines kicked in a few thousand meters out, and it sped toward the jungle.

"A champion of three planets now, it seems," Alpha said, turning toward him.

Lucas smiled weakly, but felt so dizzy he almost fell over on the spot.

"You should attend to that," Alpha said, motioning downward.

Lucas followed his finger and saw a smoldering hole in the plating of his leg armor. He'd been shot? He hadn't even noticed. Once the injury was spotted, his brain forced him to feel the pain, and he sank down to the ground. He was tired. So tired.

17

The trip back was far less intense than the journey to get there had been. They had to fend off a pair of reconnaissance fighters near one of the outer planets that spotted their escape, but true reinforcements couldn't reach them in time before the null core was fired. Zeta's men on the ground reported that it took a full hour for the rest of the planet to realize the spaceport had been wiped out. They were long gone by that time, lost in a tunnel of space-time on their way back to Sora.

When they finally managed to get long-range comms back online, they got word to Tannon Vale about the relative success of their mission, and that they were en route home. He told them that they'd been presumed dead for weeks, though that information had been kept private. Back home, the planet was still reeling from the Xalan assault on Kollux, and intelligence indicated they were keen to strike again soon. "Hurry back," he said. There was much to do.

There were only Xalan sleeping pods onboard. Those were declared strictly off limits after Asha recounted her side-effects from prolonged use of the devices, and they made do on the floor with fur blankets provided by the Oni as parting gifts.

In the end, only eighteen Guardians had survived the mission. The unit had never suffered a loss so devastating, though they'd never been assigned a task so monumental. Lucas and Asha trained with the remaining soldiers to keep in shape as Maston barked orders at them. The man could do an impressive number of exercises with only one leg.

Each night the group gathered to tell war stories about their fallen comrades. Lucas laughed as Kiati recounted a time that Silo crawled through a murky swamp during an assassination mission in the Ruined Marshes, only to discover it was the dumping grounds for the enemy's latrines. The rest of the Guardians found it hilarious when Asha recounted the story of how she and Lucas had first met on Earth, where she'd put a bullet in him after he unwisely tried to help her in Georgia. Lucas didn't understand what was so funny about that one. His shoulder still ached some nights.

Lucas's leg had mostly mended, even though the plasma round had eaten away to his bone by the time he managed to treat it. One final souvenir from the Desecrator. Lucas knew the beast wasn't dead. Monsters like that didn't die. He saw its burning eyes far too often in his dreams.

The most heartening part of the voyage home was seeing Alpha and Zeta reconnect. He'd never seen Alpha like this before, lighthearted, almost carefree. The two passed hours fixing up parts of the old ship like they were rebuilding a classic hot rod. They did sleep in separate quarters, however.

Asha had taken quite a liking to Zeta herself. The two spent many afternoons wandering the cramped halls of the ship, talking at length about the resistance, life on Xala, and what Alpha was like in his youth. Lucas only heard bits and pieces of these conversations, and Asha wouldn't fill him in on the details. "Girl talk," she said reproachfully when he inquired.

Lucas had gotten a chance to talk with Alpha more than he'd been able to since they'd arrived on Sora. His high spirits with Zeta around had made him amiable.

"So what are you going to do when this is all over?" Lucas asked him one night on the bridge as the two of them both battled insomnia. They were playing an old Xalan game on the central holotable. Alpha couldn't pronounce it in English, so Lucas just took to calling it "Squares." It involved moving holographic cubes around, blocking and parrying your opponent's advances. Lucas always lost, ending the games with no more cubes to push around, but he was getting better over time.

"Even with our current actions, the likelihood of the war ending in our lifetime is remote," Alpha replied.

Lucas rolled his eyes.

"Humor me. If it did end, what would you do?"

Alpha looked out the viewscreen for a minute. The only light in the room came from the table in front of them. They could hear footsteps on other decks; the walls and floors of the old ship were thinner than most. Lucas guessed there weren't many who could sleep soundly after what they'd experienced on Makari.

"I should like to continue the research my father began many years ago."

"What research?" Lucas asked. He grabbed three of his cubes and flung them toward one of Alpha's. The Xalan's piece disintegrated instantly.

"True terraforming," Alpha replied. "The rejuvenation of a planet."

"Doesn't that already exist?"

"No," Alpha said. "Artificially raising temperature a few degrees, or forcing plants to grow through twisting their genetics is not what I speak of here. Rather, I refer to a process that could take a desolate planet and turn it into a place like Sora. Like old Earth."

"Or Xala."

Alpha nodded. He swept his arm across the floating game sphere and a wave of his cubes advanced forward, crushing a half dozen of Lucas's own.

"That would indeed be a crowning achievement. Millions of years ago, Xala was such a place, but it would require an exceptional amount of effort and an unknowable amount of science to revert it back to that state."

"Well," Lucas said, "if anyone can do it, I'm sure it's you."

"Perhaps," Alpha said quietly. "Though war remains a focus for the foreseeable future. Perhaps my own children can see the vision come to pass someday."

Lucas raised his eyebrows. Glancing at the board, he saw that his cube count was starting to get dangerously low.

"Thinking about starting a family?"

Alpha sighed.

"Again, a lofty idea in our present circumstances. But for a long while now I have looked upon you and Asha and Noah and now your new child, and have . . . desired such an opportunity for myself. I have been alone too long."

"And who's the lucky lady?" Lucas asked, attempting to hide a grin.

Alpha chortled and took the opportunity to destroy another pair of Lucas's game pieces.

"Do not attempt to be coy. You have knowledge of my attraction to [garbled]. To Zeta."

"How's that going?"

"It is a bridge that must be built from both sides, though it may take some time. We have both endured much. The treatment Zeta suffered after capture is . . . to use the Earth word, inhumane. Unconscionable."

He paused. In the pale blue glow of the room Lucas could see a deep sadness in his eyes.

"I see the woman I once knew, but often she feels like a shadow of who she was. She likely thinks the same of me."

"Just give it some time. You have decades to catch up on."

"And yet sometimes it feels like there is nothing to say."

Alpha absentmindedly swirled one of his cubes around with his finger, seemingly pondering his next move.

"You and Asha. What binds you together?"

Lucas leaned back in his chair to consider that.

"At first it might have been, what was the phrase you used back on the Ark? 'Proximity and duress.' But it became more than that. It's a kind of connection you can't verbalize. It just . . . is."

"That is most unhelpful."

Lucas laughed.

"Sorry, but it's something you have to find on your own. It took her almost killing me three times before it finally clicked."

"I would like to avoid a similar path toward such a revelation."

"Well, I'd hardly say we're the model. And I'm no expert on the inner workings of Xalan relationships."

Lucas advanced the majority of his remaining pieces, crushing one of Alpha's strongholds on the spherical board. The move caught him off guard, and he was visibly surprised.

"Emotion is weakness on my planet. Other than anger of course. That's what we have been taught since birth. Here and now, Zeta and I exist as two of the only truly 'free' Xalans to live in thousands of years. Traitors are imprisoned or executed. They do not escape the way we have. There is nowhere to go."

Alpha brought up a secondary display, checking on the status of the ship before quickly closing it.

"The idea that we answer to no one is liberating, but also terrifying."

Alpha flicked a few of his cubes forward. Reaching a certain point of the board, they combined into a single pyramid. Lucas was in trouble now. Alpha continued his thought.

"If the war ends, I worry my people may not understand freedom; they have been subservient for so long. A vacuum may be created that another corrupt body could fill. They will need strong, but kind leadership."

Lucas folded his arms.

"Well, I nominate you."

Alpha scoffed.

"I despise politics, and am far from capable enough to be thrust into a role such as that. If only my father still lived . . ."

He waved his claw in the air.

"But enough of such talk. You have caused me to ignore our present circumstances and speculate on an all-too-ideal future. Such fantasizing is not helpful."

Alpha's pyramid advanced and crushed the last of Lucas's cubes. Another loss.

"Have faith in the plan," Lucas said as he made another tally mark in Alpha's column to recognize his latest defeat. "You'll get your future."

"How you have endured so much, yet continue to have such an attitude is perplexing."

Lucas shrugged and tossed aside the game board so that there was nothing a but a dull blue glow in between them.

"If I don't, then all of this has been for nothing. Every injury suffered, every friend lost. I'll make it mean something if it kills me."

"It might," Alpha said wearily.

"I know."

That night Lucas walked back to the cramped cell he and Asha had made their quarters. She was asleep, curled up in a pile of crimson and black furs. A few of them belonged to Guardians who hadn't made it back onboard after the assault on the spaceport. It was freezing in the cell block, as it was most places on the ship. The craft was so old that nothing worked right, despite Alpha's constant tinkering. A pair of Guardians once got stuck in their cell for a solid six hours when the door mechanism jammed. They finally just had to cut them out with a plasma torch. A female Guardian had lost the tip of her index finger to a faulty ray shield meant for emergency lockdowns only. A half second earlier and she would have likely been cut in half. The prison ship was something of a deathtrap, but if it got them home, none of them cared.

Lucas pulled the blankets over him, but couldn't stop shivering in the icy room. He could see his breath in the dim light, and curled up close to Asha, attempting to siphon some of her body heat. This was no place for romance, but some nights they blocked out their surroundings completely and made do. Lucas pretended they were back in the palace penthouse on Sora, wrapped in smooth sheets in a room stocked with unlimited food and drink and priceless treasures. It was a pleasant thought that stayed with him until he drifted off to sleep and the nightmares began again.

After another month, Sora was finally within reach. All of them gathered on the bridge as they emerged on the other side of the space-time tunnel. The green-and-blue haze slowly faded, replaced by a sea of stars in the viewscreen. Within minutes, a sizable chunk of the Soran fleet had encircled them, bringing cheers from the Guardians. The ships were there to ensure the Xalans hadn't followed them back, and to escort them through the system to Sora, just in case. The blackness of space behind them revealed no unwanted pursuers, and after a period of tense waiting, they set a course for the homeworld.

Maston stood upright on the bridge next to Lucas, which was impressive given his injury. He'd made do with a crutch for the first month, but eventually Alpha hacked together a robotic leg for him from spare parts around the ship, and had done the same for the other injured Guardians onboard who had lost limbs in the conflict. Maston's appendage was hardly state-of-the-art tech, with most of the pieces rusted and the wiring constantly shorting out. But it was better than the alternative, and through a large amount of effort he'd mastered walking on the thing. Lucas actually saw him break out in a sprint a few days prior. Soon he'd get an official robotic replacement for Alpha's makeshift device, with an organic limb to be spliced onto him a few weeks later, created from his own DNA. They'd started growing it for him as soon as they were able to reestablish contact with the planet in transit, and the Guardians all logged their various injuries that would need treatment upon their return. Over the past three months, Lucas's leg had healed well, and though Asha had had a bout with some strain of pneumonia a few weeks back, the pair were in relatively good health for a change.

Maston's gaze was fixed out the viewscreen as the fleet of enormous ships escorted their tin can back to Sora. Since Lucas had rescued him twice back on Makari, once from the Dead City and again after the battle that took his leg, the two had formed a bond that vaguely resembled friendship. It was hard to believe this was the man who had ordered him beaten nearly to death on the voyage there. Then again, Lucas was also enamored with a woman who had tried to kill him on at least three occasions. It seemed to be how all his relationships started in the current state of the galaxy.

"Looking forward to becoming whole again?" Lucas asked, nodding toward Maston's metal appendage.

Maston looked at it and sank down a bit so the coils tightened and a hydraulic contraction mechanism hissed.

"It would take more than just a leg," he said sullenly.

"It's hard to believe this could be over soon," Lucas said.

Maston scoffed.

"The war? You can't still be that naive."

"Why can't it? It's a solid plan."

A large ship drifted in front of them. It had twelve rear engines, which glowed white hot and caused the surrounding stars to twinkle rapidly.

"As much as I no longer doubt the sincerity of our new Xalan allies, putting this final stage of their idea into action would be more difficult than anything that's come before. Impossible, in fact."

He broke his gaze out the window and turned to Lucas.

"I spent three months with Alpha and Zeta, trying to come up with a workable plan to infiltrate Xalan central command on their homeworld. There is none."

"Why not?" Lucas asked.

"The building is a fortress. The city is a fortress. The planet is a fortress. If we had the ability to infiltrate Xala, don't you think we would have done so by this point?"

Lucas supposed that was true. It was odd it hadn't occurred to him.

"Perhaps Zeta will be of some tactical significance to us in decoding the enemy's transmissions, but this idea that we could broadcast Alpha's message to all of Xala without it being intercepted or interrupted is merely a fantasy. It cannot be done outside their central broadcasting unit, and accessing it is simply not in the realm of possibility."

"I've had to readjust my definition of 'impossible' over the last few years," Lucas said.

"Believe what you will," Maston said, "but the facts dictate a different course."

Maston noticed Lucas growing annoyed.

"But in any case, I will be proud to fight along with the Earthborn in coming battles. You've proven yourselves . . . adaptable since your arrival. Whether it's talent or luck, I'll take either on my side."

Forever the charmer.

Up ahead, a bright blue ball came into view among the stars. Home. Or the closest thing they had to it.

18

Lucas stood uncomfortably with his arms crossed behind his back. He was in Guardian dress blues with a winged badge on his collar that Maston had personally pinned on him, despite their past differences. The commander stood at his left with Asha on his right. Alpha loomed next to her, and there were eighteen other Guardians standing in similar poses further down the line. Camera bots orbited them like satellites. The event was in a small, ornate room in the upper floors of the palace, but it was being broadcast to billions.

He stared into the kind eyes of Talis Vale in front of him. She placed a medallion around his neck. It was silver with an engraving of the visage some long-dead warrior king.

"I present to Lucas the Earthborn the Mark of Ayon, for extraordinary valor facing overwhelming odds."

Lucas bowed slightly and the metal clinked against one of her rings as she drew her hand away. He briefly returned her soft smile, and she moved to present a similar medal to Asha. Maston already wore his.

The event was being beamed out to all of Sora—the return of the conquering heroes from their mission to one of Xala's colonies, the first ever attempted. Talis said it would help lift the spirits of the planet, which had been suffering from the recent loss of Kollux over the time they were away. Details of their mission were kept vague, and the people of Sora were content to know that the Guardians and the Earthborn had rescued a high-value target critical to the war effort and made contact with a new strain of Soran warriors, the Oni. The crowds watched in amazement as armor-cam footage was released onto the Stream showing their siege of the spaceport and bits of their duel with the fearsome Desecrator. Lucas unwillingly shuddered every time he saw a flash of the crimson creature onscreen.

The dead had already received their medallions, one rank higher than the distinction the living now wore. They'd been sent home to their families along with their Finals. The names and faces of the deceased floated behind them like ghosts. Lucas turned back to glance at the hologram.

Jat Corvin
Elys Sonotro
Mardok Axon
Yanna Hollus
Sol'tanni Silo

Lucas finally knew his first name. He turned back to face the cameras. His stomach felt flipped upside down, but he maintained his composure. The Earthborn losing it at his victory ceremony wouldn't be very good press. Lucas swallowed the lump in his throat and maintained his stone-cold stare straight ahead. He had to let go of Silo now, no matter how good a friend he had been, or how horrifying the circumstances of his death. Far too often when Lucas closed his eyes, he saw that red mist in the jungle, and the half a body that lay below it.

Talis lay a medallion around the last Guardian's neck. The crowds watching around the world erupted in cheers they could not hear.

It was surreal to be back on Sora after their latest journey to a new kind of hell. The jungles of Makari had proved even more treacherous than the wastelands of Earth, and it was yet another ordeal that would never leave Lucas. Even in the comforts of their palace quarters, Lucas still itched at his Mol'tok sting. He still saw the yellow eyes of the bloodwolf. The red ones of the Desecrator.

But there was at least one pleasant distraction from all of it. One ray of hope that burst into the room like a sunbeam.

"Lucas!" Noah squealed with proper pronunciation. "Asha!"

The child had grown immensely in the months they were gone. He was easily almost five inches taller, and the giant's blood in him was starting to show, as he was noticeably large for his age now. Noah no longer wobbled but strode forward sure-footedly. Lucas and Asha knelt down to wrap him in their arms. Behind him, Malorious Auran and two caretakers smiled at the touching reunion. Golden locks spilled onto Lucas's hands. Brilliant sky-blue eyes gazed into his. The child had been well cared for in their absence, that much was obvious.

They sat for a solid two hours as Noah regaled them with lengthy tales of his adventures over the past few months. Where there used to be mostly babbling, the child now spoke in full, coherent sentences, seemingly beyond the usual capabilities of a not-yet-two-year-old. Lucas realized that the Soran education methods of the young likely allowed them to develop cognitively at a quicker pace than children on Earth. He thought back to Noah's English and Soran lessons onboard the Ark in the captain's chair. Whatever the education process was here, it was remarkable to see in practice.

Noah gave them detailed descriptions of all his new friends from the palace day care and told them about various field trips the group had taken to cities and animal preserves. Of all the children he mentioned, there was one name, Kyra, that came up in nearly every story. Lucas remembered meeting Auran's shy granddaughter in the nursery. It seemed like an eternity ago.

Noah now spoke Soran nearly as fluently as the pair of them, though his teachers ensured that he was still keeping up with his English. They had no intention of being the ones who would let a dying tongue of a lost civilization meet its end.

Noah still had the burns on his arm and shoulder, sustained in the Norwegian nursery fire. He was deemed too young for the sorts of extensive skin grafts that would replace the damage, but it was clear he wasn't hindered by the injury. All three of them wore wounds from Earth. A family tradition.

Eventually Auran returned to the room, interrupting Noah's retelling of a particularly exciting wildlife preserve he'd been to the previous week.

"Whenever you are ready," the old man said. "They're waiting downstairs."

It was time to truly make their family whole.

Birth Day.

The event's meaning was more or less the same as it had been on Earth. "More" because a child was indeed being born, "less" because it was coming out of a fetal tank rather than a biological mother. Because of the Soran method of childbirth, the event could be a friendly gathering rather than a hysterical hospital visit.

Their child was ready to meet the world.

It had been a year since conception aboard the Ark, the result of two doomed souls grasping at comfort before they met their assured end. But today Lucas and Asha's bond was stronger than ever, held together by more than just the horrific events they'd endured as a couple.

A small group had gathered in one of the palace's many luxurious halls, this one with portraits of young princes and princesses adorning the walls from centuries and millennia past. Talis knew that, though the Earthborn were public figures, they still needed a bit of privacy. As such, the event was invitation only. In the room were Auran, Maston, Kiati, Tannon, and Talis herself, in addition to the three of them. Noah fidgeted uncomfortably in his miniature formal attire. A few other members of the palace staff were milling about nearby, medical personnel, royal guards, and the like. It was of course an event the world would love to see, the First Son of Sora, direct offspring of the famed Earthborn, but they would have to wait until the child was publicly unveiled later. It was respected tradition that Birth Days were private affairs. At least the very first one.

Maston had a new leg, fashioned from impenetrable fibro-steel and far more functional than Alpha's makeshift offering. Kiati still lacked an eye, but she had a fashionable metal plate where a bloody bandage used to be. Their organic replacement parts were still being grown somewhere in labs off-continent. Each wore their Guardian dress uniforms from the ceremony earlier. Lucas, Asha, and Noah had been given more traditional clothes for the occasion. The family usually wore green on the day, a universally recognized symbol of new life.

In the middle of them all sat their child, a little boy helpless and unaware of the chaos he was being born into. The palace was a nice facade that would protect him from the insanity outside, but sooner or later, he'd have to come to grips with being born into a war zone, as all Soran children had. Noah too, for that matter. Lucas didn't want the pair of them to endure the same terrors he had. He would fight so his children wouldn't have to. *His children.*

It was the first time in a long while he was truly thinking about the magnitude of restarting a family. He'd always been Noah's caretaker, but now, an actual father? It seemed like a part of him that was too rusted and damaged to start working again. He'd botched his first chance at being a good parent back on Earth before the war. Who was to say he could do any better this time around, in circumstances far more harrowing?

Lucas had tuned out most of what Auran was saying. Some ceremonial speech about the child being a gift to the world and a reflection of his valiant parents. As much as he admired Asha, he hoped the child wouldn't have her seemingly unquenchable thirst for blood. Though he wasn't exactly one to throw stones in that regard.

"And what is the name this child shall have?" Auran asked as he turned toward them. Noah had his arms pressed up against side of the tank and was looking up in wonder at his little brother.

"Erik," Lucas said, snapping back to attention. It had been a topic of much discussion during the long days aboard the prison ship on their return voyage. They'd finally settled on Erik as an unmistakable Earth name. It was Lucas's grandfather's name, and his father once told him that it meant "powerful" in the former tongue of their family. He'd only seen pictures of his granddad, but the burly man standing proudly atop a smoking Panzer tank seemed to fit that description. Erik would have to have the same sort of strength to survive the world he now entered.

As Auran finished his remarks, the medical attendants approached the tank. After rifling through a few controls, the viscous liquid began to drain. The child was gently laid to rest on a gel cushion at the bottom of the tank as the last of the substance was flushed out, and the tiny tubes attached to various points on his body began to detach themselves. Mild heat lamps dried his wet skin and in under a minute, the process was complete. A tiny figure sat curled in a ball as the glass surrounding him sank down into the base of the tank.

"Embrace your child," Auran said, motioning to Asha. She glanced around the room nervously and was met with small nods and broad smiles. Even Kiati had cracked a grin. Lucas saw Asha's hands waver as she approached the baby in the miniature techno-manger. He hadn't seen her this terrified in any battle they'd fought.

She picked up Erik and cradled him inside a cloth provided by one of the nearby silvercoats. A few seconds later, a tiny yet shrill cry pierced the room.

"The lungs of a commanding leader!" Auran said, drawing some laughter from the attendees. Asha jerked her head toward Lucas, motioning him to come over. Lucas felt lightheaded, but found he was smiling uncontrollably. When he reached the bundle in her arms, he gazed into the face of his child for the first time. All the anger, the anguish, the pain melted away in an instant.

Erik had wispy hair colored brown like Lucas's. His features were impossible to place from either parent at such a young age, but his skin was just a touch darker than Lucas's, hinting at Asha's genes. The child had blue eyes, as most newborns did, and they'd have to wait and see whether they'd turn green or slate gray.

Lucas suddenly felt very mortal. Was there any way he would ever get to see Erik or Noah grow up? The war had demanded so much of his blood so far. Would it finally consume him as their plan reached its final stages? Lucas looked around the room to the smiling faces of the other soldiers present. *Just enjoy the moment*, he told himself, and he rekindled his own smile to mask his unease.

The week that followed had Lucas return to a life he'd long thought left behind. It was 2900, the middle of the night, and Erik was crying again in the floating monitor that hovered over their bed in the palace suite. The child squealed and squirmed in his square, plush, crib-like enclosure in an adjacent room.

"I'll go," Asha said as she rolled out of bed and stumbled toward the doorway. Of course they had a team of servants and palace-issue nannies at their beck and call who could be calming Erik for them, but the two of them decided they wanted to do things the old-fashioned way. Neither knew when they'd be shipping out again, so the goal was to spend as much time with Noah and Erik as possible before they left. They didn't know if they had days, weeks, or months, but were determined to make every moment count. But the moments that took place at 2900 weren't exactly the most enjoyable.

Lucas was awake now and couldn't fall back asleep. On the monitor, Asha rocked Erik and was softly singing to him in French.

Un jour nous serons tous partis
Mais les berceuses restent encore et encore . . .
Elles ne meurent jamais
C'est ainsi que toi
Et moi
Serons

Lucas couldn't help but smile, despite his exhaustion. Asha had quite a beautiful singing voice, and this week had been the first time he'd ever heard it. There hadn't been much occasion for singing the past few years, he supposed.

He got out of bed, walked over to the kitchen area of the suite, and sat down at the broad stone table. Sliding the top of it open, he reached his hand inside the surface and pulled out a blue vial. *Refrigerated drinks inside the furniture. The wonders of modern technology.* He flung the container back and the liquid tumbled down his throat. His nerves started to settle within seconds. Staring around the room, moonlight glinted off the jewels of nearby artifacts.

"Bit late for a nightcap," came Asha's voice from behind him. "Or a bit early, I suppose." She was always able to get Erik down almost instantly. He had far more difficulty.

"Trouble sleeping," Lucas grumbled, staring at the empty vial.

"The kid?" she asked.

"The war," he replied.

"I'll drink to that," she said, reaching into the table for a vial herself and inhaling its contents.

"Not one of their better offerings," she said, wincing.

"What song was that?" he asked.

"One my mother used to sing to me when I was young. Haven't heard it in twenty years, but haven't forgotten it either."

"Your mother spoke French? I figured you picked it up in school."

"She was an amazing woman," Asha said with a faint smile. "In a way I'm glad she passed before the world went to shit."

Lucas spun the empty vial around on the table with his finger. Asha spoke again.

"What about your family? You never talk about your parents."

"Not much to say, really. My father was a Marine, same as his father."

Lucas drummed the table.

"But not you. Why?" Asha asked.

Lucas laughed sharply.

"I didn't believe in violence," he said, and Asha had to laugh at that as well.

"A group of my friends enlisted after 9/11, but I couldn't. I didn't believe more death was the answer. My father practically disowned me for it. Called it 'shirking my duty' to the country. To our family."

Lucas stopped drumming his fingers on the hard surface and looked up.

"A few died in the desert. A few more once they got back here and couldn't handle civilian life. The rest who stayed got cut down during the invasion, I assume."

"What about your parents?" Asha asked.

"They were in Chicago," Lucas said, and the look on Asha's face showed she knew what that meant. The city was one of the first to be completely annihilated by Xalans.

"Well, he'd be proud of you now," Asha said.

Lucas shook his head.

"Too late for that. I was an embarrassment. He felt like my wife's brother was more of a son to him than I was. All because he wore the uniform until the day he died. Do you know the last thing he said to me?"

Asha remained silent.

"'I'd take a dead hero for a son over a living coward.'"

Lucas thought back to the moment he'd heard that sentence spoken at the end of a heated argument. He'd hung up immediately rather than say one more word into the receiver to his father after that. Lucas had suffered many insults over the years, but none had cut more deeply.

"I never spoke to him again."

"He sounds like a sadistic bastard," Asha said, refusing to mask her disdain.

"Only on days that ended in 'y,'" Lucas said, smirking, shoving the memory from his mind.

"You're a lot of things, but a coward sure as shit isn't one of them," she said.

Lucas scoffed.

"And it only took murdering a few hundred humans and aliens to prove it. I suppose I should thank him for the genetic predisposition. What's your excuse?"

Asha smiled broadly.

"I'm about 80 percent sociopath."

"Only eighty?" Lucas said, eyebrow raised.

"Well, I need the other twenty to do this," she said as she leaned across the table and kissed him. Lucas forgot about crying children, his father, and the endless war. He had her, and that was all that mattered now.

It was a few days later when they were summoned to the Earth Archive by Keeper Auran. They walked down the palace halls, glancing at the wall-mounted Stream feed as they passed. It showed clips of their medal ceremony and a well-dressed newsman reported on a rumor that the First Son of Sora had indeed had his Birth Day, but it was being shielded from the public. Lucas was more interested in another story that showed video footage of a tranquil Hex Tulwar in front of some sort of tribunal. He actually seemed to be wearing a sly grin, even as every pair of eyes in the room was staring daggers at him, including Mars Maston, who could be seen seated and seething in the background. Lucas waved the Stream over to his wrist communicator so he could continue watching as they continued onward. A woman's voice spoke over the video.

"Public support for Hex Tulwar's Fourth Order resistance movement is at an all-time low after evidence surfaced that Cleric Tulwar colluded with Xalan spies to execute the assault on the Grand Palace this year. His allies in the region have withdrawn their support for his cause, and even inside Rhylos only 41 percent of the population still considers him their legitimate leader, and a mere 19 percent approve of his recent involvement with the Xalans. Since Tulwar's capture, SDI forces have dismantled dozens of Fourth Order sleeper cells and hidden bases after decrypting a Xalan data drive found during the rescue of Asha the Earthborn."

Asha scowled.

"Rescue, huh? They don't mention that I killed half the soldiers in there myself."

"And Alpha gets no credit for being the one to unearth all that intelligence. I guess life's just not fair."

The broadcaster continued. A standing figure in a white tunic was gesturing at Tulwar in the video. The newswoman continued.

"Cleric Tulwar has been found guilty of treason, collusion, kidnapping, and murder and will be executed in a month's time. Until then, he remains imprisoned at a secure location."

Lucas glanced down and thought the "secure location" was likely the palace dungeon several miles below ground. Maston had told him there was no more secure prison on the planet, and only a few of the most dangerous war criminals were kept in the cells there. Lucas wondered if they had public executions on Sora, or if they'd grown too civilized for such a thing. Tulwar was certainly a special case. Lucas pictured an energy rifle firing squad on the promenade, led by Mars Maston. *Tulwar deserves as much*, Lucas thought as he remembered the way Corinthia Vale's prismatic eyes looked when the light had left them.

At last they reached the Earth Archive and the wide doors slid open in front of them. They were waved in by a friendly attendant Lucas had seen a few times now, and the place looked exactly as it had when they'd last left it. Rumor had it eventually the contents would be moved off-site and turned into a public museum. They were of course allowed to keep anything they wanted to save before that time.

They found Auran in the books section, and he was flipping through the virtual pages of Isaac Asimov's *Foundation*, which were being projected out of its pedestal.

"Your culture produced fascinating literature," he said as he saw them approach. "I should very much wish to visit Earth some day and find more like it."

"I doubt anyone will be doing much sightseeing there any time soon," Lucas said. "Last I checked, Alpha said the coolest temperature there should be about 250 degrees by now."

Auran sighed.

"Such is the destructive nature of the Xalans, I suppose. Won't you come with me?"

He motioned for them to follow him toward a door on the other end of the room Lucas had seen before. The one marked "11."

"What is—" Lucas began, but Auran interrupted him.

"I haven't been entirely forthcoming about my role in the Vale administration. It is true I am presently its Keeper and your ward, but I was once a scientist within these walls. The most prominent geneticist of all of Sora for a time, in fact, if I'm allowed to boast. I developed the Guardian program, which was a way to bolster an ancient protective order of our people with the strength, speed, and intelligence they'd need to survive the most harrowing missions in our current war. They have saved many lives over the years, and your presence here after your recent ordeal indicates they continue to do so to this day."

Lucas glanced at Asha, who cocked her head. *Where is this going?*

"My masterpiece was a personal project for Talis Vale herself."

"Corinthia," Lucas said slowly. Auran nodded.

"With an unlimited budget, I created a Soran above all others. One who was very nearly perfect, a remarkable display of biology."

Auran's voice became grave, his eyes downcast.

"I mourned her senseless death like we all did, not just because she was my priceless work of art, but because she'd grown into a lovely person and would have been an inspiring ruler someday. She felt more like a daughter to me than a few of my own children, in fact. My heart will forever remain heavy with her passing."

He waved his hand dismissively.

"But enough history; I simply wanted to give you a sampling of my credentials. Hopefully it will assure you that I am up to the task at hand."

"What task at hand?" Asha asked, her eyes narrow.

When they reached the entryway, a scanner swept over Auran and a green light shone above them. The doors opened.

"You remember your old friends," he said with a mischievous grin. "The ones we don't talk about."

Inside the room were eleven familiar bodies. Lucas had been right; they were in fact keeping the brain-dead humans from Earth on ice here. All were now wearing skintight pressurized suits, and the liquid in which they were suspended was lime green. Below each of them, they still had a floating globe of Earth showing which country Alpha had plucked them from.

"Your scientist friend explained to me about the crash and the power loss, how all of them came to lose brain functionality. Tragic, really."

"So, what," Asha said, "you're going to Frankenstein them back to life?"

"Aha! I have read that story!" Auran exclaimed. "A fascinating tale of imagined science from your planet. But no. Even though our medicine improves upon your own, there is no way for us to wake these sleeping travelers. We could grow them entirely new brains, but they would not be who they were, and such practices are illegal and dangerous in any case."

Lucas walked over to a young girl from Iran. She had flowing dark hair that floated in the tank like seaweed. Her eyes were shut. Lucas paced around the room and did a quick check of their maps. Six females from China, Iran, Brazil, the Philippines, Australia, and Denmark. Five males from Japan, Chile, Greece, France, and Zimbabwe. Lucas instinctively touched the scar on his abdomen, where the vital organs of the sixth male, a young man from Russia, lay.

"Our tour is not yet over," Auran said, walking toward the back of the room. A door opened and he stepped inside a small tube-like lift. Asha and Lucas joined him. The doors shut and they began ascending rapidly.

"You have to understand that when we lost contact with the Spear on Makari, we thought you were dead. We were planning on getting your blessing for Project 11, but in your absence, we did what we had to in order to ensure the survival of your 'human' race."

Lucas was confused.

"What did you do, Malorious?"

"Oh god," Asha whispered, clearly just having come to some sort of realization.

The doors opened and Lucas understood.

The room before them was far bigger than the one they'd just been in, and placed symmetrically every eight feet or so was a tank like the one their son Erik had recently emerged from. In each enclosure was a tiny fetus, looking no more than a month or two old. Lucas walked breathlessly through the tanks and, making a quick count in his head, found there were thirty-six placed around the room in total. There were other scientists milling about, casting worried glances their way as they checked readouts on the tanks.

"You're *breeding* them?" Asha exclaimed. "What in the holy hell . . ."

"First you need to understand something," Auran said, attempting to calm them. "If we did not do this, with or without you, your sub-species would likely not survive past this generation."

Asha's eyes widened as she had another epiphany. "Wait, none of these are *ours*, are they?"

Lucas's stomach iced over as he considered the possibility.

Auran vigorously shook his head. "Of course not, we would never . . . Not without your permission."

Lucas breathed an internal sigh of relief. Asha breathed an external one. Auran continued.

"These are the descendents of the twelve passengers that accompanied you on your journey. A single pairing for each."

"Twelve?" Lucas asked.

"I was made aware of the ordeal with the specimen who sacrificed his life to ensure your survival, but your scientist preserved his genetic material, and so his offspring are represented here as well. For some reason, we're still calling it Project 11 regardless."

"I don't understand," Lucas said. "Why do this?"

Auran walked over to one of the tanks and put his hand on the glass. The object inside was just starting to look human.

"Study of your genetics revealed that, though you are like us, you are also *not* like us. It is a complex issue, but suffice it to say your DNA and genes have variations from ours. Regardless of our origins, we have evolved in different, subtle ways over the years."

"So what's the problem?" Asha asked, still absorbing the room.

"Early experiments showed that lab-created specimens using human and Soran DNA resulted in catastrophic failure. The offspring didn't live past a week in the faux-uteri, and data shows that the mother's life would have been terminated as well shortly after conception. This happened when either race was the mother or father, and occurred in 100 percent of all test cases."

"What does that mean?" Lucas asked.

"It appears Sorans and humans can never produce offspring together, despite our apparent similarities. The exact reasons why are still a mystery to me and my team, but the fact exists regardless of our ignorance. In short, to reproduce in the future, it would be up to the pair of you alone. Needless to say that brings . . . problems."

"Inbreeding," Asha said with disgust, thinking one step ahead.

"Precisely," Auran said. "That practice has genetic, sociological, and psychological issues that could prove disastrous for future offspring. And so Project 11 was conceived to ensure the human race does in fact live on safely."

"So what are we looking at here?" Lucas asked.

"Eighteen males and eighteen females, the first round of production, so to speak. The idea is not to mass produce humans, but to create an initial pool just large enough so that inbreeding will be a non-issue. These will be the founding fathers and mothers of the human race. Your sons are included in that as well of course, along with any other children you may voluntarily produce in the future."

"What are you doing to them?" asked Asha. "You're not going to make them hulking freaks like the Guardians are you?"

Auran shook his head.

"No. They are developing naturally, and your friend Alpha ensured that his 'collection' included physically ideal representations of your race. All the parents are in fantastic health, as are their children so far. Only preventive genes for disease and defect are being introduced into their systems, the way they were with young Erik. They require no further enhancement modification, as

Kyneth knows we don't want them to be soldiers. We have plenty of those."

"I get it," Asha said reluctantly. "But I'm having enough trouble with two kids. I'm not about to start raising thirty-six next year."

Auran laughed.

"Of course, that is not your concern. We hope you will embrace these children and help them understand their former planet and its culture, but we do not expect you take responsibility for them. After their Birth Days they will have the finest care imaginable for their entire lives."

"Yeah, well, I wouldn't coddle them too much either," Asha snorted. "It's a rather tough world out there, if you haven't noticed."

Lucas peered into one of the cases that housed a fetus about half the size of his palm. The display below read "F-Japan/Brazil," indicating its gender and lineage. *Her* gender and lineage, rather. It was hard to think of the shape as a person.

"You're just full of surprises, aren't you?" Lucas said, turning to the Keeper, who simply answered with a smile. If this is what it took for the human race to survive, then Lucas couldn't argue with the decision. It was something he hadn't given much thought to with all that was going on, but if it was true that Sorans and humans could never reproduce, the project did seem necessary, if vaguely unnerving. But Malorious Auran had always been kind, and Lucas was sure he was the man to oversee the process, as he seemed genuinely concerned about his creations, in addition to being a secret genius content to masquerade as a simple old man.

"If there was ever a time to renounce retirement," Auran said, "it was to be here and now. I will ensure that humans thrive for millennia to come. You have my word."

19

The next few weeks brought a frustrating series of meetings with top Soran military officials discussing their options for sneaking Zeta onto Xala to broadcast the message. Tannon Vale ruled out Maston's idea of an all-out assault on the planet as cover to sneak one ship past defenses, as it would cost millions of Soran lives and trillions in military hardware as it had the last time they'd attempted to invade the enemy solar system, centuries ago. Alpha proposed some theoretical planet-to-planet wormhole he could create to transport a few of them directly to the surface of Xala. The unfortunate side effect of that plan was that the concept was entirely theoretical, and the amount of power it would take could wipe out an entire continent if something went wrong.

The meetings had a tendency to devolve into shouting matches between the brightest military and scientific minds in the room, and they were making little progress. The clock appeared to be ticking, however, as reports had Xalan troops edging further into the rim systems with each passing week. Several listening posts had been obliterated entirely. Time was running out before Xala's next big offensive, which would claim untold numbers of lives. It was frustrating to know the next move to change the entire course of the war but be completely unable to utilize it.

Lucas was glad to be free of a thirteen-hour strategy session at some clandestine military base in the north of the continent, and he was gearing up for an evening with Sora's elite. It was trillionaire Madric Stoller's one hundredth Birth Day, and Lucas and Asha had been tasked with acting as Talis Vale's envoys, as it was well known she couldn't stand the man. Unfortunately, it appeared Lucas would have to brave the gala alone.

"You're really backing out?" Lucas pleaded with Asha, who lay sprawled haphazardly in bed with dark circles under her eyes.

"I'll be with you in spirit," she said. "But do I look like I'm in any condition to go to a party tonight?"

Asha had been sick all day after palace doctors diagnosed her with a relatively common form of food poisoning from something she'd eaten at first breakfast. It took about five hours of tests to confirm the lab results, but every precaution had to be taken, given her importance. She'd been given something for the nausea, but it had completely sapped all her energy as an unwanted side effect. Even sweat-soaked and sickly, she was still quite beautiful when she managed a smile.

"Fair enough, but this isn't going to be easy to do alone."

Asha waved her hand lazily, scrolling through the Stream's stories of the day.

"Stoller's harmless, and you already met half his friends at our debut."

Lucas scoffed.

"Let's hope this night goes a little better than that one."

"Well, I won't be there to get kidnapped, so that's a plus," Asha said in between short coughs.

Lucas slipped on his jacket and caught a glimpse of a familiar label inside. Jolo Houzani appeared to be content with providing them unlimited sets of clothing in exchange for swiping their likenesses for his ad campaigns.

"I don't want to do this," he said.

"You have to. You made a promise," Asha replied.

Lucas looked down at her; she was indeed something of a pitiful sight. The silvercoats said she'd be better by morning, and there was nothing nefarious about the illness.

"You going to be alright here?" Lucas asked.

"Auran's sending someone up here every ten minutes to make sure I'm not dead. If they greenlight it, maybe I'll have Noah and Erik in here for a little slumber party since I'm not contagious."

"That sounds like a more enjoyable evening to me," Lucas said.

"Can't let that suit go to waste," Asha said, winking at him. "Try not to drown in Soran fangirls."

Stoller was throwing the party aboard his private yacht that allegedly cost as much as the GDP of some of the smaller continents on Sora. Here, a yacht was not a naval vessel but an airship, and Stoller's was far above the city of Elyria so that the lights from the ground shone brighter than the countless stars above. Not a bad way to spend one's hundredth birthday, Lucas supposed.

He was taken to the festivities in one of the trademark armored palace hovercraft that shuttled him everywhere. Glancing at the helmeted driver, his heart dipped a little bit as he remembered who used to drive him around.

"Hey Silo, what's this called again?"

"Sakala. I played it in prime school before the SDI."

Lucas sighed, and stared at the empty Stream feed in front of him.

The airship was a short distance from the palace and they were there practically within minutes. The ship was circular and looked to be at least nine or ten stories tall. The underside engines emitted a dull orange ambient glow. At the very top, Lucas could see some sort of elaborate pool and . . . trees? The man had foliage growing out of his hoveryacht. Lucas saw the faint shimmer of a nearly invisible barrier shielding the highest deck from the winds that whipped around them at the high altitude.

There was a line of hovercraft pulling into the docking bay as they descended, and Lucas took a sip of a vaguely champagne-like substance he'd extracted from the back of the seat next to him. Figures wearing elaborate dresses and formal suits stepped out of their crafts ahead of him and camera bots swirled around them, shooting video as they entered the airship. This was the social event of the season, Talis had told him, which was precisely why she had begged him to go in her place. There was a time, she had said, when she relished such things, but those days had long passed her by.

Here we go, Lucas thought as he stepped out into the docking bay. Cameras spun around him like moons and there were plenty of physical press there shouting at him. He began to walk toward the entrance, accompanied by what appeared to be two private security guards who were keeping the media at bay. The questions peppered him like shrapnel.

"Lucas! Lucas! No date tonight?"

"Lucas! Where's Asha? Trouble in paradise?"

"Is that a Jolo Houzani?"

"Tell us about what really happened on Makari! Is it true you got nearly a hundred Guardians killed?"

That one hit Lucas like a brick, and he turned toward the small, mousey-looking man who'd said it. Security was already shoving him back. Lucas stomached his anger.

"I'm just here to have a good time. They say tonight will be one to remember."

Lucas walked through a pair of steel doors, which snapped shut behind him and deflected the remaining questions being hurled toward him.

"Lucas, my boy!" roared Madric Stoller as Lucas entered the inner ballroom of the airship. "So glad you could join us!"

The man was turning a hundred but didn't look a day over fifty. Such was the youth money could buy on Sora, it seemed. He was, however, one of the only overweight people Lucas had seen on the planet. His mustache alone looked like it weighed five pounds.

"Thank you for having me," Lucas said with purposeful politeness. "Asha and Talis send their apologies. My counterpart is ill while the High Chancellor is indisposed."

Stoller let out a harrumph.

"Seems to happen an awful lot when I invite her. But what do I get when I show up at one of her parties?"

Lucas waited for the answer.

"A near-death experience! She owes me a pair of hands and a liver," he said with a belly laugh as he held out his hands toward Lucas. He could see a faint line across both his wrists that indicated a graft. He'd forgotten that Stoller had been injured in the blast at the party thrown in Lucas and Asha's honor. But he seemed jovial enough to let bygones be bygones.

Suddenly, a little toddler waddled up and grasped Stoller by the knee. It was a boy who looked to be about Noah's age, with dark amber hair and blue eyes. Stoller scooped him up into his arms and he rested on the man's stomach like a beanbag chair.

"Finn, this is Lucas, our friend from another world."

The boy nodded vigorously.

"I know."

"Lucas, this my youngest, Finn. About your oldest boy's age, I do believe. We should get them together at some point."

Lucas nodded. "Absolutely. Nice to meet you, Finn."

The boy gave him a devious smile. He seemed far too young to be anywhere near a party like this. Lucas saw dancing women in the background wearing shockingly scarce amounts of clothing, given the supposed elegance of the event. A few of them appeared to be wrapped in nothing but holograms.

"Now I don't mean to talk your ear off. Come! Eat, drink, and try not to outshine me at my own party!"

Stoller flung his arm out toward the hall, which somehow looked even more lavish than the Earth Gala at the palace. The dancing girls might not have been wearing much, but each sparkled with at least ten pounds of jewelry, as did most of the women in attendance. In the center was a metal sculpture of Stoller looking a bit slimmer than he did in real life. The likeness gestured outward and at his feet was a spread of food and spirits that seemed like it could feed an entire continent. Perhaps there was a reason Tulwar and his ilk hated Sora's elite so much. Lucky for Lucas and those in attendance, Tulwar was currently buried a few miles under the palace with his army scattered to the wind.

It wasn't fifteen seconds before Lucas felt a tug on his sleeve.

"Excuse me, are you Lucas, the Earthborn?"

Before he turned around, he made sure to fix a smile to his face.

Lucas spent the next hour fleeing from admirers, gradually ascending the decks of the airship. Each floor had even more food and drink, but Lucas restrained himself from overindulging. The man he used to be on Earth wouldn't have been able to resist.

Lucas was content to sit on a carved wooden chair by the pool filled with revelers who had the good sense to pack a change of clothes to go swimming. A few wore nothing at all, but no one seemed to mind. The pool wasn't so much a pool as it was a pond, surrounded by real grass, brush, and trees transplanted by a man with apparently more money than he knew what to do with. Lucas caught a server by the arm and ordered a water, which got him a strange look, but a quick nod as the man hurried off.

". . . so what do you think about that?"

Snapping his focus back into the moment, Lucas had forgotten he was even talking to someone. A woman sat upright in the chair next to him. She was gorgeous and looked ten years younger than him at least, but who could tell? She had almost platinum hair with sparkling amber eyes and full lips. The slit in her matte black dress reached dangerous heights, and her gaze was unfocused.

"Absolutely," Lucas said with no recollection of the question. Regardless, the woman smiled and leaned in just a little bit closer to him. Lucas rested his head back onto his chair and stared up at the stars, which appeared to be moving around like fireflies. Women like this had been swarming him all night. Men too, for that matter, though most of them had less suggestive looks in their eyes.

The stars suddenly blurred as the ship shook violently. The familiar thunderclap of an explosion followed. A woman screamed on the other side of the deck.

Not again, was the panicked thought that flooded into Lucas's mind as his heart rate doubled. Everyone was racing over to the side of the ship and looking down over the translucent screen that blocked off the edge. Lucas scrambled to his feet to join them, narrowly avoiding falling in the pool as the airship lurched to try and stabilize itself.

When he reached the edge, he found it wasn't the ship that was under attack. Something had happened in the center of Elyria. A fire blazed brightly in the night below them, and smoke rose from the site. Then, another explosion, which again shook the ship, even lofted far above the area. Lucas thought he could hear the muted sounds of gunfire and more distant screams.

No one in the crowd had any idea what was happening and chattered like a bunch of frightened forest animals. Lucas ran to the door and descended to the next deck.

There he found a similar scene, as all the guests were packed against the eastern windows, the party at a standstill. Stoller was there, and with a wave of his hand an enormous display of the Stream flickered into existence above what appeared to be a ten-foot-wide hearth.

A reporter was on the scene as bloody citizens emerged from the smoke behind him. He was coughing from the debris in the air, yelling over the roar of gunfire and more explosions.

"The city is under attack by unknown forces! The disturbance began here in Tatoni Square and has—"

Something emerged from the smoke behind him. Something Lucas recognized.

The reporter was skewered through the chest and flung backward. Blood spattered onto the lens of the camera. Standing in the reporter's place was an enormous, metal monstrosity.

"*Killbot*," Lucas whispered to himself.

The machine onscreen was the same model he'd fought with his splinter team in Rhylos, though this one was painted black instead of gold. On its plated chest were the unmistakable intersecting red slashes of the Fourth Order.

How?

The smoke began to clear behind the robot, which was firing off pulse rounds toward targets offscreen. Behind him, more shapes came into view. More killbots. Two, then three, then four. The closest one eyed them with its thousand-lensed spherical head. The camera went black.

Madric Stoller was attempting to calm the hysterical crowd.

"Ladies and gentlemen, I can assure you we are in the safest place in the city. I've asked our captain to raise our elevation to the outer atmosphere, well out of the range of any possible attack."

Lucas didn't want to be in the safest place in the city. He wanted to help, but more importantly he needed to make sure that Asha, Noah, and Erik were safe in the palace. If Elyria was being attacked, the palace was certainly in danger as well.

As Lucas sprinted down back stairwells to the docking bay, he kept trying to dial Asha on his communicator, but couldn't connect. After his fifth attempt, he tried Mars Maston instead. On the second try, Maston answered.

"What?" came the loud reply. Lucas could hear gunfire in the background.

"What do you mean 'what'?" Lucas said incredulously. "What the hell is going on down there?"

More gunfire, then a brief burst of static.

"Fourth Order popped a bunch of killbots out of the sewer system. Ten, eleven maybe. They're wreaking havoc down here. Probably a few hundred dead already. Where are you?"

"In Stoller's airship," Lucas said. He had reached the bay, which was now absent of press, and there were other guests attempting to stream into their hovercraft. Lucas saw no sign of his own.

"I'm stuck up here with no weapons and I don't know where my guards went. Has the palace been targeted?"

"Negative," shouted Maston over a raucous explosion. "It's all concentrated here."

"Do you need my help?"

"You won't do much except probably get yourself killed. We've got SDI and even palace security coming down to help mop this up. It's bad, but I've seen worse."

Maston went silent on the comm for an unsettling amount of time. When he broke back in, his tone was grave.

"You need to get to the palace immediately."

"Why? What's happening?"

Lucas was in a line of partygoers waiting for their hovercraft to be brought to them. He hopped up anxiously trying to get a clearer view, but the guests and staff were all panicked, and the entire deck was a mess. Fortunately, most had stayed inside at Stoller's behest. Lucas could feel the airship starting to rise.

"This may be a distraction. Tulwar might be trying to pull something here by sending palace guards into the city to deal with this. It's a skeleton crew over there now. Even Tannon's off-continent tonight."

"Alright, I'm on my way," Lucas said, pushing his way to the front of the line.

"Shit!" yelled Maston and the comm line went completely dead after broadcasting the first half of an explosion. Lucas hoped he hadn't just been killed on the spot.

Lucas reached the front of the line. He searched for his own armored car and driver, but could find neither. Ahead of him, a well-dressed older couple was getting into a luxury hovercraft. Lucas made a split-second decision to dive in after them.

He tumbled into the back seat and was greeted with a look of shock from both of them.

"Hi, sorry, but I need to get to the palace, immediately. It's an emergency."

The man finally spoke. He had wispy white hair and a close shaven beard.

"Of course it is, it's an emergency for all of us."

"No, you don't understand," Lucas said as he turned to the driver. "Please, take me to the Grand Palace as quickly as you can."

The driver turned to him with an annoyed look on his face.

"Look, I know who you are, but I don't get paid to ditch my clients for any random alien that gets in their car."

Lucas made another split-second decision, and then dragged the driver's unconscious body into the backseat. The woman screamed.

Stoller's private security drew their weapons just as Lucas sped away, but withheld fire.

"Look, I'm sorry about this, but you'll understand later."

The couple remained silent and were visibly shaking. The driver didn't move, but his nose was bleeding onto the floormats. Lucas slid the privacy screen up.

Lucas set a course for the palace docking bay and quickly hacked the system to override the self-imposed maximum speed limitations of the craft. They would be there soon.

Tapping his communicator, he tried Asha again to no avail. Then Maston.

"What?" came the voice in Lucas's ear.

"So you're not dead," Lucas said, breathing a sigh of relief.

"Are you there yet? I was right, Tulwar's making a break for it."

"What? How?" Lucas exclaimed.

Maston sent him a video file through the comm. It started playing on the viewscreen of the hovercraft.

It was security footage from the palace showing Tulwar being let out of his cell by a uniformed palace officer. A pair of dead guards lay a short distance away.

"How the hell did this happen?"

"He's got men on the inside. I don't know how many."

The footage showed another guard joining up with Tulwar as they walked through the labyrinthine prison toward the lift.

"This was five minutes ago. Last time I saw them, they were heading toward the Palace Archives."

"Where's that?" Lucas asked.

"Next to your Earth Archive. Few chambers over. We have to assume his eventual target is Talis. She's got her personal guard, but not much else. Most of the security is here fighting these things, and the rest could be in Tulwar's pocket. I'm trying to get over there, but I'm pinned down. You have to stop him."

Shit, Lucas thought as the towering structure began to loom large in front of him. He was being hailed by palace security telling him his entry was unauthorized. He was frantically typing as Maston spoke, trying to send them his verification codes to let them know who he was.

"I have to—" Maston's voice cut out again after another hail of gunfire. Lucas immediately tried Asha.

"Thank god," she said on the other end, and Lucas's stomach unknotted itself.

"Are you alright?" Lucas asked breathlessly.

"I'm fine. I'm in the room with the kids. What the hell is going on over there? Are you far up enough to avoid all this?"

"Yes," Lucas said. "But I'm on my way to you. Tulwar's escaped. He's in the archives and heading for Talis. Palace security is compromised."

"What?" Asha cried. "I'll head him off."

"No," Lucas said forcefully. "Stay where you are. It's not—"

But she was already gone.

"Damn it!" Lucas yelled. He tried her comm again without luck. The entire network was melting down because of the attack. A green indicator informed him he'd been given temporary clearance to dock, and he swerved into the entry bay at triple the allowed speed. He skidded sideways on the deck, and the craft ripped through a support pillar before crashing into an armored transport, where it came to a stop. A pair of guards were already sprinting toward him. Usually there were a dozen here.

Lucas poured out of the craft, which was now smoking from somewhere within. The rear door opened and the frightened old couple emerged. He'd forgotten all about them.

"Stay where you are!" came the stern command from the first guard to reach him, weapon drawn.

"I need to get inside. There's a threat to the High Chancellor."

The guards didn't move. Their handguns remained trained on him. Lucas inched toward them.

"The palace is on lockdown," came the gruff reply from the first guard.

"I know. Don't you know who I am?" Lucas said, exasperated. The couple held onto each other behind him and were moving toward the back of the bay away from the standoff.

"I know exactly who you are," the guard said, his eyes narrow.

Were they actual guards or Tulwar plants? Lucas didn't have time to find out.

"I'm sorry about this."

Lucas moved like water, the adrenaline taking control of his entire body. He disarmed the first guard before he could blink, and a swift kick sent the other's pistol flying. Lucas spun around and ripped off one of their helmets, smashing it into the other's head with force enough to knock him off his feet. Whirling around, he caught the second guard with an elbow that had him unconscious before he hit the ground. One more swift kick to the helmeted man on the pavement, and neither stirred. Hopefully he'd avoided killing them if they were indeed just trying to do their jobs.

Lucas used one of their ID chips to open the doors inside the bay and made his way toward the main hall, clutching the newly acquired energy pistol.

His comm was completely dead now, and Lucas figured there must have been some sort of dampening field in effect to disrupt non-security-related communication when there was a threat inside the palace. Unfortunately, it meant he couldn't reach Asha or Maston or even Alpha, who was now in an underground research lab a thousand miles away, probably unaware of what was happening in Elyria.

Normally bustling with officials, tourists, and guards, the Great Hall was eerily silent. Lucas's footsteps echoed off the stone floor and bounced off the walls around him. The ceiling was five stories high and adorned with a massive mural of clouds, stars, moons, and other heavenly bodies. Lucas crept toward the grand staircase at the end of the hall where a series of six lifts stood. From there he could ascend to the Emperor's Refuge, as it was called, a throwback from ages past, which was where Talis had her personal quarters.

As Lucas got closer to the stairs, he noticed two slain guards tucked behind pillars, their blood just starting creep across the marble. Smoke was still rising from the charred armor, indicating they'd been killed recently.

A chime sounded from the lift bay and rang out across the room, reverberating off the stone walls of the empty hall. Ahead, the elevator doors opened and a quartet of uniformed palace guards stepped out. It was easy to decipher their allegiance once they opened fire on Lucas without saying a word.

Lucas dove behind an antique statue of an ancient king as plasma rounds whizzed by him, taking chunks out of the stone. He returned fire with his own pistol, but hit only air with his first volley.

Another chime rang out and a different lift door opened behind the troops. The rear pair of guards didn't have time to react as Asha shredded them with a pair of submachine guns. Their two remaining comrades watched their fallen bodies bounce down the stairs, but before they could move, Lucas planted a pair of plasma rounds into each of them. Asha walked down the stairs and sprayed another clip of bullets into their bodies for good measure. *Wait, bullets?*

As Asha drew closer, it was clear that she was indeed holding Earth weapons in each of her hands, though she did also have her trademark Magnum and sword. She still looked sick, but had clearly flipped a switch to not be bothered by such trivialities at the moment.

"What's happening?" Lucas asked, trying to pull himself together. "Did you find him?"

Asha shook her head.

"The Refuge is restricted access with no override. I got as far as the archive level. That's where I grabbed these," she said, motioning to her weapons. "Your gun wasn't there; I figured you had it with you."

"What was Tulwar doing there?"

Asha shrugged.

"Attendants were dead, but data logs said he spent a good bit of time digging around in some old files. I couldn't make much sense of it."

"We have to get up there." Lucas said, eyeing the lifts. The virtual controls appeared in front of him with a wave of his hand and he selected the chamber level.

"You can try, but—"

The light turn green and the lift started to rise.

"Well, that's weird."

Whatever restriction had been placed on the Refuge level had been lifted. The elevator recognized Lucas's bio-ID and allowed him access to one of the most secure floors in the building. They were rocketing up to the top of the tower.

"Erik? Noah?" Lucas asked.

"With Auran. Far underground. Safe."

Asha handed him a submachine gun. It was a relic they'd picked up at the cannibal village in Norway, but it still worked, that much was obvious. Lucas reloaded it and checked the readouts on his appropriated pistol. They came to a stop, the chime sounded, and the doors opened. There were no more floors to climb.

"Oh god," Asha exclaimed as she stepped cautiously out into the hall, which was stained with a copious amount of blood. There were no guards here, not whole ones anyway. They were just bits of pulp and gristle with the occasional limb or shattered piece of light armor.

"We're too late," Lucas said in a low voice as he crept through the gore. Blood pooled into his expensive shoes.

"What the hell could have done this?" Asha asked, looking at the devastation in amazement.

Lucas knew.

There was only one door in the hallway at the very end, and it had been blown to bits. The metal was mangled into strange shapes and had been torn away from the frame completely. They stepped through the smoke and into Talis's chambers.

Inside the vast room stood Hex Tulwar, clad in a bloodstained white suit of armor with a collar that obscured half his face. His long hair had been pulled back in a samurai-like bun, but most notably, he was aiming Natalie straight at them with his one remaining good arm.

"Shit," said Lucas, pointing his pistol at Tulwar's skull. Asha had her Magnum trained to the same location. Lucas had recognized the aftermath of Natalie's close-range carnage setting immediately in the hallway. It seemed Tulwar had made a detour at the archives to arm himself with the most powerful weapon in the palace.

"Right on cue," Tulwar said, smiling that same sickly smile that always unsettled Lucas.

"Where is she?" Lucas asked through gritted teeth.

"You mean our good Chancellor?" Tulwar said. "Right this way."

He stepped backward and to the side, revealing a figure sitting on the floor, propped up against the bed.

It was Talis, with a pair of plasma burn marks across her torso. She'd been shot. Her jade-colored nightdress was more red than green.

"Lucas . . ." she whispered, pain etched on her face. She was still alive. Lucas's gun never left Tulwar.

"What do you want, Hex?" Lucas growled.

"What do I want?" Tulwar laughed. "I want justice. Justice for my people. For my family. I know you are new to this planet, but do you know what High Chancellor Vale here did to the Rhylosi?"

Lucas nodded.

"Yes. I know she ordered the fleet to stand down at Vitalla. I know you think she's the reason you lost so many that day. Why you lost your family."

"But she didn't have a choice," Asha added. "It was either that or lose half the fleet. Sora could have fallen."

Tulwar laughed again.

"You are blind like all the rest. If it were only that, perhaps Kyneth would have allowed me to forgive her after all these years. But Talis Vale's sins run far deeper. I always knew in my heart, but now I have the proof."

Lucas and Asha slowly circled around so they could see Talis fully. She was in bad shape, and blood was pooled out all around her, soaking into the ornate rug beneath her body. She clearly needed serious medical help, but Lucas couldn't let his guard down for one second with Tulwar clutching Natalie. At this distance, one carnage blast could shred them both.

Lucas was thrown off guard when Tulwar suddenly threw a chip at him. He caught it by instinct.

"What's this?" Lucas asked as he pressed the device with his thumb and watched a hologram spring out of it. It was mostly just a string of Soran numbers and letters.

"That is a coded transmission, one long thought deleted from the archives. But I resurrected it with some degree of technological magic."

"A transmission of what?" Asha asked. Talis eyed the chip worriedly.

"Dates, times, and most importantly, coordinates. All the details of the Vitalla voyage."

"And?" Lucas asked, his head cocked.

"It is a transmission sent to the Ruling Council of Xala from our very own High Chancellor Talis Vale."

"Bullshit," Asha said curtly, readjusting her aim on Tulwar.

"It's true," he said, half shrugging in his armor plating. "Ask her yourself."

Talis was breathing heavily, painfully. She remained silent for a minute, but after a menacing glare from Tulwar, she began to speak.

"Rhylos . . . was worthless," she said. "As were the R-Rhylosi. A drain on our entire planet. Their promised work on Vitalla wouldn't have paid for a fraction of what . . . they'd cost us over the c-centuries."

What was she talking about? She'd sold the Rhylosi out on purpose? The kind woman who had embraced them like her own children since their arrival here? It didn't make any sense.

"I don't understand. You sacrificed all those people and your own father? Why?" Lucas asked.

Talis's face was ugly now. He'd never seen her like this. Blood crept over her bottom lip as she spat out her words like each one burned her throat.

"Varrus . . . was a monster. His foolish campaigns led m-my husband . . . my sons to the slaughter. I knew his arrogance would draw him to the ceremony on the planet. The fleet was to be spared . . . those were the terms."

"It can't be . . ." Lucas said slowly. He felt physically sick.

"And you just so happened to become High Chancellor yourself, how convenient," Asha said venomously. "And your daughter, Corinthia. You put her at risk?"

"I pleaded with her not to go . . . she was so stubborn, like her father. But I knew Mars would keep her safe."

"What else did you get out of it? That can't be all." Lucas pressed. "What did those millions of 'worthless' lives buy you?"

"A truce," Talis said weakly. "A decade of peace."

"Peace for you maybe, but that's when our planet was getting destroyed," Lucas said angrily.

Lucas's head was spinning. Had Talis really orchestrated the genocide of almost an entire race, and essentially ordered the murder of her own father? It seemed beyond impossible, but here she was, confessing. It was now no wonder she'd forbidden anyone to speak of Vitalla since. Tulwar spoke next.

"That data," he said, pointing at the chip, "has already been sent to every news outlet on the planet, which will verify its contents. I've also excavated some decrypted personal logs that relay the lovely back story the High Chancellor has just told you. Nothing is ever truly erased. Not really. I only needed the access to unearth it."

Talis was in tears now. The blood flowing from her wounds wasn't slowing, a side effect of the rifle's specially formulated plasma.

"I'm sorry," she said hoarsely. "I wanted . . . to be free of Rhylos, free of my father. I-I truly thought . . . it was the best path for Sora. Tell them that."

Lucas didn't know what to say; he was still in shock. Talis fell silent. Her eyes slipped shut. She was still breathing, but barely.

"Now what?" Lucas said, turning back to Hex Tulwar. "You kill us too and then die during capture?"

"Or he can die right now," Asha said, her finger quivering over her trigger.

Lucas was stunned when Tulwar grinned and tossed Natalie at him. Lucas caught the rifle with his free arm.

"What the hell are you doing?" he asked. Tulwar now appeared to be completely unarmed and raised his good hand outward in a sign of submission with the other dangling uselessly at his side, a ghost of a limb inside the armor plating.

"There is one last act to the play," Tulwar said slyly.

"I'm going to kill him," Asha said, taking another step toward him.

"Wait," Lucas said, holding up his hand. "What are you talking about?"

"A lovely rifle you have there. A truly one-of-a-kind weapon," Tulwar said, nodding toward Natalie. "One that makes one-of-a-kind wounds."

Lucas looked down at Talis. Her head was bowed and her chest was no longer rising and falling. The unending bleeding was too much. She was gone. Tulwar paid her no mind. He'd known she'd never survive those injuries.

"And it's quite a disturbance you caused here tonight."

Tulwar raised his hand, causing Asha to twitch and almost take his head off. Instead, a floating display of the Stream appeared in between them. A reporter spoke over security camera footage from the palace.

"We've just received this feed of what appears to be the Earthborn, Lucas and Asha, staging an assault on the Grand Palace."

The footage showed Lucas disarming and beating down the two guards in the docking bay. Then it switched the Great Hall where he and Asha shredded Maston's enlisted palace guards with gunfire.

"There's no word on the High Chancellor's condition, though SDI forces are en route to the palace after responding to the presumed distraction of the machines in Tatoni Square."

This was a setup.

"There's no way," Lucas said. The look on Asha's face said she understood as well. "But you've escaped, you're here. There's other footage."

"Film that has all been cleansed. And we cannot forget your premeditation of this heinous assassination!"

Tulwar pressed a button on his white suit of armor and a different video appeared in front of them. It was a high-angle shot of their room; the timestamp showed it had been filmed earlier today.

"You're really backing out?"

"I'll be with you in spirit."

It was his and Asha's conversation about Stoller's party. But it sounded . . .

"This isn't going to be easy to do alone."

A quick cut.

"I don't want to do this."

"You have to, you made a promise."

Tulwar spoke, closing the video.

"How fortunate your lovely counterpart decided to assist you after all."

Asha was seething.

"These are nothing but cheap tricks. We'll show them your body, explain—"

"You will not," Tulwar said sternly. The Stream feed reappeared and was showing pictures of Lucas and Asha with the headline EARTHBORN STORM PALACE.

"Though I thank you for your invaluable assistance in bringing me here, and helping me escape. What are coconspirators for? They'll never find me."

"What are you talking about?" Lucas asked. "There's no way out of here."

"I'm surprised you haven't commented on my armor here. Do you know its history?"

The pair of them remained silent.

"Of course not, you're new here. This is plating back from the Sacred Wars. I had my men bring it in for tonight. All the elite Rhylosi warriors wore it in battle. It provided more than just protection. It brought them *honor*."

Lucas heard the wail of alarms sounding outside.

"In the one, true faith, if a warrior's body is not burned after he falls in battle, he does not gain entry into the Blessed Forest. Only if he enters as ash may he be reassembled in a new form, which will live forever. This suit allows such a transition."

Tulwar pressed a button and a helmet shot up from behind his neck and encased his entire head.

"It is how I will enter the Forest tonight. After exposing and killing Sora's wicked leader and corrupting her two false idols. My journey is complete."

He paused, and raised his fist toward them.

"I go to my family; may you go with the gods."

"No!" Lucas shouted as he lunged toward Tulwar. Through the visor, a furnace erupted inside the suit, and the cracks of the armor glowed. Lucas winced and yanked his burned hands from the metal. As Asha looked on in horror, Tulwar was incinerated in an instant, turned to dust in a flash fire that continued to burn as the suit crumpled to the ground. Within seconds, all of the plating had turned to ash as well, and there was nothing left but a pile of gray matter that began to absorb Talis's blood like sawdust.

Lucas and Asha were speechless.

"Holy shit," she said finally. "Did that really just happen?"

"We have nothing," Lucas said frantically, thinking through what had just taken place. "He killed her with my gun, fed the footage and the story to the news. We don't even have his body. Do you have any idea how bad this looks?"

From the horrified look on her face, Asha did know. Had they really been played this well? How long had Tulwar been planning this? Since his imprisonment? Since Rhylos? Since the Earth Gala?

"We've got to get out of here," Asha said, sprinting toward the doorway. Lucas checked his wrist display.

"They're already on their way up. We have to surrender. They'll kill us on sight if they see us in here armed."

"I don't surrender," Asha growled. Lucas was racing through alternate options in his head, but none came to him.

Suddenly a blinding light burst in through the large windows at the opposite end of the room. The familiar whir of hovercraft engines could be heard from outside.

The window shattered as an armored figure dove through it, his back lit up by the flames of a jet propulsion attachment. He tumbled forward, and though Lucas's brain told him to drop Natalie to the ground, he simply couldn't. He raised the weapon.

As the figure rolled to his feet, Lucas and Asha dipped the barrels of their guns. Through his translucent visor, they could see it was Mars Maston. He stared in astonishment at Talis Vale's body, then at them.

"What . . . happened . . . here," he said slowly. "Where's Tulwar? Do you have any idea what the Stream is saying about you?"

"Maston," Lucas said, his heart in his throat. "It was all Tulwar. This was a setup from the beginning. He played us, tried to make it look like we conspired with the Fourth Order and the Xalans."

"Where is he?" Maston growled fiercely.

"You're looking at him," Asha said, gesturing down toward the ash. Much of it had been scattered by the winds whipping in from the shattered window. Only a few small piles remained.

"He had some sort of incineration suit. Combusted on the spot so we'd never have a body."

Maston whirled around in a rage and sent his fist through one of the sturdy wooden posts on Talis's bed, which splintered into a thousand shards. Lucas understood. Maston would never have his vengeance now, no justice for Corinthia. He hadn't killed Hex Tulwar, and there wasn't even a body in the aftermath. Tulwar was now nothing more than a phantom.

"Mars, you have to—" said Asha before he cut her off.

"I believe you," Maston snarled. "But they won't. We have to get you out of here. They're already inside."

Lucas collapsed inside the armored hovercraft. They sped away from the palace, from Elyria, as fast as the vehicle would take them. Looking out the rear viewscreen, Lucas could see craft similar to their own swarming the structure. Soldiers were assuredly crawling through the palace, discovering dead guards everywhere and the deceased Talis Vale next to a few inconspicuous mounds of ash.

Lucas's heart was finally slowing down from its hours-long mad racing ever since he'd heard the first explosion aboard Stoller's craft. Asha stared out the window with her hand to her mouth. She appeared to be in absolute shock, a true rarity for her. Maston remained silent in the driver's seat and had a white-knuckled grip on the controls of the craft.

The Sorans would never believe it, would they? The tale Hex Tulwar spun framing them for the High Chancellor's assassination. The Earthborn were heroes, symbols of hope. But that's why Tulwar did it, wasn't it? Take away their leader and their hope at the same time.

Lucas switched on a feed of the Stream but kept it muted. One panel showed Tulwar's evidence he'd unearthed against Talis Vale, yet another shocking part of the evening. The screen showed the text of her decrypted personal logs.

"The agreement is in place. The Xalans will take Vitalla and the Rhylosi; we will have a decade of peace to rebuild and prosper. If my father is planetside when they strike, so be it. He did not mourn for his grandchildren when he sent them to be killed at Hannaras, I shall not mourn for him. We shall be free of two evils with a strike impossible for our own armies to execute. The Xalans do not know it, but they are helping to save Sora from itself."

Lucas had felt like he knew Talis, but her warm smiles and kind eyes masked dark secrets and a bloody past. She wanted power and revenge above all else, but coped by telling herself she was acting "for the good of Sora" by killing millions of its citizens and its leader. Ordering the fleet out of Vitalla would have been a tough choice, but orchestrating the entire ambush was unforgivable. Perhaps she deserved Tulwar's brand of justice after all, though he and Asha certainly did not, nor did many of Tulwar's other victims. The Stream reported that the killbots had slain 2,043 people before their rampage was brought to an end. Lucas couldn't imagine the death toll back when there were hundreds of thousands of machines running amok during the first uprising, not just a dozen.

The Stream kept scrolling and the central story once again flipped back to the Earthborn's betrayal. They were spinning Tulwar's story that they'd been Xalan plants the entire time, and had conspired with the Fourth Order since their "debut," having fooled all the government's scientists with expertly forged genetic tests.

But what *did* the government think? The feed announced that Tannon Vale had been sworn in as acting Chancellor, but there was no official comment from the administration about Talis's death or their involvement. The media was simply running wild with

Tulwar's lies and the video feeds he'd spoon-fed them. Rhylos and its allies in the region were aflame with anger over the revelation of Talis's involvement in Vitalla, and were worshipping Tulwar, even after they'd previously distanced themselves from him. The official story was that he'd escaped custody with the help of the Earthborn and fled the palace before the High Chancellor was killed by Lucas.

Could they ever sort this out? Prove that Tulwar had set them up? Lucas's mind raced for a way, but there was nothing. Tulwar had left little to chance. The Stream was now interviewing the elderly couple whose hovercraft Lucas had stolen to reach the palace from Stoller's party. They described him as "unstable" and "violent" during their ordeal.

"Shut that shit off," Asha said grimly. "I can't handle this right now."

Neither could Lucas, and he was happy to close down the feed.

Staring out the window, he could see they were over a body of water with land only a small strip in the distance.

"Where are we going?" Lucas called up to Maston. He was met with silence.

Lucas lay back in his seat and his eyes closed like his lids were dipped in lead. No nightmare could compare to what had happened tonight.

20

Lucas found himself sitting on a floor of trampled brush, staring at a fire, unaware of how he got there. Around him, the jungle creaked and chirped and white rays of moonlight streamed in through the treetops.

Makari.

A figure emerged from the shadows. He sat down opposite Lucas, crossing his legs. He leaned toward the small fire, which illuminated his face.

"Hello Saato."

"Hello Toruk."

Lucas knew it was a dream, because Toruk was speaking broken English instead of broken Soran. Not to mention it would be rather difficult to teleport to a planet billions of miles away.

"Great problems on Mol'taavi," Toruk said, poking at the fire with a stick.

"You could say that," Lucas said, leaning back onto his elbows. Looking down, he saw that he was wearing bits of bark armor and was covered in white Khas'to tribal tattoos. In his hand he was surprised to find a long black stone knife, one with a small skull on the pommel. It looked familiar.

"Like before, eh?" Toruk said.

"When?" Lucas asked, rotating the knife around in his hand.

"New body. You forget. Many ages past."

"What are you talking about?"

Toruk threw some dirt into the fire, which caused it to smoke less. He was easier to see now.

"Back when Great Storm first create Mol'taavi and Makari, First Man Saato leader of all. Oni love Saato. Bring many years peace, food."

Lucas sat listening intently. The ambient noises of the forest were growing quieter.

"One day, Saato's men bring woman to him. They say she thief. Great beauty mask dark soul. Must die."

Toruk rubbed his hands together in front of the fire. The temperature was dropping rapidly, and bits of bark and fur weren't exactly keeping Lucas warm. He shivered.

"Saato looks in eyes. Sees magic. Great magic. Says woman must live. Tribe furious. Woman stole from rich and powerful. Evil men turn people from Saato. Seize throne. Imprison Saato and woman for many years, much torture for their crimes."

Lucas shifted as clouds began to eclipse the moon overhead. The jungle grew darker, the fire brighter.

"Soon later, sky demons come. Mol'taavi burn. Hope lost. Saato breaks free and finds woman. Tells her she must remember. Must remember who she is."

Toruk's eyes widened, full of excitement.

"Woman unleash great magic, great skill, kill sky demons, help escape to Makari. Rich men now bow at her feet. 'Who is this?' they ask. 'Who wields such power?' 'I am Valli,' she say, 'First Woman.' Blind men saw only thief, not god. Saato knew truth, did what needed to save people, even ones who cast hate on him. Saato and Valli protect Oni together many years after. First Man and Woman reunited."

Lucas nodded as Toruk finished his story and fell silent.

"I see," he said. "Why didn't anyone recognize her?"

"Saato, Valli many bodies. Always change with new era. Look like you now. Like Asha."

Lucas laughed.

"We're not Saato and Valli, Toruk. I hate to break it to you."

Toruk nodded sarcastically.

"Okay, you right. Fall from sky, commune with White Spirit, kill sky demon. Fulfill all prophecy, but not Saato and Valli. I understand."

There'd be no convincing him, it seemed. Toruk got to his feet.

"Spirit journey must end. I grow weak. Much to do on Makari. We await you return."

Spirit journey?

"We'll be back," Lucas said. "It may be a while, but we'll return to help you take Makari again."

"I know," Toruk nodded as he began to turn translucent across from Lucas.

"Do not forget past lives. Remember, even disbelievers need saving. Truth absolute, eternal. Lie fades. Always fades. Do not lose sight of whole war for sake of one battle."

And with that, he was gone, and Lucas was alone at the campfire.

He began to rise, unassisted, through the air. Through the trees, through the clouds. Lucas stared straight into the shining face of Mol'taavi. His tattoos glowed in the moonlight.

Lucas woke, being forcefully shaken. In seconds, a splitting headache found him, and his bleary eyes saw Asha sleeping on a seat across from him. Looking up, he saw the figure above him was Maston.

"Get up, we're here."

Lucas slowly unclipped his restraints as Maston jostled Asha's shoulder until she snapped awake with an angry glare. The hovercraft was stopped, its engines silent. Gray light pierced the tinted windows.

"You're going to want this," Maston said, throwing a heavy thermal blanket at each of them. When he shoved open the door, it became clear why.

The air was frigid, and as their eyes adjusted to the light, they found they were parked on a rocky shoreline. The water lapping the stones was black; the sky was a flowing stream of thin milky clouds. It was freezing, but there was no snow to be found around them. Lucas and Asha huddled in their blankets as they tried to find their footing on the rocks. They left the hovercraft behind and followed Maston up a narrowly carved path that started at the end of the beach. Lucas looked down at his communicator and saw that it had been completely wiped. It wouldn't even turn on. He did still have Natalie with him, however, and the gun was slung over his back. He soon found the rifle's targeting system was also offline, but it could still fire without power. Alpha had made sure of that during construction.

After plodding along for ten minutes, they rounded a curve and saw a structure. It was an old house, made of stone with a thatched roof that looked even more primitive than their quarters in the Oni village on Makari. When they reached it, Maston unlocked the wooden door with a rusty key and ushered them inside.

It was one large room with a fireplace, bed, table, and chairs. There appeared to be something resembling a kitchen, and an opaque screen that Lucas guessed might conceal a lavatory. The head of a large sea creature, with rows of sharp teeth and two foot-long ivory horns, hung above the fireplace with a pair of crossed harpoons beneath it.

"What is this place?" Lucas asked. His eyes were relieved to be out of the daylight, though his head was still pounding. Maston was already starting to build a fire.

"We call it a black hole," he said. "The less you know about where you are, the better. Suffice it to say you're on a very small island in the middle of a very big ocean and no one's going to find you here."

"Is that why you killed our communicators?" Asha asked, tapping her own.

Maston shook his head.

"Buried in the center of this place is a device that silences any electronics in range, other than our own greenlit transports, of course. It also shields the area from orbital surveillance of any kind. Simply put, it causes this place not to exist."

Lucas ran his hand over the carved wooden chair in front of him. On the ground was a rug made of some sort of skinned animal with the head still attached. The upturned snout indicated it might be some sort of enormous . . . boar, maybe? The place felt like an old hunting lodge.

"Where are Noah and Erik?" Lucas asked. "What's happened to them?"

"They remain under Keeper Auran's watch at the palace," Maston assured them. "Nothing has changed about their care."

"Except their parents can't go within five thousand miles of them," Asha growled.

Maston rubbed his eyes. He looked exhausted. There was no way to tell how long they'd been flying.

"We'll get all this sorted out, but it's bad right now. Half the world is rioting about what Talis did, the other half about you supposedly killing her."

"Did you know," Lucas asked, "about Talis?"

Anger flashed in Maston's eyes.

"Of course not!" he said sternly. "Knowing as much as Tulwar did, I'd have killed her myself if I had the chance. She put my fleet at risk. She put Corinthia at risk."

It was the first time he'd said her name in months.

"But that doesn't make Tulwar any less of a monster," Maston continued. "I cannot believe he did all this. I cannot believe he won."

Lucas didn't have anything to say to that. It was true. Tulwar got everything he wanted. He was burning the world down around them and shaming his enemies, all from the comfort of his grave.

"But we have a more pressing problem," Maston said, staring into the fire. "Word will reach Xala that Sora is in turmoil. They will not waste time before organizing an assault. SDI fleets are already returning from abroad to brace for a homeworld strike."

"So you're saying we need to get Zeta to Xala," Lucas said.

"Yes. There's been something we've been keeping from the strategy group that you should know now. Zeta has continued work on her algorithm. When she broadcasts the message from Xalan central command, she'll also be able to completely disrupt their communications across all ships, cities, and planets for a short while afterward. The pairing of the unearthing of the truth and an inability to communicate will throw them for a loop, and we can take advantage."

"So you want Xala to be as panicked and chaotic as Sora is now?" Asha said skeptically.

"Hopefully more so," replied Maston.

"The revelation that the existence of their entire species and the basis for a ten-thousand-year-old war is an enormous lie should send shockwaves through them that run deeper than what we're experiencing with Talis and us," Lucas said. "At least that's what Alpha has always made it sound like."

"We'll have to hope so," Maston said. "If we can't seriously disrupt their capabilities for an invasion, we'll lose Sora. They can reach us faster than we can reach them with their white cores. They'll be here in weeks."

"And we still have no way of getting Zeta to Xala," Lucas said. "Or have you been keeping that a secret too?"

"No such luck," Maston said. "We're still nowhere, last I heard."

The three of them stood in silence. The situation outside of their tiny hidden island was almost too dire to consider.

"I need to get back to the mainland," Maston said. "I'll be back to brief you once we figure all this shit out. I have to talk with Tannon to see where his head is."

"Does he think we're guilty?" Lucas asked.

"We haven't had much time to chat, but considering he's the one who pulled you off that Xalan ship drenched in Shadow blood, I'm guessing he'll be in your corner."

Maston opened the door to leave, but turned back to them.

"Oh, and the Tut-shai are friendly. They'll find something for you to eat."

"The what?"

But the door had already slammed shut behind him.

It took them a few hours before they found the Tut-shai. After locating some warm clothes and outerwear tucked under the bed, Lucas and Asha explored the rocky hill on which their cabin rested. On the other side from where they'd come, they found another path etched in the earth, one they followed for about a half an hour through the woods until they came upon a small encampment.

The Tut-shai looked vaguely Asian, but had pale white skin and glacial blue eyes. When they saw the two of them emerging from the forest path, they merely met them with smiles and waves and went about their business. It was a small community, with maybe only forty or fifty residents inside a collection of leather huts held together with handmade rope and carved wooden poles. A row of boats docked at the shoreline indicated it was a fishing village, and there were catches roasting on small fires scattered throughout the camp. Almost immediately, a round-faced woman wearing a billowing fur coat handed them two small fish skewered on pointed sticks. Friendly, indeed.

In the days that followed, they met the leader of the Tut-shai, Nanno, a short, wrinkled old man who looked to be a few days shy of a thousand. He was the only one who spoke any amount of Soran, and they learned he'd been in the SDI about eighty years ago before a mission marooned him with the Tut-shai. He'd stayed and started a family, leaving his old life behind. He told them how the tribe was ancient, and even after thousands of years, they were content to live in peace, free of the technological advancements of the rest of the planet. Nanno boasted that his adopted people hadn't seen war in twenty thousand years, though that seemed like something of an exaggeration.

The Tut-shai's lifestyle was practically prehistoric. They fished, they harvested plants from the forest, and they survived. Other Tut-shai were scattered around islands all throughout the region, and had no interest in anything other than their tiny patch of ocean. In other words, anyone the government kept here had no fear of being exposed by the locals. It seemed to be an otherworldly witness protection program of sorts. Nanno and the SDI had an understanding, and he was more than welcoming to those who needed safe haven. Lucas and Asha were starting to get sick of fish already, and it hadn't even been a week.

On their sixth day there, Nanno's wife, Janti, had tasked them with marching into the forest with buckets to extract water from one of the island's inland freshwater pools. It was only a few miles worth of hiking, though that practically took them across the entire minuscule island.

As they approached the village, they heard a high-pitched shriek up ahead through the woods. They looked at each other worriedly and set down the water before sprinting toward town.

When they got there, they found the village completely deserted. Fires were burning blackened fish. A shattered pot lay in pieces on the ground. Lucas grabbed a nearby harpoon stuck in the ground; their weapons were back at the cabin at Nanno's request. Asha pulled out a silver knife that appeared to have materialized from thin air.

Lucas peeked into one of the tents and found a mother with three small children quivering inside.

"*Ko lalo toso*!" she cried, shaking her head violently. "*Ko lalo monosi*!"

She raised her finger to point behind them. Lucas spun around, harpoon raised.

Standing there was an eight-foot-tall, confused-looking creature.

Alpha.

"They informed me I could find you here," he said through his flickering translator collar, which had somehow survived the island's dampening system. "It appears the locals are not accustomed to my species."

Of course they're not, Lucas thought. They wouldn't have had any reason to ever see a Xalan before, as the uprising and homeworld strikes hadn't touched this tiny patch of the planet. No wonder they were terrified.

"What brings you to our little corner of paradise?" Asha asked.

"Until this point, I have been kept underground in research labs as we continue to formulate a plan of action despite this . . . distraction," Alpha replied.

"What's going on out there? We've heard nothing," asked Lucas.

"The planet is still in turmoil in the wake of High Chancellor Vale's death. Commander Tannon Vale has assumed power, though many are calling for his removal in light of Talis Vale's past actions against the Rhylosi."

Some of the Tut-shai were starting to creep out of their tents now, looking in wonder at the talking creature in the middle of their village. Alpha paid them no mind.

"Why did you come here? Friendly visit?" Asha asked.

"If only it were so," Alpha said. "I am the first of many who will be joining us. Our journey to Xala is at hand."

A little girl in a fur coat far bigger than she was waddled up to Alpha. She thrust her arms upward and presented him with a raw fish as long as her arm. Alpha looked at it curiously for a minute before staking it with his claw and devouring it whole.

"If only the rest of this galaxy were as hospitable," he said. "Zeta waits at your residence. Let us go."

Over the course of the next day, a collection of hovercraft and small ships began landing on the beaches of the island, bringing familiar faces with them. First came Mars Maston, less heated than the last time they'd seen him, but clearly on edge. Kiati and a few of the Guardians who had survived Makari arrived a short while later, along with a few steel-eyed soldiers Lucas didn't recognize. Then came Tannon Vale himself with an entourage of military officials Lucas had met once or twice during strategy sessions. He looked like he'd aged ten years in ten days, and Lucas could imagine why. He told them to expect at least one more ship's arrival, but their relatively small cabin was already going to be stuffed with people. Alpha and Zeta could barely stand without hitting their heads on the rafters.

"Good to see you, High Chancellor," Lucas said as Tannon entered.

"Oh, stop it with that shit. I'm no more Chancellor than he is," he said, nodding toward Alpha. "I'm just the guy cleaning up Talis's mess."

Lucas had learned that Tannon had had no knowledge of his sister's plans for Vitalla, though much of the public didn't believe that.

"I see you brought the whole cavalry," Asha said, looking around their ever-shrinking residence.

"Well, it's a big day," Tannon said. He looked odd in plainclothes, but still intimidating.

"Now that most of us are here, someone should probably tell them what's going on," said Maston. Behind him, Kiati scratched her recently regrown eye; there was still some scarring around it. Maston had decided to keep his synthetic leg for the time being, he'd told them.

"Indeed," said Tannon. "Time for your redemption."

"Redemption?" said Asha. "We didn't do anything."

"Well, the planet still needs saving either way, and we need your help to do it," Tannon said. "May I continue?"

Asha nodded warily.

"This . . . situation may have provided a scenario to get Zeta to Xala."

"And how is that?" Lucas said incredulously. He was feeling claustrophobic, but at least the cabin wasn't freezing for a change.

"You will escape Sora. Make a run for it."

"And why would we do that?" Lucas asked.

"You, Asha, and your Xalan friends are no longer safe here. I've publicly accused the four of you of killing my sister and helping Hex Tulwar escape."

"You *what*?" Asha yelled as she shot a look toward Maston, who remained stonefaced.

"More importantly," Tannon continued, ignoring her outburst. "The *Xalan Ruling Council* now knows you've been accused of killing my sister. They may have limited intelligence here, but they'll at least hear that much."

"So we'll escape? Then what?" Lucas asked. Tannon folded his arms across his chest.

"The story will be that Alpha transplanted a white null core into a Soran ship, and the four of you are on your way to a sparsely populated rim planet to seek asylum with Fourth Order sympathizers. With the core, you will be able to outrun pursuit by the SDI."

"But not the Xalans," Lucas said, starting to catch on.

"The idea is that even with their pending invasion, they'll send at least a ship or two to intercept your craft and take all of you prisoner," said Tannon.

"One of my resistance contacts will pose as a double agent and leak the location of our escape to the Ruling Council," said Zeta. Maston cut in.

"Two of their greatest scientific minds and most prominent rebellion leaders, along with the humans responsible for killing their Shadow Commander, would be too valuable a target to pass up."

"We are not a forgiving people," Zeta mused.

"They will ambush you; we will ambush them," Maston said. "We'll secure their ship and load it up with our own troops. Then we'll head back to Xala where we'll disembark and disappear with the aid of Zeta's Xalan resistance plants before they get wise to us. They should be distracted by the invasion at that point, anyway."

"Jesus Christ," Asha said. "Alpha, did you come up with this?"

"Perhaps," Alpha replied.

"Yeah, it sounds like one of yours. Insanity, inside and out."

"And yet you live," Alpha replied smartly.

"It ain't pretty, but it's the best option we've got. The clock's run out," said Tannon. The military leaders he'd brought with him nodded silently in assent. Kiati appeared to be bored and was polishing her pistol in the corner while the other Guardians stood uncomfortably shoulder to shoulder.

"When do we leave?" Lucas asked, knowing from the beginning that no matter what they were asked to do, they would do it. He glanced at Asha, who looked riled, but he knew she was onboard. This was what they'd come here to do; it didn't matter what the planet thought of them at the moment. *Truth is eternal, after all.*

"Tonight," Maston said. "We leave tonight."

Everyone retreated to the ships and waited for the escape craft to appear. That meant there was room to breathe in the cabin again, and only Alpha and Zeta remained, conversing quietly by the fire. They were risking even more than he and Asha, Lucas thought, to save a species that wasn't even their own. But he supposed they were more motivated by hopefully freeing their people from tyranny. Lucas realized he often forgot that the Ruling Council had also butchered Alpha's entire family; he rarely spoke of it. And god only knew what Zeta had been through.

There was a knock on the door and Lucas figured it was Maston coming back to go over more logistics. But when he opened it, he found that one final group of visitors had made the journey out to see them off.

Malorious Auran stood in the doorframe, holding Noah by the hand. Beside him, a teenaged caretaker delicately held little Erik in her arms. In recent weeks he'd grown a thicker tuft of brown hair, and his eyes were starting to change from blue to Asha's bright green. Lucas's face lit up, as did Noah's.

"Lucas!" squealed Noah as he toddled over. Lucas dropped to his knees to give him a hug. Asha stood up from the table and raced over to take Erik from the caretaker. She too wore a brilliant smile.

"They wanted to say hello," Auran said. "They were very well behaved on the ride here."

"Thank you for bringing them," Lucas said, extending his hand to Auran.

"It was my honor," Auran said as he grasped it. "As it will be to watch over them until you return."

Lucas's smile dimmed a bit. Auran started backing out of the doorway.

"We will let you have some time," he said. Alpha and Zeta had come over to greet the children, and they too were now moving toward the exit.

When the door shut behind them, a realization struck Lucas like lightning. This could be the last time he'd be together with his new family. The last time he'd ever see these children. Sure, they'd survived much, and had lived through many other battles they shouldn't have, but this was different. This was a new level of danger. They were diving straight into a snake pit without a definite way back out.

"Where are you going?" asked Noah, tilting his head to the side. He seemed to grow taller by the day. His white-blond hair was starting to become more sandy-colored.

"I have to go help make sure you're safe," Lucas said, kneeling so he could look into Noah's eyes. "I have to go somewhere very far away, and I might not be back for a long time."

Noah looked anxious.

"Can I come too? I can help. I'm good at that," he said earnestly. Lucas couldn't get over how well he spoke for someone so young.

"I know you are," Lucas said, smiling. He felt the sharp sting of tears beginning to form in his eyes. "But I need you to stay here and be brave for your brother. Can you do that?"

Noah nodded reluctantly. Asha was speaking softly to Erik, who couldn't reply and was content to nap in her arms.

"Just know that whether we're here or not, Asha and I are always with you. You mother and father will always be with you."

Lucas didn't usually refer to himself as a father when it came to Noah, the boy he'd had thrust into his arms by a dying slave in a cannibal village, but it suddenly felt rather foolish not to call himself that. He loved this child like a son. If that didn't make him a father, he didn't know what would.

"You will do great things," Lucas said, placing his hand on Noah's shoulder. "You'll lead a whole new generation." He thought of Auran's thirty-six souls, waiting to emerge from their tanks.

"Can we go to the park when you get back?" Noah asked, too young to understand what Lucas was saying.

"Of course," Lucas said. "Of course we can."

A half hour later, Noah was playing on the boarskin rug with toys he'd brought with him while Asha and Lucas sat with Erik by the fire, which was starting to die down into embers.

Lucas finally spoke.

"You should stay."

Asha glanced over at him.

"What?"

"I said, you should stay."

"Like hell."

"I'm serious," Lucas said. "They're going to need a mother."

It was something that had been plaguing Lucas since Makari, where he'd thought about what would happen to the children if neither of them made it home to Sora.

"And they'll have one. A father too, when we get back," Asha said slowly.

"Do you really think we'll come back?" Lucas asked.

Asha pulled on Erik's blanket to swaddle him a bit more tightly. He hadn't cried once since his arrival.

"We always have so far."

"You shouldn't go, you shouldn't risk it."

Asha was starting to get angry now.

"I shouldn't risk it? Do you honestly think after everything we've been through I'm going to turn back now?"

"I just—"

"I'm not going to abandon you or Alpha after all this time. I'm not going to sit back and do nothing to help destroy the bastards that killed our entire planet."

"I want you to stay," Lucas said firmly, his blood starting to boil. Erik had woken up and was looking dangerously cranky.

"Why?" Asha said forcefully. "Why should I stay?"

"Because I love you!" Lucas said.

The words felt foreign in his mouth. He couldn't remember the last time he'd said them, or to whom. They might have been raising two children together, but it was the first time he'd ever spoken it out loud. Asha froze like she'd been stabbed in the chest. After what seemed like an eternal silence, she spoke.

"I love you too," she whispered. "And that's why I have to go. To make sure you come back."

"It might not be up to you," Lucas said, calming down a bit.

"But it could be," Asha said quietly. "If I don't go and you don't make it back, I'll never know if there was anything I could have done. I couldn't live with that."

Lucas looked down at Erik, who was settling down as the volume of their voices had lessened. He thought about what Asha was saying. What kind of father could he ever be if he stayed behind and Asha went off and died on Xala? It would destroy him. He understood what she meant. They needed to look after each other out there, like they always had. He sighed.

"You know, if we asked they'd probably give us a little villa on the beach somewhere on this planet. All four of us could just live out the rest of our days without a care in the world."

"If only," Asha said.

"Someday," Lucas said. "Maybe someday."

The next knock on the door was one Lucas had been dreading. He'd heard the engines outside, and knew which craft had arrived this time. He gathered up Noah and Erik, bundling them up in warm blankets and coats, and headed out into the chilly night. When he reached the shore, everyone else was already assembled.

Their ride hung in the air and slowly descended toward the beach. It was a civilian cruiser, about as big as the Ark but dramatically different in style. Jagged angles, white hull plating, and gold lighting made it look like a chunk of some unearthed rare mineral. Maston told them it was a luxury liner they were meant to have stolen in their escape, along with the white null core, and at the very least it might make for a somewhat pleasant first leg of the journey.

Alpha had split their last remaining white null core in two. It was a dangerous process, and upon completion, each half would only continue to function for another twenty days or so, when they would then be rendered useless. As the rim planet they were fleeing to was a two-week flight away, it would suit their purposes.

The other half of the core was being given to an SDI cruiser, the *Valiance*. It would fly a parallel path to their own (at the same speed, because of the core), but hide when they reached the rim planet. When the Xalans arrived to collect the four of them from the civilian transport, the *Valiance* would spring into action, disabling the ship and filling it with their own crew. Lucas tossed out the term "Trojan horse," but no one knew what he was talking about except Asha. The SDI ship was far too large to dock at the island and would be following them shortly after they left.

Lucas felt a large hand grasp his shoulder.

"As soon as this is over, I promise we'll clear your name," Tannon said. "You won't have to worry about that when you come back, or what your children will grow up thinking if you don't."

Tannon was the only one making a frank assessment of their chances of survival.

"Don't think I don't realize what you're doing for us. It's more than I could ever ask of you."

"That's why you didn't have to ask at all," Lucas said. "This is what we came here to do. Not just to save your world or avenge ours, but to stop this from spreading to planets we don't even know exist yet. Who knows how many more humans, Sorans are out there? This evil must be extinguished."

Tannon grunted.

"One thing I've learned from war is that evil is never truly destroyed. The best you can hope for is to contain it."

"Then that's what we'll do," Lucas said.

"I know you will," Tannon said gruffly. A curt nod, and that was that.

Final preparations were being made for departure. Maston and the Guardians were already heading to the mainland to board the *Valiance*. Alpha and Zeta were already onboard.

"Where are they?" Lucas asked, and Asha led him over to a nearby hovercraft parked on the beach. Inside, sheltered from the cold, were Noah and Erik, sleeping soundly. It was now the middle of the night and the pair were exhausted from traveling all day.

"Should we wake them?" Asha whispered.

Lucas shook his head.

"Nah, let them sleep. They've earned it."

"We'll see them again soon," Asha said.

Lucas placed his hands on each of them; they were warm, wrapped in heavy blankets. Noah stirred slightly but didn't wake. He'd keep this image with him. The Last Son of Earth, the First Son of Sora. He would see them grow up, no matter what it took.

21

The atmosphere was tense aboard the cruiser as they moved through a space-time tunnel toward the rim planet and their eventual ambush. It reminded Lucas of their final days on the Ark, when they were waiting for Omicron to jump out of the shadows once they reached the Soran solar system. To make it feel somewhat less like a voyage of the damned, the four of them took to telling old stories over meals, about their lives before and since they met each other.

Alpha spoke of elaborate pranks his older brothers pulled back at the Xalan science academy. Zeta talked about what it was like to try and introduce technology to the Oni, who were forever convinced she was a sorceress.

Tonight it was Asha's turn, and she was regaling them with a story Lucas knew all too well.

"So these ugly assholes have us all tied to stakes, right? And what does Alpha do? He *blows up his suit of power armor* right in the middle of them. Never mind that if it had been a few feet further forward, it would have cooked all of us."

"I calculated that action with precision," Alpha said.

"Bullshit," Lucas said, chuckling.

"Anyway, we pick ourselves up and start mowing down all these poor SOBs who had no idea what just happened. There were probably fifty in the group, but I made short work of them while these two were napping on the ground. Unfortunately, their leader survived, and was about the size of a rhinoceros," Asha continued.

Zeta stared blankly at her.

"Ah right, you don't have those. Well, he was really goddamn big, which is all you need to know. He almost caves Lucas's head in before I knife him in the shoulder and shoot him in the hand."

"Excuse me," Lucas interrupted. "I think you're leaving out the part where I remove his head with a shotgun. Credit where credit's due."

"I was getting to that!" Asha exclaimed. "But before that happens, the guy starts speaking Norwegian. He tells us that he's a schoolteacher. A schoolteacher! And now he's the chief of a cannibal village teaching classes on raping and eating people. That should tell you how messed up our planet got near the end."

"You have some unbelievable stories," Zeta said as she chewed on a piece of blackened meat. The luxury cruiser had a fully stocked kitchen, much to their delight.

"Yes, some are quite unbelievable indeed," Alpha said flatly. "And I was present for many of them."

Asha did have a tendency to exaggerate.

"Do you want me to tell the one where you got yourself captured, and your idea of a fix was to blow up yourself and a whole space station with a nuke?"

"If you had listened, I would not be here to endure such mockery," Alpha replied. "Let us not forget who persuaded our heavily armed friend here not to execute you in the middle of an ashen crater."

"Well he's just lucky I didn't shoot him in the head in Georgia."

Lucas shook his head in exasperation. It was clear this could go on for some time, though it did serve to remind him how intertwined their fates were, and how often they'd had each other's backs since this insane adventure began.

Later that night, Lucas heard Alpha approach on the bridge. Lucas was often up there to gaze into the hypnotizing blue-green glow of the space-time tunnel. He found it calming.

Alpha was clutching something in his six-fingered metal claw. Lucas recognized it immediately.

"Wow, I'd forgotten all about that."

It was the glass square Lucas had taken from Omicron's hidden safe aboard the Spear. But instead of being blank, a dim white light was shining outward from the center.

"Did you . . ." Lucas began.

"In a spare moment I acquired a tissue sample from Commander Omicron's corpse, which is currently being studied by Soran scientists as they attempt to learn about Shadow biology. I reanimated the cells enough that the [garbled] recognized his genetic signature and activated. Once switched on, I was able to sustain the process permanently."

"What's in it?" Lucas asked, staring into the white light.

Alpha set the cube down on the arm of the captain's chair and suddenly a brilliant display of Xalan symbols flooded the viewscreen in front of them.

"Many things. Commander Omicron was indeed much older than I believed. He speaks of many military battles, even the initial invasion of Makari, which was well over a thousand years ago."

Lucas was taken aback. Omicron was over a thousand years old? It couldn't be possible.

"It seems the regenerative properties of the Shadow conversion can prolong life indefinitely. A truly unsettling notion," Alpha continued.

Indeed it was, and that meant that if their production was allowed to continue, the numbers of Shadows in existence could swell to terrifying proportions.

"One passage stood out to me and appeared to be relevant for our present mission."

Alpha hovered his hand over the square and was somehow navigating through it.

"Here," he said, coming to rest on a particular data file. "Though I realize you understand basic Xalan, I have translated it into English for your convenience."

It was a dated personal log entry, though Lucas was unfamiliar with the Xalan calendar. He began to read.

1124.32[945]

Today marks a day I have long feared. My youngest son will attempt to survive the conversion process to become a Shadow. The scientists persist in telling me they do not understand why my other children perished in the transformation. The Council demands continued efforts so that they may replicate my power, and I have no choice but to continue to surrender my offspring for the slaughter. I maintain it is their dangerous new enhancements, the push of these psionic powers they've thrust upon this new generation of "Chosen" Shadows. Is speed and strength and limitless prowess in battle not enough for them? I feel myself breaking further away from the Council on this issue, even if I have been the face of the project for centuries.

But he is strong, despite his age. I have faith that he will pull through, that he will endure the way his father did all those years ago. And if he does not? The Council has no more children to take from me.

Alpha had described the brutality of the Shadow conversion process, saying only a fraction of the subjects survived, but to read about Omicron's own offspring being forced to make the attempt seemed cruel. Lucas felt just a tiny amount of sympathy for the creature who had once hunted them.

1124.32[949]

I rejoice! My son has survived conversion. It was a perilous few days, but he managed to pull through despite dire prognoses. He is not yet awake, and the scientists run their tests. They express discontent that he does not exhibit initial signs of the Chosen, but they are foolish to overlook the new warrior they've spawned. I envision a day where the two of us fight side by side as equals.

If his mother were alive to see this momentous occasion, she would be as elated as I. As would his brothers. But he is now all I have left. I will begin training him in the ways of the Shadows as soon as he has woken from his slumber.

He'd survived? Great, all they needed was another Shadow as strong as Omicron running around out there. Lucas continued reading.

1124.32[952]

Something . . . disturbing has happened with my son's transformation. The scientists do not know how to explain it. Some mutation, something gone wrong in the genetic code. Speaking to him, his mind is clearly fractured. He is prone to fits of rage, and has already broken out of restraints twice. His skin has not blackened, but rather has become crimson. I fear his affliction may be a fate worse than death.

1124.32[959]

He broke free today, and they couldn't hold him in the facility. He's grown massive, sprouted enormous claws and, stranger still, wings. The unexpected mutations allow him great power, but his mind is lost. During his escape he slaughtered half the research team and another dozen guards once he made his way to the surface. They were finally able to subdue him, and his new holding chamber is an impenetrable vault. Constant, blinding light holds him at bay.

The Council wants him exterminated, but I will not let them. I will work with him, reforge his mind into sanity. Imagine if his power could be harnessed! We may fight side by side yet.

The Desecrator was Omicron's son. No wonder he had been chosen to hunt them down. It was a more than a mission. It was revenge. Lucas looked over at Alpha to confirm and found he was already nodding. He continued reading.

1124.33[1003]

After weeks of therapy and progress, everything collapsed today. With those damnable wings, he burst through the ceiling of the training chamber and flew toward the nearest village. By the time I reached him, he had slaughtered most of them. Men, women, children, by the hundreds. We tried to contain the event, but whispers spread outward regardless. The locals won't even set foot in the village anymore, superstitious fools declaring it unholy ground. They're calling the fire-eyed beast that did it the "Desecrator." That is what my son has become.

1124.33[1022]

The Council has made their ruling, and he is to be killed. Regardless of such a thing being impossible due to his immense power, I will not allow them to make the attempt. He has been improving as of late. Coherent. Able to understand and follow my instructions. I see a glimpse of the son I once knew buried inside him. I will help him escape one last time. Escape from Xala entirely.

Makari. It is the place for him. He can hunt to his heart's content in those jungles, and they will never find him. I will claim no knowledge of his whereabouts, and may have to feign injury to assure them I was overpowered.

I believe in time they will realize his power, they will understand that he is a weapon to be wielded, not destroyed. But until then, he must be far away from here.

1124.33[1029]

It is done. And once more, I find myself alone.

"Damn . . ." Lucas said as the file closed itself. "As if we needed to consider him even more dangerous."

"Perhaps," Alpha said. "Though this could be of some use to us."

Alpha reopened the file and tapped a particular line.

"Constant, blinding light holds him at bay."

Lucas had been so shocked at the family connection that he'd missed that entirely. He was reminded how the creature had been disoriented by nearby grenade blasts when they'd fought him on Makari.

"That could be useful," he said. "But he did end up escaping and murdering a whole bunch of people in spite of that."

"Still," Alpha said. "It is more than we knew before."

Alpha, forever the knowledge seeker. Hopefully the morsel would be of some use should they encounter the creature again. Would they really call him back to Xala?

The two-week voyage felt like an eternity at the time, but once it was nearly over, it seemed like it had gone by in a flash. They were set to arrive in the rim system in a matter of hours, and all parties were making final preparations for phase two of the plan. Maston was currently taking up most of the main viewscreen, telling them what was about to happen.

"You'll arrive in the system, and I can't imagine the Xalans will be there more than a few minutes after that. The bastards are quite punctual."

Lucas knew that to be the case from their last run-in with Omicron.

"As soon as they show up, I'll take the *Valiance* out of the asteroid belt masking our signal. We'll shut their comms down and disable their ship. They may have already crippled your vessel to prepare for boarding, but it won't matter. As long as we get there before they breach, all should go according to plan."

"And then we knock them all out?" Asha said skeptically. Lucas was similarly unsure of the next stage. Alpha spoke.

"If we arrive on Xala with a ship full of Soran lifeforms and only two Xalans, they will be suspicious. We need to keep most of them alive, give or take a few that may have been killed in an imagined ensuing struggle during capture."

"That's where we come in," said Maston. "We'll flood their ship with gas, and then board and stun whoever's left. Then it's to Xala we go."

The entire crux of the plan relied on Alpha and Maston's ability to coordinate. There was also a certain amount of luck involved. The Xalans could get spooked and jet away before the ship could be captured, or they could be on a kill mission and blow them away on first contact. That's not what Zeta's spies had relayed, but who knew? And above all else, god forbid someone gave the Desecrator a spaceship.

When they arrived, they found themselves in yet another unfamiliar system. The rim world they were meant to be escaping to had barely fifty thousand residents and was a frosty little planet they would likely never even see, if all went smoothly. In the distance hung a dull reddish sun obscuring the diagonal stripe of the Milky Way.

They'd already been waiting twenty minutes or so as they shuffled toward the ice world, waiting to be attacked. The interceptor was coming, that much they knew, so where was it? Lucas felt naked without power armor, but it was part of the ruse, as they weren't supposed to be anticipating an attack. Comms were silent; they didn't want to give away the fact that Maston was nearby in the *Valiance*.

"Maybe we're not so special after all," Asha finally said at the half-hour mark. The ice planet would be in sight soon.

"Speak for yourself," Lucas shot back.

The silence was eerie. The recycled air in the cruiser was starting to feel thin, though Lucas thought he was probably just in the early stages of hyperventilation. Again, fear never did seem to want to leave him for good. Though perhaps it was part of what had kept him alive so far.

And then they appeared.

"Readings indicate a mid-range [garbled] interceptor craft. Fifty, no, sixty Xalan lifeforms are onboard. They are closing fast." Alpha rattled off the information quickly, sifting through the ship's data displays.

"Jesus, they brought the whole cavalry, huh?" Lucas said. It was hard to fault them after what had happened aboard the Ark.

"Punch it!" ordered Asha to Lucas who was seated in a captain's chair far too tiny for a Xalan to pilot effectively. He raised engine power output to dangerous levels as they rocketed through space toward the asteroid field. They had to make it look convincing.

But it was already too late. An energy pulse washed over them like a tidal wave, and Lucas felt his hair stand on end as it passed through the ship. The lights went off, then kicked into emergency mode, bathing everything in a dull blue.

"Incoming," Alpha said, and within seconds the entire ship shook as something latched onto the hull. Time to break radio silence.

"Maston?" Lucas yelled into the comm. No answer.

They had to gas the interceptor before they breached the airlock seal or—

A flashing readout indicated they were already inside.

"Goddamnit!" Asha yelled. "Defensive positions!"

The four of them grabbed their weapons and took cover behind the myriad of consoles scattered throughout the room. Visuals within the ship were offline. The only indicator someone was coming was the light clink of claws on the metal floor. It reminded Lucas of their last stand aboard the Ark, though this time they had no power armor and they weren't going out the viewscreen as a last resort.

"We're here," Maston said finally through the comm. "We took a hit from a rock, slowed us down."

"They're already onboard!" Lucas shouted.

"Shit," Maston said. "Hang on, we're disabling."

The *Valiance* could be seen out of the viewscreen wheeling around toward them after emerging from the asteroid belt with a large new gash in its hull. Alarms were surely sounding on the Xalan ship as the enormous SDI vessel came into view. Would they retreat?

A round metal object landed next to Lucas. The second it took him to process what it was almost cost him dearly. He lashed out with a kick and sent the grenade flying toward the opposite end of the room. It erupted with a flash and seared his eyes, but if it had blown next to him, it might very well have rendered him permanently blind.

Asha poked her head up and put a round through the skull of the first Xalan who dared to enter the room. Alpha cut down another with his energy pistol. Lucas recognized their sleek black armor and the symbol on them. Paragons. Xala's most deadly. He shouldn't have expected any less.

Another flash and this time they couldn't react. Xalans swarmed into the room and by the time Lucas's vision came back, there was one right in front of him, swinging a large metal pole toward him that cracked with electricity. It seemed capture, not kill, was their order. Despite both sides being committed to nonlethal tactics, Lucas knew they had a few bodies to spare.

He cut the soldier in half with Natalie's shotgun spray and turned to watch Asha disarm a nearby Xalan by slicing off both his arms with her sword.

Another flash and Lucas was on the ground, searing pain shooting through his eyes. The Xalans wore tinted visors and weren't affected by the devices. Lucas's eyes cleared and he saw Zeta and Alpha being set upon by troops. He managed to get a shot off at one on top of Zeta, and the soldier went tumbling off her. Unfortunately, two immediately took his place.

Asha had been backed into a corner and was slicing through stun batons, which were no match for the razor edge of her sword. Suddenly, a blast of light connected with her head and she went down, instantly unconscious, but hopefully not dead. Lucas struggled to his feet.

"Maston!" he screamed into the comm.

"It's too late for containment," came the reply. "We have to gas both ships."

Lucas raced over to Asha and rammed his knife into a crack in the plating of a trooper attempting to lift her. Something shoved him from behind and he crashed headfirst into the wall. As he crumpled to the ground, he found himself staring at a ventilation duct. Yellow steam began to pour out of it and Lucas was starting to fade within seconds. He couldn't feel the Xalans raining down blows on him, but soon they fell next to him.

22

Lucas woke with a sharp pain in his arm. Glancing over, he saw Kiati pulling a needle out of his shoulder. He burst into an uncontrollable spasm of coughing.

"Rise and shine," she said as she stood up and bent down again a few feet over from him. Lucas rolled over and saw she was injecting Asha with a similar cocktail. She sprang to life and started coughing up a fit. Lucas's lungs were burning and could feel a host of fresh bruises covering his upper body.

He sat up and looked around the room and recognized the architecture immediately. They were onboard the Xalan vessel. Nearby, Guardians were dragging limp Xalan bodies stripped of their Paragon armor out into the hallway.

"What's goin' on?" he asked groggily. Asha was still coughing.

Kiati extended her arm and helped him to his feet.

"We had to leave you out for a while before waking you up from the gas. Too soon and it'll fry your nervous system."

Lucas's nervous system felt frayed, but intact, so it appeared they had waited the correct amount of time.

"Where are you taking them?" he asked, motioning to the bodies being carried out of the room. They were in some sort of storage bay it seemed.

"Time to put them all to sleep for the duration of our flight. They're loading them in the cryopods upstairs. They'll be alive, but unconscious, for as long as we're here. We'll execute them once we reach Xala."

Asha had finally caught her breath.

"So everything's good then, even with you guys showing up late?"

"Don't blame us," Kiati said curtly. "You try being on time when a rogue asteroid takes out one of your engines."

Alpha entered the room, apparently already having been revived. He too had a fair amount of bruising, some of it across his face.

"I broadcasted a forged transmission indicating our 'success' from the communications bay. They believe the mission to be complete and that we are en route back to Xala. Zeta relayed what has actually transpired to her agents on the homeworld who will be the ones helping facilitate infiltration once we arrive."

Lucas lightly kicked a downed Paragon.

"What are the numbers then?"

Alpha checked a readout. "Five Xalans killed during their capture attempt. Acceptable. Believable."

He tapped a few more keys.

"In addition to you and Asha, we will depart with four Guardian troops, including Commander Maston."

"And including me," Kiati said. She was tending to a raised knot on Lucas's head.

"Only four?" Asha asked, finally able to catch her breath. "We have a whole ship full on the *Valiance*." She motioned toward a porthole where the SDI cruiser could be seen.

"Four could mean you were accompanied by a small escort in your escape who were also captured. More than that would draw suspicion. This infiltration is meant to be tactical, not an outright assault, which would surely fail."

Eight of them, then. Against all of Xala. Lucas shook his head, much to Kiati's annoyance. He looked into her stern bluish-green eyes as she sealed a cut on his forehead with gel.

"You volunteered?" he asked.

"Best case, I'm a hero," she replied. "Worst case, I'll see an old friend again."

Before Lucas could respond, Maston broke through on the comm.

"Get down here now," he said. "There's something you need to see."

"Holy shit," Lucas said as he looked down at the creature lying on the floor of the CIC. He was wearing light plated armor and clutched a fearsome-looking pistol. His skin was as black as the void of space outside.

"I should have anticipated they would send a Shadow," Alpha mused. "They likely wanted to leave nothing to chance."

Asha pulled out her Magnum and stood over him, pointing the barrel at its exposed head.

"We can't take any chances with this thing," she said.

A panicked Alpha rushed forward and swatted her pistol sideways with his metal claw. She glared at him.

"You cannot. I already relayed the casualty count back to Xala."

He tapped a few controls at the nearby holotable.

"In addition, this ship bears his signature. He is the operator. If we kill him now, they will know that somehow a Shadow captain has died despite the prisoners being allegedly secured and unconscious on a ship full of Paragons. They will not believe such a thing is possible without foul play involved. We must secure him like the others."

Maston looked at Alpha.

"I hate to say it, but he's right."

Asha reluctantly lowered her weapon.

"You're sure you can keep this thing chained up and out cold for our entire flight? What if sleeping beauty wakes up because you don't know the proper gas dosage to keep him under?"

"We have little choice in the matter, but I will monitor his state at all times to ensure he does not regain consciousness."

"Someone help me with this damn thing," Maston said as he bent over the creature. Lucas did the same and two soldiers raised his legs on the other end. It must have weighed four hundred pounds, and Lucas was the only one not wearing strength enhancing power armor. Looking down, Lucas was a bit unnerved to see its pupils moving back and forth under its eyelids. What *did* Shadows dream about?

This was it, then: one final voyage toward nearly certain death. The *Valiance* had departed, its crew with it. Only the eight of them remained to roam around the cramped Xalan interceptor as they prepared for what lay ahead.

Lucas sat on an ammo box in the armory as he cleaned Natalie for the twentieth time. In addition to every Xalan weapon they had here, the *Valiance* had loaded them up with everything they needed to infiltrate Xalan central command. More guns than they could carry. A stealth suit and a spare for each of them. Odd devices that Lucas hadn't covered during his Guardian training.

Across from him, the two lucky souls other than Kiati and Maston who had joined their assault team sat shifting through their potential loadouts. There were still weeks to go until they reached Xala, but they'd likely spend every day preparing.

One of them was named Reyes, a young, brown-skinned woman with her right temple shaved to the scalp and voluminous black curls everywhere else. She was a custom-engineered tactical assassin who had been flown in specially for the mission. She boasted about targets she'd killed across Sora and in deep space. One time, she claimed, she put down the entire crew of a Xalan scouting vessel before they even knew she was onboard. After that, they started calling her "Whisper."

The other was a lanky bald man named Kovaks. He looked far skinnier than most male Guardians, but he was recruited for his infiltration prowess. He'd been a master thief before he was caught and forcibly enlisted in the SDI, where they taught him to kill instead of steal. He was one of the few Guardians who wasn't tank-bred. Additionally, he also had been one of the few to make it back from the Makari mission alive. If there was a dead Xalan in a dark corner during the spaceport assault, chances are he was responsible, he'd told Lucas.

Kovaks and Reyes were quite competitive when it came to recounting their past kills. It was soon revealed that both had lost family in the war: Kovaks a brother, Reyes her parents. Both had happily leapt at the opportunity to join the mission when they realized its significance.

Lucas finished his maintenance on Natalie and headed down a level to go back to his quarters. He heard footsteps from down the hall and decided to investigate.

He made his way to the sleeping deck where the bodies of fifty-odd Xalans lay on ice. Maston was staring at one pod in particular. As Lucas approached, he knew which one.

"Staring death in the face?" Lucas asked. Maston was peering at the unconscious Shadow, secured and asleep behind the glass.

"Wouldn't be the first time," Maston said. "The last time I was this close to one of these, it nearly killed me."

"Same here," Lucas said. "We're in a very small club."

Lucas looked up and down the rows of pods.

"I wanted to shut off their oxygen until they were brain dead," Maston said. "That way we wouldn't have to worry about them at all."

"Can't we?" Lucas asked.

"Alpha says these pods wouldn't be enough to keep them alive after that. They need specialized tanks or something," Maston replied. He pressed his fingers to the glass.

"What would it be like, to have that much power?" he asked, gazing at the Shadow within.

"I don't know," Lucas answered. "But my guess would be terrifying. I wouldn't want to be something that was specifically bred to be a killing machine, would you?"

Maston laughed.

"Oh, I don't know, most Guardians are pretty well adjusted."

Lucas shook his head.

"They're not like this. Not like these things. I think you'd have to trade your soul to wield that much power."

"But to fight for your home, to defend those you love, wouldn't you make such a bargain?" Maston asked.

Lucas thought about it for a minute.

"I suppose I might," he answered truthfully. The Shadow's eyes were still moving underneath his lids. Lucas suddenly felt a sharp migraine coming on and took a step back.

"I'll be down the hall," Lucas said. "This place is eerie."

Maston didn't say a word, and Lucas left him staring into the pod.

Their eventual destination had Lucas uneasy already, but soon it became clear there was no solace in sleep either. Bad dreams were nothing new to Lucas; he'd endured more than his fair share since Earth. But these were something . . . else.

They went beyond nightmares to pure, unadulterated terrors that had Lucas waking up in a cold sweat screaming some nights. Sometimes many times a night.

These weren't flashbulb memories or strange dreams open to interpretation. They were simply terrifying, through and through. There was one that had Lucas strapped to a table being dissected by Alpha wearing bloodstained surgical gear. Looking down, he could see his internal organs convulsing, and each new slice brought a surge of pain that he could truly feel, despite his unconscious state.

Another night, he was simply made to sit and watch as Paragon troopers stormed into his house on the outskirts of Portland. There, they methodically tore his former wife and son, Sonya and Nathan, limb from limb before setting the entire place ablaze.

Lucas was paralyzed as the fire consumed him, and he felt every square inch of his flesh burn.

This night was different. He was back in the palace on Sora, roaming the empty hallways that were normally bustling with people. With each new turn, he found himself staring at an identical corridor, and he had no idea where he was actually going. But there was no pain, no savage Xalans nearby. What was going on?

Lucas made one final turn and found himself in a hallway painted with blood. It was the exact scene he'd found before entering Talis Vale's quarters the night of Tulwar's escape. There were corpses on the ground, and Lucas's eyes widened when he bent down to see who they were.

Corinthia Vale lay sliced open from sternum to hip bone. Silo was next to her, missing his entire lower half. Kiati's body was nearby, with her head a few feet further away. Tannon was sprawled out with his throat cut, draped over Talis, who was riddled with gunshots. Malorius Auran rested next to her, gored by stab wounds, staring blankly at the ceiling.

Lucas kept walking, splashing through the blood, which pooled like rain puddles. Again, as it had that night, the door lay mangled and torn off its hinges. When he stepped over it to enter the room, a jolt of shock surged through his spine as he found two more victims. Little Noah lay on the ground clutching Erik. Neither were bloodied, but both had turned a grotesque shade of blue. Lucas dropped to his knees in tears. He couldn't revive them, and they lay there like marble statues, looks of frozen terror etched on their faces.

Up ahead, the frame of Talis's bed was shaking. Lucas crawled forward past the small corpses and slowly got to his feet. There between the four pillars were Asha and Maston, stripped naked and very much alive. Lucas's mouth fell open as he watched the two writhe around, muscles straining, breathing shallow, not paying him any attention at all. Both were soaked in blood, as were the sheets below them, but Lucas knew it wasn't their own. Around them were discarded weapons. Swords, pistols, rifles, knives.

Blind with rage, Lucas picked up a nearby combat knife from the edge of the bed and launched himself at the two of them. He shoved Asha off of Maston and jammed the blade into his throat. Yanking it out, he turned toward Asha, who knocked the knife away. Lucas was too angry to care. Immediately he wrapped his hands around Asha's throat and threw her down onto the bed. He squeezed as hard as he was able; the blood on her bare skin made her slippery.

"Why?" he yelled. "Why?"

Despite being choked, Asha merely smiled as he shook her. Maston had blood spurting out of his neck next to them, but was somehow laughing maniacally.

"Why?" Lucas cried. Asha's smile only widened.

Lucas felt a crack on the side of his head. Pain shot through his temple and ricocheted around his skull.

He woke up on the ship.

Asha was glaring at him, breathing heavily. She rubbed her neck and even in the dark, Lucas could see there were angry red marks on her skin in the shape of fingers.

"Wha—" he began. "I didn't—"

"You didn't what?" Asha yelled. "Try to murder me in my sleep?"

She hit him hard in the face, which rocketed Lucas's head back and made him see stars. It was clear he deserved it. He tried to explain as he wiped away the blood trickling from his nose.

"I had a nightmare. It was—"

But she had already stormed out of the room, dragging most of the bedding with her.

When "morning" finally came, as indicated by the clocks, not the light outside, Lucas marched down to Alpha's quarters. The creature answered the door, looking irritated.

"Something's going on here," Lucas said flatly.

"What are you referring to?" Alpha said as he rubbed his head. Lucas could see red veins threading through his normally pitch-black eyes.

"I've been having nightmares. Truly messed-up shit. Dreams so visceral I can feel the pain in them. Tonight, I woke up trying to strangle Asha."

Alpha's reddened eyes widened.

"I have had similar terrors plaguing me. I thought I was alone in my torment. This . . . This is not a natural occurrence. It cannot be."

Alpha turned to walk back inside his quarters. It was a server room full of circuitry and holograms that sprang to life as he walked by. In a corner was a nest of blankets that was clearly his bed. Lucas half expected to find Zeta inside, but Alpha was too much of a gentleman, he supposed.

"Are you sure it's not just the stress of this suicide mission?"

Alpha shook his head. He flipped through a few screens on a nearby control cluster.

"I do not believe so. The images are so searing they feel purposefully planted."

"What have you seen?" Lucas asked.

"Many things," Alpha said, and Lucas thought he saw him shiver a bit. "I saw my family slaughtered before my eyes. I watched Zeta butchered by the Desecrator. I—"

He paused, and turned to look at Lucas.

"Tonight, I was dragged through the streets of Elyria, bound for execution in the central square. It was . . . you and Asha who carried out the sentence. I felt the rounds enter my chest as if it were actually taking place."

"Why would we both be having screwed up dreams like these?" Lucas asked.

Alpha had pulled up a view of the sleeping pod area on a floating monitor. He zoomed in on the figure.

"I suspect we are transporting a Chosen Shadow."

A few hours later, Alpha had the skeleton crew assembled in the CIC. From the rough-looking faces in the group, it was clear few had been getting much of any sleep as of late. Further investigation revealed all onboard had been plagued with the same sorts of horrifying visions. But as everyone else slept alone, no one had attempted to kill their bunkmate.

Asha had finally started speaking to Lucas again, but just barely. She still wore a permanent glare when looking in his direction.

"What have you seen?" Lucas asked her.

"I don't want to talk about it," she replied coldly. Lucas couldn't imagine much worse than what he'd been forced to witness, but who knew? He still couldn't shake the image of her and Maston and the pile of corpses, including their own children. It had sunk into him and seemed like it would be impossible to extricate.

"So you're saying this thing is putting these images in our minds?"

It was the woman who spoke, Reyes. The "Whisper." She had such dark circles under her eyes it almost looked like war paint.

"A Chosen Shadow has telepathic abilities, the full extent of which is not yet understood. Though, from our collective symptoms, this seems to be the most likely answer."

The man, Kovacs, rubbed his eyes.

"Is there any way to make it stop? We can't train like this."

Lucas wondered what career assassins had nightmares about.

Zeta chimed in. She looked less fatigued than the lot of them, but that wasn't saying much. Perhaps what she'd already endured while in captivity was worse than any terror the Shadow could show her.

"Alpha and I will try to develop a compound to feed into the pod's ventilation unit to disrupt its brainwaves. Though that poses a few risks. We could wake it, for one."

"It's worth the risk," Asha said with arms crossed. She'd already been driven insane once by maddening visions caused by Xalan technology; she wasn't about to have it happen again.

"Why is he doing this?" asked Kiati, who looked more angry than usual.

"I believe he is showing us visions based on manifestations of our own deepest fears ingrained in our subconscious. This would explain the . . . intensely personal nature of the horrors," Alpha said. "It is the only way he can torment us in his present state, without access to his physical body."

"And we really can't remove his physical body for good?" Lucas asked.

"Not without immediately alerting Xala something is wrong onboard."

Maston had remained silent through all of this.

"If he shows me her one more time, I'm going to lose it," he said. "I'll rip his telepathic brain from his skull and send it out an airlock."

"That would be ill-advised," Alpha said calmly.

"Then do it," Maston growled. "Make it stop. Or I will."

But Alpha and Zeta couldn't stop it. Not really. The compound they'd mixed up in their mad scientist lab didn't wake the creature, but it didn't stop the dreams either; it merely slowed their production. The nightmares still came, the pain still felt real, but it was only a few nights of the week now. Not a true solution, but at least something of a bandage.

Lucas had lost his roommate for good when Asha woke one night and almost slit his throat before snapping out of it. They called it even, but more serious steps had to be taken. Each night now, everyone onboard was locked in their rooms, away from weapons that could be used to hurt themselves or others.

This was torture, plain and simple. A mentally manufactured hell from which they couldn't escape. Lucas was tempted more than once to smash through the glass and cut the Shadow's head off, but he refrained, as did Maston, despite his earlier threats.

The two of them were in the cargo deck watching Asha and Reyes spar with each other. Asha had her faithful black-bladed sword and Reyes used two curved silver blades that were miraculously made out of a material Asha couldn't slice through. The two whirled around each other like the wind and clangs echoed through the chamber. Kiati and Kovacs were strategizing over virtual central command blueprints in the corner. Training was a way for all of their bodies to release the built-up rage induced by the nightmares, and planning focused their minds elsewhere, giving them problems to solve. But currently Lucas and Maston were doing neither.

"What does he show you?" Lucas asked. It was a dangerous question as he didn't want to set Maston off. But he was less angry today, and merely looked fatigued.

"It's Cora," he said quietly. "It's always Corinthia. Tortured, mutilated, battered, raped, dismembered. It's too much to take."

He put his palms to his forehead.

"Why her?" Lucas asked.

"I have no one else," Maston said. "It was only her. I never cared for anyone as much. I never will."

He stared out into the room as Reyes took a swing and missed Asha's throat by a millimeter.

"And even worse, it's always Tulwar. He's there with that serene smile on his face, committing the atrocities. And I can never reach him. Can never kill him. When I get close, he simply drifts away until the next night, and it starts all over again."

"I'm sorry," Lucas said.

Maston folded his hands together.

"Not as sorry as the thing's going to be the second we no longer need him alive."

"I meant I'm sorry about Tulwar. I'm sorry we let him win."

Maston threw up his hand dismissively.

"You didn't let him do shit. He played us, and did it well. All of us underestimated him, even before you showed up."

"If I'd let you kill him in Rhylos—" Lucas said.

"Cora would still be dead."

"And if we hadn't shown up at all?"

Maston fell silent for a minute. Then two. The only sound in the room was the clashing of metal in front of them. Asha was certainly being put through her paces from the looks of it.

"Tulwar and the Xalans would have found a way. As it happens, your presence is more likely to save us than destroy us."

He paused again.

"And you're the first friends I've had in years."

Maston gazed outward toward the duel in front of them, which was now drawing to a close. Both women were obviously fatigued, and the floor was wet with sweat and a few drops of blood from rogue swings.

Reyes dashed toward Asha, swinging her blades like a combine about to devour a line of crops. Asha spun to avoid the onslaught, whipping around her sword, which was immediately caught between the two blades. One sharp flick of the wrist from Reyes and the sword was wrenched from Asha's hand and thrown across the room, where it stuck into the wall.

"Yield?" Reyes asked with her one of her blades hovering in front of Asha's eye, the other pressed to her navel.

Asha just snorted before leaping backward and thrusting her legs forward into Reyes's stomach. She landed on her hands and propelled herself back to her feet. Her electromagnetic metal cuff had already been activated and the sword rocked out of the wall and into her hand. Reyes tried to recover, but Asha flipped the sword around so that the flat of the blade rested against her neck. With a sly smile she flicked the pommel and a quick jolt of electricity sent Reyes instantly crumpling to the ground. Not enough to fry her for good, but her hair was smoking as she lay on the deck.

"Cheating bitch," said Reyes, rubbing her head. But she was smiling. Asha extended her hand and helped her to feet.

"No such thing," Asha replied. She turned to Maston and Lucas. "You two up next?"

As time passed, the voyage toward Xala grew quieter and quieter. Evenings of restless sleep had everyone on edge, and no one bothered to talk about their latest nightmares anymore. The atmosphere onboard grew increasingly tense. With each passing day they were closer to a place they might never leave.

They now headed into the final day before they'd reach Xala. Alpha was double- and triple-checking their broadcast signatures and lifeform readouts to ensure everything was in order for the interceptor to pass inspection. There had been no incidents with the sleeping soldiers on the lower deck. Though the Shadow plagued them with visions in their sleep, Alpha believed it was not in his power to telepathically contact anyone on Xala from such a distance, especially in his current comatose state.

Everyone was itching to dive into the mission. They'd been training exceptionally hard to prepare for what was to come. Kiati and Reyes, the two tank-bred superhumans, had been putting them all through hell, and Lucas had never felt so powerful before. Combined with top-of-the-line armor and weaponry, Lucas began to feel like the eight of them could storm the whole of Xala themselves, though that was a lofty ambition. Central command would be enough of a task, as even ghosting their way into the building they'd likely meet a great deal of resistance. And getting out was another level of impossible in itself. The looks on everyone's faces as they roamed the halls suggested no one expected to make it back to Sora.

The last few hours had been all business. No room for fear or nervousness anymore. They went over their infiltration plan for the thousandth time and laid out their combat kits so they could be assembled and equipped in seconds. Once they were cleared to enter Xalan airspace, they would exterminate the crew, infiltrate central command, disseminate the message, and then escape while everything was in chaos. When put like that, it didn't sound all that bad, but the reality was likely to be far more complex.

23

There would be no dazzling array of stars or planets to greet Lucas as they came out of the space-time tunnel into the Xalan solar system. He was locked away in a windowless cell. The other six non-Xalans were in their own individual cells. When they entered the system, their ship would be scanned, and Alpha didn't want to take any chances. Everything had to look normal, and Zeta had spent a week forging the Shadow captain's biological and vocal prints that would let them pass into Xala. They had been broadcasting occasional updates to Xala during transit, but they'd be under much closer scrutiny here. One wrong word or suspicious readout and they would be boarded or blown out of the sky before they could even see the Xalan homeworld.

Lucas could feel the moment they exited the wormhole and started moving through space the old-fashioned way. Even if they were covering less distance, it felt like they were speeding up, now traveling at millions of miles an hour rather than suspended inside a place devoid of such measurements.

It was hard to tell what was taking place outside. They kept stopping and starting, presumably moving through the series of military checkpoints that Alpha warned them would be coming.

Lucas did push-ups on the floor of his cell to distract him. There was no way to know what was going on. Alpha wasn't broadcasting or translating any communication to the rest of them as he'd done previously. "Zero unnecessary risks" was his mantra for the entire mission, and everything had to be by the book to an almost insanely detailed degree.

Lucas wished Asha were here. Even though she was just in the next cell over, the thick, soundproof walls made her all but nonexistent. All the same, when he had exhausted himself, he leaned up against the wall where he figured she might be.

Then Lucas did something very strange. He prayed.

He couldn't remember the last time he'd done so. His faith had left him the moment the Xalans showed up on Earth, though in truth it had probably been many years before that. Here, with no one else to turn to, he prayed fervently to not just one omnipotent being, but any he could think of. Kyneth, Zurana, Saato, Valli. Maybe one of the stories was true. Maybe one of them out there would help them. In other circumstances, he would have felt foolish, but these were desperate times.

There was no answer, of course. But perhaps the silence was an answer in itself. Every second that went by where Lucas couldn't hear the clang of a security ship boarding them, or the explosion of a missile breaching the hull, was indeed what he had asked for. Whether luck or skill or divine intervention, Lucas didn't care at this point.

Finally, that one little word he'd been waiting for came booming through the ship.

"Go."

It was Alpha's voice, which meant they'd cleared the last hurdle required for phase two of the plan to kick into action. Lucas sprang up from the floor of his cell, the lightscreen in front of him deactivated, and the metal door behind it slid open. He tumbled out into the hall, almost crashing into Kovaks, who was in the room across from him. To his left was Asha, and next to her Maston and Kiati and Reyes followed. All had a fierce look of determination in their eyes, and no one hesitated for longer than a second as they sprinted to the armory. As Lucas ran down the hall, he could now see stars out of the ship's portholes, and in the distance a supergiant star burned bronze. Xala's sun. It looked old, ancient.

Within a matter of minutes, the six of them were outfitted in their stealth suits. Lucas felt the nanofibers of his armor turn icy, a way to slow down his pounding heart. He grabbed Natalie, a sidearm pistol, his knife, and a grenade belt, checking each one final time to ensure all were in working order. Looking over at Asha, he saw that she was already armed to the teeth and wore her familiar combat scowl. She bounced on the soles of her feet, waiting for everyone else to catch up. Soon, they all did, and the deadly fighting force before him was fearsome to behold. At least it would have been if they were about to take on anything but an entire planet.

They arrived on the bridge to find Alpha and Zeta similarly equipped. Alpha had appropriated and modified the Shadow captain's set of power armor, and Zeta was wearing Paragon plating. Both were highly functional, but also a worthwhile disguise if need be. A helmet covered each of their heads so their gray and white flesh wouldn't give them away.

"What's the status?" asked Maston, the first to enter the room and the ranking officer leading the mission.

"We successfully passed through three checkpoints on the outskirts of the system," said Alpha.

"No problems at all?" said Maston.

"It appears not," Alpha said somewhat proudly. "We underwent six separate scans, which left no doubt our manifest was as we claimed."

"What's that?" Lucas asked, pointing to a vaguely menacing-looking readout full of red dots that were slowly eclipsing adjacent green ones.

"I have begun exterminating the crew before the ship's auto-wake function activates. Half are dead already from the neurotoxin I have released, the rest will be extinguished shortly."

He said it without a hint of remorse or emotion. Alpha, despite appearing to be a meek scientist most of the time, was as stonehearted as any of them when he needed to be. Lucas thought back to when he'd ripped the throat out of his former mentor who dared to taunt him about his murdered family.

"Strange," Alpha said, tapping a floating screen that was completely blank. "The optical link down in the bay is malfunctioning."

"You're saying you don't have a visual on cryo?" Maston asked.

"I did until a few minutes ago," Alpha said. "I have been preoccupied."

"Goddamnit," Maston said.

"As you can see, the crew is—" Alpha motioned to the blinking red readout before Maston cut him off.

"Zero unnecessary risks," Maston said. "We need to watch them die."

Alpha considered that.

"Agreed. Ensure all are exterminated by the time we arrive planetside at 28:40."

Maston tapped Lucas on the shoulder plate.

"Let's go. The rest of you get down to the docking bay and prepare for rollout."

Everyone started to move, but froze when they saw what was in the viewscreen as Alpha veered the ship around to starboard.

It was Xala. The sphere was unlike any planet Lucas had seen, and the holograms didn't do it justice. It was largely brown, red, and black. There were small strips of green and blue running through it, along with a few wisps of white clouds amid the smog, but it looked almost worse than Earth when they'd left it. Yellow lights burned brightly on the surface, even at this distance, and Lucas couldn't tell if the effect was from a geological disturbance like lava flows or structures the Xalans had built themselves. The sight of the planet was chilling, and it was likely they were the first non-Xalans to lay eyes on it in thousands of years.

A few minutes later, Lucas and Maston entered the cryochamber with weapons drawn. Alpha had relayed that nearly all of the captive crew had been killed by the gas, and only a few were still clinging to life.

The lighting was dim, and Lucas felt hairs involuntarily standing up on his neck inside his suit. They were creeping through a graveyard, after all. As they kept moving through the rows of pods, Lucas saw one Xalan twitching feverishly. Lucas stopped and watched as his movement slowed, then ceased altogether. Another green light had turned red.

Lucas jerked his head to the left when he heard the sounds of crunching glass. Maston looked down at his boot, which had just turned a shard lying on the ground to dust. Further up, there were more chunks littering the floor.

"Oh shit," Maston said breathlessly as he sprinted around the corner into the next row. Lucas followed him and skidded to a halt when he saw the source.

Glass was scattered in a wide radius around the destroyed door of a pod. Lucas and Maston shared a look as they realized which pod it was.

"All units converge d—" Maston's transmission was stopped short as he was flung into a nearby wall. Lucas whipped around to find the culprit in the darkness, but he felt claws sink into his chest before he could even pull the trigger.

Lucas hit the floor and gasped for air. He looked at the Shadow looming above him. He was thin without his armor and was covered in rough patches of burns that had singed his black skin to an even darker shade.

Lucas wrenched his arm up and managed to detach the creature's claws from his chest. The armor had stopped the black daggers from going too deep, but they'd definitely punctured his skin, and pain radiated through his chest. His undersuit was already attempting to seal the wounds.

A voice in his head. The Shadow's.

"*Insect.*"

The Shadow raised another claw, but winced as a blast grazed his arm and he stumbled backward away from the downed Lucas. Maston had picked himself up off the floor and the end of his energy rifle was smoking.

Fury blazed in the ice-blue eyes of the Shadow as he thrust his arm forward. Lucas watched in astonishment as Maston's rifle was wrenched from his grasp despite the Shadow being a solid twenty feet away.

Telekinesis.

The creature flung his claw backward and the rifle launched across the room, where it shattered the glass of a closed pod.

From the floor, Lucas brought Natalie around, but another twitch from the Shadow and the gun spiraled out of his hand and cascaded across the room. Immediately Lucas and Maston both drew their sidearms, only to have them also torn from their hands. This time, the guns floated in the air, moving slowly toward the Shadow. They hung there, suspended, rotating. The Shadow cocked his head and the two weapons were instantly crushed into balls of metal and circuitry through unseen psionic forces. The compressed clumps leaked liquid plasma and finally dropped and bounced on the metal grating.

"What the hell is happening down there?" came Asha's voice screaming in Lucas's ear. He could hear metal footsteps; she was running.

"The Shadow—" was all Lucas was able to get out before the creature flashed in front of him and delivered a kick that sent him flying toward Maston. The wind was knocked completely out of him and he couldn't elaborate.

Maston launched himself at the creature, wielding a knife as big as his arm, but was caught in midair and flung backward with a wave of the Shadow's claw.

After doing so, however, the creature doubled over, coughing painfully. Even if the toxin had woken him instead of killing him, it appeared to have had some crippling effect on his insides.

Lucas took the opportunity to dive for Natalie a few feet away. He grabbed the rifle's grip and rolled into an upright firing position on one knee. This time, the Shadow couldn't react physically or mentally. He caught a trio of plasma rounds across the chest, with a fourth barely missing his burned face. He stumbled backward, but even stripped of armor, his enhanced natural plating had cushioned the blows, which would have killed any other Xalan. Lucas attempted to continue firing, but felt himself lifted from his feet and flung upward into the ceiling. His head felt like it had split open when it connected with the metal, and he was nearly knocked unconscious when he slammed back into the floor a second later.

As Lucas's vision faded back in, he saw Maston and the creature circling each other. They were at the far end of the room now, near a row of doors. One led to the upper decks, the other two Lucas couldn't place. It was then that Lucas saw Asha's face through the window of the first door. It slid open for a millisecond but was then thrust shut by a wave from the Shadow. A twist of his wrist and the controls sparked, then fizzled out completely. Mechanisms groaned from within, and it became clear the entryway was completely jammed. Lucas could hear gunfire from the group outside now attempting to blast their way through.

"I'm coming around," Asha said in his ear, and he could hear more running. Lucas was too dazed to respond. The only other entrance to the cryodeck was on the opposite end of the ship.

Lucas searched for Natalie, but the gun was nowhere to be found. Hopefully it hadn't been crushed into scrap. Instead, Lucas drew his last weapon, his knife, and raced toward the creature. He leapt at it, his armor allowing him an eight-foot vertical, but he was met with a whirling slash of claws that sent him sprawling to the floor with fresh wounds. He watched as Maston attempted to lunge with his own knife, but was telekinetically thrown backward into a door, which buckled on impact. He crumpled into unconsciousness.

The Shadow turned back toward Lucas. He scrambled for his knife on the ground, but found himself rising uncontrollably away from it as the Shadow turned his palm upward.

"You would ambush my ship?" he growled, the voice echoing in Lucas's head.

"You would keep me captive for months?"

Lucas struggled against the Shadow's influence but continued to rise.

"You would execute my crew?"

The wounds across the creature's chest were already starting to heal. There was no stopping this monstrosity. It would kill him, then tear the entire ship apart.

"You were about to do the same to us," Lucas choked out as he hung suspended in the air. Plasma was starting to eat through the door and he could see Kovaks attempting to cut through with some sort of tool, but it wasn't working quickly enough. Still no word from Asha.

The creature coughed again. His lungs wheezed audibly, but he didn't lose his concentration on keeping Lucas afloat.

"What is your plan?" the creature asked, narrowing its eyes.

Lucas remained silent. The Shadow could see Xala out the viewscreen to his right.

"What is your plan?" came the voice again. Lucas suddenly felt his back arch violently, far past its intended contour. Pain exploded up his spine and coursed through his body. The noise he made defied description, but it wasn't the answer the Shadow wanted to hear.

"Very well."

Lucas quivered as he felt his arms and legs begin to bend backward. His bones flexed and his nerves screamed out in agony, as did he. His teeth clenched so hard from the pain he could feel a pair of his molars split in half. He was about to be ripped into a thousand pieces.

Maston's knife flashed briefly before it dove toward the creature's neck. With supernatural reaction time, the Shadow jerked to the left, and the knife sank into his collarbone instead of his throat. The shock caused him to drop Lucas, who hit the floor with his bones and flesh still joined.

With every ounce of strength both he and his suit could muster, Maston wrenched himself backward as the Shadow howled and flailed his arms. Maston's feet left the ground as the Shadow attempted to summon psionic energy, but Maston kept his grip on both the creature and the knife, and fresh pain caused him to lose focus. Maston pulled him back through the now open door behind him. Lucas saw what was on the other side now.

An escape pod.

Maston kept pulling until the two of them hit the viewscreen on the opposite end of the small compartment. Lucas had gotten to his feet and was sprinting toward the pair of them. Kovaks had broken in through the door at last and he, Reyes, and Kiati were right behind him.

Blood sprayed across the viewscreen inside the pod. Red blood, not black. Maston had taken a savage strike across the neck. The Shadow started moving toward the open door, but Maston brushed off his injury and leapt on him once more. The knife was still embedded in the creature, and Maston used it to throw him back to the rear of the pod again.

This time Maston didn't lunge for the creature. He dove for the door controls. The escape pod's hatch slammed shut in an instant a second before Lucas could reach it. He hammered on the metal with his fist and caught Maston's gaze through the porthole. Lucas could only describe the look on his face as . . . acceptance. As the Shadow started to rise once more, the blood-soaked Maston entered one last command into the control cluster.

And then he was gone.

The pod rocketed out of the departure bay at hypersonic speeds, knocking Lucas back. Its engines burned blue against the vacuum of space, and the sphere of the shuttle became smaller and smaller until it was no brighter than the stars that surrounded it.

Everyone stood speechless, staring at the empty port. Alpha's mechanical voice was in his ear.

"Lucas, what has happened? Why was that pod jettisoned?"

Lucas couldn't speak.

"Lucas, respond. Anyone, respond."

"Where are they?"

It was a new voice, behind him. He turned to find Asha standing in the row of pods, out of breath. She clutched her revolver in one hand and the other was on the grip of the sword on her back. "What the hell is going on?" she demanded angrily.

"He's gone," Lucas finally said. He looked outside through the airlock door. No blue lights shone out of the blackness.

"We have to go back for him," Asha pleaded with Alpha who was gazing sternly out the viewscreen.

"Go back for what?" Reyes said. "He launched himself into space with a Shadow in a ten-by-six tube."

"With grievous injuries," added Kiati.

"He saved us," Lucas said firmly. "That thing would have murdered us all if he hadn't gotten it off the ship."

"As much as I appreciate Commander Maston's noble sacrifice," Alpha said, "we cannot alter course to retrieve his probable corpse. I have already reported the ejection of the pod as a mechanical malfunction."

"What?" Asha said.

Zeta spoke next.

"We are close to Xala now," she said, gesturing out the window. The planet loomed large in front of them and ships far bigger than their own were clustered all around them. "We cannot turn back."

"He could still be alive," Asha said firmly.

"He isn't," Lucas replied. "I was there. I saw his wounds, I fought that . . . thing. It isn't possible."

"Life readouts indicate no signatures aboard the vessel," Alpha said. "Though I have disabled its controls and blocked communications from the pod in case the Shadow survived and attempts to contact Xala."

"Unblock it," Asha said. "Your readouts could be wrong. Mars could be alive."

"We cannot take the chance," Zeta said softly.

Lucas knew she was right. If anyone had survived in the pod, it was far more likely to be the Shadow. Given the first chance, he would hail the closest ship and everything would fall apart. The look on Asha's face said she was coming to the same realization.

"We may now put this to rest," said Alpha solemnly, looking up from the ship's controls wearily. He gradually brought over a small floating window from his own display module and transferred it to the viewscreen.

"I have made a visual connection with the vessel."

The shot displayed was a wide angle of the inside of the escape pod, which made the tiny space look larger than it was. The scene was grisly. Black and red blood stained nearly every inch of the walls. The Shadow lay sprawled against the back of the central chair meant to pilot the pod. The handle of Maston's large knife rose out of his chest, and the creature was completely still.

A few feet away was Mars Maston, seated, leaning up against one of the curved walls. His chin was on his chest; wet black curls obscured his face. The front of his armor was covered in blood. He too, was unmoving.

"Unblock communications," Asha said.

Alpha didn't move.

"Do it!" she ordered. "The Shadow is dead!"

Alpha reluctantly obeyed.

All seven of them froze as they watched the screen, waiting for Maston to move, waiting for him to respond to Alpha's hails.

Silence.

"I don't know what Corinthia saw in me, but I didn't care. Every eye on a ship full of thousands was on her whenever she passed, and somehow, some way, she'd chosen me."

Silence.

"At times she barely even seemed Soran, like some sort of celestial being that had graced us with her presence."

Silence.

"It was only her. I never cared for anyone as much. I never will."

Silence.

The seconds continued to tick away.

I hope you found her, Lucas thought as he watched the unmoving figure on the viewscreen.

I hope you're with her again.

24

There was no time to grieve. Alpha had to wave away the escape pod's video feed. Their ship was now in orbit over Xala and descending rapidly. The planet reappeared in the viewscreen and a host of bright lights could be seen scattered across the surface. They were cities, judging by the patterns the lights made as they drew closer, and they were heading straight for the largest cluster.

Structures hung at various points in the atmosphere as they descended, space stations and satellites that were hard to scale. Some appeared to be no bigger than their own craft. Others were more distant and were made up of bizarre clusters of metal. Floating dwellings, perhaps? They were big enough to hold thousands, it seemed. From up here, there wasn't much of the planet that looked particularly habitable.

Alpha was communicating to the receiving crew on the ground of the unpronounceable metropolis where they were headed. Sorans simply referred to the Xalan capital as *Vas Raksis*, which almost literally translated to "The Pit." At its heart was Xalan central command, their final destination. The comm growled back at Alpha, relaying that everything was in order. These were Zeta's resistance members who were meeting them at the docking bay, and they would facilitate their hopefully uneventful landing.

Kiati was the next highest-ranking Soran officer aboard and had assumed command of the mission. It had been one of many contingency plans should Maston fall in battle, but no one anticipated he wouldn't even be there when they set foot on the planet. Kiati was handling things as best she could, but was obviously thrown off balance by Maston's unexpected death. She patched up Lucas's wounds and he changed into his spare stealth suit, one not gored by Xalan claws. Lucas even found Natalie wedged behind one of the sleeping pods, mercifully still intact. Its readouts were fuzzy and its power core seemed to be glowing hotter than usual, but the display said she would fire, and that's all he needed her to do. It would have been hard to even consider attempting a mission without her. His old friend had carried him through many harrowing ordeals; perhaps she could do the same today.

Another old friend stared out the viewscreen at the planet below. Asha was silent and hadn't said a word after seeing the footage from inside the escape pod. She didn't flinch when Lucas came up behind her and placed a hand on her shoulder.

"I imagine he's the only man to ever kill two Shadows," Lucas said.

"He was an asshole," she said curtly. Lucas was caught off guard and let out a short laugh.

"Yeah, but he liked you," he said. "He saw something in you."

Her expression softened.

"He didn't hate you. Not after Makari," she said.

"I know," Lucas replied.

"Well, just one more reason to not screw this up," she said, turning away from the window. Lucas now saw she was holding a small chip in her hands.

"His Final?" Lucas asked, surprised she had it.

She nodded and tapped the chip. It only had one name on the recipient list.

"Have you watched it?" Lucas asked. Asha shook her head.

"I saw him throw it away after the Rhylos mission. I picked it up out of curiosity, but never felt like I should actually listen. I figure if we make it back, I'll bury it at the foot of whatever monument they're currently erecting to the late Miss Vale. Hopefully they'll give him one too."

The window flickered with heat and light as they broke through the atmosphere of Xala. In a few moments, the disturbance stopped, and they could see a reddish-orange color out the window. The sun didn't appear to be rising or setting. It seemed this was simply how the sky looked here. It reminded Lucas of the angry red clouds that had surrounded Earth in its final days, but there were a few trails of white visible here.

The sky soon lost its orangish hue and they broke through a cover of brown smog as they kept heading toward the surface. It was hazy at first, but once they got low enough, they could see it. Vas Raksis, the Pit.

These were not the shining towers of Elyria. The structures were also massive, but jagged and asymmetrical, sprouting up from the ground like dark volcanic rock formations. The air buzzed with spacecraft locked into no discernible traffic patterns. On the ground, haphazardly constructed structures coated the planet like spreading mold. Milky white rivers carved paths between the buildings. There wasn't so much as a solitary tree in sight, and Vas Raksis was so sprawling its skyline spread all the way to the horizon.

This was a dying world, to be sure, though not one ravaged directly by war. But what little resources might have been here at one point were now clearly stripped bare, and it was no wonder the Xalans were forced to invade other planets and use them as fuel to keep their war machine running. Lucas thought of Alpha's dream to revitalize Xala someday. Would such a thing even be possible? It seemed like the place might be better off condemned and abandoned altogether, like Earth. But somehow thirty billion Xalans still lived there. Though many of them weren't particularly pleased about it, said Zeta.

The irony was not lost on Lucas regarding what they were about to attempt. They were the mirror image of Hex Tulwar and his Fourth Order, trying to destabilize a government though the revelation of long-buried secrets. Tulwar had succeeded, and now Sora was in chaos, a Xalan army on its doorstep. They simply had to hope that what they accomplished here would offset that chaos with chaos of their own.

Alpha slowly steered the craft into the docking bay of a massive structure. Other ships buzzed by them, giving little notice. They were simply one more craft returning from a mission like so many thousands of others. The official orders of the receiving crew were to take the prisoners to a nearby detention facility, where they'd await public execution. The group of Xalan resistance agents gathering on the monitors outside in the bay had no such inclinations.

Lucas's knees buckled as the craft came to rest on its landing gear inside the hangar. They'd officially landed on Xala. The thought was surreal.

Asha and the other Guardians were ready. Alpha and Zeta joined them in the exit bay, and soon they heard the familiar hiss of another vessel attaching itself to their own.

The airlock doors opened and the tunnel revealed a path into another transport. They'd be completely shielded from surveillance during the transfer, and the seven of them hustled into the new ship, leaving the interceptor and its deceased crew behind. Zeta's agents would ensure no one came sniffing around.

This new ship was incredibly small, a local transport with seating for only a dozen. Zeta greeted a quartet of her undercover operatives inside with a gesture Lucas didn't understand, but it was clear these were friendlies. Though their grunts couldn't be translated, a simple nod toward the humans conveyed the appropriate sentiment. *Allies.*

Lucas barely had time to fit himself with a restraint before the transport took off. He'd studied the infiltration plan enough to know exactly where they were heading next. And it wasn't to rot in a Xalan dungeon.

The trip inside the transport gave them a brief tour of the surrounding area. They flew by a shipyard constructing mammoth cruisers like the ones they'd destroyed at the Makari spaceport. Alpha pointed out the Xalan science academy, a domed building that looked slightly newer than the rest of the dust-covered shapes all around them. They flew over slums, where they could see wretched-looking Xalans living in squalor next to assuredly toxic lakes. Workers, they were told, were forcibly kept here to assemble ships and weapons for little pay. Many were former soldiers, Zeta said, deemed too old or injured to fight. A thousand feet up rose skyscrapers of sharp black metal, lofting citizens with means far above the peasants who served them. But even prime real estate on Xala meant you were constantly surrounded by thick clouds of smog and had a glorious view of a decaying planet. The place was a ruin.

Eventually, they came to rest at their destination. They landed at the mouth of what used to be a river a few centuries ago, but was now a strip of sludge and refuse. They were sunk deep into the lower levels of the city, and even the slums were above them. Out the forward viewscreen they saw a wide, round opening in a very large stone wall. The remnants of an ancient sewer system, back before that descriptor applied to the entire city.

The doors of the transport opened. He was sitting closest to the exit, so Lucas was the first to plant his foot on the rocky shore.

One small step for man . . .

The other Guardians followed suit and surveyed the area. Though the air was being filtered through their helmets, it didn't eliminate the odor. Everything smelled of burnt metal and bile, and it was enough to make Lucas's eyes water. Gray smoke poured from buildings around them, and streams of cloudy liquid ran down the walls surrounding the river, adding to the horrifying mixture pooling a few feet away from them.

Alpha motioned for them to follow him toward the sewer opening, and the group quickly obeyed, eager to get out of the open.

Miraculously, it smelled better inside the sewer than outside, thanks to its not having been used for centuries. That made it the perfect entry point into central command, though they'd have to trudge a fair distance to get there and knock down a few walls along the way.

Two of the four resistance operatives that escorted them waited just inside the entrance to the sewer while they continued deeper into the tunnel. They were stationed there to prevent any maintenance crew or random wanderers from entering the tunnel after they did, though that seemed unlikely given the remote location.

Slowly, the light of the opening grew fainter and fainter as they moved forward, then disappeared altogether around a bend in the tunnel. Lights on their armor and guns illuminated the way from there. Even though the sewer system was a complete labyrinth, they all had studied the blueprints so much over the past few weeks that each of them knew every next turn by heart. As such, they were making great time hustling through the tunnels toward their next checkpoint.

Finally, they reached an old control station for the sewer. The rusted door opened with a swift kick and they made their way inside. The station was vast and covered in a layer of dust an inch thick. It blew up around them angrily as they entered; it was clear no one had stepped foot inside for eons. Controls sat dormant and were so old they actually used physical buttons and levers rather than holograms. It almost looked like a similar facility would have on Earth, other than the tall chairs meant to seat eight-foot Xalan frames.

Rounding a corner, Lucas saw a patch of dust that had recently been disturbed. Surrounding it were prints leading off in various directions. Moving closer, he could see the remains of a deceased creature. A ribcage, a femur, a skull. Not a Xalan. It was small, and the prints surrounding it weren't Xalan either.

Lucas jerked his head around as he heard two muffled thumps, silenced plasma rounds unloaded from Alpha's rifle. When Lucas reached him, he was standing over a dust-covered ball of fur about the size of a trashcan. Alpha kicked it lightly with an armored foot.

"Wild dog," he said, using the English word. But it was no dog. Lucas shone his light on it and saw a rat-like face with three-inch-long fangs poking out over its jowls. It had four lanky legs that spread out sideways from its torso like a spider. Whether this was simply how these things looked, or it was mutated from all the toxic contamination down here, he couldn't be sure. Upon closer inspection, Lucas realized that the thing had two completely white eyes on the right half of its face, making three in total. Mutant seemed the more likely option.

Another pair of thumps echoed out from where Lucas had been a second ago, along with a painful yelp. This time it was one of the two remaining resistance Xalans who had fired. Another dead "dog" lay at his feet. Only two eyes this time. Lucas couldn't translate the Xalan's next grunt, but it was clear the idea was "let's keep moving." A sound suggestion, and Lucas kept his eyes peeled for more of the creatures as they cautiously walked forward. For a brief moment, Lucas thought he saw skittering movement across the open room, but it was far away, and this was no time to start firing into the darkness blindly. They reached another old door, this one wrenched open haphazardly, and left the cavernous room behind.

They were moving through dark hallways rather than wide-open tunnels. Lucas could only keep track of the Guardians in front and behind him with his helmet tagging them with virtual identifiers in the dark. He was happy to find it was Asha watching his back.

"We're down the rabbit hole now," she said over a private comm channel when she saw him glance backward.

"Even got our own white rabbit," Lucas replied, nodding toward Zeta at the front of the pack.

They cut holes in walls with plasma torches or blew through them with pocket-size explosives. They crept through the underbelly of the city however they could, a route mapped out by spies months in advance. Eventually they came to rest in a very cramped corridor full of pipes and wiring, where they all had to stoop to avoid the ceiling. The Xalans in the party were practically kneeling.

All of them knew where they were. Their urban spelunking over the past hour or so had gotten them past two of the checkpoints that led into Xalan central command. They were now at the third and final one before the entrance, and it was simply impossible to continue any further underground with a wall of metal a dozen feet thick at the far end of the room.

Above them, however, the floor was not quite so sturdy, and they could force their way into the room via the paneling the two resistance Xalans were currently working to quietly dismantle. No one was speaking, but each knew what was about to come. It wasn't another empty room up there. This final checkpoint was filled with guards, anywhere from ten to fourteen at a given time, according to the insiders.

Even so, the plan wasn't to go loud. Not yet. Not until they got deeper, or else they'd never get there at all.

The panel was loosened. If Maston was there, he would likely have been doing the honors, but Kiati held the pulse grenade instead. They'd make him proud.

25

The grenade bounced like a rubber ball across the floor of the room above them. It caught the eyes of a pair of Xalan guards who had only milliseconds to deduce what the device was. By the time they understood the threat, it had exploded in a flash of blue light. A pulse quickly rebounded throughout the entire room.

The device worked as intended; the explosion blinded the guards, while the pulse rendered every piece of electronic equipment in the room useless. Power weapons and armor were deactivated. But more importantly, so were comms and cameras. The room was now completely dark.

That was their cue. The group sprang up through the floor paneling, weapons raised. It took all of a few seconds for them to scramble to their feet, and only a few more to put down every soldier in the room quickly and quietly.

Lucas immediately put a pair of silenced rounds into two Xalans stumbling toward the outer doors. He turned to see Reyes opening three separate Xalan throats with her pair of curved blades and Kovaks taking out another pair of soldiers with dead-center headshots. Kiati silently snapped the neck of a disoriented Xalan while Alpha unloaded a stream of silenced plasma into a group of guards at the far end of the room. Lucas looked around for Asha, and saw her in the middle of a pile of Xalan body parts, sword in hand, dripping with blood. Lucas put one more round into a Xalan struggling to raise his weapon, and the room went silent.

By his count there were a dozen Xalan bodies littering the floor. Not one stirred and none of them had managed to even get a shot off in the chaos. The doors on either side of the room remained closed, meaning no one had heard the assault within. That didn't necessarily indicate their invasion wouldn't be discovered eventually, however.

It was time to pick up the pace.

Zeta crawled out of the floor where she'd been hiding for the duration of the brief skirmish. Though she was armed and more than capable of defending herself, the entire mission was lost if she ended up dead in a firefight. Her two Xalan escorts rose out of the ground with her and set to work on the room's security system, ending the video and audio blackout, replacing it with an old feed that would make it look like nothing had occurred within. Even if it bought them mere minutes, it would help. As a last resort, the two resistance Xalans would stay behind and barricade the entrance so that no one entered or exited. The sight of the room would instantly put the entire facility on lockdown.

Lucas walked over to the large metal door that would lead them further into the compound. Alpha was ready with an entry chip pulled from a dead guard that would open the door, but they needed to know what was on the other side first.

Lucas looked through Natalie's scope, which he'd switched into X-ray functionality. On the other side of the door, he could see the skeletons of two Xalans on either side of the frame, facing the other direction. He marked exactly where they were on the wall, and Reyes and Kovaks moved into position.

The door sprang open, and the two soldiers couldn't even turn their heads before blades were driven into their necks from behind. The two Guardians dragged the bodies into the room and tossed them onto the bloody floor like rag dolls.

The group quickly sprinted out into the adjacent hallway, the door closing behind them, sealing Zeta's two agents inside. They would work to disable security along their route as quickly as possible, but nothing was guaranteed.

Kiati drew first blood in this next phase when she rounded the corner of the hallway. Standing there were a pair of unarmored Xalans discussing something on a data pad. They had half a second to process that they were staring at a group of Sorans before Kiati's pistol tore through them. Lucas checked the map and motioned to everyone that their next move was to duck into a room to the right. The door opened without hesitation and they found themselves in some sort of control center.

Two guards inside the room were the first to go down, both beheaded by Asha with one swipe of her sword. There was another pair on the far side of the room, one of which Lucas took out with a long-barrel sniper shot, and the other sank to his knees with one of Kovak's small throwing blades embedded in his skull.

Three seated, unarmed Xalans barely had time to be shocked before they were cut down by Alpha's rifle. They slumped over their consoles like they'd suddenly fallen asleep.

As soon as everyone in the room was confirmed dead, Kiati headed over to the central viewscreen, which she promptly smashed with the butt of her gun. She and Reyes began unloading some equipment from their packs, a superheated plasma cutter that would slice through the metal behind the screen like butter. The room's outer wall was a shortcut to where they needed to go next.

The cutting tool hissed as a bright orange line slowly tore its way through the wall. Lucas took a moment to collect his thoughts and briefly leaned against a nearby console spattered with the black blood of its operator. He peered at the screen and was stunned at what he saw.

It was an enormous Xalan fleet, all moving in unison through a field of stars. Lucas saw a familiar green-ringed planet, one he'd seen when they first arrived in the Soran solar system. They were already there.

"Alpha," Lucas called out, but across the room he saw Alpha was looking at a similar scene on a larger screen.

"It appears the invasion force is nearing the Soran homeworld," he said, confirming what Lucas had seen.

"There will be massive casualties within the hour," Zeta said. "We must hurry."

"This is as fast as this thing goes," Kiati called out. The cutter had now completed roughly half of a rectangle on the wall.

Asha stepped gingerly over a dead guard as she approached Lucas. She'd removed her helmet and brushed the wet, stringy hair out of her eyes. Lucas had already taken his helmet off. His heart hadn't stopped racing since they first set foot on the planet, and it didn't seem like it was going to let up any time soon.

"So far so good," Asha said, threading her sword over her back. Lucas nodded.

"The advantages of going through the details a thousand times," he said.

Indeed, everything had gone exactly according to plan since they'd arrived on Xala, discounting of course Maston's untimely demise.

Then came a moment they had all been dreading. An alarm began wailing at the top of its mechanical lungs. The sound pierced the silence and caused everyone's eyes to widen and pulses to quicken.

"[Garbled]" came the sound from Alpha's translator, assuredly failing to convert some sort of Xalan curse word.

"Shit," Lucas said in English simultaneously, meeting Alpha's startled gaze.

They would likely never know exactly what happened. It could have been any of number of things that set it off. Perhaps they boarded the interceptor to find a tomb of dead Xalans. Someone could have come across Maston's carnage-filled escape pod. The blood-soaked checkpoint might have been discovered. Whatever the case, it didn't matter now. It was bound to happen at some point, and was built into the plan accordingly. Stealth had gotten them this far, but it would take them no further.

Every monitor in the room flashed with a warning indicator as the alarm droned on. Lucas quickly translated it.

"SECURITY BREACH SECTION SEVEN. ARMED SORANS AND REBEL AGENTS INSIDE. ALL UNITS CONVERGE TO ROOM 1250."

Lucas glanced up at a strip of Xalan symbols above the door they'd just entered. 1250.

"We have to go!" Lucas shouted. Alpha was already heading toward the door leading into the room, where he planted a pair of blinking mines on either side. Kiati was just bringing the cutting tool around to complete the red hot rectangle in the wall.

"Ready!" she called back, and the group formed up behind her. Alpha tossed out more mines throughout the room, which stuck to various surfaces with their magnetic backing.

With a hefty kick from Kiati's armored leg, the metal plate flew into the next area. Everyone froze.

The room they'd broken into was massive, with ceilings at least five stories high. The far wall was entirely translucent, a curved sheet of glass that revealed an assortment of machinery. They were looking at their final destination. A large set of double doors that led to the communications relay sat at the base of the glass. It was where Zeta needed to be in order to disseminate the message and disrupt comms. The only problem was the dozens of very angry-looking Xalan soldiers standing in their way.

With a wide sweep of her arm, Kiati threw out a half dozen grenades, mixing explosives with crippling pulse devices. They all exploded at roughly the same time, disorienting and dismembering the soldiers closest to them. It was the last time they could utilize the element of surprise.

As the grenades leveled the troops in front of them, Lucas heard other explosive thuds coming from their rear. Troops had entered the room they'd just exited and had tripped Alpha's mines. The guards in front of them had regained their senses from the grenade blasts and all hell broke loose.

The temperature in the room rose ten degrees in an instant as plasma scorched the air all around them. Both the Guardians and the Xalan guards were unloading on each other while each dove for cover behind anything they could find. In the first wave of shots, at least four Xalans went down while Kovaks took a round in the chest. He winced in pain as his suit rapidly tried to seal the wound, but it was clearly not a fatal hit. Kiati tossed him a syringe that would instantly erase the pain for the time being.

Lucas had a round whiz by his head at such close range he could feel it singe the hair on his temple. He scrambled to find his helmet, which had been knocked loose, but it was lost in the chaos.

The guards closest to them had their guns destroyed by the pulse grenades and were sprinting toward them like madmen, wielding razor-thin blades assuredly meant to be a last-resort weapon. One bounded over the console where Lucas was hiding and was blown apart with a shotgun blast from Natalie. The next one over got Asha's sword in his chest and the soldier's blade clattered to the floor next to them. Asha kicked him backward forcefully, freeing her sword from his sternum as he crumpled to the ground in a lifeless heap.

Kiati turned around to lob one more grenade into the hole they'd just emerged from. They were fighting a war on two fronts now, as all Alpha's mines had been tripped and fresh troops were trying to flank them. The blast caused a shower of black blood to erupt from the hole, and it was clear Kiati had disrupted their entry. Large pieces of debris fell in chunks over the opening, and it would take the Xalans some time to excavate.

Shots ricocheted off the clear far wall of the room. Despite being translucent, the material was something far more durable than glass. After all, it did protect the most important communications relay on the planet. They somehow had to get across the room.

The Guardians, now able to avoid an attack from the rear for the time being, began to press forward. It wasn't the type of group to hunker down behind cover for long. They were assassins, and Reyes and Kovaks were bounding across the room, dodging shots and killing Xalan soldiers with extreme precision. Asha followed their lead, no stranger to the same style of combat. Her blade whipped through the air as she cartwheeled over stunned Xalans who couldn't get a bead on a target so small and fast. The sword shredded their armor and the cavernous room echoed with wails of agony. The alarm still blared all around them.

Lucas followed closely behind her, taking out any Xalan that swung their weapon toward her. They put down creature after creature, and the pair of them were leaving a trail of bodies in their wake as they pressed forward across the increasingly slippery floor.

Behind them, Alpha was wrestling with a knife-wielding guard when Zeta walked up and put a round in the Xalan's head. Alpha looked at her appreciatively, but both had to quickly turn and unload at another pair of soldiers trying to line them up.

Kiati had taken a hit somewhere and blood was dripping from her stealth suit to the floor. It hadn't slowed her down, however, and she cracked off shots from her pistol toward soldiers attempting to end the acrobatics of Reyes. Kovaks and Reyes, despite their friendly rivalry, made a hell of a team, and the Xalans simply didn't have an answer for the pair of them.

Lucas took a grazing shot to his ribcage and doubled over in pain. When he looked back up, the assailant was already dead, Asha's blade planted in his head while she stood a few feet away. She bent her wrist and the sword ejected itself from the Xalan's body and back into her hand. She quickly ran over to help Lucas up, and he could feel his suit releasing painkillers into his bloodstream. The wound wasn't serious enough to call for Kiati's aid, so he continued forward.

The troops in the room were starting to thin out and they were able to finally reach the doorway to the comms relay. Alpha set to work hacking through the security, which was on complete lockdown after the breach had been broadcast.

Reyes was taking a few last shots at downed and squirming Xalans that weren't quite dead yet. Kovaks was clutching his chest, injured, but functional. Kiati attended to Zeta; a plasma round had eaten through her leg armor near her shin, despite constant protection by Alpha. Lucas wiped away the blood that stained his side, the wound now closed and the pain muted. They were battered, but alive. But there was no telling when the next round of reinforcements would show up.

Alpha was growing frustrated with the door controls, which were proving more difficult to override than he had anticipated. Lucas surveyed the carnage of the room in a daze; his ears were still ringing from the gunfire, and the alarm wouldn't cease its constant wailing. Finally he located the source of the sound and fired a shot that made the speaker explode in a shower of sparks. The alarm still sounded elsewhere in the facility, but was mercifully no longer echoing throughout the chamber.

Asha had her hands on her knees and was trying to catch her breath. Despite the physicality the suits allowed them, combat was exhausting, and Lucas felt similarly winded. Adrenaline flowed through his veins, warding off true fatigue.

"That was only the beginning," Asha said, and she was likely right. "The whole planet will be here soon."

It was true. They couldn't kill everyone that was about to come for them. It wasn't possible. Sora seemed exceptionally far away now. Lucas wondered if the Xalan fleet had been engaged yet. It was entirely possible that millions were dying worlds away from them at that very moment.

Alpha finally sprang the door open and quickly ushered Zeta inside. Lucas and Asha followed while Kiati, Reyes, and Kovaks remained outside as sentries.

The inside of the comms relay was like nothing Lucas had ever seen before. He could only see parts of it from outside, but within it was a stunning array of light and metal. Alpha had described the general contents of the room to him on their way to Xala, but failed to mention that it was actually quite beautiful. As they reached the center, Lucas saw a series of crystalline conductors symmetrically arranged in a column that extended far past where the ceiling should be. Rather, there was no roof in the chamber. The Xalan sky was a tiny of speck of light at least a mile up. The entrance was ray shielded, so they couldn't have dropped in that way without being reduced to ash, but it allowed the relay to broadcast across the galaxy without being overly exposed on the surface of the planet.

Green and purple electric charges jumped from crystal to crystal while light from the machinery was refracted into multicolored prisms all around them. The effect was awe-inspiring, and the room felt like the inner sanctum of some ethereal church, not merely some communication tool. Zeta had designed all this, back before she'd turned traitor, and it showed she had a penchant for artistry, not just technology.

Zeta was already hard at work on the central console of the room. Surrounding her was a complete circle of floating code that she was frantically trying to slice through to achieve the ability to broadcast simultaneously on every piece of Xalan technology with a screen. Just when she finished one section, another would appear. Alpha was trying to help share the load, but she was moving at three times his pace, well-versed in what was being displayed. It was clear that anyone else attempting the same feat probably couldn't do it given months, while she was trying to get it done within minutes.

Though Lucas was enraptured by the scene in front of him, he was jolted out of his trance by gunfire coming from the other room. He and Asha dashed back through the relay to find the Guardians unloading at a fresh collection of troops trying to pry their way through doors on either side of the room. Grenades blew apart the tightly packed soldiers in the entryway, but they were starting to run low on that sort of ordinance.

And then, silence. The Xalans suddenly stopped trying to enter the room over the mangled corpses of their fellow soldiers. Had they been scared into submission after witnessing the complete devastation in the room? That didn't seem likely. Unless it wasn't them the Xalans were frightened of.

There was a loud crash as debris rained down from the ceiling far overhead. A blur fell from the rafters and landed in front of them with such force it nearly bowled all of them over.

It was him.

26

The Desecrator slowly rose from the ground, a dozen feet tall with a wingspan even wider. His wings retracted into his back. His eyes darted across theirs, and no one dared to fire the first shot.

His chest plating had a large circular dent hammered into it by the explosive round he'd taken from Zeta's prison ship back on Makari. Around his neck was one of Alpha's translator collars, damaged, but still intact, it seemed.

"You invade the homeworld," he mused, his deep voice echoing around the chamber. "Same as me."

Everyone was silent, speechless. Reyes and Kovaks wore looks of astonishment, having only seen the creature in video feeds. He was much larger and more nightmarish in person.

"You will die now," he said calmly, flexing his mammoth claws, "like you should have in the jungle. You will answer for your crime."

"For what?" Lucas called out. "Killing your father?"

The Desecrator paused.

"I've read his journals," Lucas said. "I know what happened to you."

"You know nothing," the Desecrator scoffed.

"Your father was a warrior, like us. He died in battle, honorably. It was not murder, only war."

"The two are one and the same," the Desecrator said. "I have wanted no part in this war. The fight was not mine. A struggle between nations means nothing. Blood. Blood means everything."

He took one step toward them and everyone raised their weapons another inch.

"There will be no honor here today," he growled.

Lucas couldn't even blink by the time the Desecrator drew a weapon from his back. He felt warm blood spray his face before he even knew where it was coming from. Next to him, Kovaks lay sprawled on the ground, his head completely blown apart by the Desecrator's first shot.

The entire group shattered into every possible direction. Lucas rolled left and returned fire. The Desecrator dodged and fired again, this time his round taking a chunk out of Kiati's shoulder, which flung her into the wall. Asha was firing fission shots from her Magnum, but the creature dodged them all with ease. Finally, one caught him in the chest, but it was obvious he had survived much worse. She had to dive out of the way from a shot that would have cut her in half.

Lucas had been waiting for this. After reading Omicron's journals, he had had Alpha equip Natalie with one more special function. One he prayed would work now.

Natalie shot out a blinding beam of white light that caused the Desecrator's fiery eyes to visibly shrink into pinpoints. He howled in agony, dropped his gun, and tried to shield himself from the light. Lucas walked slowly toward him, unloading carnage blasts from his gun that knocked the Desecrator back a few more feet with each burst. Asha and Reyes converged on him, blades drawn. Lucas felt a small smile creep across his lips as he got close enough to take aim at the creature's head.

He missed.

The Desecrator ducked under the blast, almost going flat to the floor. In an instant, he lunged at Lucas and sank his claw directly into Natalie's scope, killing the shining light instantly. Tearing his claw up, the Desecrator ripped the entire scope off the weapon altogether. With the metal plating shorn away, the gun's power core was exposed. Lucas fired another blast, the weapon mercifully still working, but the Desecrator was already three feet to his left.

Reyes and Asha leapt at him from either side. He quickly caught Asha with a backhand that sent her flying into the wall and tumbling to the ground. Reyes was not so lucky and took all three of his claws directly to her chest. They pierced her armor and everything inside, and as he brought her around, Lucas could see the tips of his claws protruding out of her back. Her head rolled back, her eyes vacant. She was dead already, but that didn't stop the Desecrator from burying his other claw inside her, and tearing her body completely in half right in front of Lucas.

This creature was pure power, pure evil. They hadn't been ready for this. Not even with little tricks like the light scope. Lucas raised his rifle as the Desecrator leapt forward. He attempted to fire, but found the damaged gun had overheated and was sparking in his hands. He prepared to die.

But death did not come.

The Desecrator hung suspended in the air in front of him, one claw a mere eight inches from Lucas's head. His face was frozen in a snarl, and Lucas could see the muscles tensing in his neck. He was six feet in the air, completely frozen.

Two figures floated down from an open portal in the ceiling, each with arms outstretched toward the creature. They were Shadows, hovering above the ground, suspended by their own psychic energy. Their black skin and blue eyes were visible, but they wore actual cloth garments, something Lucas had never seen on a Xalan before. One had a long, flowing green-and-white sash wrapped around him that encompassed most of his body. The other's was red and gold. There were runic symbols on the garments Lucas couldn't recognize. They weren't Xalan in origin, or at least not the dialect he knew.

The two Shadows floated down on either side of the Desecrator, and Lucas turned to find a third Shadow behind him. This one was slightly taller and had a cloth that was pure white with gold symbols. His arms were not outstretched, and Lucas's feet remained planted on the floor. Asha was slowly starting to rise, drifting back into consciousness, and her eyes widened when she saw the three figures before them, balancing on thin air. There was a soft moan from Kiati across the room, indicating she was still alive.

It was obvious these were Chosen Shadows, but they were different than the one aboard the interceptor. Their power seemed to radiate from them like heat. It was something Lucas had never felt before. Finally coming to rest, their feet were still well above the floor. The two closest to them turned their wrists, and the Desecrator was slowly pulled upright and away from Lucas. Glancing behind him, Lucas could see that the third creature was furiously swirling through the door controls attempting to access the comms relay. Alpha had locked it up tight with a binding code only he could release, and the door was otherwise indestructible, even for Shadows, it seemed. The creature attempted to pry it open telekinetically, but it would not budge. He floated over toward Lucas. The creature's voice boomed in his head.

"*Tell the traitors to open the door.*"

His tone was icy, and its pitch cut through Lucas like a needle.

"Or what?" Lucas said defiantly. He had been prepared to die a moment ago. He was still ready. Asha looked warily at him.

"*Or we'll tear her apart in front of you,*" the creature said, turning his cold gaze toward Asha.

"We came here to die," Asha said. "You can't stop them now."

There was a look in the Shadow's eyes that said he believed them. He turned his attention toward the imprisoned Desecrator.

"*What are* you *doing here?*" he said. "*You have been banished from the homeworld for centuries now.*"

The Desecrator growled and his collar translated.

"To finish the mission. Your mission."

The Shadow to his right snarled.

"*You failed on Makari.*"

The Shadow to his left sneered.

"*The Sorans nearly killed you.*"

"I came to end this," the Desecrator said. "This was *your* task. It was meant to be my redemption!"

"*You murdered an entire battalion to get here. Of your own brethren,*" said the white-robed Xalan behind Lucas.

"They would not grant me access. And I have no brethren."

"*That much is true,*" the red-robed Xalan said. "*We thought the fact that these insects killed your father would be motivation for you to exact vengeance, but we overestimated your devotion to him.*"

"Do not speak of my father," growled the Desecrator. Lucas could see his muscles straining against their influence.

"*You are a mistake,*" said the green-robed Xalan. "*And the Council does not make mistakes. You should have been destroyed immediately after conversion.*"

The Ruling Council. It explained their immense power, their ornate robes.

"Look where you are!" the Desecrator shouted, his voice echoing around the room. "Your empire crumbles before you, brought crashing down by these . . . creatures."

Suddenly, every screen in the room, small and large, began to play a video. Lucas's heart soared in his chest as he recognized the face. Alpha's father.

"Greetings, my son," it began. *"I do not wish to endanger your life with this message, more so than I already have by causing your exile to Earth campaign."*

"It's starting," Asha said. The Council members looked furious as they glanced from monitor to monitor.

"My only hope is that if I am killed, one of you may find a way to make the truth known to our people. The truth about the intertwined histories of Sora and Xala."

Alpha broke through on Lucas's armor comm.

"It is done. Every screen, every colony. Zeta is fighting off override procedures to ensure it remains broadcasting."

The Shadows looked at each other. The white-clad one spoke urgently.

"*We must stop this,*" he said. "*Kill them all, and concentrate your energy to tear through that wall.*"

"*But it's not possible, that material is—*" started the red-robed Xalan.

"*Do not question, obey!*" the white one snarled. "*Or all may be lost.*"

"You do not see," said the Desecrator with a low growl. "You have already lost."

"*Do not speak!*" the Shadow shot back. His anger hammered inside Lucas's skull like a migraine. "*We would not* be *in this circumstance if not for your father's failure! And your own!*"

He turned and floated quickly toward the door. The Desecrator spoke to his back as the Shadows on either side of him began twisting his limbs to unbearable angles. His deep voice was shaking as he spoke through the pain.

"My father taught me many things. How to live. How to kill. How to resist."

His eyes narrowed.

"How to resist your abominable mutation."

It was like a switch had been flipped, and the Desecrator immediately dropped to the floor, his claws digging into the metal. Though the Shadows still had their arms extended, they no longer bound him. They looked even more shocked than Lucas and Asha as they frantically motioned toward him, but were unable to lock him in place. The video continued to play.

"Synthetics could evolve at a rapid rate, their intelligence dooming their creators as it expanded exponentially. But organics? Such quick evolution was impossible, and living things could be engineered to be docile."

The Desecrator swung his claw around and buried it in the abdomen of the green-robed Xalan. He flung him to the floor as black blood soaked the cloth he wore. He gasped as air evacuated his chest through new holes in his lungs. The Desecrator grabbed the other Shadow by the leg and slammed him down to the ground.

This was their chance. Asha leaped on top of the first downed Xalan and drove her blade through his chest. He swung up a claw, which caught her around the collarbone, but as she cried out in pain, she ran her thumb across the pommel of the sword. Blue electricity surged out of the blade and caused the Shadow's body to seize until it smoked. The crackling eventually stopped, and the Shadow was still save for a few last muscle spasms.

Lucas had attempted to fire Natalie at the second downed Xalan the Desecrator had pinned to the floor, but the gun still wouldn't shoot. The red robes he wore were bloodied to a darker crimson as the Desecrator ravaged the creature with claw swipes. The Shadow attempted to swing his claw up into the Desecrator's eye, but Lucas speared his palm with a knife and pinned it to the ground before it could reach its target, and the creature howled in pain. A half second later, the Desecrator removed the Shadow's head with his teeth.

"A family's personal Xalan would do housework, supervise children, whatever was required of it. They were slaves, but cheerful ones."

The Desecrator raised its head, black blood streaming out of its mouth. His wings sprang out of his back and he dove toward the final Council member, bowling Lucas over in the process.

The white-robed Xalan had managed to flex the metal of the door with intense mental strength, but he had to shift his focus as a two-ton armored creature came hurling toward him at a supersonic pace.

The Shadow drew some sort of small black dagger from his robes. He spun around quickly and jammed it into the Desecrator's neck the moment he reached him. The Desecrator lost control and crashed into the door. The Shadow lifted him up from afar by raising his right hand, and then, by thrusting his left forward, drove the Desecrator into the indestructible glass above the door.

Lucas and Asha were already sprinting at the Shadow who was distracted, but his senses were too finely tuned to ever have his attention truly diverted. They were caught by a blast of psionic energy that knocked them from their feet. They kept their hold on their weapons and unloaded at the creature as they slid along the blood-slicked floor. Natalie had finally cooled down enough to be fired, but the rifle found nothing but air as the Shadow dodged and weaved out of the path of their incoming fire.

The Desecrator was already up and airborne again. The Shadow tried to swing his dagger once more, but the Desecrator wouldn't be fooled twice. The object deflected off his armored back, and he speared the Shadow with his shoulder and the two of them crashed into a holotable on the floor of the room. Alpha's father still spoke on the display.

"The ones who remained made an oath. Their children must never know how they came to be. They swore revenge against the Sorans, but they would invent a tale about invasion and decimation of their world."

The Shadow flung the Desecrator off him with strength far greater than his size suggested. Seeing Lucas and Asha quickly approaching, he reached into robe once more. A pair of blades shot toward them at blinding speed. Asha barely raised her sword in time to deflect the one about to connect with her forehead. Lucas did not have the same good fortune.

The diamond-shaped shard buried itself between two of his lower ribs, and pain exploded through his body like he'd just been set on fire. Whatever material the weapon was made of, it had cut through his armor like paper. He gasped and tumbled forward. Asha cut her sprint forward short to run to him.

"I'm alright," he whispered, but immediately the two of them were flung backward again by another energy blast. Lucas landed sprawled on his back, staring down at the razor point sticking out of his torso. Asha was already up and unloading shots at the Shadow, who was now fending off a fresh assault from the Desecrator.

Lucas blinked and saw something he thought was a dream. It was Kiati, standing over him. She dropped to her knees.

"Slow your breathing."

Her left arm dangled uselessly at her side. Her shoulder had been nearly blown off completely by the Desecrator's blast earlier, but she'd made out better than Reyes and Kovaks, whose body parts were currently spread around the room.

Lucas almost passed out as she jerked the blade from between his ribs. She immediately reached into her armor with her working hand and pulled out a sealing tool that hissed and burned as it attempted to close the wound. Lucas looked over at Asha and saw that she was bleeding rather profusely from the chest, having taking one of the other Shadow's claws to her collarbone earlier. If she could keep fighting, so could he. Kiati hoisted him up and the sharp pain in his abdomen lessened as more painkillers flowed into him. His head went fuzzy, then cleared a few seconds later.

When he looked down, however, he found that the sealing gel hadn't worked. Some sort of bubbling foam had eaten through both it and his undersuit and blood continued to pour out of the opening. It appeared the blade had been coated in an agent that resisted attempts to close the wounds it caused. But there was no time to think about it now.

Lucas found Natalie resting a few feet away, her casing torn away and her readouts flashing danger warnings. But she was still willing to fight, just as he was. Lucas unloaded a stream of shots toward the sparring figures up ahead.

"I believe we can end this war if the truth is revealed. I understand this knowledge is a heavy burden, but despite your age, you were always the strongest of us, and I know it is something you can bear. Be well, my son."

That was the end of it. The message had been broadcast, the truth was out there for every Xalan to hear. The door to the comms relay opened and Alpha and Zeta walked out. They immediately raised their weapons when they saw what was happening.

"The Council!" Alpha exclaimed, seeing the white-robed Xalan ahead and two of his dead compatriots on the floor. The Council Shadow and the Desecrator were locked in combat and didn't seem to notice them.

"And our old friend," Lucas said as he clasped his hand over his side.

"This is our chance," Zeta said. "We can make it to the secondary extraction point. Hurry, while they are occupied!"

The group stopped firing and turned toward one of the exits. Whatever Xalan troops had been there were either dead or scattered after the message had been broadcast. Who knew what state of panic the entire planet was in right now? It was what they were relying on to make their escape. At the end of the broadcast, Zeta had disrupted all Xalan communications across all colonies and fleets for a brief window, and it was surely causing chaos in this solar system and many others. Hopefully all the way to Sora, where the deadly invasion fleet loomed.

They ran toward the exit, but were stopped in their tracks when the Desecrator slammed into the ground in front of them. He slowly extended his claw outward. In it, he held the detached head of the final Council Shadow. He tossed it to the floor where it bounced and rolled toward them.

"No brethren," he said.

"You helped us," Lucas said slowly. "The Council is finished. Xala is free."

"Xala will burn to ash," he said forcefully. "And you are not my allies. My father must find peace in your death."

All of them knew what was about to happen and preemptively unleashed a barrage of plasma that spattered off the Desecrator's heavy plating like fireworks. Undeterred, he flew toward them, arms swinging wildly.

Asha cried out as a black claw tore across her leg, upending her. Alpha took a swipe that dug into the side of his face, but very well could have taken his head off had he been a little closer. Lucas and Kiati were sent sprawling as the enormous creature crashed into them and soared up toward the ceiling.

Lucas fired a few shots but quickly turned and ran to Asha. Her leg was bleeding badly. The suit was fighting to close the wound that stretched from the top of her hip to the inside of her kneecap. She was trying to cry out, but her voice was caught in her throat. Kiati immediately attended to the injury, instructing Lucas to put pressure on the leg.

"I can't . . ." Asha stammered. "I can't . . ."

Her eyes were starting to roll back into her head. The blood was spreading out beneath her into a pool of worrying size. Lucas pressed as hard as he could on the leg, which caused Asha to arch in pain, but it allowed Kiati to seal the enormous gash that had shredded her armor and muscle tissue. The bleeding was slowing, but there was no way she could walk.

There wasn't time to dress her injury further, as the Desecrator was looping back around. Lucas sprinted forward to join Alpha, who was firing a nonstop stream toward the fast-moving target. Alpha shoved Zeta out of the way as the Desecrator buzzed by them again, this time his claws mercifully missing the pair of them.

They were in front of the comms relay now, and Lucas shouted to Alpha over the gunfire.

"We need to get to extraction, they're wounded!"

Lucas motioned to Asha, lying on the floor in a pool of her own blood, being attended to by Kiati, who only had one functional arm. That was to say nothing of his own injury from the Council Shadow's blade. There was a trickling waterfall of blood running from his wound down the front of his armor.

"The beast is too fast. He will slaughter us as we flee," Alpha replied over the din. One of his shots connected with the Desecrator's shoulder, but it wasn't even fazed. Lucas had watched the thing take a canister round from a spaceship directly to the chest. There was no stopping it.

Lucas turned back to look at Asha, who was struggling to sit up. She met his gaze, but then her eyes widened in horror as she looked to his right.

The Desecrator slammed straight into Lucas with the force of a freight train. Lucas felt the breath pulverized out of his lungs as the pair of them shot through the now open door to the comms relay. The Desecrator's wings shattered the conductor crystals inside the entrance and the sudden contact pitched him off balance. Lucas tumbled to the floor and the Desecrator spiraled into a guard rail near the central console of the relay.

Lucas scrambled to his feet and raced toward the door. But almost immediately he felt a claw sink into his shoulder and he was flung back into the room. The Desecrator now made a beeline for the entrance instead. Lucas ignored the pain and lined up a shot. Natalie's barrel extended and released a single round that buried itself in the door's control cluster. It sparked an instant lockdown of the room, and the doors snapped shut. The Desecrator flung himself into the metal, but even with all his unfathomable strength he couldn't dent it. He howled with rage, then turned to sprint toward Lucas once more.

This time, Lucas was ready and slid under the creature's swipe. He turned and let loose a carnage blast that propelled the Desecrator back into the center of the room. A second blast hurled him into the central console itself. Lucas looked out the window embedded in the door. Alpha was working furiously on the other side to let him out.

Lucas banged on the glass and pointed to his armor comm unit.

"Keep it sealed," he said. Alpha stopped working and looked up at him.

"Keep it sealed," Lucas repeated. "Get them out of here, now. It's your only shot."

"I can override the lockdown," Alpha said in a panicked tone, turning back toward the controls. "I can reseal the door before—"

But the Desecrator was already standing and walking slowly toward Lucas.

"There won't be time," Lucas said. "You'll let him out and none of you will leave here alive."

Alpha's eyes darted left and right, avoiding Lucas's gaze.

"I can . . . We can . . ."

His brain was racing through the available options. There was no plan. Not this time. No heroic save. No great escape. Lucas rapped the glass with his fist again.

"Go," Lucas said. "Keep them safe. They need you. This world needs you now."

The Desecrator was standing, waiting thirty feet behind him. Ready to dive forward if Alpha opened the door. He realized he couldn't kill Lucas if there was a still chance Alpha would try to let him out.

Alpha stopped working on the controls. He looked at Lucas and saw that he meant it. Lucas felt calm. He thought of the look Maston had given him before ejecting the pod from the interceptor. *Acceptance.*

Alpha finally nodded.

"You will kill the beast, and rejoin us."

Acceptance was escaping Alpha, it seemed.

"Alright," Lucas said. If that's what he needed to hear, so be it. "I'll be right behind you."

They both knew that wasn't true, but Alpha couldn't say it.

"Farewell, brother," he finally said.

"Save them," Lucas said. "Save them all."

Alpha gave him one last nod and then walked over to Asha's body. She was now completely unconscious, and he scooped her up in his arms. Zeta placed her hand on Alpha's shoulder, and she and Kiati ran with him toward the exit.

Lucas turned back toward the Desecrator, who now realized he wasn't getting out of the room through the door. The creature looked up to the point of light far above them, perhaps speculating on whether the ray shielding would shred him as he exited. But first, there was one last life to extinguish. He turned his back to Lucas and walked into the central chamber. Lucas followed him, strangely calm.

"Nobility is foolish," the creature hissed. "It will not save you."

"I know," Lucas said. His attention was caught by something on the central console. There was another message being broadcast, one that had been set to play after Alpha's father's video was complete. It apparently had already been running for some time.

It was Alpha, speaking to the camera this time, broadcasting to his entire species during the communications blackout. This was the only message any of them were seeing. He was mid-speech already.

". . . and now that we understand the full extent of the Council's treachery, rise up with me. Rise up and take back your planet! Take back your homes! Take back your lives!"

A call to arms. Resistance agents planted all over the quadrant were likely spearheading uprisings all across the colonies. A pair of monitors showed angry crowds massing outside central command as he spoke. Flashes of gunfire and explosions could be seen on the screens.

"Curious," the Desecrator said. "The truth exposed. The colonies in chaos. The homeworld in flames. An opportunity."

"An opportunity for what?" Lucas asked. He checked Natalie; he wasn't sure how much life the rifle had left in it.

"A new ruler," the Desecrator mused. "A powerful one. No Ruling Council. One singular pillar of strength."

"It will be Alpha," Lucas said, gritting his teeth.

"It will be *me*," the Desecrator snarled. "I tore the Council limb from limb after I learned of their lies. I will be the hero. All Xalans will ascend to glory in my image."

Lucas could see the Desecrator's new plan forming in front of his eyes. With a power vacuum, he could easily attempt such a coup. There was obviously none who could match his prowess in battle. The violent elements of the Xalan government that remained could rally behind him.

He couldn't let that happen. This had to be more than some noble gesture so that his friends could escape. The Desecrator had to die, right here, right now, or Xala could become more dangerous than ever.

Lucas pulled Natalie's trigger, but recoiled as the gun sparked violently in his arms and actually glowed so hot it began to melt the mesh fiber suit covering his hands. His old friend was on the edge of death, just as he was.

"Pitiful," the Desecrator said. "Now, step forward and you may receive the honorable death you desire. That much I will allow you for the part you played here today."

Lucas looked down at the unstable core visible through the shorn-off section of the gun. A revelation. He knew what he had to do. He was jolted by a voice on his armor comm.

"Lucas?" it said. It was Asha; she'd regained consciousness.

He was too stunned to speak.

"Lucas?" she said again.

"I'm here," he finally said.

"Where are you?" she asked, her voice weak. She was probably overflowing with painkillers. "Are you on the ship?"

"No, Asha," he said. The Desecrator was circling him slowly, and Lucas never took his eyes off the beast.

"I'm not coming back."

Asha's voice grew stronger.

"What? Where are you? What's happening?"

Lucas spoke quickly.

"Listen, I need you to go back to Sora. I need you to be a mother to Noah and Erik. I need you to tell them that what we did here was worth it. I need you to tell them I didn't abandon them."

"What? No!" her voice was getting frantic now. "Where is he?" she said, presumably to Alpha. There were whispers Lucas couldn't make out.

"No! No!" she shouted, "We're going back. We can't—"

"Asha!" Lucas yelled into his comm. "You have to go. We can't leave the boys alone in this world. They need you!"

"*I* need you!" she cried. Lucas could hear muffled sounds of her struggling, presumably trying to get out of Alpha's grasp. Fortunately she was likely too weak to succeed.

The Desecrator was growing impatient and strode toward Lucas. Alpha continued to talk on the prerecorded message behind him. The words "freedom" and "tyranny" were coming up often. Lucas was starting to feel quite dizzy. The wound in his side was draining him completely and his blood was spattered all over the metal floor. He was cold, almost freezing.

Lucas looked down at Natalie; the rifle was practically vibrating in his hands now. He ran his thumb over the etching in her stock one last time. He turned the gun on its side and arced his finger around the control panel there, increasing its power output.

Warning

"I need you too," he said to Asha.

Danger

"I'll always be with you."

Containment

"You have to believe that."

Failure

"I love you."

Core

"I love you so much."

Overload

Natalie was now so molten that the gun had eaten through his suit and was burning his palms. This was it. He flung the rifle out in front of him. It bounced once on the metal floor and slid underneath the Desecrator's legs. The creature looked down, confused.

Finally, Asha's small, soft voice spoke through the comm.

"I love y—"

She was cut off by the blast.

Lucas saw the light for a instant, reflecting through every conductor crystal in the relay like a trillion stars all going supernova at once.

Beautiful.

27

Lucas was on the Ark.

Asha lay with her head resting on his shoulder and her arm across his chest. The softness of her T-shirt was matched only by her skin. She smelled of autumn, somehow.

Ahead, Alpha was sitting at Lucas's desk in front of a pile of metal and circuitry, working on some new invention, no doubt. Noah sat at Alpha's feet, grinning at Lucas. The boy turned to rock a nearby makeshift cradle where the tips of Erik's little toes could be seen.

Asha slowly began to wake; her eyelids fluttering. Lucas found himself gazing into those brilliant green eyes that never failed to leave him breathless.

She said nothing, simply smiled. *That smile.*

This was everything he needed, right here.

He could stay here forever.

28

Asha sat propped up against the cold metal of the cargo hold. Her legs were bare after they'd stripped away the tattered remains of her stealth suit. The cut across her leg was gruesome and was currently being held together by metal stitches and organic sealant put in place by Kiati. It felt like her thigh was full of a thousand white-hot needles, but she blocked out the pain, refusing further drugs when they were offered.

Kiati had to eventually be induced into a coma, as her own injuries were far more severe than she was letting on. Alpha had a nasty gash across the side of his face, but would survive. Only Zeta had emerged from the encounter nearly unscathed, nursing only a minor leg wound. The pair of them were on the bridge, piloting their escape craft through the unsuspecting Xalan fleet anchored in the solar system, which was too busy with the chaos on the homeworld to notice them. They were simply one more military vessel, flying aimlessly without orders like all the rest. Soon, they would be far enough away to activate their white null core and head home.

Asha was locked in the room, she knew that, and had grown exhausted from banging on the door or attempting to pry open paneling to escape.

She couldn't blame Alpha for doing it. After all, she had threatened him at gunpoint to turn the ship around to go back for Lucas.

Alpha tried explaining it to her scientifically. They'd all heard the blast. Felt it as they made their escape. Alpha realized what Lucas had done, how he'd detonated the core of his weapon to kill the Desecrator. That was no ordinary gun, and no ordinary explosion. There wouldn't be anything left of him to find.

Asha didn't believe it, and leveled her revolver at her friend's head to make him take her back and prove it to her. It was Zeta who clubbed her from behind, and she woke up here with the two of them profusely apologizing. They had to leave. They had to leave or none of them would make it out.

They kept the ship's comm channel open in the hold, though Asha said nothing back when they spoke to her. Zeta confirmed that the entire Xalan comms relay had been destroyed by Lucas's detonation, and the Xalans were frantically trying to get communications back online using backup systems. Alpha contacted Tannon Vale, who reported that the Xalan invasion force had become disoriented by the transmission of the message and subsequent communication blackout. The Sorans had managed to destroy a good amount of the enemy fleet in the ensuing confusion, and the Xalans were forced to turn tail and run. Sora was saved. For now.

But Asha didn't care. She simply stared down at her communicator and listened to the gentle white noise of the static.

Any minute now.

Silence.

Any minute.

Asha felt the ship lurch and then slow to what felt like a stop. She turned to look out the window and saw the familiar multicolored haze of a space-time tunnel. The core had been activated. They were headed back to Sora without Lucas. This was really happening.

Asha stayed in the room. She wouldn't leave, even after Alpha unlocked the door. For weeks, she accepted food and water from them and allowed Zeta to change the bandages on her leg, but said nothing. Did nothing. If she slept it was only because she unwillingly passed out on occasion, only to jolt awake a few hours later.

She continued staring out the window, listening to her comm, now millions of miles out of range.

One device never left her hand. A tiny chip, only a centimeter wide. She pressed it like she had a thousand times. A familiar list of names came up.

Alpha.

Noah.

Erik.

Asha.

Lucas's Final. His last words recorded just in case. His goodbye. He'd slipped it into her armor when she wasn't looking sometime before the mission began.

Asha hovered over her name. She hadn't been able to press it so far. If she did, that was it, she thought, Lucas was really gone. Her finger drifted dangerously close to the icon, but at the last second, she closed the menu and tucked the chip back into her pocket.

Not yet.